SOHYEON AFTER MIDNIGHT

WENDELIN GRAY

Copyright © 2018 M. M. Staffen

All rights reserved.

ISBN: **1981993584**
ISBN-13: **978-1981993581**

TO SJS

CONTENTS

DRAMATIS PERSONAE	viii
PART 1: THE COUNCIL OF TEN	1
PART 2: THE CHANGELING	88
PART 3: THE HIDDEN CLAN	164
PART 4: THE ANCIENT LOVERS	290
PART 5: THE HUNTING PARTY	402
PART 6: WAR OF THE IMMORTALS	484
EPILOGUE	526
AFTERWORD	534
ABOUT THE AUTHOR	536

DRAMATIS PERSONAE

ADDISON, MD (DC METRO AREA)

Sohyeon Choi	Main character, age 18, senior in high school
Mirae Choi	Sohyeon's older sister, age 20, bank employee
Sukjin Choi	Sohyeon's younger sister, age 16, sophomore in high school
Jangsun Choi	Sohyeon's Korean immigrant father
Alanna Choi	Sohyeon's white American mother
Vince Esposito	Owner of Vince's Paintball Park in Addison
Marietta Esposito	Vince's wife, head of Addison's Welcome Wagon
Peter MacIntyre	Sohyeon's best friend at school
Doug MacIntyre	Peter's father, a professor and folklore expert
Daria Favreau	Peter's girlfriend
Phillip Wang	College student at George Washington University
Analisa Gomez	College student at George Washington University
Adam Johnson	A DC fireman
Ognjen Baram	A new resident in Addison
Todd Mazurek	A DC detective
Anton Zhao	An Addison councilman
Megumi Iwase Miller	Addison's mayor
Stephen Columbo	An Addison councilman
Terrence Brightman	An Addison councilman
Gemma Brightman	Terrence's mother
Lidonia	A sika deer clan member
Cautis	A sika deer clan member

KHABU

Minha	Khabu's high priestess
Joriya	Queen of Khabu
Birum	The Duke of Khabu, Joriya's brother
Paleya	The human child Birum had imprisoned and nearly starved to death
Litt	The ancestral first recorded king of Khabu
Gwanghui	The ancient high priestess of Khabu during Litt's time
Eoksu	Litt's long-lost love
Nominus	Litt's best friend and attendant
Liara	Litt's older sister
Zurui	Litt's father, founder of Khabu, one of the Originals
Jentzu	A minister in the ancient court of Khabu
Lessynda	Litt's oldest sister
Azantes	Litt's nephew, Liara's son
Hana	One of Minha's acolytes
Ashira	One of Minha's acolytes

EOKHMISSEUN

Pontol	The ferryman of the inner sea, servant of Minha of Khabu, and ghost-slave
Tamnyn	Cargal's daughter, one of the ruling council
Cargal	Head of the House of Elyeon, one of ruling council
Mapin	A female war pigeon, highest in command, one of the Originals

Crysalin	Tamnyn's missing mother
Kerinda	Crysalin's daughter with Birum
Laqrisa	A female war pigeon stationed at the Choi house
Tmolos	A male war pigeon stationed at the Choi house
Orach	A male war pigeon, second in command
Esram	Cargal's bodyguard
Sagar	A male knight, one of the ruling council
Naim	A male knight, one of the ruling council
Ginsam	A male knight, one of the ruling council
Yarava	A female knight, one of the ruling council
Delam	Yarava's younger brother
Gemeaux	A male war pigeon, third in command

1 THE COUNCIL OF TEN

1

When night arrived, Sohyeon Choi had already been lying in bed watching television with his earphones on for a few hours. He hadn't noticed his room had gotten dark and was now filled with the screen's blue light. The clock beside his bed read almost 10 PM.

"Go to bed. You have a calculus test tomorrow," his mother yelled up.

He hesitated, then flipped off the TV with the remote. Lying back on his pillow, his headphones still on, he closed his eyes.

Suddenly, he sat up, wide awake. Looking at the clock, he saw that it was now a little after midnight. The room felt strangely cold. Taking off his headphones, he got up and walked over to the window and pulled up the sash to let in some of the warm summer breeze. Only the air outside wasn't that warm, and his eyes were drawn to the sky where he noticed the silhouette of something against the moon.

As it drifted toward him lazily on a wispy cloud, he could see it was a silvery ship with mast and sails as in the old days. He rubbed his eyes. Surely this was a dream, wasn't it? Why would he see a ship sailing in the sky?

Curling wisps of moonbeams lapped at the ship's hull, its silhouette sharp against the full moon. Sohyeon thought he could see the figure of a man standing on the deck of the ship, glowing eerily. The pontoon-sized ship came closer, stopping only a few feet from the window.

"Who are you? Why have you come here?" Sohyeon whispered, leaping onto the window sill, looking at the man warily.

"I have come for you," the ghostly man said, his tone flat. He was very thin with sunken eyes and misshapen, almost animal-like features. Sohyeon wasn't sure how old the man was. "I am Pontol, and you must come with me."

Sohyeon nodded grimly and reached out for the boat. In a moment, he stood beside the mysterious man.

"Where are you taking me?" he asked, suddenly afraid.

"We're going to Khabu, though I can go many places."

"Outer space?" Sohyeon asked absent-mindedly, looking at the moon.

The man just laughed and touched a spoked wheel nearby, spinning it slowly with a practiced hand. The ship turned around in the air, pointing toward the dark side of the moon.

"So we sail on air?" Sohyeon said more to himself than the man, but the man corrected him.

"'Tis a river that a mortal like you can't see unless you are trained to see it," he said. "Some know it as Acherusia. The geography is not familiar to your kind, so that's as good a name for it as any."

As he settled onto a bench behind Pontol, Sohyeon noticed a sign to the right of the wheel above a plate full of gold coins. The language on the sign was unfamiliar to Sohyeon, but he guessed the coins were Pontol's payment for passage. Embarrassed to be traveling in his pajamas, an old T-shirt and sweatpants, Sohyeon walked over to the plate of coins and studied their designs. Again, the writing and pictures were unfamiliar.

"Don't worry about paying me," Pontol said gruffly, noticing Sohyeon's interest. "I am already well-paid for fetching you."

Sohyeon looked over at Pontol, suddenly aware of how tall and thin the man was.

"Someone wants to see me? In Khabu? Are you from Khabu?" he asked.

Pontol smiled slightly, his eyes never leaving the white mists they traveled through. Sohyeon noticed the mist now had obliterated the moon and stars, and they could have been traveling on the surface of the earth for all he knew.

"I am not from Khabu. Their priestess has hired my services. She has asked to speak with you."

"A priestess?" Sohyeon muttered to himself, grabbing the hull of the ship as it lurched a bit, hitting ground. They must have reached the port of Khabu already. "Why would a priestess want to talk to me?"

Pontol locked the wheel into place after the ship stopped moving, tied a rope to the dock post to keep the boat from drifting, and led Sohyeon to a short, wide plank linking the side of the ship to a wooden dock. The dock ended at a thin strip of sand eight feet wide that ran along the base of tall, reddish cliffs. Pontol led him into a crack in the cliff where a man in a rumpled gray uniform waited with a torch.

The men didn't speak but only nodded to one another as Pontol sat down on a smooth rock by the entrance. Taking out a small knife and a piece of half-whittled wood, Pontol made a sharp motion with the knife, indicating Sohyeon should follow the man with the torch. Sohyeon bowed to Pontol slightly and walked up to the man, who had been studying him curiously.

"Minha will not be pleased," the man said, turning on his heel. "Follow me."

As they walked, the corridor changed from a rough cave to an elegant, elaborately carved antechamber. The walls were covered with abstract designs of vines and flowers looped around writing resembling hieroglyphics. They approached a tall doorway framed by stone columns carved into the cave walls, its lintel draped in more stone cascades of vines and flowers with another unfamiliar symbol carved in the center. Sohyeon barely had time to look at his surroundings when they stepped beyond the doorway into a wide, high room topped with a glorious crystal dome with ten spires. Since the room was filled with light, they had no need for torches here.

The man put out the torch and retreated into the shadows, leaving Sohyeon to stand alone at the center of the airy room. An empty chair sat next to a pedestal with a large, glittering white pearl on a dais before him. This time, Sohyeon could make out the carving on the pedestal: *margaritari tis sofias*. He walked closer to the pearl, hypnotized by its shimmering beauty, wondering why the words were written in the letters of his native language. He stared at it for so long that he hadn't realized someone now stood on the dais beside him. Looking up, he was suddenly afraid.

"You weren't the one I summoned! What was Pontol thinking, bringing me this boy?"

Sohyeon's eyes met those of a woman not much taller than he, eyes as black as coal and flashing dangerously. Against her fair skin, now flushed with anger, her black hair glistened like crow feathers. Her long light blue chiton flowed down to the floor in billowy waves, accenting her voluptuousness and shimmering in the same mysterious way as the pearl. He felt there was no secret he could hide under such scrutiny, and he suddenly felt embarrassed. If she was disappointed by the sight of him, he certainly wasn't disappointed to meet her. She was like something out of a dream. Was this the priestess Pontol mentioned?

"I told that useless ferryman exactly where to find the person I sought," the woman continued, "and he has the gall to do this. I should have him executed for his mistake!"

"Surely, Lady Minha, there must be some explanation for the mix-up," the guard said from the shadows. "I will bring Pontol here to answer your questions."

"Or you can ask me what I know," Sohyeon said quickly, more afraid of leaving without speaking with the beautiful priestess than he was of her wrath.

Minha looked at Sohyeon in surprise.

"What do you know?" she asked skeptically. Sitting down on the ornate chair beside the pearl, Minha looked at him thoughtfully for a moment. "What is your name?"

"Sohyeon Choi," he said quickly. "I live with my family in Addison, a suburb of DC. Are you familiar with the United States? Or Earth?"

A look of recognition crossed her face. Her anger seemed to subside a little.

"Oh, really," she said, even more subdued. "The old fool really did make an honest mistake then. He went to the right house but to the wrong window! I thought I told him clearly that I wanted the girl. You'll have to go back."

Sohyeon looked at Minha in surprise. A girl? He lived with his mother, father and two sisters, Mirae and Sukjin. So Minha was looking for one of his sisters? But why? He wanted to stall her before she sent him back. He wanted to remember every feature of her face in case he never saw her again.

"You were looking for my sister?" Sohyeon asked.

Minha only looked at him coldly and didn't answer. Her guard returned with Pontol, cutting short their interview. Pontol knelt before the dais, begging for forgiveness in a feeble voice.

"High priestess, I was not aware of my error. Allow me to make amends and correct the matter."

"Return the boy to his home," Minha said, standing, glancing only once more at Sohyeon, who felt his heart flutter at even the slightest attention from her. "We can try again to fulfill the Queen's mission another time. It's getting late. Someone unauthorized may see you if you linger there too long. You will have to wipe the boy's memory when he returns. Do you understand your instructions this time?"

Pontol bowed his head lower, nodding. Minha dropped a gold coin on the floor before him.

"You'll get double when you bring me the girl. If you fail again, you will hang in front of the gates of Khabu where the tigers can eat away what's left of your miserable flesh! Do you understand me, Pontol?"

Pontol stood and waved for Sohyeon to follow. Sohyeon's gaze lingered over the priestess as he walked behind the ferryman, though her attention was now focused on the strange pearl. A pure white beam of light streamed out of the pearl up into the dome, and the light enveloped Minha, making her look like some dark angel. Sohyeon wondered if he had visited heaven tonight.

As they reached the sandy shore leading back to the boat, Sohyeon's body felt heavy and his heart was desperate to return to Khabu.

"Pontol, please don't take me home. I want to stay here," he said without thinking.

Dragging Sohyeon along the plank back into the boat, Pontol looked at him long and hard before he pulled up the plank, untied the rope from the post at the end of the dock and pushed off from the shore.

"I can only take paying passengers. Your fare has only been paid for tonight. How will you pay me to return here?"

"I don't know, Pontol, but I have to see her again," Sohyeon said, sitting down on the bench as Pontol took the wheel.

The ship pulled away from the shore, splitting the water at first, then everything around them turned to white mist, which suddenly reminded Sohyeon of the light from the glowing pearl. Had it really been the moon he saw behind the ship when it came for him earlier, or the pearl?

"You have to see that witch again, do you?" Pontol grumbled. "She is said to have a strange power, though I myself have never felt it, not even when she made me her slave. There is a way you can return, but you'll have to get *me* what *I* seek most in return for my services. If you can do this one favor for me, I will serve you forever."

"Name it," Sohyeon said recklessly, panicking as the mist parted and his house came into view.

"My family lost a valuable heirloom a few generations ago to the son of a powerful landowner in my homeland of Eokhmisseun. If you can steal it back from their family estate and return it to me, I can challenge Minha's spell and break free of my slavery. Then I can accompany you wherever you want to go," Pontol said, his eyes glittering madly.

"How will I get to Eokhmisseun?" Sohyeon asked. "I will have no fare until then."

"I will take you there for nothing until you retrieve my heirloom," Pontol said, the boat fast approaching Sohyeon's bedroom window. "But if you fail, you will be a slave to me as I am to Minha. Can you agree to such a bargain? If so, let me finish the witch's errand first, and I will return for you in five nights to begin your quest."

Sohyeon stepped onto his window sill and turned to look back at Pontol.

"I agree to it."

"Then give me your hand."

Sohyeon held out his hand to the ghoulish-looking man, confused. Pontol smiled strangely. Without any warning, he grabbed Sohyeon's hand and bit his palm along the edge with sharp canine teeth. Blood ran down

Sohyeon's wrist as he stifled a scream, afraid to wake his family though dawn was approaching swiftly. Yet the vision of Minha still filled his senses enough to accept the pain and their pact.

Pontol released Sohyeon's wounded hand and vanished into the lightening sky. Sohyeon jumped down into his room and slipped back into bed, his mind suddenly dark and his body too tired to move.

2

When Sohyeon woke up the next morning, he wondered if it all had just been a bad dream. Throwing off the covers, he crawled out of bed, hitting the button on his clock to turn off the alarm. Two round puncture wounds across the edge of his hand caught his eye. Bite marks. Looking back at his bed, he saw dark red bloodstains on the sheet near his pillow. So it wasn't a dream after all.

Grabbing a pair of jeans, his favorite grunge band T-shirt and some clean underwear, he went out to the bathroom to take a quick shower and think. If last night was real, then one of his sisters would soon be taken in his place. He had to find out which one Minha wanted. Why would a priestess in a faraway land be interested in his family at all? He wanted a chance to change her mind, to show her he was really the most valuable member of the family. Why didn't she want him? What did being wanted by her mean anyway?

Sohyeon dried himself off and changed quickly, nearly leaping down the stairs for breakfast. Mirae and Sukjin already sat at the table, piling toast on their plates and pouring orange juice in their glasses. His father read the paper while their mother scrambled some eggs. She was the first to look at him as he sat down at the table.

"What did you do to your hand?" she asked casually.

Sohyeon glanced down at the ragged wounds on his hand and shrugged, though his mind was racing. How was he going to explain this?

"I had a project due that I finished last night, and my hand got caught in the 3 ring binder clamps. Freak accident," Sohyeon mumbled.

"Oh," his mother said, raising her eyebrows. The first omelet was finished, and she served it and prepped the next one rather than continue her line of questioning.

Looking up to see who got the omelet, Sohyeon saw his sisters looking at him oddly. His father hadn't moved except to turn to the next page of the paper. Sukjin, the recipient of the first omelet, rolled her eyes at him and began eating. Mirae looked at him earnestly a few moments more before buttering her toast. He took a sip of orange juice and glanced at his sisters again. Which one could it be?

Mirae was 20 and worked at a bank call center during the daylight shift. Sukjin was 16 and in her sophomore year at the same school where Sohyeon was a senior. All of the Choi children were neatly spaced two years apart, though family stories suggested that Mirae had nearly died as an infant and that their mother might not have been able to have more children. Both girls had proven those predictions wrong. Did that make Mirae Minha's more likely target, or did Sukjin's miraculous existence suggest she was destined to be taken to Khabu? Sohyeon decided he would have to get up after midnight every night and watch them both to find out.

"I don't get it, Sohyeon," Pete said when they got to the lockers after gym that afternoon. No one was around, and Pete MacIntyre had been Sohyeon's best friend since at least middle school in the Addison School District. "What really happened to your hand? Those wounds look pretty nasty."

Sohyeon looked up and down the hall quickly while Pete spun his combination on the lock. They would meet up with their other friends on the way home, and he only had a few minutes to tell Pete his secret.

"I got bit by something. In my dream."

"By what? How do you know it happened in the dream and not in your bed when you were asleep?" Pete asked, keeping his voice low as he pulled out his math book to take home and study for their test the next day.

"I don't know how to explain it. I woke up in the middle of the night, and a ship was at my window with this guy in it. He wanted to take me to some fantasy world, but when we got back to my room afterward and I asked him if he could take me back there sometime, he bit my hand."

"Sounds like that videogame they released last month. Do you remember it? Moon Quest or something. Did you read about it and have a dream? Maybe you got bit by a bug or something in your room instead?"

"Moon Quest?" Sohyeon looked pensive a moment as Pete slammed his locker shut and they started to walk down the hall to the front entrance where the rest of their friends were waiting. "No, I think it was more like 'Nightmare on Elm Street' than some videogame. But what kind of monster was that guy that he bit me like that?"

"Well, then, don't let him get you like Freddy did in the movie," Pete said seriously. "Didn't the people he killed in dreams die in real life?"

Sohyeon nodded.

"Something like that."

"Why did you want to go back to the place he took you?" Pete asked, suddenly a little apprehensive. "Where did you go?"

Sohyeon smiled a little as he remembered Minha's face. He was surprised he could recall it so clearly.

"I forget the name he used for it, but I met the most beautiful woman ever there."

"You kidding?"

"Nah, why would I?"

Pete stopped him for a minute by the doors before they joined the others. The expression in his blue eyes seemed elusive.

"Be really careful then, bro. I think Moon Quest had some snake women in it. They always are beautiful on the other side, aren't they?"

Sohyeon let out his breath in a ragged sigh, aware that Pete didn't believe him. They didn't say anything further about it and walked out into the sunny afternoon together.

Later that night after everyone had gone to bed, Sohyeon had set his phone on vibrate and put it next to his pillow to wake him quietly at midnight. The hours passed slowly with Sohyeon tossing restlessly in bed, barely able to sleep. Finally, when it went off and he turned off the alarm, Sohyeon got out of bed, fully dressed, and picked up the pen flashlight he had left on his nightstand. Slipping stealthily into the hallway, he approached his sisters' room. Mirae and Sukjin shared a room, which made Sohyeon's life easier. But how would Pontol wake the right girl or even know which one was which, he thought. How did he get it wrong by taking Sohyeon in the first place?

Because Sohyeon was on good terms with his sisters and their family life was very tranquil, he had no trouble sneaking into the girls' room. He chose a spot by the door in the shadow of their dresser where he wasn't likely to be noticed should either of them wake to wait for Pontol's arrival. Listening to his sisters' even breathing in the dark, he felt himself dozing off after a while. Jerking awake suddenly, he pressed on the button of his watch to light the face up. It was ten after one! He had been waiting there an hour for the ship to arrive.

Cursing himself for falling asleep when he was supposed to be watching his sisters, Sohyeon peeked around the corner of the dresser toward their beds, but the window caught his eye first. A light breeze caressed his face, gently blowing the filmy curtains away from the open window where silvery moonlight poured into the room.

Thoughts of Minha filling him with yearning, Sohyeon jumped to his feet silently and crossed the room, noticing one of the beds was now empty. Mirae's! Sukjin slept with her back to the window.

Grabbing the window sill, Sohyeon poked his head out, glancing quickly at the ground before scanning the skies for the ship, but it was gone. Since the night air felt warmer than last night, he couldn't tear himself away from the window yet. He willed the ship to appear, but it didn't. Why would Pontol come for Mirae? What would Minha summon her for? True, she was an adult now, and Sohyeon had a certain amount of respect for Mirae's calmness and poise, but this made no sense.

Stalking back to his hiding place, he waited for the ship to return, pinching himself regularly so he wouldn't fall asleep this time.

Suddenly, Sohyeon heard a beeping alarm. In a confused haze, he couldn't remember where he was until he saw he was still sitting by the dresser in his sisters' room. He had fallen asleep again, and he couldn't risk getting caught by the girls. As he stood and tried to sneak out of the room before either of them got up, a shadow passed over him.

"Sohyeon?" Mirae asked in a sharp, low voice as she appeared beside him in the dim morning light.

When Mirae hit the light switch, he stood face to face with her. Her look of confusion changed to shock. Sohyeon saw Sukjin was still in bed and had pulled the covers over her head when Mirae turned on the light to block it out. He looked back at Mirae's face, suddenly struck by how beautiful she was. Why hadn't he noticed that before? Why would he think that about his sister now?

"Sohyeon, what are you doing here? How long have you been hiding in our room?"

He noted a trace of alarm in her voice, and he wondered what she remembered about the ship. Was she afraid that he had seen it?

"We need to talk later," he said, his mouth suddenly too dry. "Alone. Will you have time?"

"I may have to work late," she stammered, looking at him oddly.

"Make time. It's important," he said before fleeing down the hallway back to his room.

3

Sohyeon avoided Mirae's gaze during breakfast though he felt her looking at him, but no one else paid attention to them or noticed the tension between them. Everyone ate in silence and went their separate ways. Sukjin grabbed her backpack and fled, heading toward the bus stop without so much as a glance back at Sohyeon though they went to the same school. He knew she met her friends and didn't want to be seen with him. Their father got into the car and pulled out after a quick goodbye kiss with their mother, who went upstairs to take a shower.

Heading for the door with his backpack in his hand, Sohyeon felt Mirae touch his arm.

"Walk with me to the metro," she said softly.

"I'll be late. What is it?"

"Then I'll walk to your bus stop with you. I can afford to be a little late for work."

They stepped out on the front stoop together, and Mirae pulled the door shut behind them.

"This way," Sohyeon said gruffly, upset at both her and himself for some reason. Fear and jealousy of his sister mingled in his thoughts, and he could barely stand to hear what Minha might have said to her. He wanted to be the one chosen by the strange priestess, but now his sister had overshadowed him.

"You wanted to talk, didn't you?" Mirae asked, referring to Sohyeon's sullenness. "You know what happened last night, don't you? How do you know?"

Sohyeon tried not to let his anger boil over as they walked together down the street. Mirae wouldn't understand how Minha had charmed him or why he made a pact with Pontol. The demonic ferryman would be back for Sohyeon, and he wasn't sure how much he should tell Mirae about that.

"Yeah, I know. Why did Minha, that priestess of Khabu, want to talk to you? You went there last night on the ship. Don't try to deny it."

Mirae looked away from him a minute, biting her lip. Sohyeon glanced over at her, noticing how pretty she looked in her blue blazer with her long black hair twisted into the messy bun hairstyle that she liked to wear to work. Wisps of loose hair now danced around her face in the light morning breeze. Her narrow, dark brown eyes suddenly darted back to him. Their eyes met.

"Minha? How do you know what I dreamt last night? How could you know?" she asked again, her expression incredulous.

"The ship came to me too the other night, but Minha rejected me. I knew she'd come for one of you."

Mirae's monolidded Asian eyes opened wide.

"She didn't tell me she saw you. She didn't even tell me why I was there, well not really anyway. She just said she needed my help, talking like we were old friends. Why does it matter to you, Sohyeon? Isn't it just a dream?"

"It isn't a dream," he said, his voice cracking. He held his hand with Pontol's bite marks out to Mirae. "The ferryman and I have come to an agreement. This is what he did to me in that dream."

"How?" Mirae asked, shocked, her voice trailing off. She touched Sohyeon's hand delicately, running her fingers over the wounds.

It was then Sohyeon noticed a beautiful pearl ring on Mirae's hand that he had never seen before.

"Where did you get that?" Sohyeon asked, tapping on her ring as she let go of his hand.

Mirae held her hand up in the sunlight for them to admire it.

"Minha gave it to me," Mirae said, sighing in dismay.

"So you're going to admit that you knew all along that it wasn't a dream?"

"She wanted this to be a secret."

Sohyeon cut her off.

"I'll find out anyway, so you may as well tell me what it means."

"Are you interested in Minha? Is that why you resent me?" Mirae asked suddenly, teasing. "I should have realized that. The ring is merely a sign of my agreement with them to help them. Minha wants to train me as her successor. Something about serving the Queen of Khabu. It seems the Queen is at war with her brother, the Duke, and now they seem to be inadvertently sowing trouble between us, Sohyeon."

Sohyeon looked up at her suddenly, thinking.

"And you have an agreement with the ferryman?" Mirae continued. "I'm not sure I like the sound of that. Do you know which side of the war in Khabu he is on? He was rather cold, in my opinion, and if he bit you...I can't imagine what that means. Is that even a civilized thing to do?"

Sohyeon thought for a moment. The bus stop was only a block away, and he had about five minutes before the bus came.

"Probably not," Sohyeon said, agreeing. "Pontol didn't exactly talk about Minha in flattering terms. We might be on opposite sides. I don't know. No one said anything about a conflict, and Pontol is from another land altogether. Besides, I'm only allied with Pontol because I want to see Minha again."

"The priestess is very beautiful," Mirae said, looking away from Sohyeon again, "but I don't think either of us knows what we're getting into. I really thought I was dreaming when I agreed to help her. Until I woke up and saw this ring, then found you hiding in my room, I didn't think it meant anything."

Sohyeon heard rumbling up the street. His bus had turned the corner, and he had to run for it. It was a few minutes early.

"We'll go out to dinner tonight," Mirae said quickly. "Just the two of us."

"Fine."

"I'll call mom during the day and let her know we won't be joining them for dinner and not to make extra."

"I'll be waiting when you get home. Don't worry about it, okay? I can handle the rejection of a beautiful woman better than you think."

Sohyeon smiled at Mirae before turning to make a run for the bus, which was stuck in traffic a block away. He could easily make it in time. As he reached Sukjin, out of breath, the fleeting thought occurred to him that while he and Mirae had always been on fairly good terms, they had never been really close like that. Now it seemed their relationship would change.

4

"So tell me about this deal that you made with the ferryman," Mirae said when they sat down that night at a table in a shadowy corner of the Ground Round® and had given the waitress their orders. "Did you say his name was Pontol? He never introduced himself to me."

Her eyes darted back and forth as the waitress returned with their drinks. They fell silent until she was safely out of earshot.

"I guess it was pretty reckless of me to make him a promise, but I didn't know he was going to bite me. You're right that it was uncivilized. I've been thinking about that all day since you said it. Pontol didn't seem entirely human when he bit me."

"But what did you agree to?" Mirae asked, taking a sip of her coke. "Was it something as difficult as my task of stopping a war in some unknown land?" She smiled a little at Sohyeon.

"Maybe something worse," Sohyeon said, smiling back at her. "He wants me to retrieve a stolen heirloom back in his homeland."

"And what do you get out of the deal?"

"I get to see the woman of my dreams again."

"Who? Minha?" Mirae looked at him thoughtfully. "I'm astonished by how much she impressed you. She was pretty, but I don't think I'd be desperate to do anything to see her again if I were in your shoes."

After the waitress came out and set their meals in front of them, they continued their furtive talk. Sohyeon dug into his plate of fish tacos, explaining his position between bites.

"Would you be interested in Minha if she were a man? Then again, maybe it had something to do with the pearl. It was radiant, unearthly, powerful. Pete said something about it all sounding like a new videogame."

"You told Pete! We shouldn't tell anyone else," Mirae said, dropping her quesadilla back onto her plate. Her eyes were full of fear. "You don't know what people might say. This kind of thing isn't supposed to be real. Promise me you'll stop talking to anyone else about it but me."

"Okay, okay, I promise."

She sighed, thinking.

"Yeah, maybe I would be that smitten if Minha were a handsome man. I don't know. Are you sure your lust for her is all there is to it?"

"What are you talking about? I'm a gentleman with nothing but pure intentions."

Mirae snickered, and Sohyeon looked at her with a hurt expression.

"Are you sure you don't really want to live in a videogame?" she asked. "Khabu is kind of exciting, unreal, even preternatural. High school and work are boring compared to that."

"Maybe you're right," Sohyeon said, gulping down some iced tea between bites. "But Pontol kept calling Minha 'the witch' and complained that she had him spellbound. Somehow the heirloom can free him. That's why he needs me."

"So?"

"So if she's a witch rather than a priestess, maybe both of them are using magic to draw us into their world and this conflict. I wonder if Pontol's situation has something to do with the war between the Duke and Queen that you mentioned. If so, maybe neither of us really has a choice."

Mirae finished her last bite of quesadilla and pulled out the desert menu.

"You have a point," she said. "Did Pontol tell you what this heirloom is?"

"No, not yet, but he's coming back for me, maybe tonight, to begin looking for it. Hey, did you want to split desert?"

"Tell me when you find out, but don't let on to him that we're talking and comparing notes on them. Promise me, Sohyeon. I won't tell Minha either."

"Both of us are making a second pact in as many days," Sohyeon said, looking earnestly at Mirae. "Let's split a sundae and call it a deal."

"A sundae? You'd have to pick something so fattening," she said playfully, nodding. "Let's do it."

As they finished their meal, they talked about mundane things. Sohyeon was a little startled to realize again that his view of his sister was changing. Like his impressions of her during the night, he suddenly noticed how regal and wise, how grown up, she seemed. What was happening to him? Had Mirae's trip to Khabu in the night transformed her somehow? Or had it been her proximity to the magic of Minha, who now was such a draw for him to the other world? He felt uncomfortable with his observations, yet they also fascinated him, and he wondered if he also seemed different to her because of his night wanderings.

When she came back to the table after paying their bill, they took the metro home. As they arrived at their house and headed straight for their rooms, she stopped him momentarily on the stairs.

"Tell me right away what happens when he comes, okay?" she whispered before walking down the hall to her room, not waiting for him to answer.

5

It wasn't until two nights later that the ship came again for Sohyeon. He had been nervous Pontol wouldn't show at all, but the bite marks on his hand were oddly reassuring. If he had done *that*, Pontol would keep his promise.

In the hour after midnight on the fourth night after his first encounter, Sohyeon saw the shadowy outline of the ship approaching, gliding over the wispy moonbeams shrouding the imperceptibly shrinking disk of the moon behind it. Once again Sohyeon felt unsure of whether the substance the ship moved through was air or water, though he breathed in the crisp night air as he opened the window and stepped onto the window sill to meet it. After a few minutes, the ship came close enough for him to board, then Pontol spun the wheel, turning the boat away from the Choi house.

"I was afraid I'd never see you again," he said.

Pontol merely nodded.

"Tonight we're going to your homeland? Is it like Khabu? What is this heirloom I'm searching for anyway?"

Pontol nodded again.

"We are going to my homeland, Eokhmisseun." He scowled suddenly as he glanced back over his shoulder at Sohyeon. "Eokhmisseun is a beautiful land with an illustrious history, but Khabu has destroyed it."

Pontol fell silent a moment again and looked carefully at the plate of coins next to the wheel before continuing.

"It is those people who have turned it into a shadow world full of trouble and pain. You, Sohyeon, will help me cleanse it and rid it of our overlords."

"With the heirloom?" Sohyeon was afraid to say more. His mouth had gone dry, and the vision of Khabu's beautiful priestess Minha had started to fade a little. Why had he wanted to see her so badly again? He couldn't remember all of the sudden. Alarmed, he felt there was something unnatural about the way both Minha and Pontol seemed to be able to bend him to their will.

"Yes, with the heirloom," Pontol said languidly. "It was my grandfather's, and it should have been mine by rights before Khabu intervened and the new 'leader' stole it. I have never seen it, but the silver dagger is said to be of unearthly workmanship, polished so brilliantly that its light rivals your moon itself. It is said to be set with a bloodstone in its hilt, and according to family legend it has magical powers, forged by the very founders of our land over a millennia ago."

"Is that why the new leader stole it? Because it's magical?" Sohyeon asked, standing beside Pontol. The night sky they had set sail in had turned as murky and dark as a cave. Were they still in the air? If not, where were they?

"The invaders from Khabu heard of the legends, and knowing their infernal weakness, stirred up allies in our ruling council to steal it and hide it away where it could never be used against them."

"Eokhmisseun is ruled by a council instead of a monarch?" Sohyeon's voice trailed off, thinking about his conversation with Mirae. "I have to steal it back from one of the council members? Is that really difficult?"

"The council of Eokhmisseun is made up of some of our fiercest fighters," Pontol said grimly. "Since many of our people have been enslaved by Khabu, we have neither freedom nor strength to fight. Our own people have aided the aggressor and have done this to us."

Sohyeon saw the shoreline up ahead.

"Where do we start once we get there?"

"I will take you through the city to the main house of my family's ancient enemy, but first you will have to take on the guise of one of the ghost slaves so they don't arrest or kill you. It's important that you don't get caught in the city."

After they left the ship on the rocky shore, Pontol took Sohyeon to a wide, shadowy forest of gnarled trees where a tumbledown shack deep in the center added to the gloomy, mourning atmosphere. Inside the shack, Sohyeon noted with revulsion, pans full of bones, large and small, were scattered on the stove, many cracked and charred at the ends. Sohyeon walked closer to them, his eyes widening, while Pontol rummaged through a box in the darkened corner. He was afraid of what Pontol would bring him.

Only gray streams of light filtered through the grimy windows, so most of the shack remained cloaked in shadows. Finally, Pontol returned to him, holding up a long, dingy tunic with a tattered hem.

"Put this over your clothes, and take some of the soot from the fire pit and smear some of it on your hands and face. If you don't, they'll know you aren't one of the ghost slaves, and there will be trouble. I'll get you a walking stick to use to defend yourself."

Sohyeon went over to the fire pit, cringing as he put his hand into the oily-smelling ashes and noting with disgust more bones poking out of the pile. When he finished and stood up, he saw Pontol waiting for him by the door, holding a long piece of wood with a hooked metal point clumsily attached with wire to the bottom, less obvious than a spear but probably less lethal.

"What kind of weapon is this?" Sohyeon asked as he took the walking stick from Pontol.

"It's just a broken iron hearth poker fitted over the wood," the ferryman said. "We aren't allowed to have silver anymore, and any real forged weapon would give you away as one of the members of the underground, but you must look like a ghost-slave." His voice was wistful as he glanced at the tip. "Pull up the tunic's hood so no one can see your face, or they'll know."

Sohyeon quickly obeyed and followed Pontol to the door.

"Where are we going?" he asked.

"To the house of Elyeon to wait for nightfall." Pontol opened the door. "Don't speak until I tell you to."

6

Eokhmisseun was a city that seemed to have no limits. White buildings looking like carved ivory rose in terraces that stretched in every direction, delicate yet feeling deserted. Indeed, as Sohyeon walked a few steps behind Pontol through the streets, they met almost no one. Only occasionally a drab figure swathed nearly head to toe in rotting cloaks peered out of arched doorways or abandoned alleyways, receding deeper into the shadows as Sohyeon and Pontol passed.

As unsettling as these encounters were, Sohyeon was increasingly revolted as he noticed more bones lining the streets here and there, but he couldn't figure out what kind of animals the bones might belong to. They were not all the same size, and some were very large, like something he had remembered seeing in a museum dinosaur exhibit. Some even looked like they could be human.

Looking up at the carved buildings as they passed, he saw many of the facades looked like filigreed lace with no discernable windows. The white facades were unnaturally clean and whole in spite of the desolate appearance of the inhabitants and the pervasive presence of the bones. The sky also looked to be perpetually on the verge of an approaching thunderstorm. Were these hints of the disaster that befell the city?

Pontol had bade him not to speak, but questions itched on his lips, and he could not stop himself from quickening his pace to gesture to Pontol for permission to break the eerie silence. Apart from the sound of their footsteps, no sounds echoed through the city, heightening Sohyeon's uneasiness. As he neared Pontol, he must have startled the ferryman. Pontol whirled, his cloak opening briefly to reveal Pontol's emaciated but not quite human legs, which looked too skinny and curved backwards around the knee area like a dog or cat's. When Pontol's eyes met his, Sohyeon gasped, realizing too late that he had never seen the man in the full daylight.

Sohyeon could hardly understand what sort of creature Pontol was. While his hands seemed human with very long, dirty fingernails, and his figure seemed thin and wiry like a tall man, his face showed traces of something else. It was unusually elongated around the nose and jaws for a man's face, and his teeth seemed all too sharp with long fangs that had bitten Sohyeon's hand. Pontol's large eyes were the color of coal with silver slits for pupils. Altogether, it was a ghastly appearance with only stringy black hair on his head and skin approaching a gray tone.

He wanted to speak, and for a moment, he had nearly forgotten Pontol's warning not to, but seeing his fierce look, Sohyeon hesitated. The silence around them was so thick, like he remembered before church services back home, that he knew he didn't dare utter one sound without permission. Pontol grabbed Sohyeon's wrist and, pressing his bony fingers into Sohyeon's flesh, dragged him to the end of the street where he opened the door to one of the buildings.

When they entered the room, Sohyeon needed a few moments for his eyes to adjust to the dim light. Pontol watched him expectantly, and Sohyeon noticed how much more human Pontol looked now in the dark. That was why he hadn't noticed the man's odd, almost feline appearance until a few moments ago. Repressing a shudder, he smiled at Pontol, though his lips felt stiff and it probably looked like a grimace instead. Pontol nodded his head and leaned toward him.

"Say your piece here," the ferryman said in a low voice, "but don't say a word when we're out on the street, or else you will draw unwanted attention. You don't want that sort of unpleasantness."

Sohyeon was so startled by his fleeting glimpse of Pontol in the light that he almost didn't remember what he had wanted to ask. While he paused and Pontol waited, he glanced around the room. Furnished like a restaurant, the tables looked like they had once been elegant but had suffered years of neglect. Other hooded figures looking as vaguely emaciated as Pontol sat around the room alone or in small groups, all talking in low tones or sitting in sullen silence. The tables had plates of food on them here and there, but Sohyeon was so disgusted by what he saw there, he quickly looked away, pulling the hood of his cloak closer around his face.

At one table, a single patron sat before a plate where a large hairy rat lay, still alive and half-eaten. The man's mouth was ringed with blood and his fingernails covered with strips of flesh. The man gnawed at it voraciously, as if he had been starving. Sohyeon looked at the door to the establishment with longing, hoping they could resume their journey soon.

"Does this tell you what you wanted to know?" Pontol whispered grimly, quickly glancing around the room then back at Sohyeon.

"What happened here? What happened to you, to them? Are you still human?"

"No."

Pontol's chest heaved as he seemed to struggle for breath, unable to say more. His expression was tinged with sadness.

"Is this what Khabu did?"

"Silence! Don't ever say that name here," Pontol said, his voice strained. "It is enough to know our once beautiful city has been degraded." His voice trailed off.

"Then let's go get your dagger."

Sohyeon clutched his walking stick tighter and took a few steps toward the door without waiting for Pontol. Grabbing the knob with his free hand and pulling the door open, he let the cold light from outside spill into the room as he walked out. Standing in the empty street again, relief flooded his body. Pontol quickly joined him.

7

When nightfall arrived, Sohyeon and Pontol had already been waiting at the estate that was their target for a few hours. Sohyeon wondered how much time was passing back home, but his eyes were continually drawn to the ornate building that they planned to sneak into. Sohyeon was a little alarmed by the plan when Pontol had explained it to him. Never having done anything illegal, Sohyeon could barely understand Pontol's feverish excitement at the thought of the heist. Unlike their silent trek through the city streets earlier, Pontol's whispery, rasping instructions had barely stopped when they had reached the magnificent house and hidden in the small forest behind it.

Like the rest of the city, this area seemed unusually quiet with only an occasional figure wandering about, always wrapped tightly in a gray, often tattered cloak. Since they had arrived at the estate, no one had gone in or out.

Indeed, it was hard to determine if anyone was inside at all given the city's dominant architectural style. Most of the buildings had no windows but instead had facades resembling ivory carved in an intricate filigree of vines and flowers from the rooftop to the sidewalk. Behind the façade, there appeared to be places where shutters could be opened, where the people within could peer discreetly into the streets and not be seen from outside. Pontol had been agitated about this earlier, though Sohyeon could barely see whatever subtle changes in the façade the ferryman had noticed. In the darkness, whatever traces of light appeared through the gaps in the façade seemed like illusions, and Sohyeon found himself straining to catch them.

"How long do we wait before we go in?" Sohyeon asked in a low voice, glancing nervously around the grove of trees.

"You will go in alone now."

"How? They'll be watching the entrances, won't they? How will I find the dagger without you?"

"I have watched this house every day since this disgrace fell upon us," Pontol said. Sohyeon tried not to roll his eyes. This was about the fourth time since they arrived that Pontol had referred to the unnamed disaster that had struck the place and took away his humanity. "There are other ways in, including a secret entrance that the head of family uses when he doesn't want anyone to see him come and go. No one should be there right now but the servants and the girl, though you should be careful of her nonetheless. Tamnyn isn't on the council for nothing."

Pontol's voice trailed off as he seemed lost in thought for a moment.

"How will you find the dagger alone? Indeed, if I went in with you, it would sing in my presence, so I must wait here for you. We aren't allowed to have silver anymore, and in the estate, they have guardians that would announce my presence. Out here in this wooded grove, the dagger would be silent."

"So where is it in the house? How do I get it out?" Sohyeon asked in frustration, wondering if Pontol was insane. Maybe half of his hokey story wasn't even true, but Sohyeon had no idea what to do now other than go through with Pontol's plot.

"They must have it on display in their armor room where no one would be the wiser that it's silver. You see, they shouldn't have it either. The fact they do is due to a grudge between our families, not the magic of Khabu or Litt's influence."

"Litt? I don't think you mentioned that name before." Sohyeon kept his voice gentle, not wanting to set the ferryman off again since he was obviously very upset about the situation.

"Litt is the demon they put in charge of our city," Pontol said, his voice hissing into a whisper as his eyes darted around the grove. "He's Khabu's agent, rumored to be the son of the Queen, though I don't believe such a foul creature could be royalty." Pontol spit on the ground before continuing. "You need only concern yourself about confronting the guardians and Tamnyn for now. I can use the dagger on the fiend myself once we get it, and then you can do as you please with that witch."

"This dagger can kill Litt? Is that why it is guarded and why no one can have silver here? Then why hasn't this Tamnyn used it on him?"

"You'll have to ask her that yourself sometime. It seems obvious enough to me they would, but maybe Tamnyn doesn't know it's silver. It has been in their armory a long time, after all. I don't think she could possibly not know of its presence, but perhaps she doesn't. She's still a child, though a very dangerous child, but maybe she doesn't know what her father and grandfather have been up to." Pontol looked Sohyeon up and down before continuing. "Are you going in now, or what? We don't have all night to get this business done, you know? Litt prowls the streets at night rather than by day."

"Where is this secret entrance to the estate?" Sohyeon asked. "Is it near here?"

"Yes, not far at all. A small cave through the back of the grove leads down to their root cellar. Use your staff to fight off whatever may try to stop you, but spare the girl if you can. Grab the dagger then meet me back out here. We'll make our getaway before Litt's men can wander through."

Pontol dragged Sohyeon to the darkest corner of the thicket of trees where Sohyeon could smell a damp breeze mingled with the scent of some pungent, vaguely remembered flower. As they approached and Sohyeon crossed the threshold, he felt Pontol's hand slip off his arm. He was now completely alone to face the task. Steeling himself for a potential fight, Sohyeon shifted the crude walking stick in his hand so he could try to use it as a weapon and pulled back his hood so he could see out of his peripheral vision. Walking through the corridors that led to a wide storage room full of wooden barrels smelling like wine and glass containers full of various foodstuffs, he saw a set of stone stairs leading up into the house. How odd that this entrance should be left unguarded, he thought fleetingly as he quietly leapt up the stairs to the next floor. This almost seemed too easy.

At the top of the stairs was a large kitchen lit by the dim glow of an oil lamp in one corner. Sohyeon could see an arched doorway leading off to the left. Following it without pausing to look around the kitchen, he found himself in a corridor full of tapestries with more arched doorways on either side. Most of the tapestries were too dark to see. He walked slowly through the dimly lit corridor, noting only with slight interest that the few tapestries he could see depicted some order of knights in gleaming armor fighting a dragon, as if out of a bedtime story his mother might have told him when he was a young child. As he passed each doorway, he glanced into the rooms, trying to find the armory. Cursing Pontol under his breath, he realized the ferryman hadn't given him any idea where to look beyond that, and it could take all night to find such a room.

Each room Sohyeon passed was lit only with one small oil lamp fastened to a far wall, almost like nightlights, and everything they revealed showed he was no closer to finding this dagger than when he arrived. First a ballroom, then a study, then a courtyard garden, then an elaborate entryway leading to a curved staircase to the second floor, but nothing like an armory. Sohyeon paused in the entryway near the foot of the stairs, thinking. *If I had an armory, where would it be in the house? Near the door? Somewhere safer from thieves like me?* Sohyeon wasn't sure, but he thought it could be on an upper floor if the House of Elyeon was paranoid enough. He climbed up the stairs, resolute, feeling more relaxed since he hadn't seen any servants or guards anywhere so far, and he had nearly forgotten Pontol's warning that magic could be involved.

Reaching the next floor, Sohyeon paused. He saw another staircase not far down the landing leading to a third floor, and he wondered how big the mansion might be. From the outside, he guessed it could hold as many as five levels, so he had to work quickly and escape before he was caught. Would the armory be on the second floor? He took a few steps to reach the hallway that ran parallel to the landing area which hung over the entryway like a balcony. Glancing in either direction, he saw all of the doors were open, though the shadows here were deeper. Feeling a bit hesitant to intrude, thinking back to the structure of his own house and the placement of his own bedroom on the second floor, he was uncomfortable about snooping here, but he knew he had to in order to make good on his pact with Pontol. Tiptoeing down the right side of the hallway he glanced into the rooms, a little astonished that none of the doors were shut against intruders. Again, it was too easy to access this house, so was there something that Pontol had forgotten to tell him?

One room looked like it was the servants' quarters, but it was too dark for Sohyeon to determine if anyone was sleeping there. Across the hall, the room appeared to be some sort of museum of family heirlooms, which made Sohyeon pause. There were only a few more rooms in this wing of the house, and he decided he should look into those before heading back and exploring that particular room. All but one of the remaining rooms were too dim to see who slept there or what might be in the room beyond the basic sense that they were sleeping quarters. The last room he looked into before doubling back stopped him cold.

Bathed in moonlight, this room was brighter than the rest. Someone had left the shutters open so the soft light from outside filtered into the room as a filigreed shadow through the lacy facade, illuminating a white curtained bed which fluttered in the slight breeze. On a dressing table across from the foot of the bed lay some object which reflected the moonlight with a strange intensity. Mesmerized, Sohyeon entered the room, wondering if the family would keep the dagger so close at hand.

Ignoring whoever slept in the bed, Sohyeon walked past the gauzy curtains, letting one edge of the floating cloth brush against his cheek as he went straight for the dressing table. When he got closer, he saw the glittering object lay across a dark cushion, a dagger with a murky-colored stone near the hilt. Pontol's heirloom. Sohyeon was sure it was the object he sought, and he reached out to grab the hilt with his free hand and return to Pontol without delay when someone grabbed his wrist.

Fascinated, he looked at the hand that held his wrist, hardly believing it was possible that such delicate fingers could be as unyielding as steel. His walking stick fell to the floor as his right hand also lost its grip. He felt the will draining out of him. Turning his head to the left, he saw a fierce mask of a toothy animal he didn't recognize sitting on top of the head of a beautiful woman, her body clad in some sort of white armor. Was it her room that Sohyeon had disturbed? Pontol had mentioned the illustrious House of Elyeon had a daughter on the ruling council, but who was this woman? What was she? Her eyes seemed to burn into his as he felt all of his thoughts start to drift, unfocused, until all he could feel was an intense connection with this woman as she bent him to her will. He fell to his knees before her as she grabbed the dagger off the cushion with her free hand. At her touch, the dagger lit up with a flash that ran down the blade like a laser beam then popped in a small firework when it reached the tip. The flash of light lit up her face for a moment, and Sohyeon saw her long hair was bright red and her face looked as carefully carved as the ivory façade of the mansion.

"Who are you?" Sohyeon asked weakly, barely able to hold up his body. He wanted to lay on the floor and go to sleep.

Leaning over him, the woman looked at him curiously.

"I might ask you the same question," she said smoothly before carelessly dropping his hand and twisting the dagger into a defensive position as if to stab him with it.

"Oh, I think Pontol was wrong," he said rubbing his eyes. "You *do* know what kind of power the dagger has. He was going on about killing a demon."

The woman smiled coldly, relaxing her stance a bit and looking at him more curiously.

"Pontol? Minha's slave? Now why would he send you to me?" Her gaze softened a little as she tugged at his cloak to see his street clothes underneath. "A foreigner! Pontol has really done it this time."

Turning, she shouted a command, and a rustling noise started down the hallway. Sohyeon knew he wasn't going to escape with the dagger as the servants came in with oil lamps and took up defensive positions in the room.

"So you are the daughter of the House of Elyeon," Sohyeon said, trying to stand and regain his balance.

The woman smiled in amusement before answering.

"Yes, I would be Tamnyn of Elyeon. I'm surprised that the old fellow would tell you about me. Why did he send you to steal the dagger of Memnoth?"

"The what?" Sohyeon asked glancing at the dagger she held. He had to admit looking at her in her full suit of light body armor holding it like a skilled warrior that it seemed to belong to her. The power that her touch brought made Sohyeon wonder again if anything Pontol told him was even true. Did it really belong to the crazy ferryman, or did he have some other purpose behind bringing Sohyeon here?

"The dagger of Memnoth," Tamnyn said again, stifling a giggle. When she laughed, she seemed much younger than he first thought. "Didn't you know that's what it was?"

"Pontol told me it belonged to his family, and he wanted it back." Sohyeon decided it was best to tell her the truth, and in fact, he didn't sense that she was his enemy exactly. If she was on the ruling council, then maybe he could work with her.

"Pontol is a fool. Even if it was once his family's, he clearly is in no shape to wield it. The House of Elyeon is in a better position to use its power to deal with the danger we face. The dagger has claimed me as its rightful owner and stays with me until the right time."

"I see. Then maybe I should go," Sohyeon said, wishing he didn't sound so lame. Tamnyn exuded an aura of power unlike anything he ever encountered, and he was a little embarrassed he didn't cut a more impressive figure before her.

"Should you?" Tamnyn said carelessly, caressing the dagger a moment before replacing it on the cushion. Pulling off her animal head helmet, she placed it beside the dagger on the dressing table and turned back to look at

Sohyeon, her hair blowing around her in the night breeze. She looked at her servants and nodded curtly. "Prepare some midnight snacks for me and my guest. He'll be staying awhile."

"Really, I shouldn't impose upon you," Sohyeon said as he was led by armed guards back down to the inner courtyard garden where one of the female servants brought out tea and fruit.

Tamnyn sat down on an ornately carved wooden chair with an overstuffed cushion before the square table, and she gestured to Sohyeon to sit across from her in an empty chair. Glancing down at his dirty, tattered appearance, he was uncomfortable with this meeting, but he couldn't refuse her demand. She had caught him in the act of stealing the dagger, and her gracious response was the best he could hope for.

"Where did Pontol dig you up?" she asked lightly, taking a sip of tea.

"I'm not really sure where a place like this is situated in relation to my home, but we call it Earth. I'm a student there, and Pontol took me to visit the priestess of Khabu by accident before making me promise to come here and get him the dagger."

"How interesting," she said excitedly, her demeanor once again making Sohyeon think she was much younger than she had first appeared. "I don't know much about such a place, but I think we have your world chronicled in one of the atlases in our library. I have never traveled on the inner seas the way Pontol does for the priestess of Khabu, but it sounds quite exciting. Now you ask me a question."

Huh? Sohyeon thought, suddenly wondering if he got Tamnyn all wrong with his first impression. Was she still a child as Pontol had said? Her green eyes danced with mischief as she waited for him to respond.

"Well, do you always sleep in armor? What is that made out of anyway? Bone? There seems to be an overabundance of bones in this city, from what I've seen." He realized he had started to talk a little disrespectfully, but she reminded him now of Sukjin, his younger sister, instead of the formidable warrior he encountered moments ago.

She laughed merrily before answering.

"Of course not. I knew you were coming, so I was prepared for battle, though the visions didn't show me that you would be quite so charming. Now, what should I do with you now that you're here? I didn't have any direction on that when I got word you were coming."

"I should go," Sohyeon said, barely touching the refreshments laid out before him. "Pontol will wonder what happened to me."

"Don't worry about Pontol," Tamnyn said lightly, taking a bite of a biscuit. "I can send one of my servants out to see to him, though I'm sure he'll be disappointed to hear you didn't accomplish your mission."

"What good would come by me staying here with you?" Sohyeon asked, suddenly annoyed. Pontol clearly had suffered, and this rich girl was treating the theft of his family's prized possession as if it were nothing. "Shouldn't you give him back the dagger since it is rightfully his?"

Tamnyn shrugged, her expression suddenly blank and innocent.

"I have so few visitors, so it's nice to have someone to chat with while father is away. The council is no longer free to meet since Litt took over, and the citizenry has become slaves to his magic. Pontol is in no condition to handle the dagger, as I told you, plus his family never had the matching helmet that releases the dagger's power. That was in my family all of this time, not his, so is it true that the dagger is his by right?"

"A helmet? That animal helmet you were wearing when you caught me? Is that why you seemed invincible?"

"Why? Did I make you feel a little weak in the knees at our first meeting?" Tamnyn laughed, teasing him.

Sohyeon's annoyance with her grew, as did his interest in her. *What kind of woman is this?* he thought.

"Perhaps you're right that I should stay and chat with you," Sohyeon said, keeping his anger in check. "Maybe you should tell me what happened here in Eokhmisseun that it seems so sinister. Pontol's explanations are very hard to follow."

"The kingdom of Khabu, where the immortals live, invaded our country when my father was a young boy. Eokhmisseun has been in a state of emergency ever since they put a figurehead leader over the city. Some say Litt is a magician, some a demon, but Khabu enslaved the population through a series of magical attacks. Most of the citizens turned into bestial killers like Pontol. Some died because the magic was too potent. Those of us with the blood of heroes and certain geographic protections remained in our wholesome, human states, though we spend our days as if imprisoned. If we leave our estates at all, as my father has done alone to meet secretly with the other members of the ruling council, it must be under guard in carefully veiled transport. Every precaution must be taken, or else Litt's minions will strike anyone who hasn't been turned."

"Is that why Pontol had me dressed like this and stay silent on the way here? So the people of Khabu are not human?"

"No, they aren't human. They are an ancient race, full of beauty and magic, but the royal family has fallen from grace in recent centuries. Litt is among the worst of their degenerate members. Did Pontol mention the restriction they made on silver? It's true if he did. It is the only substance that can kill such beings. Pure silver must penetrate the heart in order for them to die like a mortal. This is why father will never let Pontol take back the dagger, why he has prepared me through training to do battle with the dagger and helmet. Few silver weapons remain in Eokhmisseun, though we always have agents looking for more on the black market."

"Why haven't you killed Litt yet if you have the weapon and the skill?" Sohyeon asked. "Are there a lot of you that have avoided succumbing to his magic and becoming like Pontol?"

Tamnyn's green eyes blazed a moment before a look of vagueness came over her face. She waved her hand as if dismissing the thought.

"The dagger is small, and an assassin would need to be very close indeed to successfully kill the demon, but surely you understand that no hated, oppressive king would walk around the city without bodyguards. The council has figured the best chance we have is to sneak into his compound somehow and stab him while he's asleep. Father is trying to assess if such a plan will work. The council will wait until he comes up with a foolproof plan, and I may be their chosen assassin. I would be with him to consult with them now if I hadn't had the vision of your arrival and stayed behind to greet you." She paused to study him a moment before continuing.

"The council is now made up of ten of us who resisted the magic. In all, I think we have figured between 100 and 300 citizens have not been turned into ghost slaves, and we hide out in our well-stocked, well-guarded mansions most of the time, only venturing out in the streets when we need to and taking those extra precautions."

"What mode of transport did your father take to meet the council?" Sohyeon asked.

"We use carriages drawn by mechanical horses one of the council members invented after the day of terror. Otherwise, we too stay veiled on the streets and strive to be as unnoticeable as possible, as you have done."

"Is that how you meet the council to discuss things?"

"Sometimes. But mostly we use our flock of war pigeons to relay messages. We keep them on the roof. Like the dagger and helmet, father left that responsibility to me."

Sohyeon smiled. She seemed so young, yet she was very capable.

"How old are you?" he asked boldly.

"Twenty-six."

Sohyeon was stunned. She was older than he thought, even older than Mirae.

"Where is your mother and the rest of your family? Do you only live here with your father?"

A shadow passed over Tamnyn's face for a moment.

"Dead. They all died in the war earlier during the day of terror, though we have had other skirmishes periodically since Litt loves chaos. He's always looking for a way to smoke those of us who are still whole out of the shadows to turn us or kill us. He doesn't dare hit our estates directly, because the ghost slaves still have enough of their own mind to turn against him openly if he tries. You are either very brave or very foolish to help Pontol in his task and walk through the city."

"Foolish, more likely," Sohyeon said. "Pontol didn't explain what was happening in your land but was desperate for my help."

"Maybe now *I* am desperate for your help," Tamnyn said, drinking down the rest of her tea.

"Is that why you gave me such a dramatic welcome? What is this vision you mentioned seeing of me?"

Tamnyn stood and signaled to one of the servants waiting by the entryway leading into the house.

"We can talk about it in the morning. Father will be back in three days' time from his mission, and you should stay to have a chat with him."

"Why should I do that? My agreement is with Pontol, after all, not your father."

Sohyeon looked down at the tooth marks on his hand and noticed in surprise how faint they now seemed. How had they already healed?

"By staying and helping us, you are helping Pontol, even if it doesn't seem like it. He wanted you to get the dagger to kill Litt, didn't he? We are also working on a plan to do that. He wouldn't have the opportunity since he is Minha's personal slave. We have the means to achieve his goals. Don't feel like you are abandoning him by helping us. Expelling Khabu is on all of our minds."

Sohyeon realized Tamnyn was sincere and that her aims were just, but a nagging thought occurred to him.

"You say that Pontol is Minha's slave. Why would Minha be interested in my family and send Pontol to us?"

"Khabu is interested in your family? That's odd. You met her? What was your impression of her?"

Sohyeon felt a little embarrassed to admit to Tamnyn that he was fascinated by the priestess beyond measure.

"Minha had me brought before her, but she never said why. Pontol made a mistake and brought me to her instead of my sister Mirae. Minha is very beautiful and makes quite an impression."

Tamnyn was silent a moment, looking at him thoughtfully.

"I don't know much about Minha personally. I've never met her, but I've heard about her by reputation. Father met her. He's far more well-traveled than I, so maybe he can tell you more about her when he gets back. All of the citizens of Khabu are now our mortal enemies, though I admit I don't understand the relationship between Litt and the royalty of Khabu. Rumors abound that he is a member of the royal clan, though whether that means he is degenerate or a member in good standing, I can't say. Maybe he is their ally, or maybe they hate him as much as we do."

"Your father doesn't know?"

Tamnyn smiled.

"I don't think so. He hasn't been to Khabu in many years, not since before I was born, but he told me some stories of them. The dagger and helmet were rumored to have been forged by them and brought to Eokhmisseun somehow. Father thinks the artefacts distill the essence of the immortals and bestow their power on whomever wields them. I find their magic rather intoxicating, which is why they have fallen to me to use among those on the council. Do you want to try them? We can spar tomorrow. I need sword practice anyway. For now, stay the night, and you can look through our library and enjoy the grounds until father returns. You won't find any pleasant place to stay in the city, unless you want to stay with Pontol."

Remembering his impression of the grimy, depressing little shack full of charred bones, Sohyeon shuddered.

"That's fine. We can decide how I should proceed when your father returns, but do you think Mirae is safe going to Khabu given the situation? Maybe I should send her a message through Pontol. She would never agree with Litt's rule given the details. "

"I can send a servant or pigeon to Pontol with instructions to give a message to her if you like once we have consulted with father after he returns. I don't know what they want your sister for, but it may not be good. I'll give you parchment to write your message, and the servants will now escort you to a guest room and provide suitable clothing. For the next few days, I will train you to be lord of the manor, Sohyeon."

8

The next day, Tamnyn tried to get Sohyeon to use the special curved steel swords that Eokhmisseun was known for in the hopes he could eventually try the immortals' helmet and dagger, but it quickly became clear that Sohyeon was untrained in such weaponry. When sparring together, Tamnyn overtook him in minutes, and they quickly abandoned the training. More used to studying than participating in any sort of organized sport other than videogames and paintball, Sohyeon couldn't fence with Tamnyn at all and only looked at the helmet and dagger on her dressing table with regret. Frustrated by her puzzled glances at him, as if she couldn't understand how a man could grow up without learning at least how to defend himself, Sohyeon stayed in the mansion's library the next day instead, reading official histories of Khabu and Eokhmisseun.

Tamnyn came into the library to bring him meals herself, still wearing some of her bone armor over a white quilted bodysuit, but Sohyeon was almost too distracted to eat. The geography of these strange worlds in relation to Earth on the maps he found confused him, so he could only accept Tamnyn's word they were connected to this ethereal plane through some inner sea. Otherwise, most of the histories he found in English were dry descriptions of battles and government policy changes, and all of the names were completely alien. Only a few details caught Sohyeon's attention.

The kingdom of Khabu had only had thirty kings in the span of its 10,000 years of existence, and the current ruler, known as Queen Joriya, had ruled for close to 400 years before there had been some unrest caused by her brother Duke Birum in the last century. But the passage cut off without explaining what had happened, turning to another distant land Sohyeon had never heard of.

"Do you know what happened to Queen Joriya?" he asked Tamnyn when she returned. "What is this dispute with her brother that the book mentions."

"She is still the ruler of Khabu, though she rarely is seen in public," Tamnyn said, standing beside his chair and looking over his shoulder at the book. "I believe the dispute with her brother was over the royal family's crypt, but it died down quickly."

"Why are some of these books in English?" Sohyeon asked, closing the book he was reading and putting it on the table in front of him.

"Eokhmisseun and Khabu have had dealings with your world for many centuries, though you have never heard of us. We have kept our trade and activities there quiet."

"So you're like some sort of space pirates, then?" Sohyeon asked, chuckling to himself.

Tamnyn frowned, a serious expression suddenly flitting over her face.

"We have been careful not to upset your people by our presence, but I don't think there has been anything criminal about our activities."

"I'll take your word for it," Sohyeon said, smiling reassuringly.

Both of them jumped to their feet when a commotion started downstairs.

"Oh, no, it can't be," Tamnyn said, running out of the room in excitement.

Sohyeon followed close behind her, and they both raced down the stairs to the mansion's inner garden courtyard.

"What can't it be?" he whispered in her ear when she stopped abruptly at the doorway, still in the shadows where they couldn't be seen.

"Father! He's back already. He wasn't supposed to come home for a few more days yet. I don't know if that's good or bad."

Peering around the doorframe, Sohyeon observed a tall man with silver-streaked black hair talking excitedly with the housekeeper. Dressed in worn brown leather armor with a long, shimmering light gray hooded cape over it and carrying a bow and arrows, the man appeared to have just arrived. When the man turned toward them, Sohyeon was surprised to see the man's Asian facial features. This man was Tamnyn's father? Even at that distance, Sohyeon could feel the man's charismatic pull.

Putting down his bow and arrows on a stuffed leather chair and pulling off his cloak, the man glanced back toward the house and saw them peeking around the doorframe. When he walked toward the doorway where they stood nervously watching him, Tamnyn jumped eagerly into his path.

"Father, you're back! We have a visitor that you must speak with, the one that I warned you would be coming during your trip when I had my vision."

She took a step back to present Sohyeon.

"Sohyeon, this is my father, Cargal, the leader of the Council of Eokhmisseun. He will train you with a sword so you can continue your mission to help Pontol get revenge."

Sohyeon nodded his head toward Cargal slightly, and the older man looked upon him approvingly.

"Your vision was accurate, Tamnyn. He looks like he could be very useful to us. Where does he hail from?"

"Earth," Sohyeon said quickly before Tamnyn could answer. "What was this vision exactly? You were supposed to explain that to me yesterday."

Tamnyn laughed and waved for Sohyeon and her father to come sit in the garden to discuss it further, handing her father's gear to a waiting attendant.

"I get visions of the future sometimes, and I was shown a vision a few days before you arrived that a boy would come during this full moon who would be whole and not a ghost slave. There are so few of us left here, as I told you before, and someone who can walk easily between the worlds without being caught is rarer still. Almost no one who doesn't live here ever comes to Eokhmisseun since Litt took over. Someone like you could only help our cause. It was important to the underground council to see if my vision was accurate, so I stayed behind instead of going to the meeting. But unfortunately, father, he has no training for war."

Cargal laughed, his merriment as free and easy as his daughter's. Sohyeon was struck by how relaxed they seemed given the frightening situation they lived with, de facto imprisonment in their mansion with an evil spirit ruling the city.

"Yes, we can take care of that problem, if Sohyeon is willing," Cargal said. "The council is nearly ready to move on the first phase of our plan and will need a strong young man like you."

"What has the council decided?" Tamnyn asked abruptly.

"We will risk a clandestine meeting of all of the council in a secret location in a few days. This time I only met with Ginsam, and he has sent messengers on to a few of the others regarding our plans. We need to find a way to infiltrate the palace during the day and kill Litt as he sleeps. Attacking him is too risky during the night when he is roaming the streets. The ghost slaves will do everything in their power to keep things at a stalemate even against their best interests, so it can't be handled in a public place."

"Then we should prepare for the meeting," Tamnyn said, glancing at Sohyeon. "I can get him used to handling the pigeons, and I will leave his sword training to you. It turns out he is interested in the helm and dagger. Pontol sent him here to steal the dagger so the ghost slave could assassinate Litt."

Tamnyn giggled as Cargal looked from one to the other of them in surprise.

"Pontol the ferryman? He is showing unusual independence for a ghost slave all of the sudden. Was there any event that brought about this change in him?"

Sohyeon looked quickly at his hand where Pontol had bitten him and held it up.

"He bit me, too, to make me promise I would get him the dagger. Is it possible he didn't make a mistake when he took me to Minha instead of my sister after all?"

"Minha?" Cargal asked, looking alarmed. "He took you to Khabu?"

"He was supposed to take my sister to Khabu, but he took me instead, then made me promise to help him when I wanted to see Minha again."

"How odd that he would rebel in such a way!" Cargal said softly. "And against Minha no less."

"What do you know about her?" Tamnyn asked. "Sohyeon is concerned about his sister given the situation here, which he had not been informed of when Pontol brought him."

Cargal looked at Sohyeon in dismay.

"Minha is one of the most powerful women in Khabu after the Queen herself. Anyone who is brought before her would be there on the Queen's business."

"She seemed quite upset that I was brought before her instead of my sister," Sohyeon said, his mouth suddenly too dry to speak. "What exactly is she priestess of, and what is the pearl for in her temple? It seemed to exude some magical power?"

Cargal looked at Sohyeon even more intently, his dark brown eyes flashing.

"Minha is priestess of the royal clan and is keeper of the crypt of Khabu, which reportedly no mortal has ever dared enter. She had a pearl, you say? I'm not familiar with that. I'll have to look in the library to see if it is mentioned in the histories."

"It seems to have an unearthly power, but then Minha herself also is quite bewitching," Sohyeon said.

Cargal's face relaxed as he smiled, nodding as if remembering.

"Yes, I met the priestess when I was a young man. She is intoxicating, isn't she? But then it is ever thus when a human meets an immortal, especially one of high rank like Minha. I only ever visited Khabu with my father that one time, and I remember how beautiful and enormous their palace and temples were, gleaming with light and opulence. Eokhmisseun in its day was impressive, but Khabu is in another league."

"I read that their rulers were on the throne for hundreds of years each."

"Yes, they retire rather than die, as do their subjects, though the royal family is quite special even among them. There is a mystery there that no historian ever dared write down, something to do with their family crypt. Perhaps we should travel again to Khabu to find a way to deal with Litt if we can't think of any other way to stop him."

"My sister Mirae was taken there, so perhaps she could get us information somehow," Sohyeon said.

Cargal looked up at him in surprise.

"Your sister went to Khabu and is spending time there? And you are both from Earth? How rare that is," he said, rubbing his unshaven jaw.

"Sohyeon is concerned about why they want his sister. We should investigate that as well," Tamnyn added, smiling at Sohyeon.

"She could be a good resource. Send one of the pigeons to the ferryman then, and see what answers we can get out of the girl."

Cargal nodded curtly to the servant who brought them a fluted carafe of wine and sat down on the leather chair at the edge of the garden. Sohyeon quickly sat at the table with him as the servant put small glasses before them and brought him a small piece of parchment and a quill pen to write with.

"Do you think my sister would be in any danger?" Sohyeon asked, finishing his note to Mirae but hesitating to follow Tamnyn, who was heading toward the stairs to the second floor. "They told her they want her to stop a war in Khabu."

"In danger? Stopping a war in Khabu?" Cargal asked grimly, pouring himself and Sohyeon a small glass of the purplish, aromatic wine that smelled like plums. He took a long sip of it before continuing. "Khabu isn't as dangerous as Eokhmisseun, but I have never heard of Khabu taking such interest in the children of the Earth before. Eokhmisseun and Khabu have had some quiet trade deals with your leaders over the centuries, but nothing that has caused any of us to enter your world much over that time. We must find out from your sister what they mean to do with her."

"Are they at war?" Sohyeon took a sip of the wine, and he grimaced. It tasted too sweet, too much like fruit juice rather than any wine he had ever tasted, but after a few seconds, he noticed his vision blurring a little bit and a strange tingling on his tongue. "Does Minha mean their war with you? I know they have invaded your homeland and done terrible things, but I'd hate to think my sister is in danger."

Seeing Sohyeon's earnest expression, Cargal was diplomatic in his answer.

"Of course, relations between our countries have been bad for at least two generations in Eokhmisseun. However, Khabu is an unearthly land where immortals live. Your sister is one of the few mortals to receive such a grace as a summons. It may be quite wonderful for her to be so favored, though it remains to be seen what it portends for the rest of us."

Cargal's voice then turned gentle.

"Go with Tamnyn, Sohyeon, and we will uncover this mystery. You'll find that the birds are reliable messengers."

9

Sohyeon quickly finished drinking his cup of wine and started up the stairs after Tamnyn. When he reached the top floor of the mansion, he saw that Tamnyn had opened shutters nearly the size of doors onto the darkening sky. At this height, they could see mostly treetops of the nearby grotto, though a certain type of willowy tree had grown even taller than the house and were clustered not far from the roof's edge. Tamnyn or Cargal could have used the trees to secretly leave the mansion, or perhaps their enemies could climb the trees to breach the mansion's defenses.

Tamnyn busied herself with the bird on the left side of the room where the wall was lined with 20 cages, each with one or two birds resting in them, all looking curiously at him. Their bodies were slightly plump, their feathers milky white, and their red or pearlescent eyes gleamed with intelligence. Tamnyn had already taken out one of the smaller birds and, patting it reassuringly, spoke to it in another language, which he was startled to hear the bird speak back! A small harness hung around the bird's neck with a pouch for rolled parchment where Tamnyn put the note Sohyeon handed her. Taking the bird over to the window, she let it step onto the ledge and stretch out its wings. After a moment, it flew out into the night stealthily.

Her long red hair blowing lightly in the breeze, Tamnyn stood at the window, looking at the disappearing form with an expression of wonder. Sohyeon came up beside her, caught off guard by her change in demeanor. He realized fleetingly that she was as fascinating to him as the bird that captivated her.

"So the birds also talk?" he asked, wondering if the pungent wine had gone to his head and was making him hallucinate the whole thing.

Tamnyn turned toward the sound of his voice, startled, as if he had jolted her out of a beautiful dream, and he immediately felt awkward.

"The birds speak a limited forest dialect that is based on the native language of Khabu," she said, a bit apologetically. "They are used to human interactions but can't speak a human language. Their bodies aren't built for it."

"Are they magical?" Sohyeon asked. "Is Eokhmisseun magical?"

"I don't think they are," Tamnyn said, smiling pensively. "Khabu uses true magic, while we only have some technological skill. However, I seem to recall that at the start the birds were a gift from the priestess of Khabu hundreds of years ago, not Minha but a predecessor, as a gesture of friendship long before Litt appeared and caused all of this destruction to our land."

Her voice trailed off.

"They look like doves and are very delicate," Sohyeon said, glancing back at the birds quietly nestled in their cages. "So Litt doesn't know about them? Shouldn't he if he is from Khabu?"

"I'm sure he knows about them," Tamnyn said under her breath, so low Sohyeon could hardly catch her vehement words. Her eyes were now clouded with concern. "He just ignores them. We may get caught at any time, and if we are successful in challenging Litt in any way, he may have them killed on sight."

"Is there anything in Eokhmisseun that isn't risky?"

"We will be taking greater risks than this soon enough."

They both fell silent and listened to the evening breeze rustle through the leaves for a few minutes.

"How long will it be before the bird returns?" Sohyeon asked, finally breaking the silence again.

"Mapin will return once she makes contact with Pontol. It all depends on how hard he is to find and what he knows. It may take a few trips to get all of the answers you seek from your sister, but we may be able to get at least one question answered tonight. I'll have one of the guards stay here and wake us if Mapin returns during the night. For now, we should turn in."

Without waiting for Sohyeon to answer, she started down the stairs to the mansion's third floor.

10

"Sohyeon, wake up."

Sohyeon opened his eyes, shielding them a little against the bright light in his room. Sitting up, he saw Tamnyn standing in the center of the room, Mapin on her hand. Filmy gold curtains blew on the soft breeze behind her, opening at intervals to reveal the cloudy sky between the latticework façade that blocked the window like a screen. In this room, the sunlight that seemed so thin and weak as he walked the streets with Pontol now glittered with a warm, beautiful light that illuminated the delicately carved lintels and window frames. The interior opulence of the mansion transformed the dead city into something living and beautiful.

"Did she answer?" he asked, sitting on the side of his bed and pulling on his T-shirt. "You seem excited for some reason. Was it good news?"

"I don't know what to make of it, but Mapin has explained to me the meaning of the pearl you saw in the temple when you were taken to Minha."

"Why would the pearl be of importance now?"

"Your sister was wearing a ring with part of that pearl. It has some significance to the royal family, and the pearl in the font is the light that the pigeons use to navigate like a homing device when sending messages. That's why they can run errands at night."

"What does it mean?" Sohyeon asked, walking over to Tamnyn and the bird. Though he didn't dare touch Mapin, he wondered if he would also experience whatever feeling seemed to come over Tamnyn around her.

"It means your sister is part of the royal family somehow."

Sohyeon looked up at Tamnyn in alarm, aware that her voice now suddenly had seemed flat.

"No one in Eokhmisseun knew anything about the pearl before Mapin told you this?"

"We aren't accustomed to talking so freely with the birds," Tamnyn said, frowning a little. "They don't usually tell us much about themselves, only about the task we send them on. I told you, they were once a gift to our nation from Khabu. It isn't surprising they are still connected to it in some way, or even that the pearl is connected to the royal family."

"Why would Mirae wear the ring of the royal family of some strange land? They are immortals, right?" Sohyeon asked, running a hand through his hair. He had a hard time picturing Mirae as royalty, though she never acted as childish as Sukjin even when she was younger.

"Who knows? Perhaps she is to be married into it," Tamnyn said, her eyes turning back to Mapin as the bird shifted on her wrist. "She has a bit of parchment still attached to her neck, so perhaps there is a return message that will explain it."

Sohyeon approached the bird carefully and gently pulled the paper from the pouch. Mapin only shifted once slightly, eying Sohyeon with mild suspicion. Unravelling the paper, Sohyeon recognized his sister's handwriting.

Sohyeon, I knew something was wrong when the priestess told me I was needed to help them fight a war. Tonight I accidentally met the Duke, Birum. Neither he nor Minha explained why I was there but Birum dined with me and showed me around the countryside a little. He seems to be too charming to be the cause of all of this trouble, but Minha is concerned about the Duke's interference in the affairs of Khabu. Beyond that, I have never heard of Eokhmisseun and had not been told that someone from Khabu was stirring up trouble there. Should I ask about it? Is there a way I can help? Tell me what you need me to do. Mirae.

"Should we tell her?" Sohyeon asked, wrapping the piece of parchment around his finger absent-mindedly. "Will she really be able to help us from Khabu? What do you know about the Duke?"

"Nothing much," Tamnyn said, sighing. "Perhaps we need more information about Litt's activities here so we know how to approach the Queen. Your sister really must be someone important there in order to get an audience so quickly as an outsider."

"Your idea was that she could be married off as a way of helping them," Sohyeon began. "You didn't mean to say they'd marry her to this Duke who is causing so much trouble there, did you?"

"We haven't heard anything about the Duke here in Eokhmisseun. We have enough trouble dealing with their countryman Litt to worry about their domestic issues." Tamnyn stroked Mapin's head as she examined her wing before turning to go back downstairs.

"Perhaps father will know what to ask her to do. Come with me. I need to return Mapin to her cage to rest for a while before we send our response, and then we can talk about the situation further."

They went to the rooftop where the birds were kept, deposited Mapin, then went back down to the first floor. After they had had breakfast in the main dining room, Cargal looked over the response from Mirae with interest.

"She has been taken to see the Queen herself? Then this is about more than just serving in Minha's place," Cargal said intently, his dark brown eyes resting on the flames in the fireplace. In spite of the balmy day, he had insisted the servants light the fire and was tightly wrapped in a thick coat.

"A marriage?" Tamnyn asked, picking up a slice of bread and spreading jam over it.

"It would be an unusual decision for Khabu to make, potentially diluting their bloodlines. That's not to say they wouldn't, but it doesn't seem advantageous to them on the face of things. You say she wears the ring of the royal family? That has more interesting possibilities. Sohyeon, do you recall anything unusual about your sister growing up?"

Before he could answer, the mansion's head guard walked into the room and grimly handed Cargal a slip of paper.

"Another message? My bird to Sagar has returned already? What could this mean?"

Cargal unraveled the parchment and, his eyes quickly scanning the message, he jumped to his feet, dropping his knife on the floor.

"What has happened?" Tamnyn asked, watching the color drain from her father's face.

"They are calling an emergency meeting of the council immediately. We must go in person this time, all of us."

"That will be very dangerous," Tamnyn said. "Where are we to meet them? When?"

"Tonight, shortly after dusk, at Sagar's estate."

"That's not far at least. We should take Sohyeon with us, shouldn't we? He hasn't had time to begin any sword training though."

Cargal glanced over at Sohyeon, rubbing his stubbly beard.

"I may have a weapon he can use in the meantime that won't require much skill. I can test him out in the armory before we leave tonight. We have all day before we need to leave, and the guards will need to get our carriage ready."

"Did Sagar say why he needed to call an emergency meeting?" Tamnyn asked, her eyes lingering on the parchment her father held.

"Litt has made his move. Instead of smoking us out, he has kidnapped Yarava!"

Tamnyn gasped, her eyes wide.

"What will that mean for us?" she asked, her voice barely a whisper. "Litt has never openly attacked us, yet now he has kidnapped one of the few women on the council. Will he kill her? Are we going to come up with a plan to rescue her at Sagar's meeting?"

"Would you be willing to rescue her and risk capture yourself, Tamnyn? You don't remember what it was like.

Your mother…". His voice trailed off as Tamnyn's expression turned to a look of abject terror before she looked away, her eyes drifting toward the fire.

"So we abandon her?" Tamnyn asked, her voice flat.

Sohyeon looked from one to the other, following the exchange in silence. He felt helpless and barely understood what they were talking about. Cargal didn't answer.

"Then what good is a meeting?" she asked. "Won't we be risking kidnapping ourselves by merely venturing out in the streets now that he has so brazenly taken her? We aren't ready to confront Litt under these circumstances."

"We aren't ready, but we should go to the meeting nonetheless."

"Does Sagar say anything else?"

"No, the message is just an invitation to his house. We had already planned to meet when I left him a few days ago, so perhaps he just has in mind a continuation of our earlier conversation."

"How long will it take to travel there through the streets?" Sohyeon asked.

"Not very long. Less than an hour. We must move slowly so we won't attract attention. The mechanical horses hum and clatter less than real ones, but it's still enough to be noticed if we travel at a brisk pace."

"And what if it is a trap?" Tamnyn asked suddenly.

"Do you want to rescue Yarava or do you want to hide out here at our estate forever?" Cargal asked angrily, rising from his chair. Turning on his heel, he stormed out of the dining room without another word. The parchment fell to the floor behind him, and Tamnyn picked it up, tracing over its surface with her finger absent-mindedly.

"Well?" Sohyeon asked after a minute.

"We aren't ready for this. We won't have time to plan carefully like we had hoped," she whispered.

Everyone at the Elyeon estate was sullen until nightfall, but Sohyeon managed to coax Tamnyn to send another bird to Pontol with a reply for Mirae a few hours later. He was pleased that Tamnyn let him write what he wanted without reading it.

When you return to Khabu, find out what you can about the demonic ghoul Litt who is ruler now in Eokhmisseun. I am told he is an invader from Khabu who has destroyed their land and magically tainted their people. The rulers live in hiding from him, and they can't get close enough to discover how to get rid of him apart from certain magical legends that I should not discuss here. It's very dangerous here, and I don't know when I'll be back home. Have I been gone long on Earth? Was mom worried?

Mapin took the message again around lunchtime, and Sohyeon watched her small form disappear into the cluster of trees below. The servants brought them meals separately in their rooms for the rest of the day since everyone was preparing for the dangerous procession through the city streets to the clandestine council meeting. Sohyeon had resigned himself to spending the day mostly alone and was looking through the library again when he got a summons from Cargal to come to the armory in the mansion's basement shortly after nightfall.

11

As Sohyeon reached the bottom of the staircase leading to the armory beneath the mansion and his eyes adjusted to the dim light, he saw Cargal standing in the center of a room full of mannequins wearing different suits of armor with a variety of weapons hanging on the walls. The room was lit by torchlight, and while bright, it was still dim compared to the sunny atmosphere of the upper floors. Cargal looked up at him from the weapon he held as Sohyeon entered.

"You wanted to see me?"

Cargal smiled wearily at him and motioned for him to come closer, holding up what looked to be a small crossbow.

"I called you down here to give you this." He held out the crossbow to Sohyeon. "The arrows are on the table behind me. I think it should be sufficient for an unskilled boy should we get forced to fight on our way to the council meeting. We don't have time for anything more than that. Have you ever shot a bow? Crossbows are easy to use and require no training at all."

"I've shot some of the cheaper paintball guns and a .45 once," Sohyeon said, taking the crossbow from Cargal, noting how heavy the weapon seemed. It was only a foot long with a pistol-shaped handle. He walked behind Cargal to pick up a pouch full of bolts to use in it.

"You'll also need to wear some armor and a cape," Cargal continued as Sohyeon walked back around him. "Take that armored suit there." He pointed to the mannequin across from him. The brown leather breastplate looked like a something out of ancient Rome, even down to the war skirt made from strips of leather flowing over the thighs for his legs to have a full range of movement.

"Should I get ready and put it on now? Are we leaving soon?"

"After dinner," Cargal said gravely. "We will be taking the carriage instead of walking, but we all should be prepared after what happened to Yarava. Tamnyn will be wearing the heirloom helmet and dagger, and we will take one of the house guards for each of us to serve as personal bodyguards and drive the mechanical horses. I have 50 servants who guard the mansion, so we can spare three for this evening's visit. I just want to ask you to stay close to Tamnyn for me, should something happen. Can you do that for me? I know you are still very young."

"I will do that, sir," Sohyeon said, feeling flattered.

"Then we leave as soon as we finish dinner, within the hour. Prepare however you need to before then."

The hour passed quickly, and they all gathered in their strange attire near the shadowy grove of snaky willow trees beside a smaller house attached to the main mansion.

"Is everyone here?" Cargal asked.

They didn't dare take a step out of the mansion without wearing the flowing gray capes with hoods that even covered their faces, leaving only their eyes exposed, a form of anonymity that kept Litt's men from recognizing when someone they had not succeeded at turning walked the city streets.

Tamnyn came over to Sohyeon to help him fasten the last part of the cape across his nose with her gloved hands. Sohyeon knew she wore her white bone armor with the dagger of Memnoth hidden against her torso beneath her cape, and the oddly-shaped helmet gave her head a strange appearance with the hood over it. She tried not to giggle at Sohyeon, too, as he struggled to move in all of the heavy gear and still keep the crossbow out of sight.

"You'll get used to it," she whispered, pulling him toward the waiting carriage.

More like a covered wagon with black wool covering the back compartment, the carriage was pulled by two shining steel horses with no heads that reminded Sohyeon of the Legged Squad Support System robots he'd seen photos of on the internet. He vaguely thought of what Tamnyn said about interaction between Eokhmisseun and Earth and wondered at the strange parallel.

"So these replace real horses?" he said, pausing beside one in astonishment.

Unlike the ones he saw in photos back home, these robots were taller than him by a head with no open wires or gears showing, and he noticed how intricately the joints were made with layers of small pieces of steel, how polished the metallic surface was even in the starlight light. It looked like an armored animal, yet it was not an animal at all.

"Did your father make these? Why go to such trouble when you could use real animals?"

"My father and the other men on the council are quite a skilled blacksmiths, as the knights in our city have been for generations, so we were able to achieve this level of imitation. It's too dangerous to use real animals if you can find them in Eokhmisseun because they can be so easily attacked by the ghost slaves, who will swarm and eat them if they get the chance, stranding your chariot in the middle of nowhere and killing or capturing the passengers. They discovered this problem in my grandfather's day not long after Litt arrived, and they have worked on these imitation horses ever since, though there are only twenty of them, two to each council members' household. The materials to make them are rare now that we are locked into our homes and most of the city has been turned into ghost slaves. The mechanical horses' movement, however, is driven by less scientific means."

"I'm afraid to ask," Sohyeon said, climbing up into the carriage wagon where Cargal and one of the guards already waited. The remaining two guards would stay out on the front seat to guide the horses.

Tamnyn sat beside Sohyeon with Cargal and his bodyguard Esram across from them in the covered part of the carriage. As the carriage began to move, everyone was silent, and the only sound that broke through the still night was the slow, muffled clattering of the horses' metal feet on the flagstone streets. Again, Sohyeon felt reluctant to break the eerie silence and ask the myriad of questions that flitted through his mind. Instead, he forced himself to forget his curiosity and focus on the task at hand. They would be at Sagar's castle soon enough anyway.

As the carriage turned and shuddered through the city's twisted streets, Sohyeon noted how nothing else seemed to move, no normal, stray sounds floated through the air, no indication of human activity reached their ears at all. It was so different from home where you could hear the ambient noise of car engines, radios or conversations in the distance even at night sometimes, but Eokhmisseun was under a shadow that cast a pall over life here. Even the citizens who were still whole lived as if dead, and the city sounded as quiet as a graveyard.

Finally, the carriage slowed. Cargal looked up in alarm, as if waking from a deep sleep though his eyes had never closed, and he jumped toward the driver's seat, pushing back the curtain around them.

"We're there," he said softly after a moment, sticking his head back in the compartment. "We just need to wait a moment for Sagar's summons. There is the moat to contend with."

When Sohyeon emerged from the carriage, he stood with the others on the shore of a wide moat across from a stone castle glimmering white with delicate carvings across its face, shadowy and shrouded in fog. A bridge ran from the shore where they stood over the dark, rippling water to the castle's entrance. Only a tall archway made of the same milky white stone with wide, heavy wooden doors blocked their path. After a moment, they heard a low grinding sound, and the doors opened slowly.

"Why didn't we ride across?" Sohyeon asked Tamnyn in a low voice, edging closer to her. He could only tell it was her by her white fingertips and the odd shape of her head beneath her hood. Otherwise, all of them in their party looked nearly identical in their flowing gray cloaks.

"Sagar is looking for a particular signal and verification of our identities," she said. "Anyone could come here in a chariot, though few have mechanical horses, but in the dark it's too risky to assume anything. Someone could have stolen them from our estates. He can't afford to let just anyone in. Litt would give anything to turn Sagar, and Litt's followers have tried to get to him before."

Tamnyn suddenly grabbed his bare wrist where it peeked out between his cloak sleeve and his glove, her eyes gleaming in the moonlight.

"Sohyeon," she whispered, pulling him closer to her. "Stay near me tonight. I had another vision, though I didn't tell father this time. Something will change tonight. We need to stay together. This was the point of our meeting."

Sohyeon glanced up at the two figures swathed in gray standing by the horses, but Cargal was looking at the doors instead of at them. The other guard waited in the carriage seat for permission to guide the horses over the bridge.

"Your father already asked me to watch over you," Sohyeon said softly. "I thought it was kind of ridiculous, though, since you're such a good fighter. I can't compete with you at all. Plus you have the dagger and helmet."

12

A soft whistle gave them permission to enter. The carriage slipped quietly over the threshold and across the bridge, Cargal and the two guards walking in front of it, and Sohyeon and Tamnyn walking behind it. The doors slid closed behind them, this time more quickly than they opened, and the attendants barred them against further intrusion.

Sagar's guards escorted them into the main hall of the castle, which had many of the same lacy decorative arches and thin, carved white pillars highlighted with gold that Sohyeon had come to admire at the Elyeon estate. The room was dim and smelled vaguely of freshly baked bread. A burly man with wild, curly brown hair and a neatly trimmed beard sat in the middle of a long table on a high-backed wooden chair, and behind him sat five armored, tired-looking men and one woman with raven black hair. He looked at each figure as they entered and took off their hoods and face scarves. His ice blue eyes settled on them one by one, stopping finally on Sohyeon with a look of puzzlement.

"We have a visitor from beyond the inner sea," Cargal said hastily, anticipating Sagar's question. "This is Sohyeon. We hope he will aid us in our task to rid Eokhmisseun of Litt."

"What news do you have of Yarava?" Tamnyn asked urgently, stepping forward.

"Litt's men have raided her compound and taken her and most of her servants back to his palace for the turning. It won't be long before they come for us, too, if they are willing to be that brazen. She's the first of the council members of this generation that they've gotten their hands on. We may not be able to save her without grave risk to the rest of the city's leadership."

"The ghost slaves didn't defend her?" Tamnyn asked in astonishment. The gemstone eyes of the animal head on the helmet she wore glittered fiercely in the flickering lamplight. "They have been our best protectors with their ambivalent feelings about the past, tolerating Litt but unwilling to destroy the council leaders whom they have respected in their former lives."

Cargal sighed and came over to his daughter, putting his gloved black hand on her shoulder.

"I had heard reports that the ghost slaves have been turning more bestial in the past few years. It was bound to get more dangerous as the magical influence they are under deepened. Naim had suggested at some point that they'd lose their humanity altogether and develop a taste for human flesh. There aren't many of us left here to satiate it, so Pontol's interest in Sohyeon is worrisome."

Cargal glanced back at Sohyeon, whose eyes involuntarily went to the marks on his own hand. What did it mean that Pontol had bitten him?

"So what is our next move?" Tamnyn asked, her voice wavering. "We let her die, become a ghost slave, along with her household, then just wait around until we are targeted next?"

"Perhaps Yarava will be able to fight her way out," Sagar said, rising to his feet and coming around the table to stand before them. He wore a long, luxurious blue satin robe beneath a black, fur-trimmed leather vest.

"Is it time to attempt to assassinate Litt?" Ginsam, one of the younger men on the council, asked, standing and coming over to Sagar's side. "Tamnyn has the magical silver dagger, doesn't she? She has the helmet, too, and with the power of the immortals, we can still win. We can make an attempt to sneak into Litt's lair and kill him before he tries anything else."

All of the council looked at Tamnyn, and she met their eyes with calm confidence.

"I could make the attempt soon, since my progress in learning to control the artefacts has been progressing, but we have no real plan to disarm Litt's guards, and we must consider the consequences if we fail. We only have one chance to strike and kill him. Our plan has to be foolproof. We aren't ready yet to take him on directly."

"Then we should plan for Litt's assassination within the week," Sagar said, his eyes moving from Cargal to Tamnyn, ignoring her protestations. "We can't wait any longer. Our survival depends on this."

A brief, troubled look passed over Tamnyn's face, but she quickly regained her composure.

"The artefacts are very powerful," she said, pulling the dagger out of its sheath at her waist. "They should be able to neutralize Litt if we can get close enough."

The silver blade gleamed like a mirror in the flickering torchlight. Sohyeon thought he saw a thin, laser-like beam of blue light run down the edge of the blade to the tip, but it had disappeared so quickly, he wondered if he had imagined it. Satisfied everyone had noted the dagger, Tamnyn replaced it in its sheath under her cloak.

"We'll discuss it further when we return to our estate," Cargal said, his voice uncharacteristically tight as he repeated Tamnyn's objection. "I understand the urgency of our need for action, however, an assassination attempt will require careful planning. We will send one of the war pigeons to you with details once the time is decided. For now, that is the best we can do."

The room fell silent, and Sagar nodded curtly, frowning in displeasure. The other council members looked sidelong at each other or looked at the floor.

"That's all for tonight," Sagar said, his voice gruff but ragged with emotion. "Send the message when you're ready. We will not meet in person again before the deed is done, so fare thee well!"

13

Cargal bowed deeply to Sagar and led his party out of the castle back to the waiting carriage. As the three guards prepared for them to board the rear compartment, Cargal looked back darkly at the castle and pulled the scarf from over his mouth with a sharp motion.

"He wasted our time and had us risk being caught in the streets just for this!" Cargal whispered angrily. "What is the meaning of this? Nothing was decided! Should we really risk an assassination attempt with no plan in mind?"

"Hush, father," Tamnyn said in a low voice, pulling the scarf from her face too, her eyes turning in alarm toward the castle entrance. "They may overhear you."

The six of them were alone on the bridge. Sohyeon just watched the exchange in silence, though he also ripped the face guard off his mouth, puzzled as to why Cargal and Tamnyn were being so careless as to not put their capes on fully.

Cargal sighed and climbed into the back of the carriage, helping Tamnyn and Sohyeon on behind him and pulling the curtains closed. The three of them sat with Esram in the darkness, an uncomfortable silence between them. The carriage finally began to turn back toward the road as the gate's wooden doors creaked open.

The carriage's gentle swaying and cautious, quiet gait started to lull Sohyeon to sleep after a few minutes. Feeling Tamnyn's gloved hand grab his, he jumped, now fully awake.

"Did you hear that?" she whispered as the carriage slowed even more.

"I didn't hear anything," Sohyeon said.

"I did, something faint, but I don't know what it was," Cargal said, shifting in his seat. "I should look out on the drivers to see if they noticed anything strange."

Esram woke from a light sleep and listened to their conversation with alarm.

Before Cargal could reach the curtains at the front, the carriage shuddered as something hit it low on the left side full force. Sohyeon heard something like a low growl which turned into a whining yowl at the back of the compartment as something tore at the fabric wall.

Suddenly, one of the men driving the carriage screamed. Cargal's hand froze on the curtain, and in the dim light he looked back at them.

"Get Tamnyn away from here if you can, Sohyeon. It's important she isn't captured since she's the only one who has mastered the artefacts. I'll delay them here if I have to."

"No! They'll kill you!" Tamnyn whispered emphatically, her voice breaking. "Come with us."

"There isn't time!"

He turned, and pulling out a short sword, he slit the fabric on the far side of the carriage wall where none of the odd sounds seemed to come from. "I'll take the front while Esram takes the back, and we'll hold them off. Rip it open and run."

Both men moved quickly to confront whatever waited at either end of the carriage. Without hesitating, Sohyeon grabbed the fabric and pulled roughly at the jagged tear in the cloth. In the confusion, he and Tamnyn jumped to the ground, though Sohyeon was aware of smoldering, yellow eyes peeking around the back edge of the carriage at them. Pausing only a moment to glance back at it, Sohyeon felt a sliver of fear as he saw the face bearing its long incisors at him, a grotesque mix of feline and human.

This time, Tamnyn pulled him after her before he could get a good look at the creature. From the cries of the men and Cargal's commands, Sohyeon could tell the four men were in the thick of battle. Tamnyn ran as quickly as her cloak would allow, and Sohyeon suddenly realized they couldn't escape so easily encumbered with such clumsy clothing. Without thinking, he pulled his hood off and stuffed the hem of the cloak into the belt of his armor as they ran.

After a few blocks, sensing they were no longer being pursued by their attackers, Sohyeon pulled Tamnyn around the corner of one of the buildings into a deserted alleyway and looked back toward the carriage.

"What is that?" he asked, gagging a little at the sight of their attacker again. "Is it an animal?"

"It's one of the ghost slaves," Tamnyn said, her eyes frantically scanning the scene for Cargal, who had disappeared beyond their sight. One of the guards driving the carriage hung from the seat, obviously dead. His body was covered with blood and claw marks as the half-human beast gnawed on his arm.

"Why would they attack us? Didn't you say they were mostly ambivalent in your fight with Litt?"

"They've been changing, as you heard my father say in the council meeting. We need to get back to the estate and meet up with father. We can't linger here. Why did you take your hood off? They'll see you better walking through the streets without it."

"I could barely run in it, and I certainly can't use this," he said, gesturing to the crossbow and bolts strapped across his back. "It's all fairly useless in a hand to hand fight."

"I know, but we're used to it. Put it back on for now. The cloak makes us nearly invisible to the ghost slaves' eyesight since the color makes us blend too easily into the landscape of city buildings. We need to get out of here."

Sohyeon did as she asked, and they quickly ran through the streets back in the direction of the mansion.

14

When the estate came into view, they paused at the crossroads in front of it. Tamnyn touched Sohyeon's arm and looked up and down the street, then turned back to him.

"We need to be careful. They probably expect us to come back here."

"Then maybe we should go another way," Sohyeon said, suddenly feeling uneasy as he looked at the mansion. "Is there somewhere else we could go to lay low for a day or two? I wonder if we should go back to Pontol."

"Pontol? A ghost slave may not help us if they have all gone feral against those of us who remain whole. If we get back into our house, we can prepare to defend it. If we abandon it even for a few days, they may overrun it, and then where would we go?"

"How many doors are there into the house?"

"Maybe four. I think we should try to go in through the front since we can see from here that there isn't any of Litt's men posted outside. Our bodyguards inside will know what to do when we arrive. Are you ready to make a run for it? It will take a few minutes for them to determine we aren't the enemy and let us in, so we will be vulnerable for that time."

Tamnyn held onto Sohyeon's arm and cautiously led him out into the deserted street, almost holding her breath as they snuck across the open space onto the mansion's expansive front lawn. Sohyeon felt very vulnerable and unable to defend himself in the flowing cape and face scarf, but he didn't protest and just followed Tamnyn, keeping his steps light so he wouldn't make much noise. The night was eerily silent once again, and nothing moved. Looking at the bone-like filigree carvings over the mansion's windows, Sohyeon couldn't detect any sign of life inside, and he wondered if her bodyguards were still there at all.

As they closed the distance, Sohyeon heard a soft click near the front door, but his eyes stayed riveted on the whitewashed wood, desperate for the safety of the mansion. When they were only 15 paces away from the mansion, the door opened, and the male servant who had served them dinner every night emerged, casually wearing some beaten up leather armor with his dagger still sheathed at his waist. Behind him, the house was dark. Sohyeon felt his hair stand on end as the familiar figure came out stiffly to greet them with a thin smile barely discernible in the dim light.

Tamnyn hadn't seemed to have noticed as she let go of Sohyeon's arm and took another step toward her servant, holding out her arms as if expecting to embrace him, but Sohyeon thought he detected movement to the right of the door where there was a patch of tall bushes whose ivy-bearing branches had crawled up the carved filigree façade. It was too dark to tell for sure, but Sohyeon thought he could see the outline of a tall figure there.

As Tamnyn stopped, watching her servant uncertainly, the shadow in the bushes moved with preternatural swiftness toward the manservant. Sohyeon let out a very quick, low warning whistle, and the manservant looked around in alarm. Tamnyn took a few hesitant steps back to stand beside Sohyeon, realizing something was wrong, her eyes getting wider as she ripped the scarf from across her mouth again.

The bushes rustled as the shadow passed them. Sohyeon quickly grabbed Tamnyn and pulled her against him, watching in horror as the creature pounced on the confused manservant standing just outside the front door. As the tall, solitary figured cloaked in black leaned close to the manservant, torches in the front foyer just beyond the open door behind them suddenly blazed to light, throwing the two figures into terrifying relief.

Sohyeon could see the cloaked figure wore gloves, and it tore one of them off, revealing a thin, clawed hand with chalky white skin and black veins showing through the translucent surface. When he saw the creature's monstrous hand, Sohyeon knew there was nothing they could do to save the man now and that the House of Elyeon was doomed to failure against the dark forces that ruled Eokhmisseun.

"No," Tamnyn cried weakly, her legs nearly giving out beneath her.

Sohyeon pulled her away from the drama playing out with the manservant, preparing to carry her away to safety as soon as he could tear himself away from the sight. With his other hand, he lightly pressed on her lips so she wouldn't draw the figure's attention away from the manservant onto them.

The hand floated in a cloud of darkness as the figure's cape blew around it softly in the evening breeze. The manservant's eyes were locked on the face hidden in the folds of its hood, dread slowly spreading over his features as the figure's clawed hand reached out for his throat, one of the few parts of the manservant's armored body that was soft and exposed. His arms hung nervelessly at his side as he seemed to lose all will to fight, and his eyes rolled back into his head as the gangly fingers wrapped around his throat and began to squeeze. The figure's claws dug into the man's flesh, blood dripping down his neck as they tore into it, his skin turning as pale and sickly-looking as the disembodied hand. His features began to change from human into those of some distorted, almost feline half-beast.

"What is happening?" Sohyeon whispered in Tamnyn's ear. "Is it the turning?"

He felt Tamnyn nod, and he didn't wait to watch anymore of the manservant's transformation. If they wanted to survive, they had to leave now and find somewhere safe to hide. Nearly carrying Tamnyn as he stumbled a little in the flowing cloak, he quickly went back to their hiding place across the street. The figure in black was too focused on draining the energy out of the man it held to stop them.

Pausing to look around the neighborhood, Sohyeon wondered if he could trust Tamnyn to walk on her own. Fear had gripped her to the point that she could barely stand, but it was too difficult to carry her very far in all of their battle gear, so he helped her lean against the building while they came to a decision. Suddenly, though, Sohyeon could see why the cloaks were important. It wasn't because of the ghost slave's eyesight, it was because of the turning! The monster – was it Litt? – turned humans into ghost slaves by its touch, so any exposed skin left them vulnerable to the turning. Sohyeon wondered if Tamnyn also just discovered that.

A guttural cry from the house made him look back around the corner from the alleyway, and he could see the black figure release the manservant from his grasp and replace the glove on its hand.

"Tamnyn," he whispered softly, trying not to let his alarm show as he saw the black figure turn and look in their direction across the open space. "We need get out of here. We're going to be next if we don't escape to safety now. But where should we go? It's already coming this way, so pick somewhere fast!"

He grabbed her shoulders a minute before releasing her gently, aware that the figure had started to walk across the front lawn of the estate in their direction.

"We need to get out of here now," he said again. "There isn't time to grieve for anybody."

Tamnyn's terrified eyes turned toward him, but she stood up woozily on her own, trying to clear her head. He grabbed her hand, and they ran as swiftly and quietly as they could down the alleyway in the direction of Pontol's shack. Following every twist and turn in the back streets, his eyes scanning the seemingly windowless buildings on either side of them for any signs of help or a good place to hide, he couldn't shake the feeling that the shadow was still behind them. No matter how far away it was, it wasn't far enough. Feeling like he was walking through molasses, Sohyeon tried not to despair. He knew he couldn't take the cloak off now even though he couldn't get away fast enough with it on, so he looked frantically for a place where they could throw the black figure off their trail.

"I still have the dagger and the helm," Tamnyn whispered as they ran.

"Shut up, okay, we're not fighting that kind of power directly if we can help it," Sohyeon said, dragging her through one of the few open doorways he had found as they passed, shutting the door quietly behind him. The house appeared to be abandoned and burned out, but they could run through it to another connecting alleyway or street that would make it harder for the thing in the dark behind them to follow.

"What is that behind us? What could do that to a man?" he whispered gruffly, gasping for breath as they reached a doorway at the other side of the house. Looking up and down the wide street that ran past it, confirming nothing was out at that hour, they fled down it away from the city, almost doubling back in the direction they had come. He wondered fleetingly what had become of Cargal. Would they perhaps run into him as they passed through some of the streets that led to Sagar's castle?

"Litt."

Tamnyn's answer was the one name Sohyeon didn't want to hear, though Tamnyn only confirmed what he had already guessed. So the creature who caused Eokhmisseun such misery had come to her family's door now! Sohyeon knew they couldn't go back there anytime soon if that was the case. The council was likely gone now, too. Eokhmisseun had fallen to such an evil power that there was no remaining resistance movement to stop it after tonight.

"Which way should we go?" he asked Tamnyn, stopping to take a few deep breaths before they continued running. Like Tamnyn, he pulled the scarf away from his mouth.

"I don't know where you had hoped to run to, but we can continue to the inner sea and Pontol if you like. We should cross here to that alleyway."

Tamnyn pointed to a dark area between the buildings not far from them. Sohyeon's instinct had already been to return to the ship if possible, hoping Pontol hadn't been affected by whatever was brewing among the ghost slaves tonight.

"Did you know about the real protective power of these cloaks?" he asked, grabbing her hand and pulling her into the alleyway.

Something stirred in the shadowy building behind them across the street, and he snapped his head around to look back at it, but nothing was there. They ran deeper into the alley, but it had become too dark to see very far in front of them. Slowing their steps, they walked as briskly as they could and felt their way around the corners where the alleyway crossed another narrow street.

"That Litt turned them with a touch? No, I had no idea that was how it happened. I don't think anyone knew. A lot of that happened when Litt took over Eokhmisseun 60 years ago or at night when no one would be on the streets. I had never heard anything but rumors about the process."

Repressing a shudder as he looked back toward the alleyway they had just left, he pulled Tamnyn urgently along to where the second alley reached another wide street. They stopped at the entrance out of sight to take a moment to catch their breath again.

"Is there something back there?" he asked. "I'm worried it may have caught up to us."

"How could it have done that? We have been running very fast and took a detour."

Sohyeon just looked over at her, thinking about the events of the last few hours.

"Have you ever seen Litt? Has any of the council?"

"Not anyone who lived to tell it or who wasn't turned. No, I've never seen him. Does it matter?"

"Maybe."

"Why?"

"Are the ghost slaves like him? They seem to be half-animal. Animals can track through scent. If Litt can do that, too, then we need to take different precautions. It won't be enough to just take different routes to throw him off our trail."

Sohyeon led her across the street to another alley where they paused again.

"Maybe I should consider that assassination plan now," Tamnyn whispered.

"How could you do that? We're at a disadvantage with him following us. The assassination was supposed to be one of the council members finding him at a weak moment asleep or at rest in his lair where he couldn't fight so easily. Now, we're the prey. I don't think he'll let you get the opportunity to use the artefacts against him so easily."

"There has to be a way. Perhaps we should go to his palace instead of the inner sea. We could lure him home and counterattack him there."

"You're not thinking clearly. Just a few hours ago, you didn't want to fight him at all and your father was concerned you didn't have anything remotely like an airtight plan to go against such a creature. We only have one chance, and we dare not risk it. If you are all turned, then what chance does Eokhmisseun have to overthrow him later?"

"We could go to his palace and try to free Yarava."

"Would he have postponed her turning that long? What if we get there and are captured ourselves or she is now a ghost slave and attacks us?"

"We have to do something," Tamnyn said angrily, her voice getting a little louder and showing signs of strain. "My father-."

"Silence." Sohyeon looked suspiciously back at the alley across the street where they had emerged minutes before.

Sohyeon and Tamnyn had hesitated too long. The black cloaked figure stepped out of the alley, his hooded head turning to look up and down the street.

Grabbing Tamnyn's hand again, Sohyeon pulled her down the alleyway in the opposite direction, looking frantically around for some more substantial route of escape. In this part of town, Sohyeon thought he felt eyes watching him silently from the concealed windows of the buildings they passed. This district didn't feel as deserted as the neighborhood surrounding the estate, but it seemed dirtier, and Sohyeon had to dodge debris and struggle to keep his balance on the grimy flagstone ground. Looking back at Tamnyn, he saw she was struggling too.

"Are you sure we shouldn't confront it?" she whispered to him when they reached a fork in the alley and paused to decide which way to go next.

"Didn't you see what kind of power he has? No wonder your father was afraid to send you to make the assassination attempt. I didn't understand his reluctance then, but now I do. He understood Khabu better than you, Tamnyn. We have to admit defeat for now and just get out of Eokhmisseun. Do you know where either of these alleys leads to?"

Sohyeon glanced over his shoulder to check the way they came, but the darkness was too thick to see if Litt had gained on them.

"I think the right leads to the palace, and the left leads closer to the inner sea," Tamnyn whispered, noting Sohyeon's fearful gaze. She, too, glanced back at the darkness behind them. "He may realize we will try to avoid the palace."

"Yeah, you may be right. It's too predictable if we try to go back to the inner sea and Pontol. If Sagar and the council betrayed your father, Litt knows I'm with you and may know my origins. We'll take the alley leading to the palace for now."

"Let's at least try to find Yarava, even if we don't attack or enter the palace."

Sohyeon nodded, and they ran down the right alley together. In the dim light that seemed to have no clear source, Sohyeon felt conspicuous and bogged down by the cloak again. It reflected the light too much at night to be helpful as they crawled through the city's back alleys, and Litt could see them more easily. Despair started to engulf him, leaving him with the feeling everything they tried would be futile and that there was no defense against his power. All they could do was keep running.

Finally they reached the end of the alley, which opened onto a street bordering a wooded park. The palace was at the center of this plaza, and a narrow path led from the street into the thicket where a tall glittering white tower rose above the treetops.

Sohyeon looked carefully around the corner of the buildings up and down the street before leading Tamnyn out into the open. No one seemed to be around, but Sohyeon instinctively knew that there had to be guards of some kind if this was Litt's palace. Maybe even some sort of booby traps awaited them there if they ventured too deeply into the plaza. He decided they should try to reach the block of buildings beyond the plaza on the side of the road closer to the inner sea.

As they walked toward the squat set of white stone buildings on that corner, Sohyeon became aware of Tamnyn hanging back a little, distracted by something in the street as they passed the left edge of the plaza. He turned to look back at it, too. It was a piece of parchment. Sohyeon went over to it and picked it up. It was the note from Sagar that Cargal had taken to the meeting as proof of their invitation when they rode in the carriage. Its edge was soaked in blood.

"Could Cargal have come past here?" he asked softly as Tamnyn came up to stand beside him.

"We have to go to the palace then if father has been captured," she said, looking resolutely at the palace tower.

"Is that really what he wanted you to do if it came to this?"

"We have to try to save them."

"Is it better that Litt capture all of the council or that some of you escape?" Sohyeon asked, thinking the answer should be clear, but Tamnyn was unwilling to consider that she should flee without them.

Something clattered across the cobblestones in the alley they had just walked out of, and Sohyeon grabbed Tamnyn's arm and dragged her to the bushes on the side of the palace plaza. From that vantage point, Sohyeon saw the cloaked figure emerge from the alley into the street. *So there's no way to get the creature off of our tails*, Sohyeon thought. But a sudden glint of light in the figure's gloved hand caught his eye, and he had to catch himself not to cry out and give away their location. How could Litt have gotten the dagger of Memnoth?

Sohyeon looked over at Tamnyn, who had realized the same thing. Immediately her hands flew underneath her cloak to her waist where the dagger's sheath had been strapped to her body. Pulling out the leather belt it hung on, they both looked at it in dismay. The leather at the bottom of the holster had been worn through, though perhaps not by any natural force. Sohyeon ran his bare finger over the edge where it had torn and dropped the dagger, and the edge seemed too clean. How could the leather sheath have been cut if Tamnyn was wearing it the whole time, and how could they not have been aware of losing it? Wouldn't it have made a racket when it fell on the ground as they ran?

Tamnyn looked up at the black figure through the branches of the bushes with wide eyes sparkling with tears. Sohyeon didn't dare speak with Litt so close to them, but he worried again that the creature had magic so preternatural they had no means to fight it. Did Litt have some sort of power to retrieve the dagger from Tamnyn?

15

A moment later, the cloaked figure had disappeared somewhere in the thick foliage of the plaza near its front entrance. Sohyeon warily pulled Tamnyn along the outside edge of the plaza toward the back in case Litt came too close to them as he entered the palace precincts. Knowing that their last hope to defend themselves against Litt was now gone, assuming his crossbow would be useless in a hand to hand fight, Sohyeon was sure he had to get Tamnyn to the inner sea and take the boat back to Earth with her. Her fate would surely be death if they stayed in Eokhmisseun, and neither of them knew of any safe place to hide in the city. They were at Litt's mercy until they could flee altogether.

When Litt had not reappeared, Tamnyn tugged on his sleeve and led him toward the back of the plaza, just outside of the tree line where they could more easily get a glimpse into the palace grounds without entering. The tower base expanded into a compound even more elaborately decorated than the Elyeon mansion but with windows that were unobstructed by carved screens. Inside the grove, they could see dark, hunched figures walking the perimeter, Litt's guards. A few of the rooms on the first floor were lit by candlelight, but they couldn't see what was happening in them from that distance. Tamnyn noticed them and seemed entranced by them, much to Sohyeon's alarm. She took a few steps across the pavement onto the grass toward the line of trees. He grabbed her to stop her.

"What are you doing? We don't have the dagger anymore or any way to protect ourselves. What can we do here now? We need to leave immediately and get to safety."

Tears streamed down Tamnyn's face as her eyes stayed riveted on the lights on the other side of the forest.

"Allow me at least to look here for a few minutes if I am to leave with you forever. I have to know, Sohyeon. If there's a chance he's alive, I must know. Let me just go a few steps into the forest to get a better look at what he has done to them."

"You can't guarantee you'll see Yarava or your father if you go in there."

"It doesn't matter. Let me go to as far as the inner tree line and see the palace close up for a few minutes, then I will leave and never return if you wish."

Sohyeon watched her move cautiously from tree to tree, too terrified to follow her for a moment. As she got deeper into the forest where he had trouble seeing her, he walked after her swiftly, but he only made it halfway before he nearly tripped. He rolled away without making too much noise, but Tamnyn heard him, as had a few of the guards, who looked suspiciously into the trees in their direction. No one moved. Finally, the guards returned with leisurely unconcern to their posts.

Waiting a few more minutes to make sure she wouldn't draw their attention, Tamnyn crept back to where Sohyeon sat on the grass, looking in surprise at what he had tripped over. Tamnyn looked down on the ground beside him, too, her eyes widening.

"Who is it?" Sohyeon asked, whispering as they studied the body he tripped over. While he couldn't see the face in the dark, the body lying on its back was as small as a child and wore an elaborate insignia similar to one he had seen at Tamnyn's house.

"Someone from Yarava's household. That insignia is her family's. She had a younger brother Delam who lived with her, one that had been turned but that she kept around in the hopes of finding a way to reverse the spell."

"Is he dead?"

Tamnyn leaned down, pulled off her white glove and touched the boy's neck. She quickly pulled her hand away.

"He's still alive."

"Is it dangerous to be around him?"

"I don't know. Maybe we should take him with us, escape with him and find out what has happened in the palace. He probably came here with Yarava's group and knows what happened to them."

"Fine, then let's take him and get out of here before Litt sends his men after us. Do you know how Litt got your dagger?"

Tamnyn looked at Sohyeon darkly as she knelt down beside the boy.

"Litt was looking for the dagger and knew my family had it. Perhaps he has some probing magic that allowed for him to take it, or maybe your theory is right and he used some animal sense to sniff out the silver. Silver is the primary danger to him, so he would surely be interested in knowing who still had it in Eokhmisseun. If Pontol knew we had the dagger, it's likely that Litt did too. How shall we move the boy?"

"Should I carry him?" Sohyeon asked, dreading how much taking the boy along would slow them down.

"We should each take an arm and help him up first, then we can see if he can walk down the street with us."

"He's too short. Let me just carry him."

Sohyeon glanced back at the palace and noticed in alarm that the guards' attention had now turned to them even if the guards had not moved from their posts. Perhaps they had been talking too loudly. Sohyeon paused and looked over at Tamnyn.

"They're watching. Don't move."

Both of them froze in place and waited, listening. The boy beside them started to stir a little, and Sohyeon moved his hand and put it over the boy's mouth lightly so he wouldn't cry out.

"If he's awake, we should try to question him here," Sohyeon whispered, watching the guards peering into the trees. "We'll never get out of here with him now that they've noticed us."

Tamnyn crawled a little closer to the boy's head and spoke to him in a low, soothing voice.

"Delam, are you awake? Can you hear me? Don't speak too loudly. Litt's guards are nearby and watching. What happened to you?"

The boy fidgeted a little before responding.

"The time of the purge of Eokhmisseun has come," he said, his voice dreamy and ominous.

"The purge? What does that mean?" Sohyeon asked, looking darkly at Tamnyn. "Did you expect something like this to happen?"

"No, the council wasn't aware of it, though we thought we might be attacked eventually."

"The time of the purge has come," Delam repeated softly, curling around to look at the two of them. Sohyeon could almost see the outline of his face in the dim light under the trees, boyish but somehow barely human. "Litt had determined he would be rid of those who had not undergone the turning and that we would rule unopposed at last. The bloodlust has been unleashed on the ghost slaves, and we can't resist it anymore. You must leave now, or else join us or die if you stay."

"What of your sister, and my father?"

"My sister chose prison over the turning, but she won't stay alive for long. I fled the palace to try to get away from them, but I fear Litt wants me dead as well for being close to her although I have been turned. He considers those who have not been turned as traitors unless they submit to his magic. He will not stop until he finds everyone who remains whole."

"We need to leave then," Sohyeon said, looking back toward the palace. The guards had shifted slightly, and Sohyeon couldn't take his eyes off of them.

"And my father? Have you seen him? We found a note he was carrying nearby."

"Cargal? They came back with some prisoners not long ago, but I haven't seen them. Perhaps he was among them. I had already escaped and fallen here. I feel so weak and have such a strong taste for blood that I don't want to give into. Can you give me a taste of yours?"

Delam shifted his body like a snake and dove eagerly at Tamnyn, who nearly fell onto her back until Sohyeon caught her arm. Aware that the guards would be coming for them for sure now, Sohyeon stood and quickly pulled Tamnyn to her feet, half dragging her out of the forest before the creepy boy could lunge at her again. The guards moved swiftly toward the tree line from the palace, making guttural calls that could only mean more trouble for them. Catching Tamnyn in his arms, Sohyeon fled down the street with her, his exhaustion threatening to overwhelm him.

Recognizing a building a few blocks over was the strange restaurant he stopped at with Pontol, Sohyeon suddenly knew where he was and turned so they could make a run for the inner sea and escape on Pontol's boat. Tamnyn regained her footing and ran after him, locking her hand around his.

"This way," Sohyeon said, breathing hard and not daring to look back the way they came. He could hear the guards calling to one another, and it sounded like they were getting closer. They didn't have much time to get to the inner sea, but what did Sohyeon intend to do if Pontol seemed no saner than the boy Delam?

As they raced through the city to Pontol's crumbling shack near the shore, the evening's events flashed through Sohyeon's mind, one scene after another. Cargal's face, then Sagar's, the tension in the council meeting, all of it started to make a wicked sort of sense to Sohyeon in light of the purge Delam had mention. If Litt had been planning to strike the remaining citizens who had resisted his magical curse, then Sagar's summons had been a trap to set them up from the start. Thinking back to Cargal's request that Sohyeon protect Tamnyn at all costs, Sohyeon thought perhaps Cargal had suspected something was wrong with the summons, but there was no way he could safely refuse to go to the council meeting.

They turned another corner, and Sohyeon saw the small thicket of trees leading to Pontol's shack and ultimately the shore. When they reached the trees' protective cover, Sohyeon and Tamnyn paused to catch their breaths and assess the situation. From their vantage point, they could see back for blocks in the direction they came, and there was no sign yet of Litt's men, though Sohyeon was sure they would appear soon. They couldn't rest for long, though Sohyeon's chest hurt with each breath, and his aching legs felt like lead.

"What now?" Tamnyn whispered.

"Pontol's shack is just inside here. It's not far. We need to wake him and force him to take us back to my house."

"Return over the inner sea? We'll have to take steps to ensure that Litt doesn't follow us back to your home world. We could risk leading him there. He could destroy your world the way he has destroyed mine. Is that what you want? Better to leave me behind to die with the city then."

"Stop it. I'm not leaving you here."

SOHYEON AFTER MIDNIGHT

Sohyeon was trying hard not to raise his voice, but Tamnyn seemed to be unable to maintain her composure. As her voice got louder, he cringed and looked back toward the palace. The tower top loomed over the city blocks separating them, but the tower's unobstructed windows remained dark.

Suddenly Sohyeon heard a sickening thud. Tamnyn cried out, her eyes wide in terror and searching for Sohyeon. A moment later, she fell to her knees. Sohyeon rushed over to her, pulling her to her feet and feeling something wet on her back. Running his hand up her back, it ran into something metallic halfway up. Pulling Tamnyn toward him, he saw the hilt of a dagger sticking out of her back. The dagger of Memnoth.

Laughter rang out in the empty streets. Sohyeon looked around frantically in all directions but didn't see anyone right away. No one appeared in the direction that they had come from. But the dagger had come from the direction of Sagar's castle. Looking that way, Sohyeon felt a jolt. The black cloaked figure had now appeared at the end of the street.

"We need to get out of here. He's back," Sohyeon said, clutching Tamnyn to him protectively, fighting back tears as his mind rebelled against the idea that they still weren't rid of the monster.

Half-dragging her, walking backward into the forest, Sohyeon glanced over his shoulder, seeing the path that would take them to Pontol, silently saying a prayer that Pontol would be there and was able to help them.

"I can still walk," Tamnyn said weakly, trying to stand without wobbling. "Pull out the dagger."

"There isn't time," he said, letting her go a minute to rip off the flowing gray cloak he wore at last. If he was going to have to fight Litt, he may as well do it honestly. Dropping the cloak and crossbow firmly to the ground, he crouched down before Tamnyn so she could climb onto his back, her arms and legs wrapping around him as he carried her toward the shack, walking as briskly as he dared.

Looking back over his shoulder, he saw they still seemed to have some time. None of their pursuers had appeared yet, though Sohyeon could almost feel the black figure silently gliding down the street toward the trees. It wouldn't take long for him to catch up. Forcing himself to focus solely on Pontol's shack, Sohyeon kept moving and ignored the pain. Every breath seemed to be harder to take than the next, and the forest's stuffy air was suffocating. Tamnyn's breathing also seemed to be getting more and more ragged, and Sohyeon sunk down every few steps to his knees, staggering under her weight until they were only a few steps away from Pontol's shack.

Banging up against the rough wood of the shack's door, Sohyeon pushed it open, and the two of them fell inside onto the floor. The shack was too dim to see into very far, it windows smeared with dirt and the floor covered with the bones of small animals and other unpleasant debris. Crawling out from under Tamnyn, Sohyeon pushed her into the room ahead of him and twisted back to slam the door, nearly screaming as he did. At the other end of the path at the edge of the trees stood the dark figure, but he only saw it for a moment before the door shut.

"Pontol!" Sohyeon hissed, barely able to catch his breath. He knew neither he nor Tamnyn could run very far in this condition. They only would have enough time and energy to make it to the boat, if that. "Pontol! We need your help now. It's coming. Litt's coming! And we have the dagger."

Sort of, Sohyeon thought. Surely Tamnyn would consider it an ironic statement if she could still hear him at all. Something stirred in the corner.

"Sohyeon?"

The old ferryman shuffled around in the corner before standing. Sohyeon caught a glimpse of his bestial face in the dim light, and he wondered if he could control a ghost slave even with the dagger of Memnoth under such conditions.

"We need you take us home, Pontol. In the boat. Now. Litt is right behind us, and he must not follow us back home. Can you do it? Do you have a back way out of here?"

Sohyeon tried not to let traces of his hysteria creep into his voice, but every second counted. He could almost feel Litt's strange power emanating from the door behind him.

"I don't think we can run much more, Pontol. Please help us."

Pontol looked dazedly from one to the other of them for a moment before going over to Tamnyn and helping her to her feet. When she was able to stand, he went over to Sohyeon and pulled him up, too.

"We can go out the back," Pontol said, so quietly it caught Sohyeon's attention. So the ferryman could feel Litt, too.

Tamnyn nearly tripped over something on the floor, but Pontol caught her and led her quietly over to the back door, which was almost like a large pet door. Pontol unlatched it stealthily, and pushing Tamnyn into a crouch, he patted her back to encourage her to go through it, pausing when he saw the dagger sticking out of it.

"You said you had the dagger, but I didn't think you meant *that*," he whispered when Sohyeon reached him and crouched down.

"We can talk about this later. Do you have any way to throw off Litt?"

"Let me see. I'll meet you at the boat in a few minutes. I am under Minha's enchantment, so Litt has limited authority over me although I am a citizen of Eokhmisseun. You know how to get back to the shore?"

Sohyeon nodded and left the shack, strangely relieved though he wouldn't have wanted to be in Pontol's shoes for anything. Meeting Tamnyn in back of the shack, he took her arm and helped her along toward the shore, glancing one more time at the shack. He didn't know what they would do if Pontol didn't make it. Could he navigate the boat alone? Could Tamnyn? Pushing such despairing thoughts out of his mind, Sohyeon kept walking.

Neither of them were strong enough to run, but Sohyeon felt Pontol could buy them enough time so it didn't matter. The forest soon gave way to short rocky cliffs, and the soil got sandier and softer beneath a layer of smaller rocks. They could hardly keep their balance on the uneven surface. When he smelled the water, he nearly started crying. A few steps later after they turned the corner, the shoreline came into view. The boat sat at the end of the dock.

Closing the distance swiftly with a fresh burst of energy, Sohyeon lifted Tamnyn gently into the boat, and placed her on the deck on her stomach. She moaned softly. Sohyeon saw the dark circle of blood spreading out along her back and decided it was probably time to remove the dagger. Pulling it out carefully, he put it on the deck beside her, then ripped off part of Tamnyn's cloak and put it in the water to try to clean the wound, though her armor prevented him from doing a thorough job. He marveled that the dagger was able to penetrate her bone armor and ran his fingers over the blade a moment. It seemed to thrum with life. When she was resting comfortably, Sohyeon lay on the bench near her and stared in the direction of Pontol's shack, worried the ferryman was taking too long.

16

An hour seemed to pass, but none of their pursuers appeared on the beach. Sohyeon and Tamnyn had fallen into an uneasy sleep while they waited for Pontol. Suddenly waking, Sohyeon looked around and wondered what had happened to Pontol. They needed to get back right away, before something else went wrong.

Picking up the dagger of Memnoth, Sohyeon touched the blade and point gingerly with his finger again. Pulling out the dagger that Cargal had given him and laying it on the bench, he placed the dagger of Memnoth in its sheath. He would carry the dagger for now. Looking back over at Tamnyn's helmet, he wondered at its power, but his thoughts strayed to the woman herself. She was beautiful enough, but he hadn't realized until now that his heart was no longer set on Minha, priestess of Khabu. Somehow Tamnyn had won him over, without him even realizing it. He couldn't abandon her in her time of trouble, and his heart ached when he thought of how she had lost everything because of Litt. Maybe it was an impossible match, perhaps more impossible than a match with Minha, but Sohyeon was smitten nonetheless, for very different reasons.

Leaning over her while she slept, he studied the line of her brow and the locks of red hair flowing out from under her helmet before lightly kissing her cheek.

Straightening back up, Sohyeon decided to go in search of Pontol. Retracing his steps back to the shack, he was surprised to find the forest felt peaceful, as peaceful as any place in Eokhmisseun felt that night. Pontol must have been successful in getting rid of Litt, so why hadn't he come to meet them at the boat? Opening the pet flap, Sohyeon crawled back into the shack and immediately heard the sound of loud snoring. Pontol had gone back to bed!

Walking over to the corner where Pontol was curled up on the dirty floor, he touched Pontol lightly with the toe of his shoe. Pontol's snoring stopped for a moment as he coughed and sat up, looking around in alarm. When he saw Sohyeon standing in the dim light, he immediately stood up and smoothed out his wrinkled clothes.

"Why didn't you come? We've been waiting."

"Sorry, but I had to let enough time pass to convince Litt I wasn't harboring any fugitives. He was polite when I mentioned Minha, for the beast still has some remnant of respect for the leaders of his infernal homeland. I got him to leave without any more bother. He will come back here to look for you, but we have a little time, never fear."

"Can we leave now?" Sohyeon asked. "I left Tamnyn asleep in the boat, and I don't want to be away for long."

Pontol nodded and got together a few things from his shack then led him back out the pet door, blocking it with a wooden board in case Litt returned in his absence. Pontol explained how he didn't want Litt to notice it, and the door now would look like part of the wall. They walked through the forest quickly and made it to the shore in only a few minutes.

"What happened tonight?" Sohyeon asked him once they reached the shore. "I was told there was a purge taking place, that Litt was going after everyone who hadn't been turned. Do you know anything about it? They said it also affected the ghost slaves, too."

Pontol nodded briefly.

"Litt had planned to bring them all into line. So tonight was it? I wouldn't be affected since I am in Khabu's direct employ and am protected by the witch's magic. I guess it's lucky for me after all, though I hate that woman. The council then? What happened to them? Is it over for Eokhmisseun?"

"None are left except me and Tamnyn that I know about. We couldn't determine if Cargal had been turned or killed, but there was an ambush of the council, which had been called to a meeting on a false pretext. The leadership of Eokhmisseun is no more. Tamnyn will have to lead whatever resistance she can put together from my world. Have you seen Mirae lately? I need to talk with her."

Sohyeon and Pontol reached the boat, where Tamnyn still slept. Sohyeon boarded the boat, and Pontol hopped on behind him, unwound the rope tying the boat to the dock post, then unlocked the wheel. Both of them took their places, and the boat soon started to turn away from the dock toward Sohyeon's house, the strange waters lapping at its sides and the misty moon hanging above it to pull the waters along the mysterious dimensions they would travel.

"I left her in Khabu yesterday. I'm due to go back and get her when I get her summons. They also use the magical bird messengers, and I was just waiting for instructions. She'll be back home with you soon enough, and the witch has taken good care of her. Litt can't bother her any more than he can bother me."

"But now that I have the dagger of Memnoth, we have an agreement," Sohyeon said, deciding it was only fair to remind the ferryman of his secondary obligations. "You also have to take me where I ask to complete this task. We do intend on killing Litt somehow and freeing Eokhmisseun."

Pontol looked at him anxiously and nodded.

"I will uphold my end of the agreement."

Sohyeon sighed in relief and allowed himself to relax at last. Soon his home would come into view on the horizon, and he could plan his next move.

2 THE CHANGELING

1

Shortly after midnight when the phantom boat came to Mirae's window to fetch her to the faraway land of Khabu and landed on its shore, the ferryman led Mirae to the temple of light sheltered by red cliffs and a network of caves. Looking around the big room, radiant with light from an unknown source, Mirae saw that a woman waited for her, seated on a dais next to a pedestal holding a glittering pearl. Walking toward the woman, Mirae could only stare at her extraordinary appearance. The woman's black eyes regarded her calmly, a hint of triumph reflected in them, and her long, straight black hair blew slightly as if there were a breeze flowing through the room. Her floor-length light blue chiton reminded Mirae of something out of her high school history books when her teacher had covered ancient Greece, though the woman looked Asian like her, which was all wrong for the time and place. But surely the boat had not taken her back in time but to some other mysterious place.

"Who are you?" Mirae asked haltingly, meeting the woman's gaze.

"At last, we meet," the woman said, standing. "You are called Mirae, are you not?"

"Yes, but do we know each other? What is this place?"

The woman's eyes moved around the edges of the room proudly.

"You are in my temple. I am Minha, high priestess of Khabu. We have been waiting a long time for this moment."

Mirae just looked at Minha in confusion.

"We will do our best to make you feel at home here during your stay with us," Minha said, stepping down from the dais to stand before her. "You will have to go through some training before you meet with the Queen, Joriya, but I will prepare you."

"I don't understand. Why would I be meeting with a queen? I've never heard of Khabu."

Minha smiled kindly at her.

"Of course the situation will take some getting used to," she said. "You will be training for the role of priestess for a time with me."

"Will this take long? I'll need to go back home soon."

Minha looked at her in surprise.

"Take long? Mirae, this is your new home, though you can go back to that place as much as you want. My attendants will get you suitable clothes and take you to your quarters to get acquainted with our culture. Before long, though, you will need to attend to your responsibilities in the kingdom"

"And what responsibilities would you mean?" Mirae tried not to get angry, but Minha wasn't making any sense.

"Helping us win the war. The Queen will be very pleased to have you at her side in her trials. Dealing with her brother Duke Birum's betrayal has been difficult for her, as you might image, and even I cannot comfort her anymore. "

"Do I have a choice in this matter?" Mirae asked, concerned. "I have a life back on earth. How am I supposed to help some queen of another world, which may not exist at all?"

Minha looked at Mirae with such tenderness that Mirae felt a little panicked.

"We will help you fulfill your roles in both worlds if that is what concerns you, but no, you don't have a choice to help us. It is your destiny, Mirae. You must agree to this."

In spite of her words, Minha's expression was gentle, and she held out a shimmering object to her in the palm of her hand. Mirae reached out for it, unable to control her own movements anymore. She felt as though she were playing a predetermined role in this strange situation. The object was a ring, and soft whites and pastel colors rippled across the surface of the largest pearl she ever saw set in the ring's leafy prongs. She knew she was supposed to slip it on her finger, but she hesitated.

"What does accepting this mean?"

"It means you agree to help us and are now bound to the pearl of wisdom here in our temple."

"I see."

Mirae looked up at the pearl on the pedestal and back at the ring. Minha took her free hand and led her over to the pedestal.

"Don't be afraid to take a closer look, Mirae. The pearl is a powerful source of our power and will clear your mind of all impurities. It was for this purpose that it was mined and brought here millennia ago. This is what you will draw your power from in the future as you come to our aid. This is a very prestigious position to hold in our kingdom. You should be honored to be chosen."

Mirae looked from the ring to the pearl on the pedestal, letting herself be mesmerized by the almost living, pulsing power surging through them and between them, almost physical manifestations of the light that surrounded the pedestal. Forgetting about Minha for a moment, or even her family back home, Mirae found the pulsing colors pleasant and inviting. Without thinking through her decision or the consequences of her action, she slipped the ring on her middle finger of her right hand. When the golden band settled there a moment, Mirae felt a slight jolt of electricity surge through her hand, then the ring was quiet.

The women stood looking at the large pearl in silence a moment before Mirae felt like she could move again. Even as she felt a strange joy at accepting the ring, she also felt a heaviness settle over her. It was such a reckless promise to make. Why had she let this stranger talk her into promising to help? She had no power to stop a war. She wasn't ready to stay here and learn anything from the priestess. All she knew was that she had to get back home, to her family, to clear her head and think about what she truly wanted for her future.

Turning slowly to face Minha, Mirae bit her lip.

"You are not ready to begin?" Minha asked as if reading her thoughts.

"Let me have some time with my family before I begin whatever task you had in mind. I don't want to stay here with you just yet."

Minha nodded and had let her leave with Pontol without another word of entreaty.

2

Now Mirae sat alone in a coffee shop in her neighborhood two nights after Sohyeon had revealed that he too had been approached by the midnight ship. Hardly anyone was around since it was 9:30 at night, and her family would be winding down for the evening, watching TV and getting ready for bed soon. She understood that whatever drama had been playing out beyond the night sky in the worlds of Khabu and Eokhmisseun was now entwined with her family as Sohyeon had been inadvertently lured into the war, whatever it was. The thought dismayed her. Mirae worried for the safety of her family and feared for her own future. Sohyeon, always having been the aimless one in the family and the subject of her father's concern because of his low grades, clearly didn't care as much since he was too fascinated by the exotic Minha and the adventure set before him. But Mirae was a little older, and she could see the danger lurking around them. What was she supposed to do now?

Still, at least she could count on Sohyeon as an ally. She didn't have to face the anomaly alone or wonder if it were all just her imagination since he had gone to Khabu, too. But how would they hide it from their parents? Would Sukjin be brought into the battle, too, or would they have to sneak around her as well? How would Mirae hold down a job while having these nocturnal journeys? For now, it seemed like no time passed when Pontol came for them and took them over the inner sea, so perhaps it didn't matter.

One detail that Mirae had held back during her meeting with Sohyeon over their night journeys was the parchment Minha had given her. Mirae had held back that detail because what was written on it had disturbed her so much, though she didn't understand the meaning of what it said or why it was written in her native tongue in places. The native writing of Khabu looked like a cross between ancient Greek and Egyptian hieroglyphics, beautiful but unintelligible. One of the pictographs that kept appearing seemed to be a ferocious cat facing forward with its body turned to either side wearing a crown like the old European heraldry symbol. The parchment was painted in black ink, so Mirae wasn't sure what sort of cat it might be, and what she assumed to be the translation of the exotic Khabu script above didn't illuminate the mystery.

In the day when the pearl of wonder dawns, the ancestors will climb the mountain of wisdom and rule the land of Khabu in peace.

SOHYEON AFTER MIDNIGHT

The key to unlock the secrets of the crypt has been hidden by the ancestors beneath the blue waterfalls of the north. Only mutiny can delay the time of times, only love can alter the destiny of the worlds. Who will wear the crown in the end? Will it be worn for good or for evil?

Mirae read the parchment a few times, alert to any of the coffee shop workers hovering too close to where she nursed her cup near the window. It probably didn't matter if anyone saw it, but it would attract too much attention and raise too many questions if they did. The words on the parchment sounded like a riddle. Folding the parchment back up and slipping it into a protected compartment of her purse, she finished the last few mouthfuls of coffee and waved to the barista.

Walking home along mostly deserted streets as her watch read 10:15, Mirae crossed the street when the light turned green, thinking again about Sohyeon. They hadn't talked for a few days about anything important, and maybe she should ask him for more details of his visit to Khabu than she had dared over dinner the other night. She wrestled with the question all of the way home, deciding as she arrived and entered through the side door that she should just wait a few more days.

Her mother passed the door to the garage with a tray of freshly baked cookies on her way to the family room where her father waited to deal their next round of crazy 8s. It was her parents' favorite game since their courtship, and as Mirae and her siblings got closer to adulthood, her parents had started playing again on scheduled nights to relax alone together. Alanna Choi paused to look at Mirae as she came in.

"You're coming in late. Did you have to work late tonight?" she asked, her gray-green eyes full of concern.

Mirae smiled reassuringly, taking a peanut butter cookie from the tray and shaking her head.

"No, I just wanted to read a bit without Sukjin talking my ear off. She may be quiet around you, but all she does is complain about her upcoming exams, so I can't get much done at home."

"Eventually when you make plans to move out on your own, you won't have to worry any more about sharing a room with your sister."

"Are you trying to get rid of me?" Mirae asked sarcastically, Minha's words about remaining in Khabu echoing in the back of her mind again.

"Not at all," her mother said, laughing a little. "Take as long as you need. I just feel bad that you have to stay out to avoid Sukjin."

"Well, I'm going to bed now."

Her mother smiled sweetly and walked into the family room to deliver the cookies to her father, while Mirae went upstairs to her room.

As expected, Sukjin was already asleep when Mirae slipped into their bedroom. Dropping her purse to the floor beside her bed, Mirae quickly changed into her nightgown in the dark and paused once more to look at the open window between their beds. The warm night was quiet except for the occasional sound of a car going down the street and the chirping of crickets. She still could go wake Sohyeon to consult with him, she thought. Glancing back at her bed stand, she saw the clock read 10:30. No, let him sleep for now. She got into bed and closed her eyes.

Dreams of the parchment filled her sleep. Curling letters punctuated by pictographs danced through her mind, the toothy-grinned cats overcoming and eating the other letters. Visions of a blue lake that led to a range of tiered waterfalls slowly transposed itself over images of the parchment, and Mirae felt herself wading into the cool water at the base of the falls, plunging beneath its surface, holding her breath while looking for the promised treasure, the ring on her hand glowing like the sun, a beam of light from it searching the depths of the waters like a flashlight.

Feeling something brushing against her leg, Mirae turned in the water, catching a glimpse of something reptilian with large, sharp teeth in the corner of her eye. Suddenly, the inviting blue waters turned slowly to black, like ink was being poured into them. As it touched her lips, she tasted something metallic in it. Blood!

3

Darting to the surface of the water in her dream, Mirae found herself sitting up in bed in reality. Bleary-eyed, she looked at the clock beside her bed. It was 1:30 in the morning. Shuddering as she recalled her nightmare, she got out of bed and walked toward the door. For some reason she needed to talk to Sohyeon right now. Running across the shadowy hallway to his door, she opened it slowly and went in, leaving it a little ajar. His window was also open, and the curtains were blowing into the room. Standing beside his bed, Mirae saw in amazement that it was empty. She bent down to touch the sheets. They were cold.

Walking over to the window, the wind catching her hair and thin white nightgown, she knew he had been taken. Pontol had come back and had taken him somewhere. Khabu? As she looked at the gibbous moon, she thought she saw something moving in front of it. Squinting to see it and grabbing the windowsill to lean out the window a little, she watched in fascination as the object got larger. It was coming toward her. The boat. Pontol was coming for her too tonight. Minha had summoned her again, and there was no way Mirae could refuse to go. Thinking of the parchment again and her nightmare, she suddenly was eager to go to Khabu. Maybe she would meet Sohyeon there. Either way, she could only surrender to Minha's power and hope for the best. It was time to go.

This time when Pontol arrived in the boat, Mirae studied him carefully, thinking about Sohyeon's bite wounds and pact. As he stood by the wheel and guided the boat across the sky, Mirae noticed how bestial he looked. The first time he came for her, she hadn't really paid attention to his face, only to the exhilarating feelings riding through the sky brought as well as the novelty of being in an old-fashioned boat. Now she realized the ferryman was actually quite sinister, though he seemed polite enough in their exchanges. He neither talked to her more than he had to nor stayed around when she had talked with Minha.

She tried to see his mouth, particularly his teeth, but Pontol did not turn to look back at her. Instead, the tray full of coins caught her eye, and she noticed the script on the sign and on some of the coins was similar to the one written on the parchment. Leaning toward it, she reached out to touch the coins gingerly with her finger. Some of the coins toward the bottom bore a different script. Perhaps they were from this place Sohyeon had talked about helping Pontol save. Suddenly, Mirae felt a cold, clawed hand touch her shoulder.

"Don't touch the fares, miss," he said in a raspy voice.

Pulling her hand away as if she had touched something hot, Mirae sat back on the bench. Pontol turned to face the inner sea, but the glimpse of him was enough for Mirae to feel grave misgivings about Sohyeon's pact with him. Could Sohyeon really trust Pontol?

Before long, Mirae was escorted to the familiar temple hall, but this time Minha wasn't there waiting to receive her. Another young acolyte dressed in a dark blue chiton wordlessly led her to a room behind the main hall where a stack of scrolls sat on a table. The woman smiled at her gently, motioning for her to be seated.

"You will begin your training today," she said, her bright blue eyes turning toward the scrolls. "Begin by reading these. We will bring you your meals throughout the day. We have left one of our robes here for you should you desire to change and get more comfortable."

Mirae saw a dark blue chiton lay across a flat couch on the other side of the room and thought it looked more presentable than her nightgown. Instead of sitting down, she walked over to the couch to look at it more closely. The fabric was light and silky. She turned back to the acolyte.

"Will Minha be joining me today for the lessons?"

"I don't think she had plans to stop by. The lessons should be self-explanatory. You must learn the language and history of Khabu. She has left you a copy of Khabu's ancient stone tablets listing our kings and queens and a syllabary to begin to learn to read."

Mirae thought of the parchment Minha had given her during her last visit.

"Was there anything else you needed?"

"No, that's fine. I will change and get started."

The acolyte bowed and left her.

Once Mirae started reading the scrolls, the hours passed without her noticing. The syllabary was indeed familiar, the symbols matching those of the riddle on the parchment, though the pictographs weren't explained here. When she got to the next scroll, she read through the list of kings and queens in astonishment.

The list was short. All of the rulers of Khabu had ruled for hundreds of years, some as many as 600 years, and the current ruler, the High Queen Joriya, had ruled for close to 400 years. Her rule was one of the longer ones on the list, and examining the vague details of the list even closer, Mirae wondered with alarm if Joriya was at the end of her reign. Was she an old woman? What was this war about with her brother Birum? Had Mirae been brought to protect her as they made a transition to a new king or queen? Even so, why would it involve her at all? Mirae had no answers to any of her questions, though she hoped Minha would be able to answer them.

The door opened, and the acolyte that had brought her to the room earlier appeared with a plate of food.

"Come away from the table and have some nourishment," the woman said, walking across the room and settling on the couch.

Mirae came over to join her and, sitting down, took the plate holding a few strips of dried meat and a pile of fresh vegetables from her.

"How long do I have to wait here and study? What sort of deity is this temple dedicated to?"

"We will see how long you need after a day or two of study. The initiation can occur in a month's time, if you make progress."

The young acolyte stood and walked over to the door again, without waiting for Mirae to finish eating. Mirae just watched her, tasting the odd but fragrant food. The acolyte turned to look back at her just as she put her hand on the doorknob to go, as if remembering the other part of her question.

"The temple is dedicated to the royal family and the royal crypt. We are guardians of their history and their secrets. You will learn soon enough what that means. I will return at nightfall for you."

After a few more hours alone reading the books she had been given, Mirae closed them in frustration. She had already copied the syllabary five times on the roll of parchment the acolyte had left for her, and she couldn't make sense of the strange royal history that only left her feeling more unsettled each time she read it over. None of the other temple attendants had come in to see to her needs or talk with her. All Mirae could do was sit in the room and wait to be summoned. Or was it?

She looked around the room at the sparse furnishings. Thinking a moment, she rose to her feet and walked across the room to look behind a curtain at its far end. Behind it were shelves full of books, but she already had a headache from so much reading today. Turning to a small chest in the corner, she pulled open the top drawer.

The sight of a snarling face startled her, and she jumped back, knocking the drawer onto the floor with a clatter. The face was turned to the floor now, and she saw that it was actually a mask. Picking it up gingerly, she lifted it up to her face. The light-weight material smelled aromatic, like cedar. Turning it slightly, Mirae saw that the front was painted white, and the feline features and black stripes were painted in an almost luminescent black lacquer that made the mask seem alive. A white tiger, Mirae thought. Without reflecting upon what she was doing, she placed the mask on her face.

4

As the mask touched her skin, the room disappeared, and Mirae felt as though she wore a mask of icy marble. She recoiled at its touch and, shuddering, shut her eyes tightly, taking a few deep breaths until she felt in control. When she opened her eyes, she found herself outside in a beautiful plaza on a sunny day. The plaza was bordered by three-story buildings with ancient-looking colonnades, painted vermillion and trimmed with silver and green vines. The plaza itself was inlaid with silvery marble bricks with green veins. Mirae had never seen anything quite like it on earth, but what she saw next left her even more surprised.

Movement in one corner of the plaza caught her eye. Turning to look at it more directly, her eyes met those of a cat, a large, slow animal that now seemed wary after discovering her presence. Like the mask, it was a white tiger. Wondering how the mask made her appear before the noble animal, Mirae stood still, watching it approach.

"Who are you?" it asked in a deep, male voice, never taking its eyes off of her. "Those who approach us are specifically invited. No one ever comes to us unannounced."

"I *was* invited," Mirae said, trying to explain. She suddenly felt uncomfortable in this place and wanted to take the mask off. Would the vision end if she did?

"Minha had not mentioned sending a new acolyte, though I see you wear the ring of the royal family. *Who are you?*" the tiger asked again, now halfway across the plaza and closing the distance between them much more swiftly.

"Mirae Choi," she said, nearly tripping over the words.

Feeling an uncontrollable panic, Mirae's hands went inadvertently to her face as the tiger came close enough for her to smell its breath, scented oddly of honeysuckle, and see its gleaming fangs. Peeling off the mask, the scene before her changed. Gone were the gaudy marble facades, though she now still stood in a plaza in the bright sunshine instead of returning to the room where she had found the mask. The air still smelled of springtime flowers, but the surrounding buildings bordering the plaza's red stone walkways appeared to be constructed with various types of wood and clay ceramic tiles, their sweeping, curved rooftops looking more alien than the Greco-Roman style in the visions.

A man stood before her, looking at her in consternation as she held the mysterious mask in her hands.

"Joriya! What are you doing here? You shouldn't be out of your quarters! I gave strict instructions that you should not be seen in public until we can come to an agreement."

Mirae just stared at him, uncomprehending. Joriya was the Queen, wasn't she? Why would this man think she was the Queen or talk to her so angrily? Was she under arrest? Studying the man's face, full of irritation as he continued to speak about things Mirae had no understanding of, she had to admit he was attractive in a bitter sort of way. His blue eyes contrasted with his tanned skin and dark brown hair that brushed the collar of his richly embroidered green toga. Mirae suddenly could understand Sohyeon's immediate fascination with Minha and regretting thinking his reaction was childish. The immortals had more charisma than anyone she had ever encountered.

She tried not to stare at the man. His face twisted into a look of disgust, which pierced Mirae's heart, and she felt uncomfortable knowing she had done something to displease him.

"Have you heard a word I just said to you, Joriya? You need to get back to your room and stay there!"

"I'm sorry. I told you, my name is Mirae," she said, more flustered than before. "Didn't I tell you? Was it you I was talking to a minute ago?" Her voice trailed off as she struggled to make sense of what was real and what had only happened in the vision. She realized she sounded so out of it, but the man's face softened as he repeated her name to himself.

"Yes, you said that already, but when I saw your face, you looked so much like my sister I didn't think anything of it. I'm sorry. I have made a mistake. Are you lost? Where did you come from?"

"But how?" Mirae asked almost in a whisper. "The tiger - ."

He looked at her impatiently again and then grabbed the wrist of her hand that held the tiger mask.

"The ceremonial mask has strange powers," he said. "This is why no acolytes of the temple can use it. It is only reserved for the high priestess to use and is kept in her sanctuary. The mask's power, and its secrets, are too great for the uninitiated. Did you come from the temple? Perhaps we should visit Minha and straighten all of this out."

Mirae suddenly felt very cold, as if she held ice in her hand instead of a mask.

"Go back to the temple? I think for now I would like to take a walk before I return. I've been studying all morning and came across the mask by mistake. I will probably get in trouble if I go back."

She wondered if she should say such a thing to him, but she felt reluctant to face Minha now.

"Are you new to the temple?" the man asked, his eyes resting on the ring that she wore. His jaw tightened. She remembered that the tiger in the vision mentioned it, something about it being a symbol of the royal family. Minha had not mentioned that, and Mirae had not spent time around the other acolytes to ask its significance. Perhaps it was why the man thought she was the Queen.

He took her free hand and put it on his arm.

"If you are new to the temple, let's take a stroll and talk some more. No need for you to go back just yet. What province are you from? The name Mirae is not a common one around here."

"I'm not from Khabu at all. I was brought here by ferry and am learning everything about Khabu now."

He just stared at her a moment, his expression unreadable as they walked across the plaza and turned the corner to the city's main street. Holding onto his arm, she noticed that he, too, wore a pearl ring like hers. No wonder he was interested in her now.

"I don't think you ever introduced yourself to me," Mirae said, suspicious of the man even as she felt intoxicated in his presence.

"No, I probably didn't. I thought at first you knew who I was."

"If you are the Queen's brother, as you said earlier, then are you a prince? I would be so honored to be accidentally rescued by a prince."

"A prince? In Khabu, the close family members of the reigning monarch are known as dukes and duchesses, not princes or princesses. It is a matter of respect for the fact that we are not in line for the throne, and by accepting such titles, we repudiate our right to rule. Khabu's inhabitants are immortal. Did you know that? If you were brought here by ferry, you must be from a land of mortals beyond the inner sea. You can't understand the ways of immortals in that case. Why did Minha make you a temple acolyte and give you our family ring?"

Mirae looked at the Duke in alarm. What was she doing here? Wasn't she supposed to be here to help the queen stop the Duke - what was his name? - from warring against her? Mirae had the sinking feeling she had been found out and was now being pulled into the camp of the enemy. How could she protect herself now? She felt helpless against this man's charms.

"Minha hasn't told me any details about my stay here and never explained the meaning of the ring," Mirae said, hoping he lie wasn't obvious.

They had stopped near a garden down the street from the plaza, though Mirae didn't want to let go of his arm even as he turned to face her. He seemed to be amused by her reaction. His enchantment on her was strong.

"What was your name again? Or should I call you 'Duke'?"

"Birum," he said.

She tried not to react to the name and struggled to smile. Whatever task Minha had brought her here for was likely ruined now.

"Since you are now a guest of the royal family and our temple, I should be polite and take you on a full tour of the capital. Don't worry about Minha's wrath because you escaped your acolyte trainers. I will deal with her when you return."

"What could I possibly need to see in Khabu?" Mirae asked demurely. "And I have the mask. Won't they be looking for it?"

Birum looked at it and shrugged.

"If it concerns you to have such a dangerous artefact, then come with me to my home so I can prepare a welcome feast. I will have my attendants take you and the mask back to the temple afterward and explain the situation. Minha cannot deny me your company if I choose to entertain you since I am royalty."

"Do you live far from the temple? I feel like I shouldn't go that far."

"The Blue Waterfall is a few days away from the capital city toward the central plain of our land, but I have secret ways to get there quickly. Surely you are not refusing to accept my hospitality? Rest assured that the Queen is too indisposed to make you a better offer!"

He seemed genuinely disappointed by her response, but Mirae was both alarmed and intrigued by his mention of the Blue Waterfall. That was one of the details mentioned in the parchment and an image from her nightmare which both attracted and terrified her, much like Duke Birum himself did. Looking into his eyes and reliving the memory of swimming in the soothing blue water from her dream, she knew what she had to do even though it would seal her fate with this man. Accepting his offer was also likely to be dangerous.

"If I come with you, will you let Minha know where I am and when I will return?"

"If that's what you want."

"On that condition I will come with you. Is there somewhere safe that I can put the mask until I return?"

"I can send it back with my servant when they deliver my message about our feast if you like."

The mask turned as cold as ice again, nearly burning Mirae's hand.

"I would like to keep it with me for now and ask Minha about it when I return."

"Then I will get you a pouch to keep it in until then."

He raised his hand and made an unfamiliar sign. A large, ornately decorated palanquin large enough for four people came toward them, carried by ten men dressed in black togas. One of men rushed forward, offering a velvet pouch just big enough to fit the mask in. Mirae took it, slipped the mask into the folds of the fabric, and pulled the satin strings shut, wrapping them around her wrist.

Looking up, she saw Birum had climbed into the palanquin and realized in horror that she'd have to ride in it with him in very close quarters. Hesitantly, she climbed in to join him.

Offering her his hand, he helped her keep her balance as she sat on the narrow, low bench beside him. The brocade curtain fell around them, and Mirae heard the door shut on the other side of it. It was dim in the palanquin, and it smelled vaguely of honeysuckle, reminding Mirae again of the vision of the tiger.

Birum seemed very formal, and he took pains not to jostle against her as they started to move. Leaning toward the opposite side of the compartment, he opened a thin flap to let the light in. Mirae could see some of the buildings that they passed through the tiny window. She tried not to be nervous around Birum, but she didn't know what to make of him. Everything she had been told about him suggested that he was the enemy of her allies, so what should she do now?

5

Their ride in the palanquin was a lot shorter than Mirae had expected. Much like the night ship, it seemed to move quickly smoothly without being affected much by time or distance, and Mirae thought of the way the tiger mask had moved her from inside the palace to the plaza in only seconds.

"How can we cross such a long distance so quickly?" she asked.

"I have studied magical traditions for many years, and there are ways to cross great distances, even reach other worlds, as you have experienced already in coming to our land. This is my special palanquin I use to get across

Khabu using dimensional doors. Nothing else like it exists in Khabu. It should only take a few more minutes to reach our destination. Do you come from a world that understands magic?"

"No, I don't know anything about that kind of power," Mirae said, wondering if this was part of the reason Minha had summoned her to help fight against Birum.

They both fell silent a moment as the palanquin swayed.

"So you live at the Blue Waterfall? Why is it called such a poetic name?" she asked, trying not to let her trepidation show.

Birum smirked.

"I have never looked into the origin of the name. Perhaps some ancestor felt it reflected the beauty of the land. They certainly couldn't have chosen a more dramatic place to build their estate, which is now over a thousand years old. The estate's stone manse stands not far from the edges of a block of high, zigzagging stone shelves looking like two wide steps that the river runs over before plunging down to a large pool. The top shelf is 30 times the height of a man!"

"So the water falls in broad cascades down multiple cliffs? I can't wait to see it for myself. Back home, I would have to travel quite far to see such a spectacle. I think the tallest we have in our area is Kilgore Falls, but they are only about three times the height of a man. The Blue Waterfall must be amazing."

"The water is unusually clear and bright. It's possible to swim at the base of the waterfall, though that requires a trek through the forest to get to the best location."

Birum's comment startled Mirae. She hadn't mentioned wanting to swim in the waterfall, but it was what she saw in the dream. Could Birum read her mind? The parallel with her dream reminded her he was supposed to be her enemy. The dream had ended badly, the water filling with blood. She knew she must avoid going to the swimming hole if possible.

"Surely we don't have time for a swim tonight," she said smoothly, trying to change the subject. "Minha will be worried when the acolytes find my room empty, so I should get back soon. What sort of feast did you have in mind? Did you kidnap me in order to pump me for information about the world beyond Khabu?"

She tried to keep her tone light, and Birum didn't seem to react to her gentle teasing.

"If they find the mask missing, they will figure out why you aren't there even if I hadn't sent my attendant to Minha. Don't worry about the temple tonight. I won't keep you long. I just don't see why Minha should keep such an exotic visitor to herself. We will just eat and talk a bit, though I may ask to bring you back to my estate when the weather is better to enjoy the water if you like. How long will you be staying in Khabu?"

"I don't know. Minha wants me to go through training here to serve in the temple, so it sounds like I will live here once my training is complete."

"What an odd thing for her to request of a foreigner from another dimension!" Birum said, though Mirae couldn't tell if he was suspicious enough to guess Minha's true motives. "Then I will be visiting you often now that I know you are here."

The palanquin stopped abruptly, and one of the attendants who carried it opened the door and pulled back the brocade curtain. The weak late afternoon sunlight spilled into the compartment, and Mirae shielded her eyes so they could adjust. Birum waited patiently for her to take the attendant's hand and climb out, but when he emerged into the misty air beside her, she could barely take her eyes off of their surroundings to look at him.

The water's edge wasn't that far away from where they stood, only just beyond thick bushes framed by a few clusters of trees that they could easily see through. Rising before them above the thin forest was a tall, wide cliff reaching straight up two levels with white, misty water plunging down them into an equally wide cerulean pool. It was just like her dream!

"Don't say I didn't warn you," he said, clearly pleased with her reaction.

"But you didn't warn me at all, Birum. It's breathtaking."

"You assumed I meant the estate was built near the top of the waterfall, but it's down here at the bottom where the view is much grander, don't you think? As you can see, if you take the right path through the forest a little ways, you will reach the swimming hole. For now, let's go in. Dinner will be ready, even though I hadn't announced I would have a guest tonight. Do you like deer meat?"

"It's a bit rustic for a city girl like me, but I can eat it," she replied, finally feeling in control of herself again to walk with him to the main house, which loomed in front of them in a forest clearing.

The house's was three stories tall like many of the buildings in Khabu, and its black stones looked very old. Mirae could almost believe it had been here 1,000 years. Oddly, it seemed to have no fortifications or guards. Birum and his attendants led her right through the front doors without any fanfare, and Birum took her immediately to a grand hall where the table was set for him and for his men. Mirae could smell the scent of roasted meat and baking bread and realized how the temple's food was very Spartan in comparison.

Motioning for her to sit next to him, Birum took the seat at the head of the table and poured a thick red liquid into her cup. Without thinking, Mirae took a sip. The burning sensation on her tongue felt reassuring, though she wasn't much of a drinker back home, and she relaxed a little, forgetting Minha's reasoning for training her to serve in the temple. Birum's attendants took their seats at the table, talking merrily amongst themselves and their leader about trivial household details. Apparently, the deer Birum was serving had been the prey of their hunting party the day before, which the burly men were very proud of. It had been a good hunting trip, and they reveled in their elaborate celebration dinner. Birum merely listened to their bragging with a satisfied expression.

Soon, the kitchen servants brought out trays of freshly baked bread and juicy, seasoned meat to serve to everyone present. They all ate eagerly, and Mirae found herself enjoying the men's company. Few questions were directed at her, which she found odd given Birum's insistence that he had wanted to honor her and spend some time with her. What was the real reason that he had invited her for dinner? she wondered.

6

After dinner, Birum led her into his study, a richly decorated if gloomy room next door to the dining hall. The other attendants went out to practice archery in the back of the estate although the sun was setting, leaving them alone to talk.

"Did you enjoy dinner?" he asked casually, rearranging a few pieces of parchment on his desk as she sat on a leather couch on one side of the room. "You won't get anything so luxurious at the temple."

Mirae wondered if she drank too much of the wine for her own good. Birum now seemed like an old friend. She noted again how attractive he was, and thoughts of Sohyeon's comments about Minha irritatingly came to mind. *This isn't like Sohyeon and his infatuations,* she thought. He was still a boy, and she was an adult. Surely she knew better than to fall into those kinds of traps.

"The meal they served me wasn't terrible. They just didn't cook it as skillfully as your servants prepared tonight's meal. I have to thank you for inviting me. I felt rather isolated at the temple, and no one was telling me why I was here, at least not honestly."

"Why did they tell you they wanted you to become an acolyte?" he asked, coming to sit beside her on the couch. "Did you intend on leaving home to stay indefinitely in Khabu before they asked you to?"

"I don't know why I'm here really, and I'm more confused than ever after reading the strange books they gave me to study. That's when I found the mask," Mirae said. "Your society is very old, and your rulers remain in power for an incredible number of years before disappearing. Yet you are immortals? Perhaps you can explain to me the situation as you see it in Khabu."

"Khabu is the land of the immortals, and for many centuries we have stayed close to home, cultivating our land and society instead of looking beyond our borders and our traditions," he said, smiling tightly. "It's true that our leaders serve publicly for centuries before retiring. Since you are from the land of mortals, of course this is hard for you to understand."

"When you mistook me for the Queen earlier, you said something about her confinement. Was this her retirement that you meant? She has already been on the throne for more centuries than many of your leaders, according to the history I read today."

Birum looked away from her for a moment before answering.

"The Queen is near retirement, and it's time for her successor to emerge. She is still publicly our leader, however."

"Then why is she confined?"

"It is an internal matter that only concerns the royal family," he said, his voice getting gruffer, angrier. "We don't need interference from outsiders. We just disagree on our vision for the future of Khabu."

"The future of Khabu? Do you mean that you disagree on succession? Who would normally rule in

Queen Joriya's place if she were to retire? You said the royal family took the titles of duke and duchess to repudiate their right to the throne, so who is in line to become king or queen now?"

Birum stood, his hands shaking so much that Mirae suddenly was afraid she had tipped her hand. Did he want to rule Khabu in Joriya's place? Even as tipsy as she was, she didn't want to tell him outright that she was there to settle his fight with Joriya, and she didn't want him to turn out to be the villain in this situation now that she had met him. Indeed, she found herself wanting to be with him more and more the longer they talked together. Minha would be furious if she found out.

"Never mind," Mirae said, glancing toward the window.

It was darker now, though even in the dim light Mirae could see the waterfall in the distance. Thinking of the riddle on the parchment, she stood and went over to Birum, putting her hands reassuringly on his arm. He recoiled just a little at her touch then relaxed.

"Never mind," she said again, softer this time. "I didn't mean to bring up a difficult subject after you have been so hospitable. I should go now. You said you would take me back to the temple before dark. I can come back and visit you some other time."

Turning to go, Mirae took a step away from Birum, but he suddenly grabbed her by the wrists and pulled her toward him. His face was very close to hers.

"Don't stay away too long, Mirae," he said. "We need to speak again soon."

Leaning closer, he kissed her. The touch of his lips on hers ignited something in the strange wine she drank at dinner, and she felt herself falling. Before her vision went dark, she slumped down to the floor, her legs twisted to the side, her torso facing the ceiling. She didn't have the strength to move, though she still heard and saw everything for a few minutes before losing consciousness.

Birum looked down at her in triumph and called for someone to come and take her away. As her vision faded to black, she could hear Sohyeon's voice the night they went out to dinner.

"I guess it was pretty reckless of me to make a deal with the ferryman, but I didn't know he was going to bite me. You're right that it was uncivilized. I've been thinking about that all day since you said it. Pontol didn't seem entirely human when he did it."

Now it seemed she was allied with the enemy of her keepers and had fallen into a similar trap.

7

Mirae awoke in her room back at the temple just before sunrise, her head aching as if she had a hangover. Sitting up, she looked around the room. A small candle had been left burning near her bed, but otherwise she was alone in the room. The books she had been studying still sat on the table where she left them, and remembering the mask, she jumped out of bed and ran over to the small dresser, opening the drawer. The tiger face frozen into a snarl looked out at her from it. Everything was exactly as it had been before she had her encounter with Birum yesterday. Had it been real? Was it a dream? he had to find out.

Slipping out of her room, she entered the main audience hall where Minha held court sitting next to the luminous pearl. As she had suspected, Minha was already on the dais, standing next to the font with the pearl, preparing for the day's tasks. Augmented starlight streamed through the crystalline spires of the rooftop and joined with the pearl's soft, glowing energy. Standing there deep in meditation, Minha looked otherworldly. Mirae was afraid to break the spell, but they were alone together, and she needed answers. No one would stop her, even if she angered Minha.

Stepping up onto the dais, she stood behind Minha a few paces.

"High priestess, I need some answers. It cannot wait," she said, trying to remain calm.

Minha stiffened then turned to look at the intruder.

"You! I should have expected this. Come sit down."

"What happened to me yesterday?" Mirae asked, near tears. "Was it real?"

"The mask is unpredictable, and it was partly my fault for leaving it in your room," Minha said. "But you will need to learn to control its power, so I have not taken it away from you."

"So it did happen to me! And what of Birum? Have I ruined all of your plans to help Joriya by going with him to his home?"

Minha looked at her in astonishment.

"Birum? You saw him yesterday?"

"I thought you knew," Mirae said, flustered. "He said he was sending an attendant to notify you we were having dinner together after the mask put me in his path. I was afraid you would find me gone from my room and worry."

"Birum would never send an attendant here," she said caustically. "You spent time with him yesterday? The mask took you to him? He's getting too powerful for us to control then." Her voice turned more thoughtful.

"I didn't tell him why you brought me here," Mirae added quickly. "Though I don't really understand why you think he's your enemy."

Minha's expression turned from puzzlement to alarm.

"Birum not our enemy? So he has found a way to interfere in my plans! If you didn't tell him anything, there still may be time, but we will have to deal with him soon."

"He told me that Queen Joriya is confined to her quarters, and he mistook me for her at first. Do you know what he was talking about? Are you all immortals as the histories you have me reading suggest? Who is the Queen's successor if it is time for her to retire?"

"Enough!"

Minha seemed very angry now, and Mirae looked down at the floor.

"I will answer your questions eventually, but for now, stay away from Birum. I will also look into why the mask took you to him instead of...well, you need to work on your syllabary to learn to read our language, and don't worry about these things. This is my responsibility in the temple, and I have more of our history that you need to read before your training is done. Not many of our books have been translated into the languages of the outer regions that you are native to. Birum clearly talks too much, but if his goal is to stop me from reaching my objectives, that is to be expected. I shall post a guard at your door for now until I can get a handle on the situation with him. Normally he isn't interested in temple matters."

"When will I go back home?"

"Home? This is your home for now. You shouldn't expect to be indulged a return visit to your homeland very often at this point. Before long, you will forget about them anyway."

As they spoke, a small shadow appeared in the window at the top of the hall and dropped down between them. A beautiful white bird with a piece of parchment tied around its neck perched on the edge of the font that held the pearl, waiting expectantly. Minha looked over at it as if it were a ghost, the color draining from her face for a moment before she regained her composure and walked over to it slowly. It stood still and allowed her to pull the parchment from its neck. Unrolling it but not unfolding it, Minha's eyes grew wide.

"This is a message for you. Do you know someone named Sohyeon?" Minha asked, holding out her hand.

"Sohyeon? He is my brother. I believe you met him before I came."

Mirae watched Minha's reaction carefully, noticing how uncomfortable she seemed now that she realized the boy she threw out was now in the inner regions. Mirae walked over to her and took the parchment, unfolding it and reading it eagerly after her eyes paused for a second to rest curiously on the bird.

Mirae, Pontol brought me to Eokhmisseun, and I have heard some disturbing things about your situation that I didn't think you knew from the conversation we had at dinner the other night. Did you know that a member of the royal family of Khabu has invaded and nearly destroyed Eokhmisseun? This territory is suffering horribly under his rule. His magic has turned its inhabitants into bloodthirsty monsters. Is this the duke that you mentioned the queen there was at war with? His name is Litt. You should be careful. Were you told the truth about the situation in Khabu? It may not be safe for you to stay there. Sohyeon.

Mirae looked at Sohyeon's letter in amazement. Biting her lip, she thought about her evening with Birum. Perhaps he wasn't Joriya's enemy after all, and he was trying to communicate that to her without explaining exactly what was wrong. She hoped so. She could try to find out who Litt was and what exactly had happened with the queen, even if Minha wouldn't tell her, somehow. If Minha was going to keep her under guard now, it would be harder, but she could walk out on her own or use the mask perhaps to wander more. For now, she needed to answer Sohyeon.

"Can I send a message back to him?" she asked Minha, who was watching her skeptically.

"The bird is waiting. I will bring you parchment to write a message. What news does he send?"

"He's in some place called Eokhmisseun. Have you heard of it? Something terrible is happening there."

Minha walked across the hall to a corner that Mirae hadn't noticed before and pulled out some well-concealed drawers. She took out a small portable writing desk and brought it back to her.

"Sit there and use the brush and paper inside to write your response. I will wait for you."

Mirae took the writing desk and sat down on the chair on the dais while Minha went to feed a small morsel to the bird. It jumped onto her hand as she fed it, cooing contentedly. Before she started to write, Mirae thought fleetingly that Minha seemed used to handling the bird.

Taking out paper and a brush, Mirae wrote her answer out to Sohyeon, her heart in turmoil.

Sohyeon, I knew something was wrong when the priestess told me I was needed to help them fight a war. Tonight I accidentally met the Duke, Birum. Neither he nor Minha explained why I was there but Birum dined with me and showed me around the countryside a little. Minha is concerned about the Duke's interference in the affairs of Khabu. Beyond that, I have never heard of Eokhmisseun and had not been told that someone from Khabu was stirring up trouble there. Should I ask about it? Is there a way I can help? Tell me what you need me to do. Mirae.

Reading it over one more time, she folded the paper and rolled it up small enough to fit in the bird's collar, handing it back to Minha. Minha placed it in the bird's collar and tossed the bird into the air. It took flight and floated up to the hole in the ceiling. The two women watched it return to its master a moment before resuming their conversation.

"What did your brother say about Eokhmisseun, Mirae?" Minha asked, coming over to where she sat on the priestess' favorite chair. "It's odd that a bird messenger from there would come over the inner sea to us here instead of staying in their territory. I seem to recall they were a gift from our country to Eokhmisseun many generations ago, so it's curious they would return now."

"Eokhmisseun is suffering due to some member of the royal family of Khabu. Have you heard about it? Perhaps that is why the bird wanted to come here."

"Eokhmisseun? What business has Khabu had with Eokhmisseun in recent years? I do not know."

"Is the royal family large? Someone named Litt has taken over Eokhmisseun and has claimed to be from here. Is it possibly untrue?"

Minha turned back to her, looking at her strangely.

"Litt? The royal family is large enough that one of the men could have taken it upon themselves to cause trouble abroad, but none bear that name."

"An alias?"

"Perhaps."

"Would Queen Joriya know?"

"Why do you ask?"

Mirae paused, thinking. What was her next move in unraveling the mystery? Everyone in Khabu seemed reluctant to give her any information willingly.

"Perhaps I should meet with the Queen and hear her side of the story. She would know her family members better than anyone, wouldn't she? Maybe she would know about Litt when the rest of Khabu would not."

"As the high priestess of Khabu, I would know all of the royal family members," Minha said mildly. "But I see no reason not to grant you an audience with the Queen. Come with me."

8

Mirae and Minha walked down the corridor to a disused part of the temple on one of the upper floors. Mirae had been surprised that Minha had suddenly relented and offered to take her to see Queen Joriya, but Mirae was puzzled as to why the Queen was quartered there.

"I didn't get the impression the Queen was being confined in the temple. Birum-."

"Birum may pretend to know everything we do, but I assure you he is a blustering fool and a troublemaker," Minha said, her tone milder than her words. "The Queen trusts us more than her palace attendants given the situation within the royal family. I'm only taking you to see her because I think she would want to counter his influence. Here we are."

They reached a door near the end of the corridor. Minha pulled out a large skeleton key and placed it in the lock. The door swung open, revealing a multiroom suite with large windows overlooking the temple plaza where Mirae had met Birum.

"Go ahead. I will wait for you out here."

Mirae stepped into the parlor and looked around as Minha shut the door behind her. At first it didn't look like anyone was in the room, but after a few minutes as her eyes adjusted to the light, she saw a slender woman sitting in the corner, the light from the window shining on her face. Mirae took a few steps toward her, unable to tear her eyes away from the woman. Birum was right. Queen Joriya looked like her, at least enough for the resemblance to be noticeable. The Queen seemed ageless, and her layered multicolored silk brocade clothing suggested someone of high status. The style was quite unlike the temple acolytes' garb, yet it also seemed somewhat old-fashioned in a way Mirae couldn't put her finger on.

Stopping a few paces away from the Queen, who had not acknowledged her presence or turned toward her yet, Mirae waited uncomfortably.

"Is it time for us to finally meet?" the Queen asked pensively, her eyes still riveted on the window. "I hadn't expected Minha to bring you so soon. I'm afraid I'm unprepared for this, Mirae, though I am glad you are here."

"Do we know each other, your highness?" Mirae asked. "Is there something you have to tell me?"

The Queen turned toward her and smiled sadly. Standing, she walked over to Mirae and studied her a moment. The Queen's gown was predominantly green silk with silvery vines embroidered around the front collar with inner layers of yellow and gray underneath, and her black hair was pulled away from her face and piled on her head. Mirae's eyes were drawn to the pearl ring on her right hand. Holding out her own hand wearing the same ring, she felt a sense of trepidation coming over her. She almost didn't want to know the truth and steeled herself for Joriya's revelations.

Joriya saw the ring on Mirae's hand and nodded.

"Why am I here?" Mirae asked. "Is it really because there is some war?"

"You are here because it's time for me to leave the throne of Khabu," Joriya said, smiling slightly again. "You have been told the truth that there is a war in Khabu over who my successor will be. My brother Birum has taken it upon himself to challenge our traditional rules of succession and has put me here to prevent my interference in his plot to take over."

"And what does that have to do with me?"

"It was time to bring you here because I need to stop Birum. He believes he has nearly killed my successor, but we have played a trick on him so he has the wrong person!"

"I don't understand," Mirae said, her sense of trepidation turning to dread. "Who has he nearly killed?"

"The woman he believes is the true successor to the throne, my official daughter Pareya. Birum attacked her not long after her birth and had her imprisoned during my rule for the past twenty years."

"But this is not the truth? This Pareya is not the true heir to the kingdom?"

"No. Minha and I knew of Birum's plan to betray the clan and seize the kingdom for himself, so we came up with an alternate plan. We sometimes had secret dealings with a world beyond the inner sea, and Minha came up with the idea that we should send the child I had borne to them for safekeeping. We put my child in a home there and took a child of theirs in exchange to be our counterfeit."

Mirae could only stare at her in disbelief. She thought of Sohyeon's complaint about how Minha had angrily rejected him when Pontol brought him instead of Mirae.

"No, it can't be. What are you saying? You can't mean what I think you're implying."

Joriya looked at her with tears glittering in her eyes.

"You are my daughter, Mirae. I have waited a long time to see you again, but I at least knew you were safe all of this time. Now we can stop Birum's plan in its tracks. "

"There was another baby born to my family then?" Mirae asked, thinking back to her family's stories about the birth of the Choi children. "I was supposed to have died as a baby. There was a child, then, who nearly died."

"Yes, Pareya is the Choi's daughter, not you. She was always weak, but Birum weakened her further. Still, even as a human she lived among immortals, so he wasn't able to destroy her completely, and I protected her however I could."

"Where is she now?"

"We have other things we must discuss and attend to, Mirae. Why concern yourself with a girl you never met and who is of no consequence to our plans for the kingdom?"

"We can talk about Birum later," Mirae said, feeling an almost physical pain at the thought that he was indeed her enemy and also her uncle. "Let me meet the girl first."

"What will it solve?" Joriya asked gently.

Suddenly, Mirae thought of something Sohyeon had brought up that provided a glimmer of hope the situation wasn't so dire.

"If you want to change the subject, then let's discuss Litt. Is he also another brother of yours? Who is he and why have you allowed him to invade Eokhmisseun?"

Joriya looked at her in astonishment.

"Eokhmisseun? A brother named Litt? I had heard there was some unrest in that land maybe fifty years ago, but it has nothing to do with Khabu."

"That isn't the story they tell over in Eokhmisseun. My brother is there now, and he sent me a letter warning that the situation is bad. He mentioned the land is ruled by an evil man claiming to be from Khabu."

"I don't have a brother named Litt. I am unaware of any of our people who could have done such a thing."

"Is there anyone from Khabu named Litt at all? Anyone who isn't a member of the royal family?"

Joriya's brow furrowed as she thought a moment.

"The name sounds familiar, but I don't think it was anyone in the royal family."

"But he could be from Khabu?"

"Yes, I suppose it is possible. Regardless of who he is, he has now made Khabu and me personally responsible for his transgressions, now hasn't he?"

"How can we stop him then?"

"I have no power over the internal situation in a foreign land," Joriya said, sighing. "I understand now why you want to see Pareya."

"Nothing is what it seems in this situation. How did the fight between you and Duke Birum begin all of those years ago?"

"I can't say I remember that well. I haven't seen him since you were born, maybe not since he had burst into the family crypt to make his claim to take my place. The ancestors banished him from the temple since the crypt is forbidden for him to enter, but he found a way to hamper my rule and destroy Pareya."

"What? You haven't seen Birum in more than twenty years?"

Joriya's eyes widened.

"I don't see what difference that makes. He has spent many years causing me trouble from his fortress."

"The fortress at the Blue Waterfall? I saw it yesterday. It was beyond beautiful. I can well understand why he would be entranced with ruling Khabu if all of the land is so beautiful," Mirae said.

Joriya froze and seemed to be speechless. She looked at Mirae in sheer terror.

Before Mirae could say more, the door burst open. Minha stood there with her assistant.

"Come quickly to the main hall on the first floor. We have news from Eokhmisseun!"

Mirae and Joriya quickly followed the women through the corridors and down the stairs to the room with the pearl, Joriya no longer concerned about being caught out of her luxurious jail cell for the moment. The four women stood in the hall, looking up in wonder at the dome where daylight now poured through the ceiling. The room was filled with fluttering white birds, close to fifty of them. Rays of luminescent light emanated from the pearl, holding the birds in place as they struggled to find a place to land. Mirae squinted to see if any of them bore another message from Sohyeon.

"Minha, what is the meaning of this?" Joriya asked, staring at the birds in alarm. "These are our sacred ancestors from the Forest of Bliss near our southern border."

"They are not, my lady," Minha said breathlessly as she gently caught one of the birds in her hands. "These messenger birds were our gift to Eokhmisseun a very long time ago. They have been whispering since they arrived that a purge has begun in Eokhmisseun and that they are too afraid to stay there. What should we do? This isn't our war."

"Purge? What could they mean by such a thing?" Joriya asked, walking over to the bird Minha held.

The bird spoke a series of strange sounds to Minha, whose face transformed with grief.

"He is killing all that are left to oppose him."

"Who is killing them?" Joriya asked.

"Litt," Mirae said, not needing an interpreter to explain the birds' distress. "What of my brother, Sohyeon? He was there not long ago."

"We can find Pontol and ask what has happened," Minha said, setting the bird gently on the arm of her chair on the dais. "Bring some of the special cages we have for the messenger birds when we use them so they can settle down," she said to her acolyte.

"I should go to Birum and see what he knows about this," Mirae said. Minha and Joriya looked at her in horror.

"Forget going to him for help," Minha said. "You don't seem to understand the threat he poses to the kingdom after your little tête-à-tête with him last night. I will think of something once I find Pontol and get his report."

Joriya looked at Mirae with sudden understanding.

"Let's take this one step at a time," she said, walking over to Mirae slowly.

"What do you mean?" Mirae asked.

"You asked to see Pareya. Her cell is not far from here. If we must deal with the war in Eokhmisseun before settling issue of Khabu's succession, then it's better for you to see the truth. Especially if Birum has seduced you. The Blue Waterfall? How the world has changed so much in twenty years if he should do something like that."

9

Joriya and Minha led Mirae down another floor to an entire complex built underneath the temple. Here the ceilings were even higher than on the temple's main floor, and the colonnaded rooms were grander than the ancient temples of Egypt and Greece back on earth. Mirae could hardly walk through the wide room connecting the four precincts without stopping to gape in awe.

The women quickly led her to the eastern precinct, but Mirae had noticed the western precinct had a familiar design next to the corridor leading toward it. The tiger mask! It was repeated in a bas relief larger than the mask she had back in her room. Suddenly the urge to run down that corridor to meet her fate felt so strong, she stopped and turned back momentarily. Joriya and Minha quickly grabbed her arms and pulled her along toward the eastern precinct, the glance between them telling Mirae that they had noticed something strange about her attraction to that part of the temple.

In the eastern precinct, the corridor led to a gate of thin bars, looking more like prison doors. Minha opened them with her skeleton key and pulled Mirae along. The sharp scent of garbage made Mirae recoil, but Minha led her down another set of stairs to another corridor lined with barred doors. Joriya remained on the upper level.

"Don't," Mirae murmured, struggling against Minha.

"You wanted to see her, didn't you? This is what your beloved Birum did to her. You need to see it."

"I didn't say I loved Birum," Mirae said in a low, emphatic voice.

"No? But you are clearly under his spell. Time to see him for what he is."

Minha pushed her gently against the bars of one of the cells.

"Pareya, you have a visitor."

Leaving Mirae there, Minha walked back down the corridor and waited, her anger apparent from her gait. Mirae couldn't look into the cell right away, though she could hear the rough breathing of the girl.

"Do I know you?" Pareya asked in a weak voice.

The echo of her own question not long before to Joriya brought tears to Mirae's eyes, and she closed them a moment. This girl, a stranger, had taken the punishment meant for Mirae had she remained in her homeland of Khabu. The girl belonged to the Chois, the family that raised Mirae from birth, whom she loved deeply. It was hard not to feel as if she had betrayed them somehow by letting their real daughter suffer while she, an imposter, had been pampered by them. Finally, she looked up at the girl.

Not far from the bars sat a human, though one could hardly call her a girl. In fact, Mirae's first impression was that she looked strikingly like the unwholesome ferryman Pontol. Barely more than a skeleton with skin, Pareya's body was bent and emaciated, her sparse hair now mostly white with a few black streaks though she was nearly the same age as Mirae. Her dingy dress hung in tatters and was so dirty Mirae couldn't tell what color it actually might be. A small bowl of foul-smelling food sat beside the girl.

What could she say to Pareya now? Their fates were sealed by Minha and Joriya's decision years before.

"No, I'm sorry. I thought maybe we did know one another, but I was mistaken."

Pareya's hopeful expression fell.

"I'll see what I can do for you, though. Is there some food you like, or something you want to make your stay here more comfortable?"

The girl sighed and shook her head.

"Better not let Minha hear you. She has strict instructions from Birum not to give me more than this."

"But she is an immortal. What consequence could she be afraid of?"

Pareya looked up at her in surprise.

"Don't you know? Immortals can be killed with weapons made of silver through their heart. They aren't completely immortal. So the traditional execution rite awaits her if she disobeys."

Mirae didn't mention what Pareya told her about the execution of immortals when Minha and Joriya walked her back through the main level of the temple's underground corridors. Neither woman asked Mirae what they had spoken about. It was enough for them that she had seen Pareya. The three women walked back together in grim silence until they came to the corridor with the carving of the tiger's face. Mirae stopped. Walking up to it, she ran her fingers over it. She looked back at Joriya and Minha.

"What does this corridor lead to?"

"The crypt," Minha said.

"May I see it? I am a member of the royal family, after all, am I not?"

Joriya nodded sadly.

"It is within your rights to see the crypt, though most of the family never enters it."

"Why? We are immortals. Why wouldn't we want to speak with the ancestors face to face?"

"It isn't normally done until we retire from public rule," Joriya said.

"Only the high priestess enters the crypt before retirement for very special feasts held only once every hundred years, when certain stars align with the pearl in the hall," Minha said.

"Once they enter the crypt, they don't like to be reminded of their life in the kingdom and don't involve themselves with kingdom business," Joriya said.

"The mask in my room is connected with the crypt, isn't it?" Mirae asked.

"It is what the priestesses who serve in the temple wear for the 100 year ceremony," Minha said. "We are discouraged from entering the crypt in our human form. What you are suggesting goes against all of temple protocol."

"But if we are at war, isn't this an emergency?" Mirae asked. "If I am to help you settle this war, and if I am truly to take the throne after Joriya abdicates, then I should have the right to meet with the ancestors and seek their counsel!"

Without waiting for either of them to respond to her demand, Mirae walked resolutely down the corridor past the tiger mask carving to the door of the crypt. When she reached it, she stopped, puzzled. It was a solid wall with an elaborate carving that looked like a map. Minha came up beside her, looking at the map with an air of nostalgia.

"What is the meaning of this?" Mirae asked. "How do we enter if there is no door?"

Minha smiled slightly, turning toward her.

"This is an ancient map of Khabu. Don't you think it's a fitting decoration for the portal? You see, the crypt isn't accessed by a normal door that we are familiar with in everyday architecture. It is a dimensional portal that can only be opened on the inside. Perhaps the ancestors will be impressed with your determination and let you enter. Put your fingers here and wait to be summoned across the threshold."

Minha indicated two spots on the map that looked worn down. Placing her hands over the grooves, she found her fingers fit over the worn spots perfectly.

"What is this over here, Minha?" Joriya asked, indicating a wall a few paces down the corridor.

Minha turned to look back at place where the queen stood and gasped in astonishment. Rushing over to Joriya, she studied the wall.

"The list of kingship spanning our 10,000 year history," she said finally. "All of them should have retired to the crypt. Your name will go here at the bottom once you enter."

Joriya studied it a moment and pointed toward the top of the list, her eyes wide.

"I was wrong, Mirae," she said. "The name Litt isn't a name I recognize from the royal family still outside of the crypt, but his name on the list of kings! He ruled Khabu 8,000 years ago! I didn't think of it at first when you mentioned it. He should be in the crypt now!"

Mirae didn't move from the portal and focused more strongly on Litt in her mind.

"I didn't think of the list either, but you're right. I did read yesterday in Minha's sanctuary, too, but I read Sohyeon's note later when I was no longer studying in my room and hadn't made the connection. Why would one of the ancestors who had retired from the world thousands of years ago turn up in Eokhmisseun?"

"What about Birum breaching the crypt all of those years ago?" Minha asked, turning back toward Mirae. "Litt may not actually still be in the crypt, so maybe you're right that it's time to speak with the ancestors to verify his whereabouts. "

Joriya nodded.

"Yes, that's right! Birum had caused quite an uproar when he violated the temple's rules and invaded the crypt. When was that now? Maybe 20 or 30 years ago? Oh, maybe it was 60 years ago. At my age, I don't recall exactly. I think it wasn't many years before I gave birth to you, Mirae. My brother was already showing his ambition, and he had made threats against my heir even though I didn't have one yet. It was this incident that made me see I had to send you away to keep you safe and find a way to throw Birum off of pursuing you.

"Birum and I were never close, but he was closer to me than the rest of my siblings. Many of them I did not even know by name, but Birum was always a presence in my life. Perhaps that was the root of his dissatisfaction. He didn't remain at the palace in later years but built a fortress by the inner sea, not far from the ferry service between the worlds. I never visited him there, though I heard stories of his wandering. A few of my ministers suggested I put a stop to his activities, but I couldn't bring myself to do it. Too late I realized he was a menace to me and concocted my scheme to hide you with Minha as a last ditch effort to protect the kingdom."

"Birum reportedly got drunk one day and came to the temple unannounced," Minha said. "Forcing his way into the crypt, he disrupted the ancestors before I could have the acolytes arrest him and calm them. I closed the portal even more tightly than ever before after the ancestors' complaints, but it never occurred to me to check among them to see if any of them were missing. Birum seemed incompetent and boorish, not cunning. What could he have done in that condition? I thought."

"And now will they let me in?" Mirae asked. "Are there guardians inside that I must impress and pass?"

"Not quite, though since you are a member of the royal family who intends to re-emerge and rule Khabu one day, I would advise against entering more deeply than the antechamber past the gates. You will recognize the gates immediately. They are made from a slab from the same quarry that the pearl in my ritual hall and the rings of the royal family come from. It is a special substance reserved for the temple and royal clan. Do not walk beyond it, or you will never come back to reign. Not even the priestesses who have served in the temple have ever entered so far."

As they spoke, Mirae could feel the map beneath her fingers getting warmer and smoother, like she was sinking her fingers into warm taffy like she used to make with her mother in the summer when she was a little girl.

"I think it's opening. Will you come with me, Minha?"

Minha hesitated.

"You should go with her," Joriya said from across the corridor behind them. "I cannot enter, and she shouldn't go in alone. They might inadvertently lead her across the threshold, and I need her to return to rule Khabu in my stead."

10

The wall began to dissolve before their eyes, though the portal opening was only visible a few paces away from it. Joriya couldn't see anything happening from where she waited. Minha came to stand close to Mirae and linked her arm through Mirae's so they could walk into the crypt together. In moments, they were standing in a shadowy antechamber built of the same gray marble as the lower levels of the temple but ending in a shimmering pearl gate before them. The portal seemed to have closed behind them, and none of the torchlight that lit the corridors on that level illuminated the antechamber.

Mirae strained to see as she looked around the antechamber, but nothing was visible except gray storm clouds beyond the gate ahead of them.

"When will they come to speak to us?" Mirae asked. "Should we call for them? Or do we wait?"

"It won't be long before one of them is alerted to our presence. I used to serve the king before Queen Joriya a short time before his abdication and entry into the crypt, so my scent will be familiar. I often have talked with him."

"You are older than Joriya?" Mirae asked, astonished. "Isn't she 400 years old or more?"

Minha chuckled to herself.

"Of course I am older. In addition to being the temple priestess to the previous king, I gave birth to his heirs. I am Joriya and Birum's mother, and your grandmother."

"Such a strange world!"

"It is customary for the temple priestess or priest to marry the ruler."

"And my father?"

"One of the male temple acolytes who has gone into seclusion here already. Only the temple acolytes and royal family end up here. Civilians of Khabu later change into the magical pigeons you have already seen. They can either remain in service as messengers or go to live in the Forest of Bliss at the edge of Khabu."

As they talked, Mirae became aware of a shadow coming into the antechamber through the gate toward them. Studying it a moment, she nearly fell to her knees in shock. The ancestors! Instead of a human, Mirae was confronted with the beautiful beast she saw in the plaza while wearing the mask, a white tiger with crystal blue eyes ten feet tall at the shoulder and twenty-four feet long. It came closer, its eyes steadily upon her. Mirae took a step back.

"Don't be afraid," Minha said, holding onto her arm. "It won't come too close. Didn't you say you saw one when you wore the mask yesterday?"

The tiger came forward to the center of the room and sat in front of them.

"Who is this, Minha?" it said in an oddly masculine voice.

Mirae was surprised to be able to understand it.

"Ah, your majesty," Minha said in a formal tone. "This is your granddaughter, Joriya's daughter, who has come to investigate a mystery we have encountered in Khabu. We are on the verge of war with Birum, but now there seems to be complications. Someone named Litt who claims to be from Khabu has invaded a nearby land. We are struggling to make sense of it all."

The tiger's brow furrowed in dismay.

"Litt? Birum? The clan has been concerned ever since that boy has come in here that something like this would happen. You should have taken stronger measures to control our son, Minha. Perhaps I retired too early. But Litt is another matter!"

"So Litt was here at one time?" Mirae asked hesitantly.

The tiger turned his attention fully to her.

"Litt was one of the first of us to enter the crypt. When Birum broke in, many of us had noticed his absence, but the crypt distracts us from the problems of the world with its dreamsleep, and we had no means anyway of discovering what may have happened. I can only surmise, knowing my son as I do.

"None of us saw him go. He just wasn't among us after Birum was thrown out of the crypt and the crypt was resealed. Birum was always skilled at black magic, especially traveling between the dimensions, and I suspect his resentment of Joriya fed his interest in it after the pearl chose his sister to rule instead of him. However, he knew the rules of the kingdom and how it was run. He still had more advantages than any in the known worlds as an immortal of the royal house of Khabu even if he wasn't king, yet that wasn't enough for him! I'm sure he had the skill to come in to abduct Litt, to smuggle him back out into the outside world. I fear that for any of us in the crypt returning to the outside world would bring a certain insanity to even the best of us. If that's what happened, it was Birum's primary goal in coming here that day.

"The magic would have been very strong for him to keep Litt from his beloved Blue Waterfall, where his home once stood thousands of years ago. It no longer was standing by the time I entered the crypt four hundred years ago, though. He would be very disappointed at our world now, if he has returned."

"There is a mansion there now," Mirae said softly, thinking back to her dinner with Birum and his men and the beauty of the waterfall. "I can understand why he was so drawn to the waterfall. I saw it myself yesterday when I visited Birum. It was astonishing."

"Excuse me," the tiger said, standing and looking at her more intently than before. "Did you say it was rebuilt and Birum is there? How strange! My son Birum didn't have a romantic bone in his body, and a love for the Blue Waterfalls requires a romantic soul."

"We have reason to believe that Birum is using Litt as a puppet in the destruction of the human land of Eokhmisseun across the inner sea," Minha said. "Messenger birds from the Forest of Bliss returned from there after centuries of service, afraid of some purge. Mirae's adopted brother sent a letter about it too."

"Yes, he said Litt had taken over and turned the inhabitants into bloodthirsty monsters," Mirae said.

The tiger was silent for a while.

"Birum always was interested in the worlds beyond the inner sea," the tiger continued after composing himself. "His fortress was near there so he could explore them better. When he broke into the crypt, the ancestors and I were able to glean enough of his memories to know that he had gone to both Earth where you had hidden Mirae and Eokhmisseun as well as many others. Perhaps since Khabu was beyond him, he found them interesting places he could plot to take over more easily.

"But his kidnapping of Litt is disturbing. His actions are more than monstrous if his black magic has turned one of our oldest ancestors into a murderer and a tyrant. This must be stopped at all costs, Mirae. As the heir to the throne, it is your duty to put an end to his madness, if it is in your power to do so."

"And what of Litt if I should find him? Can I really fight against Birum's black magic if it's so powerful?"

"Litt cannot come back here until he is purified," the tiger said. Minha nodded in agreement. "Birum's black magic and his renewed exposure both to Khabu's and human lands will make him too vulnerable to return here, even if he is willing. We should bring him back to the temple and palace to test his spirit and prepare him to rejoin us in another 500 years. If he is guilty of the serious crimes that you refer to, then he must then undergo execution."

"Your majesty!" Minha said, shocked. "Must it go that far? None on the list of kings has ever been shamed by execution, and we don't even know what happened to the helm and dagger of Memnoth in the first place."

"Was it Birum's doing again? When did they go missing? If it turns out to be the same time as his break in here, then he knew what punishment would await him in the future when he was discovered. In that case, he too shall undergo the execution and be beheaded additionally. Such an immortal shall not be tolerated, especially if he has used his magic to corrupt our ancestor Litt. Litt was a fine man worthy of the crown long ago. It pains me to think what Birum might have done to him."

11

As their audience with the ancestral king ended, Minha and Mirae rejoined Joriya in the corridor of the western precinct as the portal shut behind them.

"What have you learned?" Joriya asked.

"Litt was the man on the list, and both he and Birum need to be captured and brought to account for their crimes," Minha said gravely.

"Then I only have one choice now," Mirae said. "I need to go back to the mansion at the Blue Waterfall and confront Birum about all of this."

"What power will you use against him when you confront him?" Minha asked, genuinely worried. "He has great skill in the black arts, and I was concerned when I heard you were with him yesterday for that reason, but you have no power to counter his attacks. I don't think it's safe."

"But don't you think it's odd, Minha, that Birum would now be at the Blue Waterfall?" Mirae asked. "Even the ancestor told us that was Litt's favorite place, not Birum's."

"What do you mean?" Minha asked.

"When I put the mask on yesterday, I had a vision of a completely different plaza with a large white tiger there who was walking toward me and talking just like he was human. Just like the crypt now. When I took the mask off, I was still in a plaza and talking to a man, only the plaza had changed slightly and it was Birum who was speaking to me."

"Birum is a member of the royal family, after all," Joriya said suddenly. "Of course he would look like one of the ancestors in the mask."

"Not so fast," Minha said, her face so ashen and expression so livid that Mirae nearly jumped out of her skin. "The mask doesn't work that way. Not at all. It doesn't see the true nature of the immortals who live in the city. It was magically calibrated to only detect the ancestors in the crypt. If Mirae saw a tiger in place of Birum with its power, then it couldn't be Birum at all she was talking to."

"Then who was I talking to?" Mirae asked, confused. "Did I somehow see into the crypt and then find myself with Birum when I took it off?"

"Not at all! Don't you see?" Minha asked, putting her hands on Mirae's shoulders and nearly shaking her. "It wasn't Birum yesterday. It was Litt! You saw his true nature as one of the ancestors in the crypt. Didn't you say he took you to the Blue Waterfall? Birum lives in the fortress by the ferry at the inner sea when he stays in Khabu."

"But how could it be Litt?"

"What did this man who told you he was Birum look like?" Joriya asked, the truth slowly dawning on her. "I haven't seen Birum in years, and Minha hasn't seen him lately either."

"He was handsome. He had brown hair and blue eyes."

"It is Birum then," Minha said. "We can verify it by looking at the portraits in the hall in the northern precinct here. Litt's portrait should be among them. Come with me."

The women walked swiftly in silence as they retraced their steps back to the main hall on the crypt level and raced down the corridor to the northern precinct. The corridor opened onto a wide room lined with paintings of kings and queens. Minha led them to the left side of the hall where the earliest portraits were. It didn't take long to find Litt's.

"A-ha. As I figured," Minha said, pointing toward the painting of a beautiful blonde man wearing the recognizable dark blue silk tunic embroidered with the symbols of the royal house.

Mirae stepped toward it, studying it carefully.

"Are there portraits of Birum anywhere?" she asked. "This is not the man I met yesterday."

"In the center of the room are wooden boxes with more recent paintings," Joriya said, turning around and walking over to one of the marble tables. Pulling out a small box full of unframed paintings, she spread them out across the table and pointed to one. "These portraits are from my reign and show my immediate family. Here is Birum when he was younger."

"That's the man," Mirae said, her heart sinking.

"Then you should proceed with caution if you go to confront him," Minha said, heading back toward the corridor. "I should prepare the temple for war with Eokhmisseun now. If Litt and Birum are working together, it's only a matter of time before their crisis becomes our own."

When she had disappeared down the corridor, Joriya turned back to Mirae.

"Why do you want to confront him now directly when it's so dangerous? Tell me the truth."

Mirae looked at her sheepishly.

"I had hoped he wasn't the one responsible for all of this."

"You hoped he was actually Litt instead of Birum like he claimed? How can it be that my brother has seduced you in so short a time?"

Mirae turned back to the portrait of Litt and walked over to it.

"It seems I may have inadvertently formed a pact with him last evening when we dined together. He kissed me, too. What did that mean? He seemed so likeable, and the waterfall…".

Mirae remembered her dream and Minha's strange riddle on the parchment. *The key to unlock the secrets of the crypt has been hidden by the ancestors beneath the blue waterfalls of the north. Only mutiny can delay the time of times, only love can alter the destiny of the worlds.*

"He will need to be rehabilitated in the end, so perhaps it will fall to you if the mask's vision was the correct one and he is not Birum. Try not to lose hope. But what will you do if you are wrong when you confront him and it *is* Birum?"

"I'll think of something," Mirae said vaguely, aware that she didn't have a plan at all. "I'm a member of the royal family, after all. I am immortal, too, like Birum and Litt."

Joriya looked at her a moment, biting her lip.

"That's such a cavalier attitude to take going into such danger. You need to be careful, Mirae. You are the heir to the throne of Khabu, and you have a responsibility to that future."

"But Birum and Litt are part of the future of Khabu, too, aren't they?" Mirae asked hotly, a little startled by her own rising anger. "There's no way to save the kingdom without dealing with them and whatever crimes they may have committed. They still don't know I'm the heir to the throne, so the danger is minimal. Or do you suggest they would kill me with silver according to Khabu's execution protocol?"

"Being immortal doesn't make you invincible. You have a lot to learn about yourself now that you know the truth." Joriya sighed. "Yes, it would take them killing you with silver, and we don't have much of that in the kingdom beyond the execution implements that have gone missing decades ago. Still, there are worse things than death, and Birum is a magician of the darkest sort. Don't underestimate him."

"I know that what I'm doing is risky, but someone has to take a risk to make the situation right," Mirae said. "Perhaps the tiger mask can protect me with its power now that I understand somewhat how to use it. Is it true that we all will look like the ancestors in the end? Are we also part animal even now?"

Joriya nodded, smiling a little.

"Yes, we give up our human form in the crypt. I think the ancestors have forgotten what it's like to be human, it has been so long since they have taken that form. If you intend upon using the tiger mask as protection, you should talk further with Minha about its power and study more of your books. Do you really need to rush to confront Birum at this point? "

"I heard from my brother that Litt was in Eokhmisseun, which has been overcome and degraded by his magic, so the need to do something seems urgent. Unless you are willing to let that human land be lost entirely. Don't forget I have lived all of my life among humans, and my allegiance is not entirely to Khabu and the immortals now, even if I find the idea of being immortal useful at this point."

"Does it explain some things about your childhood?"

"Yes, somewhat."

Joriya looked back at Litt's portrait, sadness filling her eyes.

"Perhaps you are right in your foolhardiness," she said slowly. "I have been too complacent and inattentive to my kingdom and my brother to see the need to do more. You may be able to make things right. Go then, if you feel you must stop Birum."

Neither woman spoke for a long time but just looked around the room at the paintings of the ancestral kings and queens. Finally, Mirae wordlessly bowed to Joriya and ran down the corridor back to her quarters.

12

Back in her room, Mirae went to the dresser and tore open the drawer. The tiger mask sat there, staring out at her with its fierce scowl. Now instead of scaring her, it made her feel a bit stronger. Picking it up, she noted that it felt like any normal, wooden mask might feel, neither hot nor cold. She sighed in relief. Whatever triggered its magical response, she wasn't entirely sure, but it was dormant now.

Thinking back to her meeting with Birum when she put it on, she could only guess that wearing it activated a certain type of magic. Did it have any power beyond taking her to talk with the ancestors? Why did it take her to Birum if it had some ceremonial function connected with the crypt? She guessed the man had to be Litt then, just as Minha had suggested.

She giggled a little at the thought of all of them actually being tigers in human form, scarcely believing such a thing was possible. Maybe, just maybe, part of her wanted to challenge Birum now and get to the bottom of the mystery of Litt's abduction because she didn't really believe all of this nonsense about immortality and talking tigers! Was she really Joriya's daughter, switched at birth? What did being immortal mean to her anyway? Nothing felt any different after the revelation. She needed to know the truth, and she didn't completely trust Minha or Joriya.

Knowing it was the only way to be sure, Mirae turned the mask and placed it over her face, waiting.

In a flash, the scene changed. No longer in her austere room at the temple, Mirae found herself immediately standing in front of the Blue Waterfall, a thick wall of trees behind her, and the water crashing down alarmingly close to her right. This was the closest edge of the cliff to Birum's mansion, and she could see where the path led back through the trees toward it. Realizing this was the place Birum had indicated was a safe swimming hole beneath the waterfall, she thought he might be nearby. The mask would only take her to him, or at least that was what she had surmised. A rocky ledge leading up the cliff to her right had been weathered into steps, and she was aware of a shadowy shape lurking there. Blue eyes met hers, though the face was that of a tiger, not a man. As expected, the mask had brought her to him, whichever man he was, and showed her his tiger form.

Moving closer to the cliff, the tiger leapt into action, jumping down the rocky staircase to stand not far from her at the edge of the water.

"Who are you?" she asked him as he sat in front of her.

She studied his feline face and sleek body carefully to note any hints of his true identity.

"What do you mean? We met before. Don't you remember who I am now?" he asked.

"Yes, I know you said you were Birum, but I don't trust men who are tigers in the spirit world. This mask lets me see you differently than you are when I take it off."

"Which is it you don't believe?" he asked, amusement creeping into his voice. "That I'm a man or a tiger? This is the gift of Khabu's royal family, to have such a dual nature. The average citizen of Khabu, too, has such a gift, though they have a bird nature instead of the tiger. I'm sure Minha would have explained this to you."

"In the world where I am from, people are just people, with no animal nature. Well, at least not a physical animal nature. Their attitudes and behavior may be another matter."

"Are you afraid to encounter a man who is not merely a man then?"

"Now you're teasing me," she said, laughing a little. "Perhaps I should come closer to take a better look at you."

"Remember we are members of the royal family, not pets."

She took a few cautious steps forward and reached out to touch the fur on his neck. It was as soft as she imagined in the crypt talking with the former king, though she would never have dared to ask the old king to allow her to touch him. But did it give her any insight into Litt's whereabouts? She pulled back, standing again.

"Finished?"

"I should take this off now," she said, running her fingers down the side of the mask, her voice serious.

Birum didn't say anything more, so Mirae pulled the tiger mask off of her face with both hands. The scene changed only slightly this time. Birum was no longer a tiger but a man, the same man she had met the day before.

"So you wanted to know who I am," he said, his tone now as serious as hers. "Why is there any question?"

Mirae suddenly felt like it was too confrontational to mention her suspicions directly, so she took a different tack.

"Why did you move out here to the Blue Waterfall to live?" she asked. "I heard from Minha that you used to live in the fortress near the docks at the inner sea. The Blue Waterfall is beautiful, but somehow it doesn't seem to suit you. You don't seem like someone relaxed enough to enjoy such a natural setting."

"Ah, so you have had a talk with Minha about me and have continued your studies of Khabu's history, have you? That explains your confusion. Minha doesn't know everything about me. I try to keep the royal family guessing. They all are too boring anyway."

Mirae giggled nervously at his comment, and he smiled slightly.

"The Blue Waterfall has had a mystical significance in Khabu's history, and maybe I just like to be near the water. The inner sea is interesting for other reasons, because it is a portal rather than actual water, but there is something special about the raw power of falling water."

"So you crave power?" Mirae asked, trying not to burst out laughing.

Birum laughed as well at her suggestion.

"Why is it you came to see me today? You have learned that the mask brings you to me, so you came here for a reason, didn't you?"

"Minha told me that the temples priests and priestesses often intermarried with Khabu's royal family. So now it seems I could be a candidate. Why did you kiss me yesterday? Does it seem fortuitous in some way that the mask should keep bringing me to you even though that's not its ceremonial purpose? Perhaps it's playing matchmaker with us."

She kept her tone light, careful not to reveal her true identity as the heir to Khabu's throne. This was a much better tactic to get answers, though Mirae knew herself well enough to know she wasn't only asking out of curiosity.

He looked at her in astonishment before answering.

"Marry into the royal family? You mean you want to marry me?" He glanced back at the falls before giving her a sly look. "It's true I have not taken a concubine from the temple as is customary for the royal family, and now that you are an acolyte there, this is a possibility. I kissed you last night to seal our bargain. The wine I served you also was a sign of that pact."

"What?" Mirae asked, laughing again. "You didn't tell me anything about making a pact with you. What reason could you have to do that?"

"Maybe the same as yours. You came here today to ask about a royal marriage with me, didn't you? I merely saw an acolyte I liked in the temple for the first time in hundreds of years. I've been looking for someone for a very long time."

"Actually, I came here today because I was hoping you would tell me some of the forbidden stories of the kingdom. I can't get Minha to tell me certain things, and now that we are linked together by your mysterious ceremony, don't you have to do what I ask?"

Birum's expression turned to surprise.

"What story won't she tell you that you want to hear?"

"She mentioned something about you breaking into the ancestral crypt many years ago, which scandalized everyone. It sounded rather interesting, but she wouldn't tell me any details. Did you really break into the crypt? Or is that just family legend? I wanted to go in myself, but she wouldn't let me near it. I saw the corridor leading to it, though."

"Ah, so we are birds of a feather so to speak, you and I, Mirae," he said, very amused. "You are really a rebel at heart, as am I! Yes, I did break in, much to Joriya's dismay. I could tell you about it if you like."

Playing her part to the hilt, Mirae took a few steps forward and, grabbing Birum's arm, she leaned forward and lightly kissed his cheek in encouragement. He smiled, pleased at her response.

"Yes, tell me all about it," she said.

"I guess it's safe to, though you must not tell my sister or Minha all of the details. This is only for you."

"Okay, I promise."

"Well, first of all, the only people in Khabu who have the right to go into the family crypt are the high ranking priestesses of the temple and royal family members themselves when they retire from public life. The rest of the citizenry are prohibited. I took advantage of a gray area, you might say, since I am permitted to go in after I retire, though I had no intention of retiring when I entered.

"I had always been curious about the crypt," he continued, a faraway look coming into his eyes. "But it was only when Joriya was neglectful of the kingdom and no heir to the throne seemed to be forthcoming that I decided I needed to go to the ancestors to have a talk with them. I wanted their advice about how to handle my sister, for the good of the kingdom."

"Neglectful? How was the queen neglectful?"

"She never seemed curious about what was going on in the countryside of Khabu, so she had no idea that the magical forest where the citizens go after they retire was under attack from rapacious outsiders, for one thing. Reports were that she rarely even went to discuss kingdom business with the palace ministers but left them run the country while she sat around the palace garden. She had no dealings with the outer or inner worlds, no trade or treaties that would enrich Khabu and bring us more wealth and happiness. Instead, she cut us off from the rest of the known worlds. She also seemed reluctant to take any of the temple acolytes as a husband, so she had no hope for an heir. When she finally acquiesced, she gave birth to a sickly child whom she kept imprisoned from nearly birth in the dungeons of the temple. What mother does that? She seemed altogether incompetent."

"She put her child in the dungeon?" Mirae asked, wondering how Birum's story could be so different from Joriya's. According to the Queen and Minha, it was Birum's threats that forced her to keep the girl in prison so he could take the heir's place. Who was lying?

"I decided I needed the ancestors' advice, and traveling the known outer worlds, I found books on magic that gave me a way to force open the portal long enough for me to sneak in and get the information I needed. I didn't need any of the priestess' rituals or permission to enter.

"The spell worked, and although I didn't enter that far into the crypt, one of the ancestors came out to meet me and find out why I had breached their defenses. He wasn't angry, and I was a little afraid when I saw how they appeared in animal form there. It was the first time in my life I was ever confronted with the reality that we were essentially animals and would live as animals in the end. Never before had I met anyone in the royal family who had turned into beasts before their time, so this was difficult for me to grasp at first."

"And did the ancestors help you?" Mirae asked, mesmerized by his story.

"The ancestor who greeted me was a former king from the early days of the land, and he was both willing to speak but also somewhat confused by my questions and my anger. The ancestors know nothing about the kingdom once they leave it. They live in a world of dreams and never take human form again, so he had forgotten a lot. It alarmed me that he seemed so unhelpful. I felt pity on him, wondering if Minha was drugging them somehow to keep them out of Joriya's business."

Mirae was aghast at his suggestion.

"Would such a thing be possible? Could Minha do that to them?"

"No, perhaps not, but much to my chagrin, I believed she could at the time. Since I saw the ancestors had some strange power and felt angered by what I believed was the temple's abuse of them, I remembered that the books on magic I found also had other useful spells, and I went into action.

"Without thinking about the consequences, I decided it was the right thing to do, to take the ancestral king with me and help him escape from their bondage. I grabbed him and recited the spell to change him and free him from the crypt."

"Did he recognize the spell at all?"

"No, it was far beyond him since it was from the human world, and he had been in the ancestral crypt a very long time. The spell turned him into a small jade statue that I could fit in my pocket and escape with undetected. I don't know if any of the priestesses ever discovered one of the ancestors was missing. This is why I don't want you repeating any of this to Minha, understand? It is a high crime, what I have done."

"But Minha did discover you had gone in obviously. How did that happen?"

"The acolytes are very attentive to the crypt. It is the whole reason for the temple's existence. So they will get dreams and visions from the ancestors if anything goes wrong there. The acolytes were on to me as soon as I opened the portal and stepped in, though it took a while for them to assemble to apprehend me. As it was, I fled in time, before the temple guards could catch me in the act. Perhaps it was because of the ancestor I took with me that I was given some special grace of speed to escape them.

But I also escaped punishment. My sister was so embarrassed I could successfully slip through their security that she let it go."

Mirae thought about this a moment. Was that true? If Birum had threatened them into keeping Pareya in the temple dungeon, couldn't he have also threatened Joriya so she would not punish him for his transgression?

"My sister has a lot of secrets that she doesn't want known, and it would be a scandal to the public for the royal family to have such an incident be generally known. Joriya thought better of making an issue of it. It was not long after that that she took one of the acolytes as her concubine and had the child that now is so weak and useless they could never rule Khabu. However, she tried to stop me by providing an heir."

"What do you mean? Why would providing an heir make a difference?"

"The line of royal kings and queens would end if she didn't fulfill her duties and provide a child."

"Who would rule in such a situation then?"

"That was what I needed to ask the ancestors. Never in 10,000 years had Khabu faced such a situation."

"What was the answer the ancestors gave you about Joriya?" she asked.

"As I said, the ancestors all seemed to be very easily confused and were not given to handling the politics of the realm anymore, so all that the ancestor I abducted told me was that I should find my fortunes exploring the inner sea rather than topple the throne of Khabu outright by initiating a power struggle with Joriya. I had, of course, already ventured beyond the inner sea a little before he gave me that advice, but I became more adventurous in my travels."

"It's astonishing she tolerates you living so close to the capital out here. Does Joriya know that you leave the kingdom like that?"

"No, she never did even before I took the ancestor. I've been traveling the inner and outer worlds for centuries now, and in the past fifty years or more since I took the ancestor, I have gone even further and seen more wondrous things than Joriya could imagine. From those foreign ports, I could consolidate enough knowledge and power to challenge Joriya when the time was right, if need be. But as you have noted, she doesn't care what I do or where I go. She is as apathetic about that as she is about the kingdom itself."

"And what became of the ancestor after that?" Mirae asked.

"I lost the statue, much to my shame."

Mirae cried out in disbelief.

"But you said he was confused and unable to understand the real world after living in the crypt so long. Do you know what sort of danger he would be in all alone out here?"

Birum merely nodded, looking uncomfortable.

13

For reasons she couldn't name, Mirae felt he was lying about the whereabouts of the ancestor. They were at the Blue Waterfall, after all, the place Minha and Joriya had said was intimately connected with Litt. This couldn't be a coincidence.

"When did you move here to the Blue Waterfall? Surely if the ancestor told you to sail the seas, your fortress near the docks would have been more advantageous. Why come so far away if that was the plan?"

"I already old you," Birum said, his tone getting sharper, even angry.

"It seems like an odd reason given your goals. Which of the former kings did you abduct from the crypt?"

Birum spun toward her, furious.

"What does it matter now? He's gone," Birum said dismissively, looking so intently at the water at his feet that Mirae drew nearer to him instinctively.

"Did you find other lands to rule beyond the inner sea?"

Birum didn't answer. Instead his body stiffened, and for the first time, he didn't seem entirely human. He was clearly suspicious of her questions, so she went over to him and put her hand gently on his arm to reassure him.

Mirae noticed he trembled violently at her touch. When he turned to face her, she saw his eyes were turning bluer and bluer until the whites of his eyes had been swallowed up by them entirely, and their overall shape was becoming rounder. The edges of his mouth shifted to look more feline, and his skin was growing the soft white covering of hair she had touched earlier when he was in his tiger form. His hair turned from brown to white blonde and grew in length until it looked like a wild mane around his face.

Suddenly Mirae felt uncertain. Did the still-living royal family change into tigers outside of the crypt, she wondered? What did that mean? She couldn't remember what Minha had said to her about that.

Looking down at his fingers, she saw they had curled into clawed paws of enormous size. Though he still stood on two legs like a human and still had the overall shape of his human form, he was changing. Nervously, she watched him slowly transform. The forest felt a little colder as the wind picked up and the shadows deepened. For a moment, there was only silence between them as they listened to the rushing of the waterfall, which was also turning a deeper blue. Something was wrong. Unsettled, she let go of Birum and took a few steps back.

Unable to tear her eyes from him, feeling a little more than hypnotized by the sound of the rushing water, Mirae lost all sense of caution. Suddenly, she couldn't hold back the words anymore.

"Aren't you really the ancestor? What was his name? Litt? Isn't that who I am truly meant to marry in the royal family, after all?"

As soon as the words left her lips, the mask in her hand turned so cold it seemed as if ice were crawling up her arm, and she screamed in terror, dropping it. Crouching to find it in the brush, she was horrified to find herself face to face with the weretiger again, only this time, Birum had become even larger and more menacing than he had looked in his fully tiger form when she wore the mask. She didn't dare touch the mask again. She slumped into the grass in defeat, her whole body alert to the primal danger of the animal-man who stood before her, ready to attack.

"So you know about Litt?" the creature before her said, his voice sounding deeper and hollower than when he was entirely human. "Why didn't you say so earlier?"

"You were always careful in telling your story not to say his name, weren't you?" Mirae asked accusingly, her voice soft but lethal as she slowly stood up. "Why is that? Are you really Birum? Why do you look like Birum if you aren't?"

Standing slowly, the creature stopped in a more humanoid pose, exuding a fantastic power. Time seemed to move so slowly, she wasn't sure if it hadn't stopped at all. The waterfall behind him convulsed as the air around them shifted. It was like the portal to the crypt again. What was this place? The Blue Waterfall had mystical power, Birum had said only moments ago, but he hadn't explained what kind of power.

"How do you know his name, Mirae? No one in Khabu knew I took him from the crypt."

"The ancestors told me Litt was missing. I too went into the crypt, though I told you I hadn't. Litt particularly loved this waterfall. His home was here 8,000 years ago."

He lunged at her, but she dodged him, nearly falling into the water. They both stopped again, hunter and prey, their eyes locked in battle. The forest behind them seemed to be waiting.

"Stop!"

A woman's voice broke the silence. Someone was coming behind them. Mirae tore her eyes away from the weretiger long enough to look into the dim forest. Minha and four of her acolytes emerged along the path beneath the trees, all of them wearing versions of her own tiger mask lost on the ground. So Minha had traced them here using their magic?

Each woman carried a small lantern emitting a weak light, throwing shadows on the rocks to the right of the now glistening stream of water running down its edge. Night had fully taken hold of the Blue Waterfall, and a full moon rose above them, though Mirae hadn't noticed either before now.

"I didn't expect you to follow me here," Mirae said, not recognizing her own voice. "Why did you come here? I told you I could handle it."

Minha's eyes rested on Birum a moment. Filling with pain, her expression growing more alarmed, she took a step in front of the group.

"You are not my son, are you?" she asked, as if already knowing the answer. "He has done this to you, hasn't he, ancient father? I am so sorry. I had no idea what he had done until we entered the crypt tonight."

The weretiger didn't answer. Minha looked back at him, wondering how Minha could be so sure which man was standing before them.

Minha came closer to her so she could catch her whisper.

"None of the citizens of Khabu typically turn into their animal form before death without using abnormal magic, yet this man shifts easily to only a half form none of those living in or out of the crypt has taken on, as would be expected if he were an ancestor from the crypt. He has far more control over his presentation of our human and animal features than the average citizen of Khabu, a feature of his great age and proof of his tutelage under Birum with his forbidden magic. I had wondered about this when you said the mask showed you Birum in tiger form. This is Litt standing before us now. Am I not correct?" Minha asked, turning to him.

As Minha said the name, the tiger-man's face twisted into an expression of such anguish that Mirae unthinkingly rushed forward to comfort him. As she placed her hands on his arms, his body shuddered. The spell had been broken at the sound of his true name, as if he had forgotten it. Shockingly, his facial features shifted, and though they kept a feline cast, Mirae could see it was the man in the portrait that now stood before her, not Birum. So it was Litt who had lured her here. It was Litt that she was now bound to. Relief and despair washed over Mirae at the same time.

"Why am I here?" he murmured, looking around the shadowy grove.

"What do you remember?" Minha asked, concerned.

"I only remember the crypt and a man touching me who said strange, dreadful words that filled me with pain and made me sleep."

"The spell," Minha said under her breath. "Why would he need to go so far as to wipe your memory for fifty years?"

"He was impersonating Birum," one of her young acolytes said suddenly. "Perhaps Birum needed a double so we wouldn't know he was missing. But where is he now?"

Litt couldn't answer, but Mirae remembered Sohyeon's letter.

"Litt is supposed to be in Eokhmisseun leading the purge of their country," she said quickly. "He has been terrorizing the inhabitants there in Litt's name for a very long time, more than fifty years."

"No one in the modern world, not even in Khabu, would have recognized the name, even had they been familiar with the list of kings and queens," Minha said, nodding. "He wanted some anonymity when he took over the other country, and perhaps Litt gave him some royal authority when he enthralling him and sucked him dry of his memories. This is a high crime that Birum cannot escape execution for. Harming any of the ancestors from the crypt alone would be unforgiveable. He should never be allowed to set foot in Khabu alive!"

"What do you remember of Birum since you came here?" Mirae asked Litt.

"Nothing. I came from the crypt back to my home and lived as I was expected to, hunting and enjoying the forest with my attendants," Litt said, his eyes still misty with confusion.

"So you never saw Birum again?" Minha asked sharply. "Not since the abduction?"

"No."

"Then you are not his collaborator and your innocence in this will be accepted by the temple leadership."

Before Minha could finish her sentence, Litt cried out in pain. Mirae was so startled that she jumped away from him, afraid to touch him as he flashed his fangs at her. The six women could only watch his suffering in terror. Panting, he struggled to remain standing, sometimes bending over on all fours. Moving ever closer to the edge of the water, he waded into the pool beneath the fall's edge.

Whimpering as the water touched his body, Litt trembled as the remaining color drained out of him into the pool, like ink flowing into clear water. Birum's black magic was losing its hold on him with the strange manifestation, the substance rippling through the pool of water until the water was a solid mass of onyx sludge. Inexplicably, even the water falling down the cliff across the span of the Blue Waterfall had started to run an unwholesome black.

Something unsettling tugged at Mirae's mind. A memory? The dream! As Litt struggled to stand in the water, the black waves of the spell now staining his skin and hair instead of remaining hidden within him, Mirae knew she had to make a choice. None of the other women moved but just silently watched the ancestor, afraid of the black water.

Anger rising in her, Mirae quickly closed the distance between her and Litt, stepping into the black water, unconcerned about the consequences. Her chiton grew heavy as the black water creeped up her body like snakes, and her hair and bare arms were covered with grimy streaks. As she splashed through the water to reach Litt and threw her arms around his waist, they nearly fell into the water together. The turbid water started to boil around them, and Mirae watched it bubble in alarm though she resolved she wouldn't let go of Litt no matter what it meant.

"It isn't over, Mirae," he said only loud enough for her to hear." You can't free me from Birum this way. Save yourself!"

"No, I won't leave you!" Mirae screamed.

The water around them began rising, as if to drown them if they would not cooperate by sinking under the pool's surface.

Behind them on the shore, Minha and the others yelled a warning. Something was coming out of the water in front of them in the shadow of the waterfall. Mirae looked up, straining to see in the darkness what was rising there.

At first, all she could see was the mist at the bottom of the falls catching the moonlight like diamonds. Then suddenly even the mist was blocked out by a black form that was growing larger and larger. Whatever it was, it spanned the whole width of the falls, and once it rose high enough above them, Mirae could see it more clearly in the moonlight.

Clinging to Litt in terror as he fell deeper into a disquieting trance, Mirae took in the creature looming over them in disbelief. The shadow stretching from one end of the waterfall to the other was the creature's wingspan, and above the wings rose a horned head with fiery eyes and a sharp beak. It had iridescent scales rather than feathers, like a large, leathery bird, perhaps more like the dinosaurs back on Earth or maybe a dragon. When its wiry body emerged completely from the water, black droplets dripped in a curtain from its wings around them as it hovered over the pool searching for them. Its taloned claws flexed in anticipation of finding its prey.

Mirae was certain it was looking for them. The spell had transformed itself into a living, magical creature who existed to serve Birum. There was no easy way of escape for Litt, and she wasn't going to give him up without a fight.

Behind them on the shore, the acolytes were consulting with Minha in panicked voices, trying to come up with a plan to stop the dragon before it attacked them. She didn't know what kind of weapons the temple acolytes might have, but Mirae knew looking at the bird as its gaze found them that they were doomed.

Swooping down with a high-pitched shriek, the dragon's claws closed in on them and lifted them out of the water together. Since the beast was careful not to nip their skin, the dragon's hold was not painful, though Mirae knew their destination could not be pleasant. Surely, they would be face to face with Birum himself soon. Their enemy would be very aware that Litt had been released from his spell somehow and that an interloper had interfered with his plans for the ancestor. Mirae herself would be in danger, especially if he knew she was Joriya's daughter. Yet she saw no way to fight against her fate.

Litt was completely unconscious now, and she clung tightly to him, barely aware of the screams of the priestesses on the shore now far below them. At that dizzying height, they quickly entered the misty clouds close to the stars, and the sound of the rushing waters below grew ever fainter. She felt her own eyes closing, unable to fight the dragon's magic.

14

"They're gone," the second ranking temple acolyte said, her voice nearly hoarse from screaming. "There's nothing we can do now, Minha. Do you have any idea where that thing might be taking them? We have to get Mirae and the ancestor back!"

Minha thought for a moment, aware that Mirae's abduction would also be very dangerous for Khabu though no one knew her true identity. There was only one place the dragon could be going. Eokhmisseun.

"It's going to a human land across the inner sea to Birum's true lair," Minha said at last, ripping the tiger mask from her face and pulling out a satin sack from her belt to drop it in. She held it out to the rest of her entourage to do the same. They immediately complied. "Take off the masks for now. We can't risk its magic taking us again to Litt's destination when he arrives. It would be too risky yet to use that shortcut, and I need to take care of a few things first and check something in the temple library before I'm ready to confront Birum in person. We need to plan carefully."

"He has gotten so powerful, hasn't he?" her assistant acolyte said. "How could a broken spell turn into a living thing like that and stop their escape? I have never heard of such a thing."

"And this land it is taking them to," another acolyte said, "do we know where it is specifically or anything about it? Is it somewhere our people have ever explored before?"

Minha looked at her followers grimly.

"I know which land it is, though only because Mirae's brother sent us a tip with that letter through the pigeon messengers earlier. Otherwise, no one in Khabu has been there for years, though it once was a tributary land for Khabu. They would send a delegation of leaders here once a generation, no more. For now, let's get back to the temple and make our preparations."

As they turned to go, Minha's foot bumped against something on the ground. She looked down at the grass and saw Mirae's tiger mask. Crouching swiftly, she picked it up and put it thoughtfully in the satin bag before pulling the string and following her acolytes back to the waiting carriage.

When the women arrived back at the temple a few days later, Minha went straight to the main ritual hall, alone, handing the bag of tiger masks off to her assistant. As she reached the dais, she pulled off her cloak and stood near the pearl, holding her hands out a few inches over its surface, as if warming her hands by a fire. Taking a few deep breaths, she felt the tension drain out of her. Images of the ancestor, Litt, floated into her mind, and she felt an aching sense of loss. For the first time, she felt reassured that he was also with Mirae, whatever terrible fate awaited them both.

Finally, her mind focused on the pigeons, and after a few moments of picturing them the way they were not long before, swarming through the hall in the warm sunlight, she was sure the pearl sent her message. Returning to her seat nearby, she picked up a small writing desk standing on its end next to it and started to write. They had no other choice now but to take desperate measures. Chagrined, she knew she would have to rely on the repulsive ghost slave who served as her ferryman.

Pontol, she wrote in the common dialect of the inner sea, *I need your services at the temple. Come right away. It is an urgent matter. I will make it worth your while as always. Minha of Khabu.*

Setting aside the quill, she folded and rolled the parchment, then waited. Before long, the small, graceful figure of one of the pigeons flew into the room from the main corridor of the temple. Mapin. Minha recognized her as one of the most intelligent birds they had among the messengers, and though Mapin had spent many years in Eokhmisseun, Minha had become reacquainted with her when the birds fled the doomed land.

She perched on Minha's hand and allowed her to place the note in her collar. The bird and woman regarded one another a moment before Minha stood and held the bird up toward the opening in the ceiling high above them.

"Make haste to Pontol. Our lives depend on this."

Mapin flew up to the hole and disappeared into the night sky.

Her first task done, Minha walked through the now silent temple to the upper levels. At this time of night, the acolytes who weren't working directly on her orders after returning from the Blue Waterfall were all sleeping. A light, cool night breeze wafted through the cold marble corridors, pleasant, but a stinging reminder of their loss that evening. The torches ensconced in the walls flickered at intervals as the air was disturbed by her passing. Tonight, the temple felt more like a tomb. Shuddering, Minha rubbed her bare arms, trying to keep warm and wishing she hadn't discarded her cloak so soon.

Finally, she reached the door she sought. Knocking lightly, she pulled out the skeleton key and opened it without waiting for a response. As she entered and let her eyes adjust to the darkness a moment, a candle burst to light in the next room of the suite.

"What brings you here so late?" Joriya asked, her long hair falling around her face, a blanket tossed around her shoulders casually as she walked out of her bedroom.

Minha regarded her with satisfaction, smiling a little. She looked much younger in such a casual pose, even much more like her daughter Mirae. That would make tonight's task much easier.

"I need you to get dressed and come with me."

"At this hour?" Joriya asked, looking toward the corridor apprehensively. "Has something happened?"

Minha looked down at the floor a moment.

"Oh, no. It isn't Mirae, is it? I knew she shouldn't go to confront Birum. What has happened?"

"It wasn't Birum. As I suspected, we discovered the man living at the Blue Waterfall was actually Litt. Birum has held him spellbound by his black magic all of these years, fooling us into thinking Birum was still here."

"So where is Birum?"

"In Eokhmisseun, one of the human lands across the inner sea. You may not remember it that well since their delegation hasn't been here in a long time and only came rarely. I seem to recall it had some noble leaders, but apparently they all may be dead now that Birum has taken over. We need to deal with this situation, Joriya."

"And Mirae?"

"Gone. When Birum's spell over Litt was broken, a monster appeared and took them away. I assume they will be held captive in Eokhmisseun, though I will need to confirm that is where they ended up. In the meantime, I have a problem. Come with me. I will not abide by Birum's demand for your house arrest any more to protect our secret. Let me find something suitable for you to wear. Your royal attire will never do for the task I have in mind."

Joriya watched Minha in amazement as she went into her bedroom and opened her closet to find something suitable. Tossing out some of the clothes, she finally emerged with the items she sought hanging over her arm.

"It isn't quite what I had in mind, but it's the best we can do until you get there."

"What are these?" Joriya asked, looking at the clothing in surprise as she dropped the blanket and put down the candle to take them. The clothes were plain and not very feminine. Putting on the long, flowing purple skirt, she quickly pulled the light blue blouse over her head. Minha fastened the gathered sleeves at the wrists and tied the drawstring at Joriya's neck, then went back to the closet to take out a long, dark blue sleeveless vest that laced up the front. When Joriya was completely ready, she waited while Minha looked her over.

"Leave your hair loose for now," she said, motioning for Joriya to follow her.

"Where are we going?" Joriya asked as they started to walk down the corridor together.

"To the docks."

"At this hour?"

"There's someone I want you to meet there."

15

By the time they got to the docks, Pontol still hadn't arrived. Irritated, Minha found a place along the rocky shore where the women could sit while they waited for him.

"Are you planning on sending me away somewhere?" Joriya asked, finally unable to take the uncertainty any longer. They had walked all the way here from the temple in silence, and she felt it was time Minha gave her some answers.

"I'm sending you to Sohyeon," Minha said firmly.

"Sohyeon?"

"Mirae's brother. I met him once when Pontol first was sent to get Mirae, and he wrote her from Eokhmisseun just yesterday about the troubles there, mentioning Litt. He will have a better idea of what may be happening."

"Was he in Eokhmisseun when he wrote her? Is that where I'm going then?"

"No, I think we shouldn't go to Eokhmisseun just yet. That's Birum's base of power now. It's too dangerous without good intelligence and a plan. I need to gather some information before I dare make a move against him on his own turf. That's where you come into things."

Joriya looked at her, eyebrows raised.

"I'm on an intelligence gathering mission?"

"I'm sending you to Earth, to the Chois, to be precise," Minha said, agreeing. "I know that as queen you ruled over a peaceful land and have never been forced to do anything dangerous. Even so close to your retirement, we have to act. Even if it means you have to walk into the snake's den, then so be it, Joriya. Just accept that now we have no guarantee of peace or safety. You will have to be very careful and devious. You must convince the girl's human parents you are Mirae, though Sohyeon understands our world enough that you can tell him your true identity and what became of his sister. He will understand and perhaps know what to do. In the meantime, I will have to deal with that idiot!" Minha suddenly spat.

"Who?" Joriya asked.

"Pontol! There he is now. You'll see what I mean. Just say very little to him, and send any message you need to get back to me through him."

The small ship glided through the night sky to the ethereal waters lapping the dock where they waited. After he tied it to the post along the edge of the dock to anchor it, Pontol jumped over the side of the boat onto the rocks to meet them. Joriya studied him a moment and recoiled in horror, unable to understand the odd, animalistic deformity that he seemed to have. Minha grabbed her hand and dragged her over to meet her new keeper. Joriya quickly recovered her composure and smiled weakly at the slave.

"Pontol," Minha said, feigning friendliness, "I need you to take Mirae back to Sohyeon tonight. She has some important information that he needs. Am I right in guessing he is there and is no longer in Eokhmisseun?"

Pontol nodded wildly.

"Indeed, ma'am, he fled Eokhmisseun with the lady of the Elyeon estate. The demon was even at my doorstep looking for them. It was all I could do to fend him off and get them back to safety. He will be glad to see his sister. Go on into the boat and have a seat, miss."

Pontol's languid voice seemed friendly enough to Joriya, who quickly did as he requested. He turned to follow her, but Minha put her hand on his arm to stop him.

"You said a demon was looking for them," she began. "Would you mean this leader named Litt that Sohyeon referred to in his letter? What did he look like?"

"Yes, the demon is known by that name around Eokhmisseun, my lady. No one has ever really seen him up close, though no one ever forgets an encounter. Evil exudes from him, so no one gets close to him willingly, and those that have are rumored not to live to talk. His magic is what done this to me. I was human like you before his interference, but now all of us look like this and have a horrible taste for…well, it's better I don't say."

"In that case, before you go, let me ask you for a favor," Minha said, her voice smooth and conspiratorial. "Deliver Mirae back to Sohyeon for now, then return to Eokhmisseun and do a little spying for me. See if you can find anyone who has ever seen this Litt and get a detailed description of him and any conversations or magic or whatever that he has been seen doing and bring them immediately to me at the temple. Can you do that?"

"I can ask some people I know who have served in the palace if you like."

"Good. I also need you to look for someone for me who may be in Eokhmisseun now. We believe a woman may have been kidnapped there along with her boyfriend. The boyfriend is a tall, blonde man, and his girlfriend resembles Mirae. Would that be possible to find out?"

Pontol looked back at Joriya and studied her face a moment.

"I can have a look around. I have no restrictions that those who have not been turned live under, and Litt can't really do anything to me since I am under your protection. If I find them, what should I do? Did you want me to talk to them, or rescue them?"

"Nothing. Just come back to me and tell me where you saw them and try to keep an eye on them in case they are moved."

Pontol started talking excitedly about his new assignment, but suddenly Minha was unable to follow the conversation. The ancestor's transformation at the Blue Waterfall now came unbidden to Minha's mind's eye as she watched Pontol's animated face and mannerisms. Joriya also looked dazedly at the ferryman but said nothing.

No wonder she had always found Pontol so repulsive, Minha thought fleetingly. The turning? He was a normal human once before this evil magic had been done? That could only mean Birum's black magic had the power to create and destroy at a much deeper level than Minha had surmised. The evil cast of Pontol's features jolted her for the first time into noticing the resemblance the ghost slaves had to deformed versions of the ancestors. Pontol's feline features weren't normal, however, and so they were not immediately apparent to any observer, but now it seemed clear, once Birum was identified as the source of the twisted, degraded magic that created them. Just what had he intended by using such magic?

Minha thought a moment about what she had said earlier to Mirae about how the immortals didn't turn into their animal forms before retirement into the crypt or the magic forest. Was Birum experimenting with shapeshifting before he returned to the crypt? Was that dangerous? What did it mean that he was transforming humans into twisted caricatures of the ancestral animals?

Pontol jumped into the boat, untied it from the dock and unfastened the wheel, not waiting for any further instructions from Minha. As the boat turned back toward the moon for the journey to the Chois' house, Joriya cast a quick glance in her direction with a soft smile, reassuring her. Minha smiled back, feeling a little of the tension drain out of her. The boat glided along the shafts of moonlight toward the moon until the ferryman and his charge were too small to see on deck anymore. Sighing, Minha turned back toward the path leading to the cliff and cave entrance to the temple.

Taking a few steps, she paused, noticing a well-worn path that veered up the side of the cliff to the forest. Birum's fortress was along that path. Too angry at her wayward son to leave a search until morning, Minha took the path, knowing that the fortress was the likeliest place in Khabu where she might find the secret to whatever black magic Birum had used to create the ghost slaves. Minha decided then she would find out what he had done, even if she had to force the temple guards to rip the doors off of the fortress to let her in.

Still, she paused, wondering if going there and making demands would tip him off more than he already was that they knew about him. Perhaps Litt's release from the spell wasn't specific enough for Birum to know that the leadership of Khabu knew about his tricks. In turmoil, she realized she was too tired to think clearly and determine the best action to take. Retracing her steps, she resolved to return to the temple for now to get some sleep.

3 THE HIDDEN CLAN

1

"Who's there?"

Sohyeon awoke with a start, sitting up in bed and looking toward the open window. The chiffon curtains floated lightly in the night breeze, and the streetlights made up for the lack of stars and weak light of the waning moon. Surely, Pontol wouldn't come again tonight. There couldn't be news so soon from Eokhmisseun. So what had awakened him?

Sitting on the edge of his bed, he waited for his eyes to adjust to the light. Glancing toward the place on the floor where Tamnyn had set up a sleeping bag until they could figure out how to explain her presence to his parents, Sohyeon saw she hadn't stirred. Her wounds were healing nicely since their arrival back on earth a week before, which relieved him, but she wasn't the source of whatever sound had awakened him.

Walking over to the windowsill, he felt chilled in the late spring air. It had been colder than usual last night, but he had left the window open out of habit. Putting his hands on the windowsill, his fingers traced lightly over a footprint on the wood. Somewhere in the back of his mind, he remembered that they had wiped down the windowsill since their last night journey. So whose footprint was this?

Silently, stealthily, Sohyeon walked across the room back to his bed and snapped on the night stand light. Squinting in the bright light, he looked frantically around the room, his eyes finally resting on the figure of a woman standing in the shadows near the window where she wouldn't have been noticeable in the dark. She looked back at him, her eyes full of fear. But Sohyeon smiled.

"Mirae? What are you doing here? Did Pontol drop you off at the wrong window again?" Sohyeon asked in relief. "Did you get my message in Khabu about the fall of Eokhmisseun?"

He walked over to Mirae and started to embrace her, but she stepped away from him, her body stiff, her eyes wide. They stared at one another a moment before Sohyeon pulled his hands away, chagrined.

"I'm sorry. It's kind of dark in here, and you look so much like my sister, but you aren't Mirae, are you? What are you doing here? Is this some kind of joke of Pontol's?"

The woman smiled slightly and nodded.

"So you are Sohyeon? I am not your sister, though I know there is a resemblance between us. Now isn't the time to get into that, however. The situation is dire. Minha sent me to you because I look so much like Mirae. We need your help."

"Then this isn't about Eokhmisseun after all?"

"It is about Eokhmisseun, and Khabu, and your sister," the woman said, looking at him sadly. "I don't know where to begin. I have never left Khabu in all of my days, not in more than 400 years."

"That's right, all who live in Khabu are immortal. Most of them never leave their land for the inner or outer worlds," Tamnyn said, suddenly joining the conversation.

Sohyeon hadn't noticed Tamnyn was awake, but she sat on the sleeping bag, looking intently at the woman.

Wearing one of Mirae's pajama sets, Tamnyn looked like any of an assortment of Mirae's friends from school or work. Her long red hair was tied back at the nape of her neck.

"If the priestess sent you, then who are you?" Tamnyn asked, her voice gruff. "Why would you just happen to look like Sohyeon's sister, and why would that make Minha send you here?"

"Tamnyn, don't," Sohyeon started to say, but the woman nodded.

"It's alright. These are the questions I anticipated. I only hope I can answer them satisfactorily. I am Joriya, and Mirae and I are related by blood. Mirae has gotten into some trouble in Khabu, so Minha thought it best that I come to enlist your help, Sohyeon, since we believe she may have been abducted to Eokhmisseun. This girl is right. In Khabu we are not known for our travel through the worlds, and we know next to nothing about Eokhmisseun. Since you have been there, you would know how to get her back and make the situation right."

"Joriya?" Tamnyn asked, her tone sharp but low. "Do you mean you are Queen Joriya of Khabu? How would Sohyeon's sister from Earth possibly be related to anyone in Khabu, let alone be a member of the ruling royal family there?"

Joriya looked at Tamnyn in amazement.

"How would you know who I am?" Joriya asked, irritation creeping into her voice. "The people of Earth wouldn't have any idea of Khabu's existence let alone the name of its queen!"

"Tamnyn isn't from earth," Sohyeon said quickly, stepping between the women. "She's the daughter of one of the illustrious houses of Eokhmisseun. Both she and her father Cargal were on its ruling council until the purge by the demonic creature that took power there a few decades ago. We fled the purge and have no word on the situation. Cargal is possibly dead, as is the rest of the council. Now only evil reigns in Eokhmisseun."

"The demonic creature that rules there is likely to be my brother Birum," Joriya said softly. "We only just figured it out with Mirae's help."

"The creature's name is Litt," Tamnyn said shortly, standing on the sleeping bag, her hands on her hips. "Now explain to us who Mirae is to you."

"Mirae is my daughter whom I hid here on Earth because of my brother's threats. It's coming to the time of my retirement to the crypt, so she had to return to Khabu to take her place -."

"As Khabu's queen?" Tamnyn asked, incredulous.

"I would never have guessed Mirae wasn't my sister," Sohyeon said, whistling softly at the news. "How did she get abducted to Eokhmisseun?"

"We believe that my brother released one of our ancestors, an ancient king named Litt, from the crypt, and had him masquerade as my brother in Khabu while my brother was in fact subduing Eokhmisseun. Mirae discovered Litt's true identity, but she couldn't release him from Birum's magic. She fell under the same curse and was taken back to Birum by a magical creature. Or that is what Minha surmises anyway."

"Then we have to go back in," Tamnyn said with finality. "I've told you as much, Sohyeon. Now you can't keep saying we have to wait or shouldn't go back. While we're there looking for your sister, we can see if my father is still alive."

As Tamnyn started rummaging around in her box of things beside her sleeping bag, Sohyeon shook his head.

"You know that would be suicide. We barely escaped Eokhmisseun the last time, and Litt nearly killed you. Your wounds haven't even healed yet."

"But we have the dagger and helm of Memnoth." Tamnyn lifted the dagger and helmet up out of the box.

Joriya looked at the artefacts in horror.

"Where did you get those?" she asked breathlessly. "Who are you again?"

"They have been in my family since my grandfather's generation. It is said they were forged in Khabu, but otherwise all I know is that they have great power when wielded together."

"Your grandfather's generation?" Joriya said to herself thoughtfully. "In human terms, how long ago would that have been? Fifty years? Sixty?"

"Wait a minute," Sohyeon said. "Pontol said the dagger was originally his family heirloom, so it was probably longer than that."

"It can't be. Somehow you're family has the missing executioner's dagger and helm from the Ministry of Punishment at the palace in Khabu. These would never be given as gifts to anyone, especially outside of the kingdom. Memnoth was a minister of Khabu in ancient times who was thought to be the first executioner to use them in dealing with our criminals. The dagger particularly has been forged to deal with wayward immortals."

"Because it's silver?" Tamnyn asked, looking at the dagger more carefully as she set the helmet back down into the box.

"We can only be killed using silver through the heart," Joriya said, not taking her eyes off the dagger.

"Could Pontol's family have stolen it from Khabu? You said it was missing. When did this happen?" Sohyeon asked.

"They went missing maybe around that time. I had thought perhaps they were lost more recently, but Birum was probably the culprit, and they likely fell into Pontol's hands or the hands of this woman's family after that. It is a good omen that they have turned up now."

"Why is it a good omen?" Tamnyn asked, replacing the dagger in the box and sitting back down on the sleeping bag.

"Because we'll need to execute Birum at least, perhaps even Litt, too, though we are hoping it will not come to that. We have no other implements to use for the task in all of Khabu."

"You have no silver in Khabu?" Sohyeon asked in amazement.

"Silver is carefully controlled since it is the only way to kill us," Joriya said.

"Which means that as it stands, neither Khabu nor Eokhmisseun have any way of killing Birum then," Sohyeon said. "That's outrageous."

"What are we going to do?" Tamnyn asked. "We have to go back to Eokhmisseun. If you want to see your sister again, if I want to see my father again, there's no other way."

"What did Minha suggest we do?" Sohyeon asked Joriya.

"She plans on using Pontol as a spy in Eokhmisseun."

"That's actually a good idea," Sohyeon said, nodding. Suddenly, he turned his attention to Joriya and looked her up and down. "No matter what we need to do about this situation, for now we can only wait here and come up with a plan until Pontol gets us the information we need. You look enough like Mirae, even in those wild clothes, to pass for her, Joriya, but I don't know what you'll do about her job. Tamnyn, we need to talk to my younger sister and come up with a way for you to pass as one of Mirae's friends from out of town. Sukjin is only sixteen, but I think we can trust her to help us, and I can't hide you in my room any longer. For now, we need to act like everything is normal and that you are both from Earth. Go back to sleep, and when mom and dad leave in the morning, I'll talk to Sukjin."

2

When morning came, Sohyeon was careful to keep the door to his room shut so no one would notice anything unusual going on. He had been doing it all week since he had come back with Tamnyn, and it had worked so far. Since he was graduating from high school in another month, his mother had already told him he would be responsible for cleaning his room and washing his own clothes, as she had set the rules down for Mirae at her graduation, too. Adulthood was looking to be very convenient right now. Dressing and washing up in the bathroom after breakfast, he waited for his parents to leave for church since it was Sunday. He, Mirae and Sukjin had been going to a later service, so they had some time alone in the house to get organized.

"Come on out," he said, pulling his bedroom door open once they had gone. "I'll get Sukjin downstairs for a 'family meeting.' Try not to scare her with too many details about Khabu or Eokhmisseun or any of this story about Mirae not really being our sister and just let me do the talking. I'll get you some breakfast when I come down with her."

Joriya and Tamnyn nodded, and they went downstairs as he approached Sukjin's door.

Her door opened just as he was about to knock. She looked at him skeptically for a moment.

"Who were you talking to just now? And don't deny it, or I'll tell mom you've got someone hiding in your bedroom."

Sohyeon smiled at her tightly.

"I knew you were a smart one, Sukjin, that's why I had it in mind all along to let you in on my little secret," he said, keeping his voice light and conspiratorial. "Mirae and I have a special project we've been working on that we need your help with."

"Mirae didn't come home again last night," Sukjin said, biting her lip.

"She's downstairs now," he said, hoping she wouldn't notice that Mirae had been replaced by Joriya. "You can ask her about the details later. Right now I need you to help her friend Tammy. Mirae has been trying to help her through some personal troubles and said she could stay here until things get sorted out, but we don't really want to upset mom with all of Tammy's problems. What do you think?"

"They're downstairs now?"

"Yeah, I told them to get some breakfast. Would you be okay with sharing your room with Tammy for a while? You won't feel too crowded, will you?"

"I get it," she said, walking past him toward the stairs. "I don't care. The more the merrier."

The two of them ran down the stairs to the kitchen where Joriya and Tamnyn were waiting for them at the table.

"You could have at least gotten breakfast started," Sohyeon said in mild irritation, knowing that neither woman had ever have made breakfast with their own hands in their lives. "Never mind. I'll be your slave for today. You'll owe me a big favor later, so I won't complain."

He took out a box of cereal and some bowls, poured them each some and put milk on it. Sukjin got her favorite toaster waffles out of the freezer and set up the toaster, so she had her back to them for a few minutes. Sohyeon silently mimed for the women how to eat cereal until Sukjin came back to the table with her toasted waffles and a carton of orange juice.

"I'll get the glasses," Sohyeon said, pouring some cereal for himself.

Sukjin sat down across from Joriya and looked at her a moment.

"Did you go to a Renaissance festival with your friend last night, Mirae?" she asked at last. "I didn't know you had that kind of clothing in your wardrobe, or I would have asked to borrow it at Halloween last year. It's really pretty." Sukjin looked over at Tamnyn, who was wearing one of Sohyeon's old Metallica t-shirts and Mirae's powder blue pajama bottoms. "So you must be Tammy. Sohyeon tells me you need to stay with us until you get some family matters straightened out."

Sohyeon sat down with them and started to eat.

"Yes, my situation is quite difficult, and your sister has been kind enough to ask me to stay with you," Tamnyn said quietly.

"When we're done here, why don't you find them some more comfortable clothes to wear?" Sohyeon asked Sukjin. "We need to go out for a while and take care of a few things before church."

Sukjin found Tamnyn one of Mirae's frilly emerald green mini dresses that she layered over a pair of jeans, though she looked curiously a Joriya, figuring that Mirae should know her own wardrobe. Seeing her confusion, Sukjin took out Mirae's favorite plaid blouse and long denim skirt from the clean clothes she had left folded in the laundry room the week before. When the girls were ready, they rejoined Sohyeon at the front door.

"We're going out now, okay, sis?" he said lightly, noting Sukjin's irritated look. "We'll talk some more when we get home. Let me and Mirae explain the situation to mom when we get the chance, though."

Without waiting for a response, Sohyeon took the keys to their second car and went out to the driveway. Opening the doors for the girls to sit in the back seat, he got in the driver's seat and started the car. It was early Sunday morning, and the paintball facility he liked to go to with his friends would be closed, but the grounds were safer than most for them to talk freely about their plans to return to the other worlds without being overheard. Only ten minutes from the Choi house, it had both an indoor and outdoor course. In the back of his mind, Sohyeon thought maybe when they figured out what to do next, he could ask Tamnyn to teach him some fighting moves since his knowledge of paintball guns wasn't really that helpful for fighting in Eokhmisseun.

He parked the car at the edge of the parking lot away from the main entrance not far from the spectator benches overlooking the outdoor course. As expected, no one was around. He led the girls over to the benches and bid them to sit down.

"This looks like a war field," Tamnyn said, looking around as she sat down next to Sohyeon. "

"It's where my friends and I come to play games," Sohyeon said. "The owner should be by to open it up in a few hours, so we have time to talk uninterrupted. Let's not beat around the bush. What should we do about Birum and saving Mirae from his clutches?"

"We need to find out what Pontol has discovered since Minha asked him to spy for us," Joriya said. Her voice was firm, and it was apparent she was used to giving orders. "Minha will know what to do with the information. Then we should arm ourselves and prepare to land on Eokhmisseun's shores."

"That's pretty vague," Sohyeon said, scratching his arm. "I can only imagine what information Pontol will have for us. Eokhmisseun was a terrifying place, and Tamnyn and I couldn't wait to get away from it. We were lured out of hiding and ambushed in the streets on the night of the purge, when the citizens of Eokhmisseun were struck with an unnatural bloodlust. Litt followed us through the streets, and there seemed to be no way to shake him off our trail. How do you plan on contending with that?"

"But you said it isn't Litt, didn't you?" Tamnyn asked, looking at Joriya thoughtfully.

"Yes, it is actually my brother Birum who has taken over Eokhmisseun. He seems to have stolen the identity of our ancient king whom he abducted from the crypt."

"Why was Mirae with him?" Sohyeon asked. "She was supposed to stay in Khabu, wasn't she, and help you with some trouble there?"

"Birum was the trouble we sought to tame," Joriya said sadly. "When she met with him unexpectedly, he bewitched her. Though the man she met is really Litt, our former king 8,000 years ago, he is still as dangerous as Birum since he is under my brother's spell. Mirae was vulnerable, and I should have foreseen his allure. In the end, she couldn't free him from Birum's magic but became ensnared in it herself. Perhaps she didn't want to escape it if it meant giving up Litt."

"Why does Birum's magic turn the citizens of Eokhmisseun into beasts?" Sohyeon asked, a little amazed to hear about Mirae's situation. "Birum himself seemed to be half animal as he pursued us, and I wondered if he had some sort of enhanced sense he could use to track us."

Joriya's eyes were fixed on something in the distance beyond the outdoor field. A thicket of trees ringed the edges of the field, concealing the housing development that was a few blocks away. She didn't answer Sohyeon's question, and he squirmed a little at her silence.

"It's very likely he is holding Mirae and your ancestral king at Eokhmisseun's palace," Tamnyn said. "He probably has my father and whichever other council member had survived the purge there as well. Joriya, why would your brother, a member of the royal household of immortals, attack our land like this? Is this magic some sort of heritage in Khabu?"

Joriya suddenly seemed to snap out of her reverie as she looked at Tamnyn.

"Birum was jealous of my power and sought a pretext to have me deposed so he could take my place. I don't know what sort of magic he is using. Khabu doesn't have such a tradition, but I had heard rumors that he had been traveling the inner sea and even the outer worlds searching for knowledge. Perhaps he found this black magic in one of those lands. It's clear he will not be an easy foe to defeat. While it helps that we have the executioner's helm and dagger, we will need more weaponry than that. Each of us should have something to defend ourselves. Pontol should be given a weapon as well."

"Won't they have to be silver?" Sohyeon asked. "Will any other sort of weapon do damage to an immortal?"

"It should be silver to kill, though other weapons can inflict pain and cause damage to our bodies," Joriya said. "You can mutilate Birum to some degree with any weapon even if you can't kill him, but he will regenerate. How quickly will depend on the severity of the wound. Losing blood won't affect him."

"How long would we have if we beat him with a bat or cut him in a vital area with a regular weapon?" Sohyeon asked.

"I don't know firsthand," Joriya said, a slight smile playing over her lips. "We do have old war manuals, but I've never witnessed anything like that in my lifetime to know for sure. The old manuals suggest that deep flesh wounds to vital organs will take months to regenerate. Lesser wounds, maybe a fortnight. Small cuts, barely an hour. It can at least buy us some time, but it won't kill him or even stop him much. His magic would probably make that even less effective. Do you have any weapons we can use?"

"I think getting any silver weapon is going to be out of the question," Sohyeon said. "A projectile would be best so we wouldn't have to get close to Birum or even be seen by him, but you can't just walk into any store in the US and get silver bullets. We'll have to come up with some other alternative."

"Then my father was right to give you the crossbow. That is the perfect weapon for you. Could we dip the arrow tips in silver somehow?"

"Is it only silver that will do the job? Is there some other substance?" Sohyeon looked at Joriya hopefully.

"I don't know anything about weapons," she said apologetically.

"I'll have to do some research then," Sohyeon said, standing and putting his hands in his pockets as he glanced back at the road. A few cars passed by though none turned into the facility's parking lot yet. "My friend at school knows about things like that, gaming and folklore, so he can help. What about armor or disguises or something? I mean beyond the cloaks and gloves we have to wear in Eokhmisseun to avoid being touched by him so we won't be turned."

"Can an immortal be turned, I wonder?" Tamnyn said, looking at Joriya. "If Birum touches anyone with his bare hand, skin to skin contact, they turn into degraded half-man, half-beasts like Pontol. We saw him do it to one of my household servants. Until then, I didn't really understand why we always went out covered so completely. It was an old law that originated in my grandfather's generation not long after Litt took control. Sohyeon was clearly uncomfortable in the unwieldy garb when we left that night."

Joriya looked at them in surprise.

"When Birum touched a human this happened?"

"You didn't know your brother could do such things?" Tamnyn asked.

"It's the black magic, not anything from Khabu, but…".

"Yes?" Tamnyn said as Joriya fell silent.

"I don't know if any of this magic could work on an immortal exactly, though Birum was able to use his magic in a different form on both Litt and Mirae, who are both immortals too. It's possible, I suppose, that this 'turning' could be used on us, though it would have a different effect because of our royal lineage. Still, I shouldn't just walk into Eokhmisseun like this even if I am immune to this deformity he inflicts. Birum would recognize me, and I would probably be arrested. I will need to wear the cloak, too."

"It's horrible, you don't want to. How are we supposed to fight in clothing like that? Tamnyn, how did your father do it?"

"The council never tried to fight the demon directly. We only snuck around after he took control, and the cloaks and masks were helpful so we wouldn't be recognized as council members, then later as residents who had not been turned. It wasn't ever meant for us to fight in such garb."

"Then how do we do this?" Sohyeon asked in frustration.

"It has to be projectiles, nothing hand to hand, just like you have suggested," Tamnyn said, sighing. "I wish there was some other way."

"Pontol gave me a crummy spear with a hook tied to the bottom when he took me to your estate," Sohyeon said thoughtfully. "Is that homemade weapon even good enough for him to use against Birum? It certainly allows him to inflict some damage from a safe distance, though it's not as good as a bullet or arrow, and I'd say it wasn't sturdy enough to withstand a real fight."

"Didn't you say Pontol wanted the dagger?" Tamnyn asked, glancing at Joriya. "Of course, now that we know what it is and who its rightful owner is, we can't return it to him. But was he thinking that he needed it to deal with Birum on his own with a real weapon, right?"

"Probably," Sohyeon said grimly. "He must have figured out he needed silver, that it was a weakness of Birum's. He mentioned knowing about Birum's vulnerability to silver somehow. Maybe we can get him to do our dirty work."

"Minha will not allow you to use her slave as cannon fodder in this battle, even if she wants him to be our spy," Joriya said, standing as car pulled into the parking lot.

Sohyeon recognized the driver as the owner of the facility and waved.

"I guess our consultation about how to assassinate a demon is now officially over," he said.

"Maybe that part is," Tamnyn said, watching the car with interest. "But we should still be able to talk about fighting techniques. Both of you need more training. You said this place was some sort of training ground for warriors?"

Sohyeon laughed a little and nodded sheepishly.

"It's nothing like you and your father would recognize as real fighting. We only use toy weapons that shoot paint so no one gets hurt. This place is mostly for parties and just having fun, not serious weaponry training. Still, it wouldn't be out of place to discuss those sorts of things here, within reason. Vince won't care if he overhears that kind of talk, and maybe he has a few foam weapons of a more traditional sort lying around."

"We will need soldiers from my land when we finally go in to Eokhmisseun to rescue Mirae and Litt," Joriya said in a low voice, watching Vince get out of the car and walk over to them. "We shouldn't assassinate Birum ourselves but have my soldiers arrest him and return with him to Khabu for sentencing and execution."

"So that's what you're thinking?" Tamnyn asked in astonishment. "Can it really be done to a creature so powerful? Sohyeon, show me what weapons you use in a place like this. If I have a better idea of your training, we can prepare properly for this task."

3

"We can talk about this later," Sohyeon said tersely. Vince had nearly reached them, and they had to be careful not to talk about anything strange around him.

"Hey, what are you doing here so early, Sohyeon?" Vince said, looking curiously at the women. "If you had wanted to schedule some time today, you should have called me. You have my cell phone number, right?"

Vince Esposito was a graying, slightly overweight man in his forties, but Sohyeon always liked to talk with him since he knew a lot about video games and baseball. He had a ready smile and always laughed at Sohyeon and Pete's jokes, his mustache twitching with amusement, and he was very enthusiastic about his business venture with the paintball park, which was thriving in Sohyeon's upscale neighborhood.

"Maybe not today, Vince," Sohyeon said, feeling his cheeks burn as he realized how shady it looked for him to have brought two women out there when no one was around and the place wasn't even open. He hadn't really considered anything this morning but the issue of Mirae's abduction. Now he was faced with earthly complications.

"So what did you guys come all the way out here for this morning?" Vince asked lightly. "Want to introduce me to your friends?"

"I don't think you've ever met my sister Mirae," Sohyeon said quickly, gesturing toward Joriya who smiled nervously at Vince. *At least she doesn't look too awkward*, Sohyeon thought. "This is Mirae's friend, Tammy. We just were looking for somewhere out of the way to talk. The house is a bit crowded right now, and it was a really nice morning."

Vince nodded approvingly.

"You'll be graduating soon, won't you? You should bring the family here for your graduation party."

"Yeah, I might just do that."

"Ah, Sohyeon," Tamnyn said suddenly. "Didn't you say Vince had some fake weapons we could use?" She turned toward Vince, taking charge of the situation. Sohyeon was a little taken aback, forgetting for a moment she had been a leader of Eokhmisseun. "We wanted to practice a little, too, while we're out here."

"What did you have in mind?" Vince asked, smiling.

"Tammy said she wanted me to show her the paint guns, but she's good with a sword and wanted to teach me and Mirae a few of her signature moves."

"Oh, is that so," Vince said, clearly intrigued. "I do have some foam *katana* swords and some five and seven foot *naginata* pole blades. I don't get much chance to bring them out with all of the kids' paintball parties I do, though your father brought his friends from work by the one night we were slow and did pretty well with the *katana*. I guess I should expect as much from a *kumdo* sword expert, right, Sohyeon?"

"Your father is a sword expert?" Tamnyn asked Sohyeon in astonishment. Suddenly thoughts of Cargal flashed through Sohyeon's mind, and he realized he never really thought about his father the way that Tamnyn did hers when it came to martial skill.

"Well, yeah, he and Sukjin are really into that. My family is Korean, and *kumdo* is a traditional martial art. I never really cared for it, though, and mom never made me learn it."

"She should have," Tamnyn said flatly.

"If you're interested, Tammy, you really ought to talk to Jangsun about it. I'm sure he'd love to give you some pointers," Vince said, looking slyly out of the corner of his eye at Sohyeon.

"We can talk about that later when we get home," Joriya said, picking up on Sohyeon's cues that this was supposed to be her father, too, that Vince was talking about. "For now, let's take a look at your collection, and maybe Tammy can show us a few moves out here. I never learned *kumdo* either."

"Good, good, let me go unlock the door and bring out a few of them. Do you prefer swords or the bladed spears?"

"Bring two of each," Tamnyn said.

Vince went down the concrete path to the front door, fishing in his pocket for his keys to the door.

"They aren't real weapons, you know, so don't get too excited," Sohyeon said. "There's only so much you can teach Joriya and me in an hour with fake weapons anyway."

"Can I really talk to your father about this when we get back to your house?" Tamnyn asked, eagerness glittering in her eyes.

Sohyeon winced in embarrassment.

"If you really want to, but just be forewarned that you'll never get him to stop once you ask him about it. Just don't give away you aren't who you are pretending to be, and don't say anything about Eokhmisseun. Things are difficult enough without you getting all friendly with dad."

Joriya giggled a little.

"Maybe we don't need to worry too much about finding bodyguards, soldiers or assassins if your father is a trained warrior," she said.

"Hey, no one ever said he was a trained warrior. At all. He just does this in a club for fun. It's not serious, not like when we fled from Birum when he tracked us through the city. My father was never in the military or anything, never saw any active duty, so don't get don't get your hopes up."

4

"Sohyeon? Mirae? Can I have a word with you in the living room?"

Sohyeon's mother Alanna was standing in the kitchen looking at them with concern when the three returned home hours later with Sukjin after church.

"Sure," Sohyeon said, knowing Joriya wouldn't know how to answer his mother's probing questions. He had already gotten the third degree after his strange absence last week when he was in Eokhmisseun, so he had some idea of what his mother might say to Joriya now.

The three of them walked into the living room while Sukjin and Tamnyn went upstairs to wash up before a late lunch. As his mother shut the sliding French doors between the kitchen and living room, Sohyeon realized his father Jangsun was also sitting in one of the leather wingback chairs flanking the fireplace, his refined features set into a stern expression as he looked at them over his wire-rimmed reading glasses. Alanna came over to stand beside Jangsun and gestured for them to sit on the couch across from them.

"Is something wrong?" Sohyeon asked casually, trying to signal Joriya they were in trouble in case she had not noticed the signs any American teenager might have caught right away.

Alanna sighed, flipping back her long brown hair impatiently.

"Sohyeon, you and I had this conversation just last week, and I was hoping we wouldn't have to have it again so soon, if at all."

"Oh, yeah, that. I've done everything you asked me to do since we had that talk, mom. Why am I in trouble now?"

"Oh that? That's all you have to say about it? You were gone from school for days, and your father and I hardly saw you even come and go. If Sukjin hadn't seen you, I would have called the police."

Good thing Sukjin was fast thinking enough to cover for him during his absence, Sohyeon thought. He had tried to talk with her about what had been happening, but she was as irritated as his mother was, though she promised not to tell anyone he was gone the entire six days.

"And now your sister has been doing the same thing!" Alanna said. Jangsun just glared at him and Mirae with the same rocky expression. "Mirae, I got a call from your boss, and he said you haven't been to work at all this week. I didn't know what to tell him other than lie and say there was a family emergency, but he was gracious enough to let you take the vacation time you had saved up and not fire you. You need to go to work tomorrow and straighten all of this out. What were you doing all week that you haven't come home or gone to work?"

Joriya smiled uncomfortably, and Sohyeon knew she was out of her league with his mother.

"Mirae has been helping her friend Tammy through some personal problems," Sohyeon said quickly, trying to cover up Joriya's confusion. "Tammy is having some problems with her father, and she was staying at a nearby hotel, so Mirae and I have been trying to help her out."

"I didn't ask you, Sohyeon, so will you please let your sister answer for herself?"

Sohyeon fell silent and looked at the floor.

"So this Tammy is the redhead I've seen around here the past few days?" Alanna asked, looking at Joriya.

"Yes, she was injured running away from home," Joriya said. "I'm afraid my other responsibilities must have slipped my mind in the face of her serious situation. I apologize for causing so much trouble."

Sohyeon noticed an odd expression in his mother's eyes as she looked at Joriya, and he knew listening to Joriya that she really didn't sound that much like Mirae even if she could pass for her physically. What would they do if his mother figured out the deception?

"Fine. Get things back to normal in this house starting tomorrow, and we'll let it slide this time. Now, how long will this Tammy be staying here? You haven't even introduced me to her yet. When were you planning on doing that, by the way?"

"She'll be here until we can figure out a way for her to safely return home," Sohyeon said, glad he could at least be partly truthful about Tamnyn's situation.

"So she'll be staying for meals? I'll be sure to make extra for lunch. Is that all we needed to discuss, Jangsun?" she asked, turning to his father.

"Let me just add a reminder that I will not stand for you slacking in your grades this close to graduation, Sohyeon," his father said, his voice not as stern as his face had been. Jangsun took off his glasses and laid them on the table beside his chair. "You still have a few weeks to go, and you also have some decisions to make about your future. We need to have a talk about it before summer ends."

"Tammy has actually expressed an interest in speaking with you about your hobby," Joriya said suddenly.

Sohyeon cringed. The last thing he really wanted was for an extended conversation between either of the women from the inner worlds with his parents. The less said the better, otherwise they might give away their unearthly origins, and then they'd really be in for a confrontation.

"My hobby?" Jangsun asked, his posture now relaxed as he sat back in his chair and smiled slightly. "What hobby do you mean?"

"*Kumdo*," Sohyeon said gruffly. "You can talk about it after dinner or something. Right now, let's just have a quiet lunch, so we can take a walk this afternoon since the weather is nice."

"Ah, so she's a swordswoman?" Jangsun chuckled. "Perhaps having a guest won't be so unpleasant in that case. What did you say her family problem was? Where do they live?"

Sohyeon looked furtively at Joriya before he answered.

"Abusive family. She almost had broken bones. They live out of state, and she's trying to get settled here in Addison and make a fresh start."

"She probably would find *kumdo* useful for self-defense in that case. Perhaps Mirae and Tammy would consider moving into an apartment together at some point. For now, it's okay that she stays here as long as there's no trouble."

"Lunch will be served in 15 minutes," Alanna said, walking back to the doors and sliding them open. "Go get your sister and Tammy, and your father and I will get everything set up in the dining room. Tacos good today? Ground meat was on sale at the store."

"You know I love Mexican," Sohyeon said, standing and grabbing Joriya's hand surreptitiously as they left his father alone in the living room.

5

"What am I going to do, Sohyeon?" Joriya whispered when they reached the top of the steps. She pulled him into his room and shut the door. "I don't know anything about Earth, and we need to talk with Minha and enter Eokhmisseun for a rescue mission. How can we cope with this sort of situation?"

"They weren't too happy when I didn't come home for a week when I was in Eokhmisseun either," he said grimly. "On the brighter side, Mirae is supposed to become queen of Khabu in the end anyway, right? She won't need her job anymore when that happens. In the meantime, I can give you some tips on what to say and how to act on the job. Mirae worked in a call center for the bank, so you may be able to wing it until we can deal with the situation in your homeland and save Mirae."

"Wing it?"

"Look, you have to have a job to get money to live in this world. It's not like Khabu, and none of us here are immortal. It's going to take a little time for us to figure out what to do, and I can't return to Eokhmisseun until I graduate in four weeks. I have finals to study for in the meantime. That will buy us some time to plan and gather what we need to fight Birum, plus Pontol needs time to figure out what is going on in Eokhmisseun. We're just going to have to be patient and cope with the situation the best we can."

"Then we can't go back to Khabu for more than a few hours," Joriya said, looking toward Sohyeon's bedroom window.

"We're going to have to be very careful how long we are gone until we're ready to move on this. I'll be freer once I graduate since I won't get a job right away, but you won't be able to call in sick much and will have limited vacation time. I need to talk with Sukjin after lunch. We'll have to trust her with the truth so she can cover for us. In the meantime, let's get the girls and go downstairs for lunch."

When everyone was seated at the table for lunch, Sohyeon noticed his father studying the women and worried that their excuses wouldn't be good enough. As his father's eyes lingered over Joriya, a look of puzzlement crossed his face for a moment before turning toward Tamnyn. His father smiled slightly then returned his attention to his plate of food.

"Coffee, dear?" Alanna asked, putting the pot on the trivet in the center of the table.

"I'll get some in a minute."

As everyone passed around the platters of food and took what they wanted, a gentle silence covered the room. Sohyeon looked furtively at everyone, grateful that there weren't too many questions, but then Sukjin shattered his peace of mind.

"Aw, no, it's raining now! There goes sword practice."

"You were going to go out in this?" Alanna asked. "The forecast had thunderstorms and torrential rain all afternoon and evening. Didn't you see that earlier in the week? I can't believe you planned practice knowing that."

"Well, we had hoped the weather man was wrong."

"Do you have a tournament soon?" Jangsun asked, his eyes turning once again toward Tamnyn as he seemed to think of something.

"No, but I need to find time for drills. I feel like I haven't practiced in ages, and now that finals are coming up, it's hard to find time for it."

"I hear Mirae's friend Tammy is interested in sword-fighting, too," Jangsun said, smiling cordially at Tamnyn as she looked up in surprise at the mention of her name. "Is that true, Tammy?"

Tamnyn glanced at Sohyeon quickly before answering his father. Sohyeon noted with a sinking feeling that his father also saw her glance. She was supposed to be Mirae's friend, right, not Sohyeon's?

"Yes, I have studied sword for long years," she said awkwardly.

"What school of sword fighting?"

Tamnyn looked at Sohyeon again, hesitating. He knew he had no choice but to jump in and rescue her, no matter what questions his father might have regarding his behavior. There was no way Sohyeon could risk anyone bringing up the inner worlds with his parents.

"Wasn't it the Italian school? It was more historical re-enactment than modern fencing if I recall from the way it looked," Sohyeon said, meeting his father's gaze steadily. "More warlike and less tournament style."

"Is that so?"

"Yes, I'm not really an expert on the details of origins, but I do know some effective moves with a sword."

"Effective? You have been battle-tested, have you?" Jangsun asked good-naturedly. "I also study Eastern historical sword techniques, so perhaps when the weather is nice again, we can have a bout."

Sohyeon quickly kicked Tamnyn under the table. She wouldn't know enough about Earth to realize that no one actually fought with swords here anymore, and saying more would look suspicious.

6

After that, his father let the subject drop, and everyone left the table to go their separate ways when lunch ended, putting their dishes in the dishwasher as his mother put away the remaining food.

On the way back upstairs, Sohyeon grabbed Sukjin and gestured for her to come to his room. Joriya and Tamnyn had already gone in, but Sukjin looked at him suspiciously.

"What's going on? Why do you need me?"

"We need to talk. Something has happened, and it's important that mom and dad not find out about it, at least not yet. Come in, and we'll tell you."

Sighing impatiently, Sukjin went in, and Sohyeon closed the door behind them. Tamnyn and Joriya had already sat down on Tamnyn's sleeping bag, while Sukjin sat down on the edge of his bed, studying the two women.

"You're not really Mirae, are you?" she asked Joriya softly before looking back at Sohyeon for confirmation.

"You're right, she isn't," he said, coming over to stand in the middle of the room. "These women aren't from Earth at all. Mirae and I had been meeting someone, something, at night these past few months, and now Mirae has disappeared. They had to come here because of what's happening in their homelands far away."

"So the man at the window wasn't a dream?" Sukjin asked softly, the shock apparent in her eyes. "I had asked Mirae about it, but she told me it was nothing, that sometimes she also had strange dreams that had seemed real."

"You saw Pontol?"

"Yes, one night I did. I saw Mirae climb through the window onto some sort of boat, but he didn't seem interested in me when he saw I was awake and looking at him."

"When did this happen? I was in the room the one night he took Mirae, and I didn't think you were awake."

"It was around the time you disappeared, too," Sukjin said, her voice breaking a little. "So Mirae left with that strange-looking man and hasn't been back since. Where did she go? Who are these women then?"

"I don't know exactly where it is, but there are lands beyond the sky that Pontol can take us to. Mirae and I have been traveling there for the past few weeks, and we met these women. Their lands are going through a crisis, and they need our help. Tamnyn is the daughter of a prominent warrior in her land, and she herself was a leader there. Joriya is the queen of second kingdom."

"Joriya? She looks like Mirae, though not enough to fool me. She probably isn't really fooling mom and dad either. You know it's only a matter of time," Sukjin said. "What kind of help could we possibly give leaders of some world beyond the sky? We're just kids. What kind of trouble are they in exactly?"

Sohyeon paused and looked cautiously at Sukjin, wondering how much he should trust her with at this point. She didn't really need to be involved at all. What they needed to do would be dangerous, and Birum was some sort of scary magician. Sohyeon wasn't even sure he could do anything to help them.

"I am Mirae's real mother," Joriya said before he could stop her.

"Wait a minute! What?" Sukjin said, her eyes growing bigger. "That's impossible, isn't it? She's our sister, isn't she, Sohyeon?"

"I don't know anything, Sukjin. All I know is that Mirae is there and in some sort of danger we need to rescue her from, and a great evil is spreading through their lands. We just need you to cover for us until we can figure out what to do to save Mirae and end the threat. Somehow."

"So then 'Tammy's' interest in sword-fighting isn't just for fun," Sukjin said, her face growing thoughtful. "I know some moves, too, though I'm not sure how good my skills would be in a real war. I know Sohyeon only knows modern stuff, not the old, traditional methods like dad and I study. I could help when you go to rescue Mirae."

"No. You're too young, and besides, we need you here to cover for us."

"Could you help me so I can go to Mirae's job and not make anyone suspicious?" Joriya asked. "We may be here awhile before we can rescue her, and it sounds like she will get in more trouble at her job because of me."

"I'll go to school late tomorrow and take you to her office," Sukjin said. "I don't know a lot, but she did tell me enough that I could teach you a few things, like what a telephone is and how to use it and the names of her boss and coworkers. You could pretend to be too sick or addled from the problems at home to remember everything clearly when you're there."

"Good, then that settles it," Sohyeon said. "No one is looking for Tamnyn here, so she can stay with either me or you out of the way so mom and dad don't realize she doesn't work anywhere. But the first thing I need to do is talk to Pete's dad. I can invite myself over to Pete's for dinner to discuss folklore and killing monsters. I need time to figure out just what we're dealing with since Birum is some kind of monster, so I may as well prepare to take my exams and graduate before we go."

"Some guy named Birum is a monster?" Sukjin asked, looking really interested again.

"Stop. You aren't going anywhere near him, so don't worry about it."

"Jeez."

"Let's get started on those preparations before morning," Sohyeon said, looking around the room at everyone before they each went their separate ways for the rest of the afternoon.

7

It was almost Friday before Sohyeon could get a minute alone with Pete to ask about coming over. Worried that Pete was avoiding him after their strange conversation about Sohyeon's bite and his subsequent disappearance for a week, Sohyeon texted him that he needed some help preparing for his calculus final. It took Pete a long time to respond, however. Every time he saw Sohyeon, he was flanked by a new gal pal, Daria, whom Sohyeon had taken an immediate dislike to. All Sohyeon could do was go home and complain to the girls about how things weren't coming together, and he was almost too distracted to study for finals.

"At least you aren't having as much trouble as Joriya," Sukjin said, whispering as Tamnyn and Joriya talked together in the corner of her bedroom. "She looks like she won't make it through the week without getting fired. She could work the phones at least, but she is having such a big 'memory loss' about what to do there that her boss told her he won't put up with this much longer."

"Does mom know?"

"Not yet."

"Can't you help more? What did Mirae do exactly anyway? It's not like she'll need her job if she stays in Khabu, but we should at least maintain the appearance that nothing is going on."

"I don't know that much about what Mirae did every day at work, or I would teach her," Sukjin said, sighing. "There's not going to be any way to hide this in the end. It may already be too late. Didn't you see the news?"

"What are you talking about? There's something on the news about us?" Sohyeon looked at her in horror.

"Not exactly, but didn't you say that you were fighting a monster? Tamnyn told me a little about your flight from Eokhmisseun and the way Birum stalked you. Take a look at this."

Sukjin pulled out her phone and opened up her web browser to a local news reel of a meeting of Addison's city council. Sohyeon sat down on the bed next to her and took the phone. A crowd of people stood in the meeting room, but one figure in the back particularly caught Sohyeon's attention. The tall figure cloaked in black did remind him of Birum's appearance when they were fleeing Eokhmisseun. The sight sent a jolt of fear through Sohyeon, but he quickly told himself that it was a pretty thin comparison.

"It's just a guy in a black coat," Sohyeon said, still feeling inexplicably uneasy. "Why would it mean anything? I mean, people wear black coats all of the time. It's really not so unusual, is it?"

"It has been pretty warm out lately, being almost summer and all," Sukjin said. "Let's see what Tamnyn thinks when I show it to her. Maybe she'll feel differently."

Sohyeon grabbed her arm.

"Don't do that."

"Why not? Don't you want to know if he could be here? Isn't it reasonable to believe he could come here too, if you can go there?"

"He didn't follow Pontol that night. There's no reason why he should come here now. Pontol has stayed away since he brought Joriya, and we haven't tried to contact Minha yet to get him back."

"But Mirae is there, isn't she, with *him*? What makes you think he couldn't torture her or something and find out about us? Maybe he knows something about Joriya coming here from the grapevine at the palace in her homeland. I would imagine if his ultimate goal was to take over her country that he would have spies around her. Isn't all of this reasonable to assume?"

"You read too many books, Sukjin," Sohyeon hissed, handing her the phone back firmly, remembering fleetingly Tamnyn saying that Khabu's people might have been something like space pirates on Earth.

"No one in the council meeting seemed to notice the odd-looking man there, though you would think someone would have objected to how completely he had his face covered or even asked about his presence."

Sohyeon looked over at the women talking in the corner of the bedroom, oblivious to the video of the demonic figure.

"I need to talk to Pete's father now."

"Invite yourself over for dinner."

"That won't go over too well if I don't talk to Pete first. What will I do if his new girlfriend Daria is there, too?"

"Why don't you like Daria?"

"I don't know. I just don't. Pete and I haven't had girlfriends around to get in the way of our friendship until now, so maybe it's that."

"You have Tammy now, right? You two are a thing, so why can't he have one?"

"She reminds me of that guy on the video you just showed me," Sohyeon said, joking, but it clearly fell flat.

Sukjin merely looked at him with wide eyes full of fear.

"Go over now. Tell him that you need to figure out how to kill this thing. You can't take a chance now that we have reason to believe he could be here."

"But we don't have evidence of anything, just a video of some creepy guy who's overdressed for the weather at some local council meeting none of us care about. It was probably all about boring stuff anyway. Why were you watching it in the first place?"

"Dad was looking for something on it because of Vince's place. I think some of the people in the neighborhood aren't too happy with the zoning or something, but no one ever talked about it anyway. Then this guy showed up in the middle of the proceedings."

"What were they talking about when he appeared there?"

"I don't know. Maybe it was welcoming new residents. Isn't that creepy? It fits, doesn't it?"

"Your imagination is getting the better of you." Sohyeon stood up and put his hands in his pockets. "Just go invite myself for dinner, is that it? Maybe I should."

8

Fifteen minutes later, Sohyeon was standing on Pete's stoop, hitting his doorbell. It was still light out, but Sohyeon could see the partial moon clearly enough even in the daytime sky, and he wondered again about the inner sea. Maybe Pete's dad, a literature professor at a local university with an expertise in folklore, would have some idea of what it all meant. Still, Sohyeon didn't really want to have to tell anyone about what he had seen or where Mirae really was. He just knew he didn't have the information he needed to help anyone at this point, even if he went back to Eokhmisseun.

The door opened, and a tall man with short sandy hair stood there, his blue eyes sparkling brightly when he saw him.

"Is Pete home?" Sohyeon asked, his voice cracking a little. "We were supposed to work on calculus for the upcoming test, but he never got back to me."

"Pete's out right now, but he should be home in the next half an hour when dinner is ready. Would you like to stay and have some grub with us before you hit the books?" Mr. MacIntyre asked, letting Sohyeon in the house.

The foyer smelled like garlic potatoes and roast chicken. Mr. MacIntyre led Sohyeon into his study.

"Actually, I'm glad to have a minute alone with you, Mr. MacIntyre."

"Oh? Why is that?"

They made themselves comfortable in leather chairs in the room, which was lined with bookshelves and held exotic ornaments, like a stuffed rabbit in the corner and statues from Cambodia. It looked like a cross between a library and a curio shop.

"I was wondering, given your area of expertise, what you knew about werewolves and things of that nature."

"Ah, so this is a professional call," Mr. MacIntyre said, smiling in his friendly way. "Now, I should ask first off if you and my son were planning on hunting werewolves, or if this is just some new video game strategy you were working out."

"I don't know. It's just really curiosity I guess. My sister and I have been playing some of the Elder Scrolls and a few other games, like the new Moon Quest, and we have a dispute about how traditional folklore perceived some of the creatures, how it differs from the games. Looking on the internet didn't settle the question but only made me more confused."

"You and your sister? Yes, I've heard that the two of you have been having some difficulties lately. Is this related to that somehow?"

Looking at him, Sohyeon knew better than to lie completely.

"Well, we did get in trouble for playing video games too much, but the one visual novel is about killing a monster that only dies if you hit it in the heart with silver."

"Okay, if it's a werewolf, silver is pretty standard. What sort of question did you have?"

"Actually, I don't know what kind of animal it is. Maybe it isn't a wolf. It's sort of human-like but has some animal features. I just thought the idea that silver could kill it might make it more like a werewolf. But in the game we couldn't get much silver weaponry, so what other alternatives historically could a person fighting such a thing use?"

Mr. MacIntyre squinted at Sohyeon a moment before answering.

"You may need to reconsider your interpretation of the monster, depending on the kind of animal it actually is a hybrid of. You see, wolves have a special connection to silver through ancient moon lore. If it isn't a wolf, then that old lore isn't relevant, and your magical weapon might be useless."

"Why does it have to be a wolf? Can't silver and the moon be connected without wolves?" Sohyeon asked, realizing Joriya never answered his question about Birum's animal attributes when they were at the paintball field. He made a mental note to press her harder on the issue the next time it came up. "Can silver be dangerous to other sorts of monsters?"

"Perhaps. The old legends about silver bullets really came from ideas about sympathetic magic. Since wolves were connected to the moon, and the moon was silver, silver was a precious metal, the use of silver to kill the beast all seemed like a logical conclusion to come to. Of course, in the modern world, we don't think like this."

"By that logic, then, would you suggest that any silver object could kill a werewolf? If it just had to be silver-colored, why not use steel or some other shiny silver-like metal?"

"You could consider that possibility. If you're sure a silver weapon is what you need, you could also look at something more modern like titanium arrows, though that tends to look more gold than silver as a coating."

"Do they make crossbow bolts with titanium heads? Steel would be more common, wouldn't it?"

"I don't know. I'm not a hunter, but I think part of the attraction of silver bullets was that the silver was not a commonly used substance for various reasons. You would want to consider scarcity in your calculations."

Suddenly, there was a commotion at the door. Pete had returned and walked into his father's study.

"Sohyeon, what are you doing here?" he asked, a look of surprise crossing his face.

"We were supposed to study for the math final together, but since you never came up with a time, I thought I'd stop by."

"It's almost dinner time, so I invited him to stay," Mr. MacIntyre said, getting up to go to the kitchen and check on the food.

When he had disappeared down the hall, Pete's look of astonishment turned to anger.

"What are you doing here?" he hissed at Sohyeon, throwing his duffle bag down on the floor and coming over to where Sohyeon sat.

"I already told you."

Pete grabbed the front of Sohyeon's collar and twisted it a little as he pulled him out of the chair and onto his knees on the floor. Sohyeon looked up at him, terrified.

"What's gotten into you?"

"You know, a lot of people around here have asked the same question about you, haven't they? And your sister is missing now? What have you gotten yourself into, Sohyeon?"

Pete leaned down and grabbed Sohyeon's hand where there were still faint marks from Pontol's bite.

"You asked me about this last month," he said, anger and fear reflected in his eyes as he studied the marks. "I didn't take you seriously back then when you did. It happened when you were sleeping? I should have known that was a bad sign."

Pete dropped Sohyeon's hand as Sohyeon stood up, grasping the side of the chair and picking his backpack up off the floor.

"What are you really here for? Did you come to pump my father for information about your little problem? You'd better tell me the truth, because I can check with him and find out anyway."

"I just came to find out a little about hunting folklore."

"And what are you hunting?"

"I don't know. Some animal in a game Mirae and I were playing. I haven't been able to figure it out yet. Your father suggested I check out some modern hunting gear. Is that okay, Pete?"

"Dinner is served," Mr. MacIntyre said, walking back into the room. Seeing his son glaring at Sohyeon, he frowned. "Come on, guys, I know finals and graduation are a stressful time, but what's the trouble?"

"Sohyeon won't be staying for dinner this time," Pete said, not tearing his eyes away from Sohyeon, his gaze full of contempt. "Sukjin just texted him that he has to go home for dinner."

"Well, that's what I get for not asking first," Sohyeon said, meeting Pete's gaze with as much defiance as he could muster and pulling his jacket closed. "We can pick another time to study. Give me a call."

"It's a shame you can't stay," Mr. MacIntyre said, looking in alarm at the boys.

"I have a date with Daria tonight anyway."

Mr. MacIntyre rolled his eyes as Sohyeon started toward the foyer.

"When am I going to meet this girl anyway, Pete. You hardly ever spend any time at home anymore. I'm not sure your late mother would be too happy to hear that your first girlfriend has monopolized your time like this, and right before you go away to college."

"Mom isn't here, so what does it matter?" Pete stormed off into the kitchen before his father could reply.

Sohyeon looked back over his shoulder at Mr. MacIntyre before he opened the door to leave. Seeing the look of worry as his gaze followed his son, Sohyeon thought again about Sukjin's comment about the strange council video. Could this Daria be part of a larger problem connected to Khabu?

"Sukjin has lost her mind," Sohyeon said under his breath, shaking his head. "I'll see myself out, Mr.

MacIntyre. Don't worry about it, okay? I'll stay for dinner next time."

Mr. MacIntyre smiled weakly at Sohyeon as he stepped out into the night and pulled the door shut behind him. Standing on the stoop again for a moment, he drew in a long shuddering breath.

"What has gotten into him?"

As he took a few steps down the street toward his house, he had an idea that he needed to take a long walk before returning home and started down the street in the opposite direction.

9

Before long, he found himself in front of Vince's house. Sohyeon didn't know why, but he suddenly needed to talk to Vince. When the door opened, the smell of spaghetti wafted out, and Vince smiled at him broadly.

"Sohyeon? What brings you to my neck of the woods tonight?"

"Hey, I'm sorry to interrupt your dinner, but could I talk to you a minute? It's not about anything important, but I just suddenly had this idea that I wanted to run by you."

"Sure, come on in. Want to stay for dinner? My wife makes great homemade pasta, and we just sat down. Marcus isn't around today. He's on a business trip in India and won't be back for a few months."

Marcus was Vince's 30 year old son, and his wife Marietta, a pleasant-looking, plump woman with a gray-streaked brown bob, was sitting at the table waiting for them.

"Marietta, you remember Sohyeon from the party? He's one of my regulars, Jangsun's son. You remember Jangsun and Alanna Choi from the paintball shop's grand opening, don't you?"

Marietta smiled at him warmly and motioned for him to sit down. Sohyeon sighed in relief as he pulled up a chair across from her while Vince returned to his seat at the head of the table, a big plate piled with spaghetti and meatballs in front of him. He ground some parmesan cheese over it and poured Sohyeon a cup of lemonade as Marietta handed Sohyeon a platter of pasta.

"So what was it that you wanted to ask me?"

"Well, it was two favors really. I need you to help me learn how to shoot a crossbow and teach me about arrow types for one thing."

"Okay, it's not my specialty right now, but there isn't a weapon I don't know how to use, so that's a good proposition. And your other request?"

Sohyeon glanced at Marietta a moment.

"I'd like to know how to get on the local borough's welcoming committee."

Vince looked up from his plate in surprise mid-bite. Marietta laughed and clapped her hands together in happiness.

"Oh, so you want to join my committee?" she asked excitedly. "It's such a rare thing for you kids to get involved in local government these days."

Sohyeon laughed nervously.

"I didn't say I wanted to run anything, just help out and meet some new people. I probably won't cause much trouble on a committee like that."

Marietta waved her hand, dismissing his comment.

"You just need to get your feet wet. Start off with the Addison Welcome Wagon, and before long, you'll be running for council. We could use some new blood. It's good for everyone. I've been trying for years to get Marcus to run, but he's too busy running around the world with his business dealings to really put down roots in Addison. I think maybe he wants to leave this town anyway. As close as we are to DC, it's still a little too familiar to him to be exciting. I wouldn't be surprised if he moved to Bangalore."

They all laughed.

"So when is your next Welcome Wagon meeting?" Sohyeon asked, taking a bite of Marietta's pasta. "Man, you should give my mother some tips on cooking like this," he said without thinking.

"I'll send you a text about the next meeting date. It should be in two weeks. I'm sure your mother will be glad to hear you're getting involved after that incident a few weeks ago. And now your sister is back after her sudden absence. Your family has had enough drama for the year."

Wow, word really gets around in Addison, Sohyeon thought.

After spending a few hours joking around with Vince and hearing from Marietta about the events the Welcome Wagon put together for new residents of the city, Sohyeon finally felt calm enough to go home. It was close to 9 o'clock, and the next day was Saturday. He could sleep in, spend some time studying and maybe even relax a bit with Tamnyn, who had been bored hiding around the house trying to evade his mother. He felt bad about her predicament and thought he owed her some attention.

When he arrived at his house, most of the lights were on upstairs. Slipping in the front door, he felt he could make a quick run up the stairs to his room without drawing too much attention. As he took off his shoes, however, he was startled by a sound in the next room where his father suddenly appeared in the darkness.

"Sohyeon, could I have a word with you for a moment?"

Sohyeon nodded wordlessly and followed his father back into the shadowy living room. A small reading light attached to his father's favorite chair was the only thing on in the room. Sighing deeply, his father sat down in the chair and motioned for Sohyeon to sit down on the sofa across from him.

"What did you want to say?" Sohyeon asked nervously, trying not to let his irritation show.

"First of all, you are about to graduate from high school, and I wanted to hear what you had in mind to do after that. I was going to wait to have this discussion, but after giving it some thought, I decided I shouldn't. After all, Mirae went to work at the bank right after she graduated. Perhaps she could get you a job there, too, if you like."

Sohyeon remembered Joriya weeping and apologizing to him that she was going to get his sister fired before long and realized how out of touch his father was regarding the situation. Not that Mirae would really ever need her job again. Would she ever come back now that she was supposed to take over the throne of Khabu? He could only imagine what his parents' reaction would be to that news when the time came.

"I haven't really given my future much thought," Sohyeon said truthfully. "Maybe I should take a few months off before I make a decision since I've never been as focused as Mirae or as good in school as she was. I could ask Vince if he needs some help out at the paintball park. I just was over at his place talking with him over dinner, but I didn't think to mention it."

"Vince Esposito is a good guy. He'd make a good boss and keep you in line, I think," his father said lightly. "It's too bad there's so much negativity about his new business there."

Sohyeon remembered the video Sukjin had shown him of the creepy man in black at the council meeting where they were supposed to be discussing the paintball park. Uneasiness washed over him again, and he suddenly felt an urgency to ask his father about the meeting.

"Hey, Sukjin told me you had her looking up council meeting videos. Was there something going on about the park and Vince?"

Jangsun Choi looked up at his son in surprise, then smiled.

"We have some trouble makers in the community who aren't too happy about the way war games are being marketed to local children," he said nodding.

"Trouble makers? You mean people like that freak who dressed up in his Halloween costume at the meeting? He looked like a wraith. Sukjin got a good laugh out of scaring me with the video of that guy."

His father's expression looked pained for a moment, as if he were trying to remember the man Sohyeon meant.

"Uh, didn't you see it?" Sohyeon asked, an icy feeling moving down his back. Maybe he and Sukjin were the only ones who could see it on the video. "You should ask Sukjin to show it to you. I want to know if I win my bet with her that it's Jackson Sorenson at my school pulling a prank. He looked pretty creepy. I'm surprised no one threw him out."

"There was no one at the meeting who was wearing a Halloween costume that I recall," his father stammered as he frowned.

"Oh, never mind then. It was probably something Sukjin cooked up to troll me. I shouldn't have mentioned it."

"What was something I cooked up to troll you?"

Sohyeon jumped to his feet at the sound of Sukjin's voice as she walked into the room, clearly irritated to discover she was the topic of their conversation.

"Sohyeon said you had a video of a creepy guy in a Halloween costume at the recent council meeting. Would you mind showing it to me?"

Sukjin looked at Sohyeon in alarm, and he just shrugged in response. Pulling her phone out of her pocket, she quickly pulled up the video and held it out to Jangsun, who had already jumped to his feet to take it. Watching the video intently, his brow furrowed.

"I don't know who that is. I'll have to ask around. You're right, though, he sure looks weird. I wonder why no one escorted him out."

"So you can see him, too?" Sohyeon said, partly to himself.

"Why wouldn't I be able to see him?"

"I don't know. I guess I just thought it was weird that no one else seemed bothered by his presence, like you said."

"So you thought there was something supernatural going on?" Jangsun asked, smiling in bemusement.

"By the way, why did you come down here anyway, Sukjin?" Sohyeon asked in annoyance, changing the subject.

"Mom was wondering why you were taking so long, dad," she said earnestly. "She has your bath drawn and is ready to give you a massage, but you're still down here."

Sohyeon rolled his eyes as Jangsun looked pleased and handed the phone back to Sukjin.

"What?" he asked, noticing Sohyeon's grimace. "Can't I enjoy a relaxing evening with your mother?"

"There are some things I don't need to know about the two of you."

Laughing a little to himself as he walked upstairs, Jangsun disappeared into the kitchen, leaving Sohyeon and Sukjin alone in the dim room. Sukjin went over to turn off the book light.

"Dad probably couldn't tell, but you look pretty shaken. What happened to you tonight? You didn't come home for dinner. Did something happen with Pete?"

"Things went really bad there," Sohyeon said, nodding a little. "I had a few minutes to talk to his father alone, so I have some leads on weapons we can use against Birum when the time comes. I also went to see Vince about learning how to get and use the weapons Mr. MacIntyre suggested, then I asked his wife if I could help out with the council. So I can get near that thing and see if it really is something dangerous and not some prankster."

"But what happened with Pete?"

"When he arrived, he was really angry to see me there. He's upset about my and Mirae's disappearance, and he was very accusing, even touching my wounds from Pontol's bite. He knows something unnatural is going on. He nearly threw me on the floor, and of course Daria was his excuse. He basically asked me to leave."

"I'm sorry to hear that," Sukjin said. "Is that why you said something to dad about the video? I can't believe you did that! You could give away everything, though admittedly, we aren't going to be able to hide the truth from them for long anyway, not with Joriya about to be fired from Mirae's job."

"I don't know why I told dad. I just can't get that figure out of my mind, even though I want you to be wrong about it, Sukjin. Birum can't come here. He's busy running Eokhmisseun into the ground, and he couldn't follow us because of Minha's magical protection on Pontol. Right? I'm just over-reacting. But what will they do, mom and dad, if they find out the truth? Will that really help anything?"

"Why exactly was Pete upset about your disappearance? Only because he knew about Pontol before you left? Or was it because of the gossip going around about our family now?"

"What gossip? I haven't heard anything other than comments about my and Mirae's disappearance. Nobody has anything else to say about it, because they don't know anything about what happened."

"Of course, no one will say it to your face, Sohyeon. Some of them are criticizing our family for being too different from the other suburbanites. They blame a bad upbringing on you and Mirae flaking out, or so it seems to them. Some people say Mirae is on drugs and that you ran away because you got involved with a bad crowd. None of it is true, but most people don't care about truth that much."

"I had no idea," Sohyeon said grimly. "I noticed the weird looks in school, but I didn't really think about why people were reacting like that. So that's why dad decided to have our talk tonight. Has any of it gotten back to mom?"

"Probably."

"What are Joriya and Tamnyn doing now?"

"They're playing a card game in my room to relax. Tamnyn has been bored cooped up in the house, and Joriya is just relieved to not have to go back to Mirae's job tomorrow. I think we'll be going to bed soon. Say, tonight's going to be a full moon. Did you see the moon on the horizon after dinner the past few nights? We don't need to wait until dark to go with Pontol to return to their worlds and fight. Maybe he'll come tonight."

"We? You'll be staying here regardless of when it is, but there's no plan to leave just yet. I need to finish my finals, get some training and equipment from Vince to try to kill this thing, and then wait on intelligence from Pontol. We're stuck here until then, so they might as well make the best of it."

"Tamnyn was out in the yard practicing her sword moves after dinner, and dad seemed impressed watching her. You'd better hang around to cover for any mistakes she makes in explaining what she's doing. She could give away the whole thing with some exotic explanation that doesn't make sense in the real world."

"Keeping a secret is an awful lot of work. Maybe I should consider telling at least dad the truth."

"Are you crazy? What if he doesn't believe you and thinks you all are really on drugs?"

"It's a hard decision, I know. I just wish I knew what to do. I feel so helpless. You weren't there, Sukjin. You didn't see what kind of creature they're fighting in Eokhmisseun."

"Well, it's the weekend, so for now let's get to bed and forget about it."

Sukjin flipped off the light, and the two of them retreated upstairs for the evening.

10

Sohyeon spent the next day at his desk in his bedroom, cramming for his calculus and French exams. It was a warm, sunny morning, and he left his window open, the scent of freshly cut grass wafting through the window as his mother and father took care of the yard work. Sukjin had taken Joriya and Tamnyn to the mall to shop and get out of the house. Alone in the house, Sohyeon became more and more bleary-eyed and caught himself dozing more than once as he stared at his textbooks.

By lunchtime, the sound of the hedge clippers and lawnmower had ceased, and Sohyeon heard his parents' car pull out of the driveway. Going downstairs to grab a microwave pizza pocket and some coffee, Sohyeon retreated back to his room for an afternoon cram session on physics and English. Sitting back down at his desk, he felt aggravated at the thought that this would be his life for the next few weekends until finals were over.

As the hours passed, the shifting sky in the window caught his eye. It had gone from sunny to overcast during the afternoon, and now it looked like a storm front was on the horizon. He thought again briefly about seeing the moon in the daytime and accessing the inner sea even then, but now the cloud cover was deep and thick. Thin threads of lightning appeared in the sky on the horizon at slow intervals, but it was too far away to hear the thunder. Roiling gray clouds gathered over the neighborhood, their purplish cast contrasting vividly with the shivering green trees lining the yard. *I should take a quick walk around the block to clear my head before the rain starts*, Sohyeon thought, but he was undecided about actually doing it.

Suddenly, a small white bird landed on his windowsill. Sohyeon looked at it a moment, wondering why it would be there, but then he remembered. Mapin! Rushing over to the window, nearly knocking his chair over as he leapt across the room, he reached the bird as it calmly started to chatter in a language unknown to Sohyeon, who recognized the cadence from when he had watched Tamnyn talk with her.

Mapin's arrival could only mean one thing.

"Tamnyn isn't here to talk to you, Mapin, so I'm afraid you're out of luck for a few hours until the girls return."

Mapin just looked at him curiously while Sohyeon checked the pouch around her neck for a message. Would anyone over there know how to write in English anyway? It was probably hopeless unless the message was from Mirae herself.

Pulling out a small piece of rolled parchment, Sohyeon flipped it open with his free hand while Mapin shifted into a more comfortable position on his other hand.

"I found them at Litt's palace," the note began in a shaky script. At least it was in English, somehow. Glancing quickly at the bottom of the paper, Sohyeon saw it was from Pontol. "Need to confer with you over some details I discovered. Multiple captives are being held there, but Litt has left the palace temporarily."

Litt, or Birum? Sohyeon thought. *Would Pontol know the difference?* He couldn't remember what Joriya said she had told Pontol about the switched identities of the men, but either way, that meant Birum could have followed them to earth. Then what would they do if he had? Maybe it would be easier fighting such a monster on familiar home turf with conventional Earth weaponry after all, but Sohyeon wasn't sure. He just knew he felt vulnerable.

"You should stay until Tamnyn returns so she can question you," Sohyeon said to Mapin. Mapin made some more strange warbling noises in response.

Looking around the room, he decided to let Mapin sit on his nightstand to wait for an audience with the remaining councilwoman of Eokhmisseun as he went back toward his desk. Sohyeon chucked to himself a little, thinking of Tamnyn like that, but then he stopped cold.

Tamnyn *was* a member of the ruling council of Eokhmisseun, wasn't she? Birum somehow had wrested power from the council decades before, but what did that mean? Now there was a strange figure appearing at Addison's council meeting. Could there really be a connection as Sukjin suggested?

Taking out his phone, Sohyeon quickly texted Sukjin, asking her to return and telling her to let Tamnyn know that Mapin had come. Sukjin answered immediately. It would take more than 30 minutes for them to get back since Joriya was getting a manicure. Impatient, Sohyeon could no longer concentrate on his study session. The clock read three forty-five. He had already been at it over seven hours, so he was entitled to a break.

"They'll be here soon," Sohyeon said reassuringly to Mapin. "I'm going to go downstairs and wait for them a little while, so you stay here until I bring them up to talk with you."

When he got down to the living room, he was startled to find someone hanging around the back door. He hadn't heard anyone knocking. Looking out the sheer curtains cautiously, leaving the lights off so he wouldn't show up in silhouette, Sohyeon didn't recognize the person standing outside, a middle-aged man with oddly irregular features who was dressed in an old English-style trench coat that seemed tattered in places. His curly dark brown hair flew around his head like a clown's wig, and dark circles ringed his bulging eyes. A vagrant? In Addison? Sohyeon felt uncomfortable and left the room without answering the door, retreating back to his bedroom on the second floor.

Taking out his phone again, he texted Sukjin about the man at the door.

"Maybe that's your person from the council meeting," she texted back. "Just stay away from the door now and mention it when dad comes home. We'll walk around the block a few extra times if we see him still hanging around on our way home."

"It looks like rain," he texted. "Did you take an umbrella? You won't be walking around the block for long if it hits at the right time."

"☹."

Sohyeon laughed nervously when he saw her response. They might not have any choice but to deal with the visitor. Could it be Birum at the door? Sohyeon didn't think so, but there was definitely something off about the man. Birum was part animal, wasn't he? Again, Sohyeon remembered he needed to ask Joriya more firmly about that when she got home. But for now, all he could do was wait.

Opening his textbook up, he started reading the page, but this time a rough knock at the door made him jump. The intruder had now come around to the front of the house beneath Sohyeon's window. Sohyeon looked at the window, wondering if he should try to peek out again at the visitor, knowing he could give himself away, but he couldn't stop himself from walking over to it under Mapin's now silent, interested gaze.

When Sohyeon got to the window, he looked down at the front door. The creepy-looking man who had been pounding on it was the man Sohyeon had seen at the back door moments before, and he stepped back off of the front stoop to look up at the house just as Sohyeon had appeared at the window. Their eyes met, much to Sohyeon's chagrin.

"Looking for someone?" Sohyeon yelled down to him. At least from the second floor he could talk to him without any pressure to let him in.

"Is this the Choi residence? I'm looking for Sohyeon Choi."

Sohyeon hesitated, startled to discover that the man was looking for him. He knew he probably shouldn't deny it.

"Yeah, this is the Choi residence," he yelled down. "Who are you?"

"Detective Todd Mazurek with the Metropolitan Police Department of the District of Columbia." He held up a flat wallet with his badge toward the window.

Sohyeon was even more shocked and dismayed to hear it was the police. He couldn't dodge inviting the man in now.

"Is Sohyeon Choi here? I have some bad news for him."

"I'm Sohyeon."

"Can you come down so we can have a chat? We shouldn't stand out here shouting in the street."

Sohyeon paused, but he knew he had no choice. Whatever this was about, he didn't want the neighbors overhearing it. According to Sukjin, there was already enough gossip going around.

"I'll be down in a minute."

Shutting the window and patting Mapin lightly on the head, Sohyeon dashed down the stairs to the front door.

11

His mind racing, Sohyeon opened the front door and let the creepy man in black into the house. In spite of the man's shabby coat, he smelled of spearmint gum and cheap cologne rather than like the street person Sohyeon mistook him for earlier.

"Detective Mazurek, let's go into the kitchen," Sohyeon said, waving him into the next room. "Would you like some coffee?"

Detective Mazurek nodded slightly and walked into the kitchen. Before he followed the detective, Sohyeon's eye caught movement at the top of the stairs. Mapin had flown over to the half wall at the top of the stairs and looked down at him with intelligent eyes. Feeling mildly relieved that he wasn't completely alone in the house with the police, Sohyeon strode dutifully into the kitchen and took out two clean mugs. He was glad he made extra coffee for his marathon study session now that he had company.

"Black is fine," Detective Mazurek said, his voice low but friendly.

Sohyeon poured the coffee and handed him the cup before sitting at the table across from him. The two men eyed one another warily for a moment.

"So what did you stop by to talk to me about?" Sohyeon asked casually.

"Are your parents home?"

"They stepped out buy groceries and should be back soon."

"Good. I'll also need to speak to your father and sister later. In the meantime, I'll get down to business. You have a friend named Peter Seamus MacIntyre, don't you?"

Alarm bells started going off in the back of Sohyeon's mind, but he forced a smile at the detective.

"Pete and I have been friends for years, though since we hit high school, we only have math and science classes together."

"Would you consider yourself close friends?"

"Yeah, we've always been pretty close, though maybe we're drifting apart a little now that we're graduating and he's going off to college soon."

Detective Mazurek made a few notes in a small notebook he had flipped open. A small pen appeared out of nowhere in his hand.

"You visited him at home last night, didn't you?"

"I was there for a short time, but I didn't stay for dinner. Pete had a date or something."

"What was the purpose of your visit?"

"We're studying for finals, and I thought we could study together for a little bit."

"On a Friday night?"

"We could more easily have a late night study session on a Friday than on other nights during the week when we have school."

"I see. Was that the only reason for your visit?"

Sohyeon paused, knowing the detective's questions were getting into dangerous territory. How could he tell the truth and not raise the man's suspicions?

"Pete's father is rather famous around here, and I've always found him fascinating to talk to, even as a kid."

"What's so fascinating about him?" Detective Mazurek asked, squinting as he looked up at Sohyeon from his notebook.

"He knows a lot of folklore, and we always thought he was a good source for advice on video game strategy."

"So you wanted to talk to him about a videogame? Which one?"

"Moon Quest," Sohyeon said, not knowing as much about the newly released game as he would like to in order to keep up the ruse. "It just came out a few months ago, but Mirae and I have also been playing Skyrim, so we had some questions relating to game play for both. Excuse me, Detective Mazurek, but what is all of this about? Are you a gamer?"

The detective finished jotting his notes down and looked up at Sohyeon soberly.

"Peter MacIntyre disappeared last night a few hours after you left. This morning we found the half-eaten body of his girlfriend, Daria Favreau, in a DC park, which is my jurisdiction."

Sohyeon looked at Detective Mazurek in astonishment.

"*Daria's* dead? Half-eaten?"

"We haven't released the details publicly yet, so keep them to yourself. We're still working on time of death, but they think it happened around midnight." Detective Mazurek studied his reaction a minute before continuing. "Doug MacIntyre said you were there inquiring about werewolves last night. Is that true?"

Sohyeon suddenly realized what the detective was getting at, but he wasn't willing to play along.

"Yeah, it was part of my video game research, but I was mainly just waiting for Pete to get home. Are you suggesting that Daria was killed by a werewolf?"

The detective paled visibly, aware of the absurdity of his accidental suggestion.

"Did you know Miss Favreau?"

"Only to see her. Pete and I haven't talked much since he started dating her."

"Did you like Daria?"

"I didn't know Daria," Sohyeon said firmly. "I didn't even know her last name until now. I think she was a recent transfer to Addison high, plus she's only a junior."

Detective Mazurek took another sip of coffee before continuing.

"I heard through the grapevine that both you and your older sister disappeared briefly yourselves recently. Do you mind telling me where you went?"

Sohyeon knew he was in big trouble. There was no way to account for his disappearance, and Joriya was completely unable to maintain the ruse of pretending to be Mirae under such intense scrutiny.

Just then, a bird flew into the room and sat down on the table between them, her eyes riveted with great interest on the detective as she started warbling.

"What's this?" Detective Mazurek asked, pushing his chair back from the table in alarm.

"My pet bird," Sohyeon said. "Mapin got loose again. I'm sorry for the distraction."

Mapin took a few steps toward the detective, and he slumped forward in his chair as if hypnotized. Wondering if it wasn't exactly the distraction he needed just in the nick of time, Sohyeon heard a commotion at the front door and remembered that Sukjin should be due back with Tamnyn and Joriya. He needed to get them out of there before the detective snapped out of it and tried to question Joriya.

A stampede of quick footfalls coming toward the kitchen echoed down the short hallway, and Tamnyn appeared in the doorway, her eyes wide and her long red hair slipping out of its hairband. Seeing Mapin on the table, she called to the bird using the same unusual tones. After Mapin responded, Tamnyn turned toward Sohyeon in alarm.

"This man has brought danger here to us, hasn't he?" she asked, gesturing to the detective.

"My friend has disappeared, and his girlfriend was murdered. The police want to question me and Mirae. You know why we can't let that happen. Where is Joriya?"

Joriya and Sukjin came into the room behind Tamnyn and looked curiously from the bird to the man in black passed out in his chair. Sukjin sucked in her breath.

"Sohyeon, is that the man in the council video?"

"He looks a little like it, doesn't he? But I don't think so, Sukjin. He's a policeman here to investigate a murder."

Sohyeon noticed Joriya's odd, intent look at Mapin. Like Tamnyn, she had some bond with the bird that went well beyond anything Sohyeon had felt around her. Again, he was reminded they needed to have that talk about animals and Birum, though now wasn't the time.

"Joriya, you need to get out of here. Now. They want to question you about Mirae's disappearance, thinking you are my sister. They also are asking about my disappearance when I was in Eokhmisseun. Neither story will stand up to a police investigation."

"So what do we do now?" Sukjin asked, looking at the bird in fascination. "What kind of bird is this anyway?

And what happened to him?" She looked back over her shoulder at the detective. "Did you put something in his coffee to knock him out or something?"

"No, Sukjin, I didn't, and please stop making those unhelpful remarks before someone overhears you. It's the bird! It's some sort of magic."

"Mapin is my pet," Tamnyn said, holding her hand out to gently stroke the bird's head. "But she's from Khabu. Joriya can tell you more about the magical messenger birds, but they have helped my family cope with house arrest once Litt, er Birum, took over my land. They are very special and speak a magical language."

"Then you were just talking to her?" Sukjin asked, coming closer to look at the bird. Only Joriya hung back.

"We don't have time for this," Sohyeon said. "You need to take Tamnyn and Joriya somewhere safe for the rest of the day. Don't come back until 10 tonight when the police are sure to be done here."

"How do you know he'll wake up again?" Sukjin asked.

Sohyeon looked at Tamnyn, and she smiled.

"Mapin just put a minor spell on him to make him go to sleep for a little while so he wouldn't interfere until we can figure out what to do."

"Joriya, what is this bird?" Sukjin asked, reaching out to touch her gingerly, clearly intrigued.

"We don't have time for this right now," Sohyeon said again, more insistently this time.

"The war birds are my subjects."

All three of them turned to look at Joriya in surprise. Even Tamnyn had been unaware of the birds' origins and was now puzzled by Joriya's claim.

"Your subjects?" she asked, pausing thoughtfully. "But the people of Khabu are immortal, aren't they?"

Joriya's eyes remained locked on Mapin even as she turned pale.

"Immortality in my land means something different than what you assume, Tamnyn. We live forever, but not as humans. Khabu's commoners turn into a special sort of bird that lives in the Forest of Bliss in Khabu when they turn 600 or 700 years old."

Her voice turned dreamy, its pitch low and full of emotion.

"Then Birum is also an animal, isn't he?" Sohyeon said, realizing why he had such a strong impression of that when Birum was chasing them through the streets of Eokhmisseun.

"You said the commoners turn to birds," Tamnyn said, looking at Joriya curiously. "What happens to the royal family at that time then? They don't turn to birds?"

12

Just then, they heard a car arrive out front. Sohyeon's parents had returned.

"You need to leave now, through the back door. It's imperative they don't see you until after this guy leaves. We can talk about this later."

Sukjin grabbed Joriya's hand and ran down the hall toward the living room and the back door. Tamnyn hesitated a moment, her eyes searching Sohyeon's face with concern.

"Can you handle this? I can stay if you need me to try to get you out of it. I don't want you to be carried off like my father was, not with the war that's brewing, that we're preparing for."

"Go. I'll be fine somehow. Trust me."

"Mapin will stay here to watch over you, out of the way. Make him wake up now, Mapin. No more time for playing tricks."

With one more lingering glance at Sohyeon, Tamnyn followed Sukjin and Joriya to the back of the house. Mapin perched on the edge of the table near the detective and whispered a few rhythmic words before flying back into the hall and up the stairs to a safer vantage point.

Suddenly, Detective Mazurek started to grunt and yawned. Shaking his head a little to clear it, he looked around the kitchen in confusion.

"Ah, what were we talking about?"

"I think Moon Quest, the new video game, sir. But it sounds like my parents just pulled into the driveway, so you can talk with my father next. Was there more that you needed to ask me? I'm not wanted for anything, am I?"

Detective Mazurek quickly covered up his embarrassment of not knowing what he was doing for a few minutes and smiled reassuringly.

"No, you aren't wanted for anything, though I do want to talk to your father. I just needed to get a feel for how the younger generation thinks about things these days, to get some insight into where Peter MacIntyre may be. We're organizing a search party for him later tonight, so maybe you'll want to help out. In the meantime, think of everywhere your friend could possibly go. That's the sort of thing we need help with."

A few moments later, Detective Mazurek met Jangsun at the front door, and they went into the living room together, shutting the door behind them. Sohyeon stuck around downstairs and helped his mother bring in the groceries from the car. It was a little before dinnertime, and Sohyeon's mother had gone into the kitchen immediately after the police interview had begun. Sohyeon went up to his room to wait awhile for the interview to end, then came down to sit on the bottom of the stairs near the hallway by the front door when he heard the men's voices echoing in the foyer.

"Where are your sisters?" Sohyeon's father asked after Detective Mazurek had left.

"I don't know for sure," Sohyeon said, pulling out his phone to text Sukjin that it was safe to return. "I know they spent some time at the mall today shopping. The weather was good, too, so maybe they went for a walk afterward. Let me see where they are."

Sohyeon looked up at his father after sending the text and was dismayed to see he still looked rather unsettled by the detective's visit.

"So what else did Detective Mazurek say to you?" Sohyeon asked gently.

"I'm sorry you were home alone when he came," Jangsun said in a low voice. "We should have been present for something like that. He told you about the girl's death?"

"Yeah, I was surprised. I can't imagine where Pete might have gone or that he could have killed her, but then again, he hasn't been too friendly to me lately."

Jangsun looked at his son a moment as if uncertain how he should proceed. Sohyeon thought in the uncomfortable silence once again of Sukjin's warning that they couldn't hide the truth from their parents forever. Detective Mazurek didn't remember wanting to question Sohyeon and Joriya about their disappearances for now, but he would be back before long once someone reminded him. How would Sohyeon answer him? How could he protect Joriya from being exposed? If the police found out about her unearthly origins or Mirae's kidnapping in the other world, it would be a disaster.

Searching his father's face earnestly, he knew he couldn't handle any of this alone. Realizing that the situation, and maybe even Birum himself somehow, was backing him into a corner, Sohyeon made his decision.

"Dad, we need to talk somewhere alone. It can't wait."

His father sighed deeply as a look of fear mingled with resignation flickered over his face. Sohyeon felt chagrined by his reaction.

"It's bad, but it's not what you think," he said quickly. "Let's go upstairs to my room and talk."

Jangsun sat on the bed as Sohyeon shut the door and came over to stand beside his desk. Mapin perched quietly on his nightstand near his father, looking more like a stuffed animal than a real bird. Sohyeon was sure his father hadn't noticed it was real yet.

"What is going on, Sohyeon? Are you somehow mixed up in this girl's murder? If so, your mother and I have some money saved up, but I can't guarantee we can get you the best attorney available even with that."

"Dad, I'm not involved in Daria's murder, though I may know who is. The problem I need to talk to you about is a little more complicated than that, and a lot wilder." Sohyeon struggled a moment trying to figure out where to start his explanation. "It's about Mirae."

Jangsun's face froze and looked even more haggard than before.

"Your sister? I know she's been having a hard time since her disappearance," he said. "I think your mother said she's on the verge of losing her job."

"Mirae never came back after she disappeared," Sohyeon said flatly.

Jangsun looked shocked.

"What are you saying, Sohyeon? That girl isn't Mirae?"

"Hadn't you or mom noticed? We know there's a strong resemblance, but Joriya can't pull off living as Mirae. Mirae will never come back anyway now. She has been kidnapped, and we're trying to save her, but even when we do, she won't return here."

"Joriya? Is that the girl's name? She is pretending to be Mirae then?" Jangsun asked angrily. "Why try to deceive us in this way, Sohyeon? Where is Mirae now?"

"We needed to buy some time to find Mirae, so they sent Joriya here instead for now to throw off suspicions. It's important no one find out that Joriya isn't Mirae. Do you understand now why the involvement of the police is a problem even though we aren't involved in this situation?"

"Where is your sister?" Jangsun asked again quietly. "Where did you go when you disappeared? Is that where she is?"

"Do you remember what I said when I showed you the weird council video yesterday?"

"You mean when I said you seemed to think there was something supernatural about it? Yes. This is something supernatural then?"

"I think the person, the creature, who has Mirae may have killed Daria. It isn't human, though it looks human. I'm not sure if Pete would be connected somehow to her death or not. If it was this creature, that would mean things are now very dangerous for us because he followed us here. We've been trying to figure out how to kill him and rescue Mirae."

"And that's why the detective came here asking questions about why you went to see Doug MacIntyre about werewolves? Is this what kind of creature we are talking about?"

"I know it sounds silly, but that's the only lead I have on what the creature is. Until Joriya tells us more, we can't pinpoint the best way to stop it."

"Where did you go when you disappeared for that week?" Jangsun asked again, this time more forcefully.

"It's a place called Eokhmisseun in another dimension I think. That's where Mirae is now. It's Tamnyn's homeland, too. She and Joriya could perhaps explain it better than I can. She said people from their lands had dealings with our world in past ages."

"Do you have proof that any of this is true? If I'm supposed to help you keep this secret about Joriya from the police, I want to be assured it is really true."

"I'm working on it. Can you also keep it from mom, too, for now?"

Before Jangsun could answer, Sukjin burst into the room.

"Sohyeon, we know what animal Birum is. Joriya finally told us," she said excitedly but stopped as soon as she saw her father sitting on the bed. "Oh, are you in the middle of something? We'll come back later."

Sukjin started to retreat back into the hallway, but Jangsun stopped her.

"Wait a minute!"

Sukjin froze where she stood and looked helplessly at Sohyeon.

"It's okay. I told him."

Sukjin's jaw dropped, and she quickly came back into the room, shutting the door behind her.

"Did the policeman leave?"

"For now," Sohyeon said. "That's why I decided to tell dad some of the details."

Sukjin looked at her father out of the corner of her eye.

"Does he believe you? It's pretty far-fetched?"

"That depends," Jangsun said. "I'm not going to rule out the possibility of paranormal things happening or inexplicable monsters appearing, but it's going to have to be more than just your word for it."

"Well, there's Joriya," Sukjin said, thinking. "She looks a lot like Mirae, but you and mom should have picked up right away that it wasn't her. They don't look *that* similar, and she's totally awkward here in our world."

"I will have a word with her to verify this when we're done here," Jangsun said. "But you realize that anyone can playact and be mentally suspect."

"But did you tell dad *why* she looks so much like Mirae?" Sukjin asked Sohyeon. "That in itself ought to be suspicious."

"Not yet. This is going to be hard enough to prove without getting into that. I was thinking that Tamnyn's helmet might convince him, maybe the dagger…".

"What about the magical bird? She's right there on your desk. Have her hypnotize dad the way she did the cop earlier."

Jangsun gasped in exasperation as they all looked at Mapin.

"It hypnotized Detective Mazurek? Are you trying to get us all killed here? Sohyeon, this is a murder case!"

"That could work," Sohyeon said, ignoring his father. "Go get Tamnyn and have them come up with a convincing demonstration."

"Joriya might know some way, too. Wait here while I get them."

A few minutes later, the two women entered Sohyeon's bedroom with Sukjin.

"I told them dad knows," she said once they were behind closed doors.

"My father wants you to give him proof that our story about your world is real, that there really is another world where Mirae is being held," Sohyeon said to Tamnyn. "Sukjin suggested using Mapin's hypnotic trick. Can you ask Mapin to help?"

Tamnyn looked at Mapin in astonishment.

"They're magical birds, that is true, however, my father and I only ever used them as messengers so we wouldn't risk the danger of traveling in our city streets."

"I can ask her," Joriya said, stepping forward, her expression grim. "If it's proof you want, there are things the birds of Khabu can do. She is actually from my homeland, not Eokhmisseun."

Joriya held out her hand to Mapin, and the delicate white bird stepped up obediently. As its clawed feet touched her flesh, both Mapin's and Joriya's eyes lit up like fire. Gone were the whites and pupils of their eyes. Fierce flames pulsed within the hollow spaces, as if Sohyeon and the others were looking through a hole into a furnace. The lamp on the nightstand flickered and went out as the air in the room crackled and grew heavy. Tamnyn cried out and clutched her chest, falling to her knees in the darkness, gulping a few times for breath. Light blue bolts of static electricity shot out as Sohyeon grabbed her arm to help her to her feet, but she pulled him down to the floor with her. Sukjin and Jangsun watched the effect in horrified fascination.

Joriya and Mapin turned slowly to face Jangsun, their flaming eyes weaving a soft glow around their faces. Jangsun brought up his arm to shield his eyes from the light.

"Do you want to know the truth, Mr. Choi? Feel the power of the immortals and gaze upon their slumber through the eyes of Mapin, one of my loyal subjects!"

Jangsun's whole body trembled as Joriya raised her free hand level with his head, the palm of her hand facing him. A bolt of static electricity flickered blue between them, and Jangsun flew flat on his back on the bed, his eyes wide open. A look of wonder passed over his face as his eyes seemed to focus on something far away in the flickering, dim light in Sohyeon's room. The air pulsed with even more power than before Jangsun fell, making the hair on Sohyeon's arms stand on end. It seemed alive, velvety, even solid.

"What are you doing to him?" Sohyeon whispered.

"He will walk among my subjects in their land of peace, look upon the birds in the Forest of Bliss," Joriya said, her voice growing terrifyingly low and inhuman.

Seeing her transformation, Sohyeon had to wonder if Joriya told the truth when she said Khabu had no tradition of magic and that Birum had learned his magic elsewhere. Now, he could believe they were brother and sister. Had Joriya fooled them all with her helpless behavior? Even Tamnyn seemed taken aback by her outrageous display of power. How could any human fight such a force?

"That's enough," Sukjin said, pleading.

"It will only take a few minutes more," Joriya said. "Then I will release him."

The seconds ticked by. No one moved. The light emanating from Joriya and Mapin started to weaken and fade until only the moonlight coming through the window illuminated Sohyeon's room. Finally, Jangsun began to cough and his eyes seemed to refocus on the room. Sitting up, he looked around.

"Do you believe now?" Joriya asked caustically as Mapin flew back to her spot on Sohyeon's nightstand.

"What was that I saw?" Jangsun asked dreamily. "Such a beautiful land, full of unearthly birds. It was like being in paradise, and the trees seemed as alive as the animals."

"Yes, it is that and more, the forest of eternity where our commoners rest once they transform from their human form into their animal form."

"Commoners? Who is the ruler there? You?" Jangsun asked, fear returning to his voice.

"That's right. I am their queen, the queen of the immortals!" Joriya's voice had a quality that Sohyeon had never heard her use before and was startled to hear. She sounded strong, commanding. He marveled again at how unexpected this was. "Sohyeon didn't tell you everything, but I am the leader of a fierce race."

"That's right, Sohyeon," Sukjin said, unconcerned with interrupting the Queen of Khabu. "I started to tell you when I came in before. Joriya told us that the immortals of Khabu are half animal. Their subjects become birds after time, but the royal family transforms into a different animal. The white tiger."

13

"Were you going to help out with the search party for Pete?" Alanna Choi asked as they finished up dinner and she scooped the last of the leftover kimchi and rice into containers.

Saturdays were their usual day for traditional Korean fare, and Sohyeon's mother cooked a mean plate of *japchae*. But no one had said a word since they all came down to eat.

"I think Detective Mazurek said they're supposed to go out at 8PM and just take a quick look around Addison," she continued, dismayed at their silence. "If you hurry up and eat, you can make it in time."

Sohyeon glanced at the clock on the microwave. It was already 7:30, and the meeting point for the search party was at Pete's house. He had already given up studying for the night.

"Sohyeon, Tammy and I will be going to help out," Jangsun said, getting up from the table abruptly and going into the foyer to get his blue windbreaker. Tamnyn looked up in surprise as he said her name. She and Sohyeon also rose and followed him into the foyer.

"Do I get to go, too?" Sukjin asked.

"No, you stay here with your mother and sister. We need adults and people with some ability to fight in case there's trouble," Jangsun said, picking up his gnarled walking stick and setting a gray tweed flat cap on his short black hair. "Would you like to take one of my practice *mokgums*, Tammy?"

Tamnyn looked at Sohyeon, uncomprehending.

"He means his bamboo sword," Sohyeon said.

"Okay, but shouldn't I take mine?"

Sohyeon glanced at his mother before answering. She had walked into the living room with Sukjin, who was still begging her to go.

"It might raise suspicions since most people around here don't carry real weapons," Sohyeon said, putting on his baseball jacket. Jangsun handed Tamnyn one of his wife's ponchos along with the *mokgum*. "The wooden sword would be safer, at least if the community notices, though it may not help you much in a fight compared to a metal sword."

"Let me do the talking," Jangsun said, waving for them to follow him. "We'll walk to Doug's house since they are expecting a fair number of helpers tonight. There won't be anywhere to park."

They reached the MacIntyre place to help with the search parties before too many people had arrived. Mr. MacIntyre was cool toward Sohyeon as he greeted them and began talking with Jangsun about his garden, showing him around the front lawn where he had some new landscaping planned. Before long, Jangsun surprised everyone by bringing up the police visit. Doug MacIntyre looked uncomfortable and avoided meeting Sohyeon's gaze.

"The detective came when we weren't home, and I wish he would have waited until I was there to proceed with his questioning," Jangsun said.

Sohyeon wanted to listen to the whole conversation, but Tamnyn pulled him toward the opposite side of the lawn to talk as more people pulled up to join them with the search.

"You didn't bring a weapon, did you?" she asked, looking at him with concern. She had changed into jeans and a sweatshirt and had braided parts of her long red hair to help keep it out of her face. "This whole situation feels familiar somehow, and I feel like it's a bad sign that you don't have any way to protect yourself."

"Familiar? How would it be familiar?"

Tamnyn looked down the street, her worried expression deepening, but she didn't say more. Small clusters of people walked down the front sidewalk to where Jangsun stood with Doug MacIntyre.

"I have my phone and am ready to take a photo at a moment's notice," Sohyeon said, pulling her gently back toward where the growing crowd waited so they could get instructions on what to do.

"We should stay with your father as much as possible while the search is going on," Tamnyn said, her voice oddly full of tension.

"Why are you so edgy? You didn't know any of the victims here."

"I don't know. Maybe because I got separated from my father during the ambush that night," she said. "Will they split us up into groups to do this?"

"I think so. We'll cover more ground that way. Look, we'd better go listen to them and stay by dad then."

After they split into seven search parties of about six people each, they were given maps of which part of the borough to look around. Jangsun made a point of keeping Sohyeon and Tamnyn in his party, and they took the map covering the forested area not far from Vince's paintball facility. The other people in their party included a thirty-something volunteer fireman and a couple of college students. Sohyeon had never seen any of them before, but he overheard the students talking about how they had met Pete at an open house at George Washington University not long before. Seeing how many of their helpers were coming from outside Addison to look for Pete, he felt a little guilty over how badly their encounter had gone the night before.

Jangsun took charge, and they decided to take the fireman's car to Vince's place where they could park and access the area on their map.

"I'm Adam Johnson, by the way," the fireman said. "I'm not from Addison, but I usually try to join these search parties as part of my fire department activities. It's good to learn the neighborhoods, and we're used to dangerous situations, though of a more natural sort."

"Jangsun Choi," Sohyeon's father said amicably. "I'm an engineer in Arlington, and this is my son Sohyeon and his friend Tammy."

The two college students introduced themselves as Philip Wang and Analisa Gomez. Within a few minutes they were at the paintball park, which had already closed for the evening since bookings were light with finals coming up. The sun was just setting, and in the twilight, the thickly wooded suburban area already would be too dark to walk through without flashlights. When they got out of the car, Adam went around and opened the trunk, pulling out two camping lanterns and a few lantern flashlights for them to take.

"I came prepared with the most powerful lights in my collection," he said, slamming the hatch shut again.

Jangsun took one of the camping lanterns in his free hand, carrying his walking stick deftly in the other. Sohyeon took one lantern flashlight, leaving the remaining two for Philip and Analisa.

"We'll have to share," he said to Tamnyn, who only nodded.

"I'm not used to electronic torches anyway," she whispered to Sohyeon as Adam led the way, looking over the map to see what ground they needed to cover.

"The most obvious and dangerous place to look would be places like those woods behind this outdoor paintball track," Adam said. "Sticking to the sidewalks won't take us anywhere a person could reasonably hide or be hidden."

"I'll take the rear," Tamnyn said.

Adam looked at her in surprise, but Jangsun nodded in agreement, knowing that she was not an average woman from the city and had some real experience in battle, as Sohyeon had explained after his father had come out from under Joriya's spell.

Sohyeon stayed just a few steps in front of Tamnyn and kept a close eye on her as they walked to the other end of the paintball field where the tree line began. Suddenly, his hair stood on end, as if kicked up by a cool, unexpected breeze though the air was still. He had to agree with Tamnyn that this felt ominously familiar somehow, but Sohyeon pushed the distracting thought out of his mind. What did it matter even if it was shaping up to feel just like that night they fled Eokhmisseun? Apprehensive, he waited a moment for Tamnyn to catch up with him to take her arm and guide her as they entered the small forest bordering an area of Addison that had large tracts of land between the houses.

The group moved slowly, staying fairly close together in a disorganized clump, the beams from their lanterns moving across the ground and the trees bordering the narrow path they took through the undergrowth. The glow of Adam's and Jangsun's lanterns was broader but still soft and weak compared to the lengthening shadows as night set in. Adam led them to walk the length of the forest before moving deeper into the trees so they could study the uneven ground and gullies. The only sound they heard was the crunching of twigs, then later the gurgling of water in a shallow creek running along the edges of the property where the forest opened onto a residential lawn.

"Do they think your friend is dead or hiding?" Tamnyn whispered to Sohyeon as Adam turned to lead them deeper into the trees. "It's hard to know where to look."

"I imagine Adam would be looking at the ground more closely since he's trying to find us a safe path to walk. Maybe you should look at the trees to see if they have any odd markings or clues."

"Why are we coming out so late at night anyway?" Analisa asked, overhearing their conversation and drawing closer to them. "Shouldn't they have organized this earlier today or waited until tomorrow? We could break our necks out here, even with Adam's help in navigating this."

Analisa's question left Sohyeon feeling more unsettled than before. She was right, of course, that it seemed silly to try to comb the neighborhood in the dark.

"I think it's because they had to wait 24 hours after he was missing to report him," Philip said. "Even though there was a murder connected to his disappearance, the last time anyone saw him was around 8PM last night, so I think the idea was to get started as soon as the waiting period had ended and they had police department support."

"Have you been on these sorts of things before?" Sohyeon asked. "This is my first time searching for anyone."

"Yeah, I've been on a few searches. Nighttime search parties aren't unheard of. I think this time it is just the urgency of the situation that made it turn out like this, but there will be more searches for at least the first week after Pete MacIntyre's disappearance, I would expect. Was the missing boy your friend?"

"He and I were childhood friends, and I saw him last night before he disappeared."

"I'm sorry to hear that."

Their conversation was cut short when Adam and Jangsun stopped to wait for them to catch up since they had fallen behind.

"What was that all about?" Adam asked. "Did you find something?"

"No, we were just talking about how search parties are run generally since we have a few newbies on this one. Did you see anything so far that looked suspicious?" Philip asked.

"Not yet. In about another 25 paces that way, we'll be in the back of someone's residence and will have a break from this rough terrain."

"But we'll have to come back this way to get the car again, right?" Analisa asked.

"We can walk the perimeter of this area instead of going back through this forest to get to it, so don't worry," Adam said, smiling a little.

"If the body was found so far away in a DC park, why are we looking here for the boyfriend anyway?" Analisa asked.

"They don't know where he disappeared," Adam said. "They think it's possible he could have disappeared closer to home since he hasn't exactly been implicated in her death. It's a logical place to start a search. If he were also killed or injured, we could find him here."

The search party resumed its work, slowly walking the number of blocks they were assigned on their map in around two hours. Finding nothing, they relaxed a bit on the way back to where Adam's car was parked. Turning off their lanterns and flashlights since they were under the streetlights and the full moon, they walked along the sidewalk bordering the main artery through the borough. Traffic had lightened considerably as 10PM had passed, and most of the other residents were home watching TV, which the little group detected from the blue glow visible through their first floor curtains.

"It was nice meeting you, Mr. Choi," Philip said. "It's too bad it was under such circumstances. So where do you practice your sword technique? I'd like to see it sometime."

"He practices at a local *dojang*," Sohyeon said, looking at his father with an indulgent expression. "But you really should try Vince's Paintball Park where we left the car for some real fun. My friends and I go there all of the time. Sword fighting is rather old fashioned."

Jangsun smiled and nodded as Tamnyn threw Sohyeon an irritated look and shook her *mokgum* at him, reminding him of her own skill with the sword.

"I forgot, my girlfriend as well as my dad like the sword."

They all laughed. Vince's place was just up ahead, and everyone quickened their pace, eager to get home for the evening though they would disappoint Mr. MacIntyre with their report. But when they turned the corner, Tamnyn and Sohyeon stopped abruptly at the sight of a small group of people who had arrived at the parking lot in their absence. The others in the search party continued to the car without noticing the couple hung back, and they greeted the group without any particular wariness.

"Did you come out tonight to search for Pete MacIntyre?" Marietta Esposito asked Adam and Jangsun as they passed and nodded in response. "Such a shame what happened to his girlfriend."

She stood next to Detective Mazurek, who was still in his tattered black trench coat, and an impossibly thin, tall man also swathed in black, even wearing the hood of his coat up in spite of the balmy evening. Marietta didn't seem disturbed by the men's odd appearance, however.

"It's the man from the video, isn't it?" Tamnyn whispered to Sohyeon. "What do we do now?"

"I was thinking that, but I didn't know Sukjin showed it to you. We need to find out who he is and why he's with Marietta and the police," Sohyeon whispered back. "It seems my first idea of joining the Welcome Wagon to find out who this guy is was correct. Marietta brought them right to me, and I didn't even have to go to one meeting. Come on. They'll wonder what's wrong with us if we stay back here and avoid them."

"Sohyeon, there you are," Detective Mazurek said, turning around as they walked past him toward the car where the rest of the group now waited. "Did you have any luck finding your friend?"

"Not yet," Sohyeon said, pulling Tamnyn a little closer to him, though he knew she could take care of herself. "What are you guys doing here? We didn't see you when we arrived earlier. You could have joined us in the search."

"Detective Mazurek and his friend wanted to have a look around the facility," Marietta said cheerfully, as if she was just having lunch with one of her friends instead of showing the police around in the middle of a murder investigation.

"His friend?" Sohyeon asked casually. "You didn't mention you had a partner when we talked earlier, Detective Mazurek."

"No, I didn't," Detective Mazurek said. "This is Ognjen Baram. He's new to Addison, though he has lived in the DC area for a while. He and I were associates there."

"Were you planning on booking a paintball party?" Sohyeon asked, trying to keep the sarcasm out of his voice. Ognjen Baram? Sohyeon wondered if there was any way to verify who this man was, but then he remembered that no one had seen Birum's face either. How would they know if this man was their enemy?

Sohyeon felt Tamnyn's fingernails digging into his arm and winced in pain, but he managed to smile at the men, who hadn't answered his question.

"We'd better go," Sohyeon quickly stammered. "It's getting late, and I have to get back to studying for my finals. See you later, Marietta."

They headed back to Adam's station wagon where everyone was already inside watching them. Sohyeon and Tamnyn piled in the middle seat, though Sohyeon caught his father's eye in the front seat and shook his head. As Adam pulled out of the parking lot, Sohyeon saw Marietta enter the building with the two odd men and shuddered. Of course, he thought, even if it was Birum, nothing would happen to her. That would be too obvious, and he would need time to make his move, wouldn't he? Sohyeon sunk into a cloud of depression as the others were making plans to go back out to search Sunday afternoon. When Adam finally dropped the three of them off at the Choi residence, he still hadn't snapped out of it and just wanted to go to bed. How could this be happening? What a crazy day it had been.

14

When Sohyeon woke up, everyone was already downstairs eating breakfast.

"How did I manage to oversleep this morning?" he said as he joined everyone in the kitchen and sat down at the table. He met his father's gaze, and seeing the grim expression there, he poured himself a bowl of cereal without saying anything more.

"Since the search didn't go well last night, do you really think you'll find anything this afternoon?" Alanna asked suddenly, eating the last bite of her waffle. "How many of these things do they normally do when someone is missing anyway?"

"Can I go this time?" Sukjin asked, interrupting the conversation.

"No, you're too young," Jangsun said. "We'll do as many searches as it takes to make Doug MacIntyre feel more at ease. With his son missing, he just wants to be doing something constructive to try to bring him back, and I think he's concerned that Pete might be hurt or dead out there where no one has discovered him yet. I felt the same when Sohyeon and Mirae went missing, though we had no reason to believe it was foul play and Sukjin reassured us they were just with their friends."

Jangsun's gaze shifted to Sohyeon and Joriya.

"And if he really is responsible for the girl's murder?" Alanna asked. "Then what?"

"But wasn't she eaten or something?" Sukjin asked carelessly, taking a bite of a sausage patty. "Would Pete have done something like that?"

"I think she was killed first, dear," Alanna said matter-of-factly. "Wild animals must have gotten to her later. The detective suggested she was murdered around midnight, and it was a good six or seven hours before her body was found."

Jangsun sighed in frustration and stood up, throwing down his cloth napkin on the table beside his empty plate. Alanna looked at him silently in surprise.

"Sohyeon, we need to have a talk right now. You, Tammy and J-, er Mirae, must come with me."

"Sure, dad. Where did you want to talk? I'll bring this with me."

Sohyeon grabbed a few pieces of buttered toast and tossed it on a saucer, and placing his cereal bowl over it, he jumped up to follow the three of them into the living room.

After motioning for the girls to have a seat on the couch, and as Sohyeon sat in one of the leather wing chairs, balancing his plates on the arm as he finished eating, Jangsun slid the doors shut and took his favorite chair in the corner.

"What did you want to talk about?" Sohyeon asked between mouthfuls of cereal.

"The murder. And that man last night."

"The one in black," Sohyeon said wryly. "Yeah, Tamnyn and I were really freaked out when we saw him there with Marietta."

"He's the guy in the video from council chambers, isn't he?" Jangsun asked.

"Well, that's the assumption, isn't it?" Sohyeon said. "All we know is that we have some random guy wearing black from head to toe running around Addison who looks a bit similar to a random guy wearing black from head to toe running around Eokhmisseun who happens to be a black magician immortal beast of some kind who took over that land and turned everyone into monsters. I think that pretty much sums up what we know and suspect."

"So you're saying we can't know for sure who he is?" Jangsun asked.

"The detective told us the man's name," Tamnyn said. "Ognjen Baram."

"Baram, Birum, pretty close, don't you think?" Sohyeon asked. "But that's pretty thin stuff to go on, and we can't just go attacking people based on that kind of evidence, not in this world anyway. Even if we saw his face, it wouldn't do any good. Has anyone actually seen Birum's face?"

"I have, of course," Joriya said. "He is my brother, after all, and I lived with him three hundred years before he fled our world."

"Oh, that's right, so one of us has seen him," Sohyeon said, thoughtfully. "But you never saw him in Eokhmisseun, right Tamnyn? Only wrapped up in that black cloak when he killed your family's servant the night we fled?"

"That's correct. My father or grandfather might have seen his face, but by the time my generation came along, we were confined to our estates and feared traveling outdoors where Birum or his henchmen could find us and turn us."

"Then getting Joriya around him to see his face would be our best way of identifying him?" Jangsun asked.

"Not really," Joriya said, looking at him in alarm. "My brother would recognize me in a moment. He has never seen Mirae and I together, and if he noticed the resemblance when she was brought to his palace with Litt, it may not have meant anything. Seeing one of us here would make him think of me, and since we are enemies, it would give everything away. If he is active here, I need to be very careful leaving your house."

"Mirae could have told him that you were here and that you looked alike," Sohyeon said. "It's possible given the situation that he talked with her. Mapin's message from Pontol stated as much yesterday. He said he found they're being held at the palace."

"If she told him any more than that, he would have instantly killed her," Joriya said, worry creeping into her voice.

"There is another way to identify him potentially," Tamnyn said. "It would be very circumstantial though."

"What way?" Jangsun asked.

"The old stories of how Birum took over Eokhmisseun."

They all looked at Tamnyn in surprise. No one had thought of that.

"What old stories?" Sohyeon asked.

"It would have been in my grandfather's time that Birum first appeared on Eokhmisseun's shores. Even then he was prone to wearing a black cloak and masking his face, from what the histories tell. The capital's ruling council has been in power for a few centuries, and in my grandfather's day, they met regularly at the palace, where their leader lived with his family. For some reason, they brought this odd drifter into their confidence. Does this sound familiar at all? Isn't the video you first saw him in also connected to the ruling council of this place?"

"Well, they aren't exactly the biggest power brokers in society or the world," Sohyeon said, almost laughing. "It's just the local city council where we have a few bureaucrats running things like garbage collection, snow removal and the Welcome Wagon, of course. If Birum wanted to take over America, it would be a strange place to start."

"Maybe someone from another world wouldn't realize the power dynamic," Jangsun said. "Making a tactical error like that might be quite easy if he doesn't know much about our society."

"You mentioned that Khabu had dealings with us before, Tamnyn," Sohyeon said thoughtfully. "Could they have more information on us than we're assuming given that previous contact?"

"I don't know. I'm not sure what Birum knew about Eokhmisseun when he took over, but he got in with our ruling council and gained their trust. The histories note that his magical skill impressed some of them enough for them to argue that he should become a member of the council and a citizen of Eokhmisseun.

"His champions were ambitious in their own right and saw him as a useful tool against their rivals on the council. Dissention among them eventually led to their downfall. Birum was able to exploit it and take over completely during the final years of my grandfather's tenure. My father, who watched the takeover when he was a boy, quietly helped my father organize a new ruling council in the shadows as more of the still whole people in our land kept off of the streets and dared only whisper against our strange new leader. Birum had declared himself king and sought to destroy the remnants of the council not beholden to him."

She fell silent a moment, overcome with emotion.

"What did he do to them?" Joriya asked softly.

"After his crowning as king, Birum pursued them as they fled into the shadows and executed the council members who had once welcomed him publicly. The ones who had helped him became his most loyal aides. He heard rumors about the clandestine council opposing him among those of us still whole, led by my father, son of the man who opposed him most vigorously, my grandfather, and he plotted to bring him down one way or another. Shortly after I was born, he found a way to punish him without killing him."

She stopped again, her voice becoming strained.

"How?" Joriya asked, her voice commanding this time.

"He kidnapped my mother," Tamnyn said, her voice cracking as tears ran down her face. "I just narrowly missed being taken with her. My father had to meet with the council secretly, leaving me and my mother behind, but he suggested I always sleep with an old servant of his who had served him as a child. She was very old, almost eighty then, but very kind. Because I was in my nurse's room that night when Birum's henchmen broke in, they only got my mother. I'm not sure if Birum ever figured out that I was Cargal's daughter or that he even had a daughter. We never heard from my mother again, but there were rumors."

"Rumors?" Joriya asked pointedly. "What kind of rumors?"

"That my mother had become his concubine," Tamnyn said, her voice barely a whisper.

Everyone fell silent for a moment.

"Did they have children?" Joriya asked, finally breaking the silence.

"There were rumors that they had."

"So you may be related to Birum's offspring?" Joriya's eyes turned toward the windows of the living room that looked out onto the rolling lawn. With the lights off in the living room, she could easily see out through the sheer curtains. "Did your father ever tell you that you looked like your mother? Is there any way he could recognize you as a leader in Eokhmisseun? You met him last night, did you not? Would he have recognized either you or Sohyeon from your time there?"

"Yes," Sohyeon said. "I think he could have recognized me, though it was dark last night as well as the night we fled Eokhmisseun. I think when we were running away from him that night, my cloak hood flipped back a few times, and I stripped it off at times as well, so he might have gotten a good look at me. Maybe not so much with Tamnyn. The people not affected by the turning in Eokhmisseun were not as careless as I was about wearing the cloaks and masks when they walked the streets."

"What you are suggesting, Tamnyn," Jangsun said, "is that this sinister figure at the council meeting may be using the same methods that Birum did when he took over your land. Is that correct?"

"There are some undeniable parallels," Sohyeon said. "Though I agree that he's barking up the wrong tree if he wants actual power. Local council is pretty small beans in the larger scheme of things. What could he be up to in trying to take over that?"

"We need to figure out how to confirm that this man is someone from Khabu," Joriya said.

"As an immortal, we have no chance of really killing Birum anyway, so would accidentally wounding him be any help at determining he isn't human?" Sohyeon asked.

"He could get us in trouble by our own laws if you do something like that," Jangsun said grimly. "We already are on the verge of being drawn into this murder case, which reminds me of another question I had. Daria Favreau was half eaten. Unlike my wife, I wonder if it was an injury that was inflicted after the girl's death. Sukjin said the royal family of Eokhmisseun is related to tigers somehow, and Sohyeon said Birum was half-animal, like a werewolf. I'd like to hear more about this, please."

"Yeah, we never discussed Sukjin's statement last night when she said that," Sohyeon said, putting his dishes on the end table and stretching a bit in the chair. "When we saw Birum kill Tamnyn's servant, he didn't use any natural force to do it, yet when he turns humans, they become more animalistic and do kill in more recognizable ways. What is their connection to the tiger, Joriya? You have to tell us now, though I know you don't want to. You always seem evasive when the subject comes up."

"Although we are immortals and are born in human form, we are actually a tiger clan," Joriya said flatly. "Like our subjects, when we reach the age of six or seven hundred years, potentially earlier if we choose to, we change into our animal shape and enter a liminal state in an interdimensional land."

"Which means?" Sohyeon asked.

"We transform into white tigers and return to a suspended state between sleep and wakefulness in the crypt beneath the palace of Khabu. Only the priestesses may enter before her time of retirement."

"Minha!"

"But Litt was taken out and is now with your sister under Birum's control," Joriya said, anguish filling her voice.

"Do you need to eat human flesh?" Jangsun asked.

"No, so I don't know why Birum would be connected with this woman's death," Joriya said. "In fact, I don't know why he would seem animal-like since he is too young to make the transformation and enter the crypt. We usually don't transform into our animal shape until then. It's not like we are always shifting from one form to the other throughout our lives. We are human for centuries with the tiger part of our nature held at bay, though we can transform if we want to, then we transform into our tiger shape for the rest of our existence and never return to our human shape.

"Now it seems Birum has broken this unspoken rule and even caused our ancestral king whom he kidnapped from the crypt to as well. Litt has been a tiger for the better part of 7,500 years, but emerging from the crypt, he has taken on an almost exclusive human form, which your sister is now so enchanted with. But what good does it do for Birum to transform into his tiger shape at this stage?"

"I think humans would find it really terrifying under the right circumstances," Sohyeon said. "Maybe it's just a way to provoke fear in his subjects now that he has gained all of this power in Eokhmisseun. Can he shift to be half and half, like our werewolf? I think that would make him an easily recognizable threat, a monster by our definition, more than him just turning into a wholly animal form. If he has studied other worlds and forbidden magic, he may know that association, know what scares us most, and play into those fears."

"No wonder you like to go talk with Doug MacIntyre," Jangsun said, smiling indulgently at Sohyeon. "You sound a lot like him. But never mind all of this. We need to come up with a solid plan of action to discover what is going on and who this Ognjen Baram really is."

"Then there's only one way I can think of to do that," Sohyeon said. "I talked to Marietta Esposito the other night when I went over to Vince's for dinner, and I asked her if I could join the Addison Welcome Wagon. I can go back over to talk with Vince about getting a job at the paintball park once I graduate and pump Marietta for information."

"When will you do this?" Jangsun asked. "We have to go on the search party this afternoon for a few hours, and you need time to study."

"Let me see if I can run over there around dinner time and catch them," Sohyeon said. "We should be done with the search party by then, shouldn't we?"

Tamnyn stuck close by Sohyeon as they all came to an agreement and dispersed through the house. He had intended on going back to his room to get a few more hours of study in before lunch and the next search party assembly. Sukjin and Joriya stayed downstairs with Jangsun and Alanna, so the two of them were alone on the stairs.

"Did you think of something?" Sohyeon asked, grabbing her hand and pulling her gently up the stairs with him.

"Maybe the immortals of Khabu don't eat human flesh, but there are those who do," Tamnyn whispered, looking troubled.

As they reached the upstairs hallway, he stopped her and thought for a moment.

"What do you mean? Do you mean the purge on the night we left Eokhmisseun?"

"After the citizens were turned by Birum's magic and became ghost slaves, they acquired a taste for all sorts of flesh out of proportion to normal human needs, even human flesh as the magic replaced their humanity altogether."

"You're probably right," Sohyeon said, remembering the boy they encountered as they fled from Birum that night, and even Pontol when he bit Sohyeon's hand. "But that would mean some of my people were turned by Birum's magic somehow, wouldn't it? Birum has power here then if that has happened."

He walked into his bedroom and sat back down at his desk, letting the warm afternoon breeze blowing through his open window calm him. This situation was getting so out of control. What could they possibly do if Birum had arrived in Addison? He closed his eyes a moment.

Tamnyn put her hand on his shoulder, and he looked up at her.

"Maybe some of the ghost slaves from Eokhmisseun have come here," she said softly. "Maybe they followed Pontol's route, like you feared. But if Birum has come here, it won't be long before he overtakes your land. Unlike Eokhmisseun, Addison doesn't have any knowledge of magic or any power that can stop him."

"We have technology. Even your father made use of that against Birum."

"Did he? We lived like prisoners on our estate. I'm not sure how helpful any of his inventions ever were compared to Birum's craftiness and power. I will go with you to talk with Marietta later and ask questions too, if you will let me."

Sohyeon nodded.

"You should go back down now and show my father your real sword techniques, stuff he can really use in battle, not the tournament stuff he knows to look cool in public."

Tamnyn smiled and went back out to the hallway, shutting Sohyeon's door behind her, leaving him to stare at his textbook.

15

"Searching for Pete in the daytime will be much easier, I would presume," Doug MacIntyre said after everyone had arrived at his house to begin their afternoon reconnaissance.

"So the police haven't come up with any new leads as to his whereabouts since we were here last night?" one of the older men standing near the front of the group asked.

"Nothing more has come up." Doug MacIntyre's voice broke mid-sentence, and he paused a minute to take a deep breath and collect himself. "Would everyone please get in the same groups and cover the same ground you looked over last night? That would make it easier, I think."

"Not everyone came back today, and we have some new people," Detective Mazurek said from the back of the group of about 50 people.

"That's fine. We can make do with whoever we have and fill in where we need to. I'm just grateful we have this many people to help today."

Everyone moved to the makeshift tables where the gear and maps were laid out for them again. Jangsun got their map and came back to stand with Sohyeon and Tamnyn, while Analisa and Philip joined them. This time, Adam wasn't helping out.

"I think I heard he got tied up at the fire station," Detective Mazurek said when he got to their group after checking in with the others starting to depart.

"Then I'll have to take my car today," Jangsun said, turning to go, then stopping mid-step as if he thought of something. "That reminds me, how did you like the paintball park? Sohyeon told me he spoke with you outside of it right before we left after the search. Were you planning on hosting a party for the people in your precinct? I would imagine for professionals like you, it would be a lot like work. We had a nice party there a few months back for our *dojang*, just to socialize together for once outside of tournament preparation and to try on new skills. I can't recommend it enough."

Detective Mazurek looked at him blankly and nodded.

"Umm, something like that. I'll have to ask her again when the facility is available." He started to drift away from their group, but Jangsun wasn't quite finished using the opportunity to find out what was going on.

"Sohyeon told me we had a new neighbor who came with you to the paintball park last night," Jangsun said in his friendliest tone. "His name sounded very foreign when Sohyeon said it, and I have to admit I'm always curious when I hear someone with an exotic name like mine has moved into the neighborhood. Will he be coming to any of the borough functions? Where is he from?"

Detective Mazurek gave him a tense smile and paused.

"Ognjen is from Eastern Europe, I believe, and I'll be sure Marietta invites him to the borough hot dog bash over Fourth of July, but remember, I'm not a resident of Addison. You'll have to talk with her later about that. Good day, Mr. Choi."

Detective Mazurek made a slight saluting motion to Jangsun as he left them and continued on to greet the leader of the last search party preparing to leave the MacIntyre house. His eyes meeting Sohyeon's, Jangsun waved for the group to follow him to his car parked a little down the street. As Sohyeon got in the passenger seat beside him and the rest piled into the back, Jangsun turned to him.

"Did you hear all of that? Remember to ask that, too, tonight when you speak with the Espositos," he said in a low voice so the others couldn't hear.

"Yeah, I heard. I can hardly wait to invite myself over for dinner tonight."

"Just be careful. You might run into him at dinner if Marietta Esposito is escorting him around Addison."

He drove the car down to the paintball park and found a space on the far end of the parking lot near the edge of the property where the forest began. This time the parking lot was full of cars closer to the door.

"There must be a party booked now," Sohyeon said as they started to get out of the car. "Vince should be here now."

"Do you want to run in and make sure he will be home at dinnertime?" Jangsun asked as the others grouped around them.

"It can wait until we're done here. They'll probably still be here by the time we finish."

"In two hours? It's two now, so that will be around four, close to dinner time."

"Don't worry about it. I'll figure something out later. Who is going to lead the group?"

"I will this time," Philip said, and Analisa fell in behind him with her high-powered flashlight.

Jangsun took up the middle position with his walking stick, and Sohyeon and Tamnyn took up the rear, Tamnyn wielding her *mokgum* and Sohyeon also carrying a walking stick this time.

In the sunny afternoon, the little forest separating Vince's paintball park from the housing development was shadowy but not too dark to see into. Analisa didn't need to turn her flashlight on except to examine a few dark crevices they came across. Philip had his phone out to take photos in one hand and the map in the other. Leaves and twigs crunched under their feet pleasantly as they enjoyed the warm day.

"At least it didn't rain overnight," Sohyeon said nervously to his father. "We'd have a muddy mess to slog through if it had."

His father laughed a little too loudly, startling Philip and Analisa, who looked back at them in surprise. Sohyeon wondered why they should all feel so jumpy. No one seemed that tense when they walked this route in the dark last night, so what exactly was the problem today? He didn't know Analisa or Philip well enough to know why they seemed more nervous this time, however, for the Chois, maybe it was meeting the man they suspected was actually Birum. Now they had a focal point for their concerns.

It took about 45 minutes to walk the forest, searching every tree and ditch carefully for signs of Pete. Next they emerged from the trees to walk along the far edge of the housing plan's expansive backyards, a mark of upper middle class suburbia. Sohyeon didn't know anyone who lived on this side of Addison, but he looked at the backs of the houses with mild interest as they walked along the neatly cut grass past them. Each house had its own special porch design and landscaping. A few people who were sitting outside waved, and one came down to talk to them.

Jangsun had the group wait for the young man dressed in a shirt and jeans, carrying a stack of Styrofoam cups and a pitcher of punch for them.

"I had heard there were search parties out around the neighborhood today looking for that missing boy. Are you one of them? Any luck? I brought you some refreshments in case you were thirsty."

"Thanks," Jangsun said, nodding politely but not taking the man up on his offer. Analisa, however, poured some for her and Philip. Tamnyn also poured a cup. "Yes, we're searching for the boy, but nothing so far. The police thought the woods here might be an important place to look. Have you seen anything unusual going on over the past few days around the neighborhood?"

"Not that I can think of," the man said. "I know a lot of people are upset because it was such a gruesome crime, and if the boy did it and is hiding somewhere here, then we're in a lot of trouble."

"I think there is also some concern that he may have been a victim of whatever killed Ms. Favreau," Jangsun said hastily, though Sohyeon turned away, thinking of the ghost slaves.

They quickly continued their search as the man returned to his porch to read the paper.

"I wonder if they will do a house to house search next," Philip said when they paused to study the map to see if there were any more places a person could hide or a body could have been dumped that they hadn't looked over yet.

"House to house? Why would they need to do that?" Jangsun asked, alarmed.

"If the residents are really worried Pete is alive and dangerous, they may demand something more thorough." Philip paused and ran a finger over a spot on the map. "Wait a minute. Did we check here last night? I don't remember going to any storm drain down the street. Isn't that where the little creek we saw in the forest flows?"

Jangsun looked at the spot he was pointing to and frowned.

"I don't think we did. It was too dark outside, and Adam steered us clear of it so we wouldn't fall or get hurt there. Even with flashlights, it would be a treacherous place to walk, if it's the place I'm thinking of."

"We should definitely go there now, shouldn't we?"

"This time we shouldn't avoid looking anyplace," Jangsun agreed, waving for the others to follow him further down the tree line at the edge of the street.

They quickly covered the distance and passed the last house on the block, turning down a winding path to a creek bed on a lightly forested piece of land. The place definitely didn't look familiar to Sohyeon from their walk the night before, but then too in an odd way, it seemed very familiar. Suddenly, he grabbed Tamnyn's arm as a small house came into view, set deeper into the trees so it couldn't be easily seen from the road.

"What does that remind you of?" he whispered, pulling her closer to him and pointing at the house.

"That house?" she asked, her eyes growing wide.

"It doesn't look like any of the others on the street. It makes me think of Eokhmisseun. Do you see?"

Tamnyn gasped.

"Pontol's shack!"

"But it's not Pontol's shack, now is it? Could there be more than one way to reach Eokhmisseun from my world?"

Tamnyn looked at the house in astonishment, shaking her head.

"I don't think there would be. It can't really be his house. This house looks far too well-kept compared to

that old place where he lives. The woods around it were denser too."

"Hey, aren't we supposed to stay together?" Philip called from the front of the line. Sohyeon and Tamnyn had fallen far behind them as they turned the corner and were starting down a set of natural steps to the large, man-sized concrete storm drain on the property.

"It's daylight, so is it that important now?" Sohyeon asked. "Did you see the house up here?"

Philip doubled back to talk to them while Jangsun and Analisa waited.

"I don't think it's a good idea to split up right now, but what did you have in mind? Did you want to question the people living here?"

"It just seems really out of place, doesn't it? A house like this in a neighborhood this ritzy?"

"That must be why Adam led us away from it in the dark. I can see why you are drawn to it, though. We should investigate it further, but first, let's all go down to the storm drain and look around. Then we can go up to the house and see who is around, together. I have an uneasy feeling about us going separately."

"I can respect that," Sohyeon said slowly, also feeling uneasy about the house. Holding Tamnyn's hand tightly, he pulled her along behind Philip to join the others.

Analisa reached the storm drain first, though she didn't get close to the large opening. The concrete beam that it ran under ultimately met the sidewalk at the end of the street, and the bed of the drain was still covered with tree branches from a storm they had last week. Sohyeon noted how cold it seemed here compared to when they were out in the open crossing people's lawns.

"We should maybe dig around here," Philip said. "This would be a prime location for a person to hide something."

The five of them all stood in the drain bed and began pushing the branches out of the way. Analisa took her flashlight over to the drain to see inside the dark passageway.

Suddenly, Jangsun gave a strangled cry, his eyes riveted on the branches at his feet.

Philip ran over to Jangsun, his phone out and set on record. Sohyeon and Tamnyn ran over to him too, while Analisa hung back, watching apprehensively from the drain pipe opening.

"What have you found?" Philip asked.

"It looks like bloody clothes." Jangsun picked up a long branch from the stack nearby and poked at the cloth lying on the concrete drain bed.

Sohyeon studied the clothing carefully, noting it probably was Pete's size.

"Wait a minute, dad," he said. "Turn it over so I can see the pocket. Pete like a certain brand of shirt, though this is pretty formal and not what I saw him wearing before I left his house Friday night."

"The missing person's report had a description of him wearing a dress shirt and dress slacks out on his date with Daria," Philip said. "He must have changed for his date after you saw him."

Jangsun moved the stick to flip the fabric over just enough to see the front of the garment, revealing an embroidered crest.

"That was also on the report," Philip said.

Sohyeon nodded.

"It looks like Pete's shirt. Can you pull it out of the muck, or is that against crime scene protocol?"

Jangsun didn't wait for an answer but turned the stick so it caught the shirt by the collar and lifted it up. Sohyeon could see streaks of blood running down the front of the shirt, and the cuffs of the sleeves were tattered and torn up. Otherwise, it seemed intact, as if Pete had taken it off and discarded it.

"How would it end up in that condition?" Jangsun asked. "Does the blood look like it was from wounds he may have sustained?"

"I don't think so," Tamnyn said, looking at it carefully. "I would say someone wiped blood on him, as if they were trying to grab him or stop him."

"Were Daria's hands bloody when they found her?" Sohyeon asked.

"I don't know," Jangsun said, putting the shirt back down where they found it. "Did the report say anything about that?"

"It only discussed Pete's appearance when his father last saw him and some potential places he may have gone," Philip said, turning off the video recording he was making.

A snapping twig up on the ridge from the direction they had come made them all jump and turn.

No one was on the ridge. Everyone stayed quiet, looking around frantically to find the source of the noise, but all was quiet. After a few minutes, they all relaxed and turned their attention back to the shirt.

"We should report this to the police right away, shouldn't we?" Philip asked, typing quickly into his phone. "I'll let Mr. MacIntyre know that we found something and send him the link for the uploaded video I took in case they need it right away."

"Maybe we should get out of here," Jangsun said. "Now that we've found this clue, I think we should let the professionals take over searching the area. It may be too dangerous for us to stay here now."

"I know what you mean," Philip said, turning. "Analisa!"

Everyone turned to look toward the storm drain. Analisa was gone.

"Did she go into the drain while we were looking at the shirt?" Jangsun asked, his voice growing shrill though he was almost whispering.

"We can't leave without her," Philip said in a tight voice, moving toward the drain opening, calling to her.

Jangsun looked back at Sohyeon and Tamnyn helplessly.

"We should get out of here now before something else happens," he said quietly to Sohyeon. "If she went into the drain herself when we weren't looking, she's stupid. If someone grabbed her, then we will be in great danger if we continue looking for her. Stop him, and let's get out of here."

"If she's his girlfriend, we won't be able to stop him," Sohyeon said, walking past his father toward Philip, holding his walking stick in a ready position. "Hey, Philip, the police should be here soon since you sent that text, so why don't we leave. I'm sure Analisa is fine. She couldn't go that far, right? It's too dark for us to follow her in here."

Sohyeon stood next to Philip at the edge of the drain pipe, looking in as far as the light would let them. Analisa was the only one of them with a flashlight, so they couldn't see far very into the pipe. Why would she enter it all of the sudden? Feeling his hair stand on end, he grabbed Philip's upper arm.

"Let's get out of here now, man," he said emphatically in Philip's ear. "What good will it do her if you follow her and you get hurt, too? We need to get to safety and let the cops take over. Let them look for her. Why would she think to go in there at all when we found something out here?"

Philip looked at him, his face pale and visibly shaken. Biting his lip, he turned to go with Sohyeon. The four of them scrambled back up to the ridge above the drain pipe, all feeling uneasy. Philip whipped out his phone again and typed some more while they looked down at the drain.

"I sent Mr. MacIntyre another text telling him Analisa is missing, too. At least someone knows."

They turned toward the road and started to walk past the sinister little house. Sohyeon looked at it in fascination again, and Tamnyn noticed the direction of his gaze.

"Now isn't the time, Sohyeon," she said.

"Philip," Sohyeon said softly, walking more quickly to catch up with him. "Take some video of that house before we leave."

"I don't want to hang around here any longer," Jangsun said, clearly on edge, a note of warning in his voice.

"I can do it while we walk," Philip said. "Hold on to me so I don't trip, Sohyeon."

Sohyeon and Tamnyn each took an arm and guided him as he started to record the house.

"No one seems to be around," Tamnyn said.

"Odd, don't you think, that Adam steered us away from this place?" Sohyeon asked.

His father looked back at him, his brow furrowing even deeper than before.

"Odd or a blessing? We might not have seen the shirt, and maybe something worse would have happened to us if we had come here last night."

Philip turned off the video recording after a few minutes, and the four of them picked up their pace, nearly running to get back to the main street. Once they reached the street, they walked quickly back toward the paintball facility, past the thickest part of the forest, only now they eyed it nervously.

"Mr. Choi, can we go back the other way where there are more people?" Philip asked suddenly, his voice cracking with the strain.

They all stopped and looked at Jangsun.

"I can have Doug or your mother bring me back to get the car later," he said, eying Philip in concern.

They doubled back the way they came, walking briskly past the drain and the little house until they reached a 7-11 on the corner of a block of shops and restaurants at the edge of Addison's business district. It was close to 3:30.

"Why haven't we seen any police coming here or heard sirens or anything?" Sohyeon asked, unnerved by the silence even in town. "Shouldn't Mr. MacIntyre have gotten in touch with them by now? He was supposed to be waiting for any report from the search parties."

"We'll find out when we get to the house," Jangsun said as they quickened their pace to reach a popular pub across from the 7-11. "I'll call your mother from here and have her come get us."

16

When they got to the pub, the four of them went straight back to sit in one of the larger booths, then stared at one another in shock for a moment.

"What do we do now?" Sohyeon asked in a low voice. "Did Mr. MacIntyre ever answer you, Philip? Why we haven't we seen or heard any police."

"You already asked that. Do you really think any of us knows what's happened?" Philip said tensely, pulling out his phone and looking over his texts again. "Nothing. Maybe we should swing by his place and talk with him in person on the way back to your house. Is he a really tech-savvy guy?"

"Probably not, but with all of this going on, I can't imagine he couldn't have read a simple text message," Sohyeon said.

Jangsun held out his hand toward Sohyeon, gesturing to the cell phone.

"Let me call your mother to come pick us up, and we can drive past there," he said as Sohyeon gave him the phone. "Get whatever you want in the meantime, and I'll pay for it, but get it take out since we won't be here long."

"I don't really feel like eating right now," Tamnyn said, gripping her *mokgum* tightly.

"Let's order pizza and take it home with us," Sohyeon suggested.

"There are seven of us," Jangsun said, waiting for the phone to pick up on the other end. "Get at least two."

Sohyeon waved the waitress over, and she took their order. By the time he was finished, Jangsun had handed the phone back to Sohyeon and turned to Philip.

"Come home with us tonight until things settle down," he said. "Something about all of this feels wrong.

My wife is sending my daughter Sukjin over with the car, and she should only be a few minutes. How long will we have to wait for the pizzas, Sohyeon?"

"It should be ready by the time she gets here. Ten or fifteen minutes. I got the thin crust."

"Okay, then what should we do next. Call Detective Mazurek?" Jangsun asked.

"Call Vince and tell him that we'll be by later to pick up the car at the paintball park," Sohyeon said. "I guess my plan to stop by his house is off after this. You know, I can't figure out why, but I agree with you that something about all of this feels wrong, in a big way. I wouldn't call Mazurek, though. Something about him makes my skin crawl. I know I shouldn't feel that way, but I do."

"Yes, I think we should get home as soon as possible," Jangsun said. "Get the pizzas, run quickly past Doug's, then go home and stay home. That sounds like the best plan. I'll call Vince when we get there."

"We need to lock the doors and windows," Tamnyn said, looking very tense and distracted. "I'm surprised you feel it, too, Mr. Choi. Sohyeon was with me the night that it happened…".

"Not here, Tamnyn," Sohyeon said softly, looking over at Philip nervously.

"Detective Mazurek seemed okay, though I can understand why you'd think he was a little off," Philip said, thinking. "He didn't look very professional any of the times I saw him. But if Mr. MacIntyre didn't call him for some reason, we definitely should. Analisa is missing now along with Peter MacIntyre, and I really am worried about her."

"Was she your girlfriend?" Jangsun asked gently.

"Not really. We had a few classes together, and we were both volunteer guides for new student tours. We just hit it off and became friendly. Still, it's freaky to watch someone just vanish into thin air like that, especially in the middle of a murder case in such a scary location."

"Could she have run into the pipe on her own?" Jangsun asked.

"Why would she have done something like that?" Philip asked pensively. "I don't know her well enough to say, but maybe. Regardless, she could get hurt in there and will need help if she did. It's funny, though, that she didn't call out to us if she was inside and merely injured. That suggests something much more sinister has happened to her."

They sat in silence until the pizzas came. A few minutes later, Sohyeon got a text message from Sukjin saying she was outside. Grabbing the pizzas, Sohyeon and the others went out to the car, Jangsun getting in the front seat with Sukjin and Tamnyn, Philip and Sohyeon piling in the back.

"Why is it so dark out already?" Sukjin asked, turning down Doug MacIntyre's street once everyone got in. The smell of pepperoni and mushroom pizzas filled the car and made Sohyeon's stomach growl. "It's only a little after four."

"It looks like there's a storm coming," Tamnyn said, pointing out the back window toward the steely clouds sweeping across the sky. "We shouldn't get the other car tonight. Leave it for later. We need to get in the house and wait it out right now."

"Is it somehow connected to this murder case?" Philip asked in astonishment. "I have to admit, everything feels kind of distorted right now."

"Distorted how?" Jangsun asked.

"I don't know. I can't describe it. It's almost like we've stepped into another world."

"We didn't, but something has definitely arrived," Sohyeon said ominously, pulling up the local news on his phone. "There's nothing on the news so far about the search parties or anyone calling to report what we found."

"Doug's house is up ahead," Jangsun said.

A few minutes later, Sukjin slowed the car as they reached Pete's house. The MacIntyre house, now dark and shut up tight, looked deserted. No one waited on the front lawn where the flimsy search party tables were still set up, the last few missing person fliers fluttering under a paperweight in the breeze. She stopped the car in the middle of the street.

"What are you doing, Sukjin?" Jangsun asked, looking around frantically.

"No one's here at all," she said, clearly spooked. "The whole street looks deserted. Didn't you say there was a big crowd conducting the searches today?"

"Shouldn't one of us go out and take a look around?" Sohyeon asked. "Maybe Mr. MacIntyre got cold and went in to get dinner. Let me go up and knock on the door at least to see if he got Philip's message."

An uneasy silence filled the car. Without waiting for a response, Sohyeon handed the hot pizzas off to Philip as he opened the door and jumped out, leaving the car door ajar and his walking stick behind. Sprinting across the lawn to the front door, he reached out to press the doorbell and noticed the door was slightly ajar. Sohyeon froze. What should he do now? Touching the door lightly, he pushed it open very slowly and stepped into the foyer.

The house was dark, and it stunk of wet animal. Feeling for the light switch, Sohyeon flipped it on and nearly fell back onto the stoop as he recoiled from the sight. The foyer walls had been slashed, perhaps with a long knife or claws, and on one wall something had scrawled words in blood, only the letters looked so alien Sohyeon was sure it was written in either the language of Khabu or Eokhmisseun. Seeing a small, black rectangle on the floor near the threshold between the foyer and Doug MacIntyre's study, Sohyeon slowly walked over to it, staring at it in fascination. Leaning over it, he touched the smart phone's screen and saw the notification for unread messages on it.

He never got Philip's messages, Sohyeon thought in despair. They had first tried to text Doug MacIntyre at least an hour ago. Had the house been like this for that long? What had happened to the other search parties when they returned, if they had returned? Sohyeon felt like he should search the house to see if Doug MacIntyre was just missing or if he was dead, but something wouldn't let him move. He felt overcome with such a sense of terror that it didn't matter which it was. He just wanted to get out of there.

Leaving the foyer lights on behind him, he stepped out into the much too dark afternoon and ran back to the car, jumping into the open door and slamming it behind him. His hand shook as he locked it.

"Lock the doors, all of you, and let's get home."

"What did you find?" Jangsun asked. "Why did you leave the lights on?"

"He's gone. Something happened in there. He never got Philip's messages, and we need to get out of here before whatever got him returns. Sukjin, take us home. Now!"

Sukjin didn't need to be asked again. She immediately shifted gears and hit the gas pedal, turning down the street that would take them back to the Chois' house.

"Is he dead?" Jangsun asked, clearly in shock.

"I don't know, but the place was ripped up, and there was something scrawled in blood on the wall. I couldn't read it, but I'm sure Tamnyn or Joriya could."

"Really?" Sukjin asked. "Then they're here?"

"Shut up and drive," Sohyeon growled, looking behind them to see if anyone was on the road. The streetlights were now coming on, but the neighborhood showed almost no signs of life. Only a few windows here and there in some of the houses were lit. Many were dark. Too dark for Sohyeon's liking.

When they arrived at their house, everyone spilled out of the car and ran in as Sukjin shut off the car, hitting a button so the garage door would close behind them. It was so dark outside, it looked like midnight even though it was only around 5PM. Sunset wasn't supposed to arrive at this time of year until almost 9PM. When the garage door was firmly closed, Sohyeon turned off the light and closed and locked the connecting door. Sukjin and Tamnyn had already enlisted Joriya and Alanna in shutting and locking all of the doors and windows in the house while Jangsun and Philip got out plates and served the pizzas. At least nothing had happened at their house, Sohyeon thought in relief.

"We have too many big windows," Jangsun said as he walked around the downstairs a moment with Sohyeon, making sure the window blinds were closed and the curtains drawn. "When we're done eating, I'm going to reinforce the windows and tape the window blinds down so there are no gaps on the first floor. I think we should have a little time before anything else happens, and the second floor should be okay for now. Was this the way it was in Eokhmisseun?"

"Yes. Tamnyn's family estate was still easy to enter if you knew how, but they rarely left and were careful when they did. The upper floors were left much more open. They also had a lot of weapons and armor, and the house had gardens planted in an inner courtyard so they didn't have to go out and buy food anywhere."

"I have some extra practice swords in the basement that we can all use, though I can't do much about the food situation. We're dependent on the grocery stores for that."

"Tamnyn has the executioner's dagger, too. But is that enough? We need to call Vince."

"And what do you think Vince will be able to do?"

The women came back downstairs and gathered in the kitchen with Philip. Jangsun and Sohyeon joined them. They all ate eagerly in silence.

Finally, Alanna looked at Sohyeon in concern.

"Did you find anything during today's search?" she asked, trying to sound as light and normal as possible.

"We did find something," Jangsun said cautiously, his face grim, "but no one seemed to be around to investigate it further, and one of our search party members disappeared while we were out."

"Something is wrong then?" she asked, a note of fear in her voice. "Is that why you had us shut the windows and lock up everything?"

"Yes, but we'll talk about that later," Jangsun said. "Right now we have a lot of preparation to do."

Sohyeon realized they had not gotten around to telling her the truth about what was happening and made a mental note to tell his father it was time to bring her into their confidence, maybe Philip too since he was now stranded at their house. When they finished eating, Alanna started toward the stairs with Joriya.

"Let me get the spare blankets out for you, Philip. You'll have to share a room with Sohyeon if you're going to be staying the night. "

"Sohyeon, we should go downstairs and get out my extra swords for everyone," Jangsun said, standing. "We need to talk anyway."

The two men went down the stairs off the kitchen while Sukjin, Tamnyn and Philip stayed in the kitchen, drinking coffee.

"I didn't expect things to get like this," Sohyeon said as they opened up the chest where Jangsun kept all of his *kumdo* gear.

"Perhaps you should have. From the story you told me, this seems to be the inevitable outcome if whatever was happening in the other world is pushing into ours.
You should get a weapon you are more comfortable with than that walking stick."

Sohyeon looked around the room a moment and saw his old wooden baseball bat in the corner. That was more his speed than spears or swords.

"Tamnyn has a real short sword with her that she brought when she fled Eokhmisseun," Sohyeon said. "I guess at this point we need to use weapons that can do actual damage. I was hoping to get those arrows and crossbow training from Vince before anything happened. We should call him, shouldn't we?"

"At some point, yes, if we can get through. Who knows how long the electricity will be on and the phone lines working. I need to tell your mother what is going on and the truth about your sister."

"Yeah, I think that's a good idea, too, and I was going to suggest it."

Sohyeon put his walking stick in the pile of weapons his father was making in the center of the basement floor and went to get the baseball bat. Suddenly, his phone rang. He pulled it out of his pocket and looked at the display. A call was coming in, rather than a text message, but the number shocked him.

"Pete!"

"What?" his father said, looking up from the chest of weapons in alarm.

"It's a call from Pete. I should take it, shouldn't I?"

"Answer it, but don't tell him where you are. Try to get answers from him about what happened."

"Hello?" Sohyeon said warily into the phone after hitting the answer button.

"Sohyeon? Thank God I finally got someone. I've been trying everyone for the past few hours, but no one has been picking up," Pete said.

"What's going on, Pete? I'm kind of surprised to hear from you after our talk the other night. You didn't seem too happy to see me."

"I'm sorry about all of that," Pete said sheepishly. "Did you hear what happened?"

"Not really. I just heard you were missing."

"Not even about Daria?" he asked, his voice wavering. He started to sob into the phone. Sohyeon wondered if maybe Pete didn't know what was happening and suddenly felt sorry for him. "She's dead, Sohyeon. The love of my life is dead."

"What happened that night?" Sohyeon asked, looking at his father with wide eyes.

Jangsun pulled out a real single-edged steel sword, a traditional *hwando*, and quickly unsheathed it to look at it, ignoring Sohyeon but clearly aware of the conversation.

Pete was crying so hard, he couldn't answer Sohyeon for a moment.

"I can't believe she's dead, Sohyeon, and in such a horrible way. It's dangerous to be out tonight. Do you see how dark it is already? It's not natural for summertime. I should come over and tell you the whole story. You're home, right?"

"Come over?" Sohyeon looked up at Jangsun in alarm, and Jangsun vigorously shook his head no. "I don't think that's a good idea, Pete. We have company tonight, mom's got friends over, and aren't people looking for you? If you're in some kind of trouble, it would be best you stay away for now until things die down."

"I really need your help, Sohyeon. Don't abandon me now after all the years we've been friends. I can risk all of that and come over. I can come to the back door where no one will know I'm there."

"Where are you? I'll come to you instead."

There was a long silence.

"At home."

Sohyeon thought of the way the MacIntyre home looked when he had gone in and shuddered. Was this really Pete? Had he done that to his own house? Perhaps his father was dead too?

"Really? So you have talked to your dad? I know he was worried about you and had people over to try to find you."

"They all must have gone home. Now I'm here alone. I don't know where dad went. Maybe he's with the police.

If he brings them back here, I'll have to leave. Can I stay with you for a while, Sohyeon?"

"Let me run over there, and we can talk, okay? Mom's little tea party won't be over for a while, and the Detective is supposed to stop by later tonight to take our statements. It's too dangerous for you here if you're trying to avoid the police for some reason."

"It's so dark out," Pete said in a whiny voice.

"Yeah, I'll bring a flashlight. It will be okay, Pete. I'll be there in a few minutes. Just stay there and wait for me. I'll come around to the back porch."

"Ok, ok. I'll be here, Sohyeon. Don't take too long. All of this has been pretty frightening, and I don't know where dad is."

Sohyeon hung up the phone and looked at his father grimly.

"Did you hear that?"

"You have to go over there?"

"If I don't, he'll come here, and I don't trust what is going on with him. He told me he's at his house, but I told you what it looked like when I went in. If he's there, then he's lying about what's going on. Maybe he even did that. He didn't even mention the condition of the house, though he did mention that his father was missing."

"You shouldn't go alone. Do you want me to go with you?"

"If you come with me, who will guard our house? No, I'll get Tamnyn to go. She's got the real, edged sword, too, and she's used to battling these things."

"I can go, too. I know how to use a sword. A *mokgum* can inflict some damage even if it doesn't have an edge."

The men turned around and saw Sukjin on the stairs. Jangsun looked at her fearfully, biting his lip but not objecting.

"She should stay here," Sohyeon said. "She did good driving our getaway car, but I'm not sure how she'll do fighting monsters. I'm not even sure *I'm* up to it."

"I'm too young, I know," she said, coming down into the basement and grabbing one of the wooden swords. "But I at least know how to fight."

"Dad," Sohyeon said, but he saw his father studiously examining one of the bamboo *jukdo* swords. "I guess you could, Sukjin, but do mom or Philip know how to use any weapons? Joriya might, but I'm sure she hasn't ever seen a real battle. We need a few competent people to remain here at the house should trouble come to our door."

"I know how to fight some, though not with swords," Philip said, coming down the steps behind Sukjin. Tamnyn was with them, too.

"How much did you overhear?" Sohyeon asked, looking at them in alarm.

"Not much. Just enough to know we will need to fight…something," Philip said, coming down to stand next to Jangsun in the middle of the pile of weapons.

"Pete called," Sohyeon said, slipping his phone into his pocket. "He said he was home now, but he wants to come over. Tamnyn, we need to go there and keep him away from here. Something isn't right about this. I saw the house, and the condition was terrible, but he didn't seem to notice. I just have a bad feeling about this."

"I'll get my sword."

"We should go now before Pete gets impatient," Sohyeon said, starting up the stairs after Tamnyn.

"Don't go on foot," Sukjin called after them. "Take your bike so you can make a fast, quiet getaway. Dad, I think we should turn off the lights and probably stay on the upper floor until morning."

"There are a few more preparations I want to make downstairs, but that sounds about right. Sohyeon, text me if you can when you return so I can be ready at the door to let only you and Tamnyn back in."

He nodded and followed Tamnyn back to the kitchen. As she ran upstairs and returned with her steel sword , Sohyeon put his windbreaker on and grabbed his baseball bat.

"Ready?" he asked.

"It's going to be Birum," Tamnyn said. "You know that, don't you?"

"Don't say that. We don't know for sure who that creepy new resident is. My bike is in the garage. You can ride behind me since the seat is big, and I'm good at riding with a passenger. I used to take Sukjin on it with me when she was little. We can go out the side door with it so no one will hear the garage door opening or have a chance to sneak in the house through it."

He secured the bat with a hook and loop sling like a yoga mat strap so he could fasten it around his torso. Since he was steering the bike, he handed the bat off to Tamnyn to carry along with her sword which had a similar device on its sheath. Both fit around her well enough, though Sohyeon thought the arrangement might be a bit awkward if they found themselves in a real fight. At least for now, they wouldn't need to wear the capes they had in Eokhmisseun and could still move somewhat freely.

"Come on," he said, leading her into the garage and bringing the bike over to the garage's side door.

17

It only took a few minutes to reach the MacIntyre house by bicycle. Sohyeon parked it near a shrub at the edge of the front lawn so it wouldn't be as noticeable to anyone walking around the neighborhood. After flipping down the kickstand, he and Tamnyn headed stealthily for the back door. The house was dark, the front door now shut. Sohyeon wondered again how Pete could be here, how anyone could have closed the door and not seen the damage that had been there only an hour or two before. He felt his phone in his pants pocket vibrate, but he ignored it for now, taking his baseball bat from Tamnyn and casually carrying it propped up on his shoulder as if he were going to a game. He saw Tamnyn also had her sword unsheathed and was carrying it casually like she had the *mokgum* earlier, with the blade down where it could easily be shifted into a defensive position.

When they rounded the corner, they snuck toward the back porch. Although Sohyeon had been to Pete's house before, he had never been in the backyard. As he would have expected of the MacIntyres, big pots holding a few types of the exotic flowers his father had favored lined the porch's far side and the edge opposite the house, providing some cover. Its concrete slab was even with the grass with no stairs, so it would be easy to fight and flee if necessary. A line of bushes on either side of the yard separated the MacIntyre's yard from their neighbors' and gave them a moderate amount of privacy. The backyard disappeared into a grove of trees.

"It looks like no one's around," Tamnyn whispered to him, slipping her hand around his upper arm as she crept closer. "Should we knock on the door?"

"I don't know. There aren't any lights on, so it looks like no one is home. Someone has been trying to call me, but I'm not answering the phone right now."

"Maybe it's your father."

"I don't have time for that now, and he knows it. No, it's probably Pete, but I'm not answering it. Let's try knocking a little."

Sohyeon and Tamnyn walked up to the back door, Tamnyn looking around in all directions behind them as he guided her across the patio.

"The other houses are all dark, too," she said. "Isn't it a bit too early for that?"

"It is. All of this is so strange and unusual."

Reaching out to knock on the door, a sudden motion to the left of them startled Sohyeon, and he jumped back into Tamnyn's arms.

"Who's there?" Sohyeon whispered sharply as a shadowy figure emerged from behind the bushes near the yard's boundary. Pulling a small flashlight out of his jacket pocket, he snapped it on and pointed it at the figure. "Who are you?" he asked in astonishment as the light played over the features of his friend. "Pete?"

Tamnyn sucked in her breath behind him.

"Ghost slave," she whispered, using the ancient tongue of her nation so Pete couldn't overhear.

Sohyeon knew the word well enough from his time in Eokhmisseun to know what it meant. He had seen the strange, evil cast to Pontol and could see his old friend was now also afflicted. Then it was true, he thought, that Pete had probably killed Daria when he was turned. Running the light up and down Pete's body, he saw that Pete was only wearing a torn undershirt stained with dirt and his dress pants, also torn in places. This time he could recognize the vaguely catlike traits melting into Pete's own human features. Tigers, Joriya had said. Yes, Sohyeon could see that. It wasn't prominent veins that covered Pontol or Pete then, it was stripes. Very subtle, but unmistakable once you were in on the secret.

The three of them stood rooted to the spot, not speaking for a long while. Finally, Pete broke the silence.

"Who did you bring with you, Sohyeon? You didn't come alone?"

"She's just a friend. She felt too scared with everything going on to stay by herself." Sohyeon stared at Pete's mouth, now full of sharp, dirty teeth. "Have you heard from your father? I tried looking for him here earlier. I saw the inside of the house. It looks like he isn't doing too well."

Sohyeon knew that was an understatement, but he still wanted to see Pete's reaction. Nothing but a fleeting glimmer of contempt flickered across Pete's grotesque face, which increased Sohyeon's wariness.

"What are you doing out here? Shouldn't we go in where it's safer?" Sohyeon asked, knowing the house was probably a death trap if they went in. Outside they could flee easier in any direction and had the space to fight. Inside was another matter.

Pete seemed to be in no hurry to go anywhere. He took a few cautious steps toward them, blowing his noxious breath in their direction. Sohyeon really didn't want him to come any closer. More threatening than Pontol ever was, Sohyeon felt a strong revulsion he hadn't around the ferryman even though they both had been turned. The animal nature had taken over Pete with a ferocity Pontol didn't display.

"Don't let him touch you," Tamnyn warned quietly in his ear as she pulled him tighter against her chest. Her sword slowly moved up his legs toward a defensive position across his body against the creature.

The beam of the flashlight fell over Pete's hands, and Sohyeon gasped. His fingers were long and bony, capped with lethal-looking claws flecked with dried blood. *Pete could have been the one who clawed the walls of the foyer*, Sohyeon thought.

"What happened the other night to you, Pete?" Sohyeon asked, trying to keep his voice from trembling. "You look terrible."

Pete smiled.

"I made a new friend, Sohyeon, someone who said he'd like to meet you. Daria and I were out on our date when we first saw him. We decided to show him around town since he was new to Addison."

"A new friend? Don't tell me. It's that Ognjen guy, right? Sukjin saw a video of him that was pretty suspicious."

"Ognjen? I think that's his first name, but he prefers to go by Baram. You need to meet him, Sohyeon."

"Well, we can plan a night out when all of this is over."

"Oh, no," Pete said, taking another slow step toward them, his voice growing louder. Tamnyn's blade moved a few more inches over Sohyeon's body toward his chest to ward off any sudden attack by Pete, though Pete didn't seem to notice. "Tonight you will meet him, Sohyeon. Turn around. He's right behind you."

"The Red Tiger of Eokhmisseun is now residing in Addison," came a familiar female voice behind them.

Sohyeon looked back as he tried to tamp down an almost uncontrollable feeling of dread. Tamnyn had already turned to see who was behind them. Her jaw had dropped and her sword hand now hung limply at her side at the sight of the newcomers. Sohyeon just stared at the scene in shock.

The tall, thin man who had troubled them so in the video now stood before them, his tattered black cloak only carelessly resting around his gaunt shoulders over a rich red robe with thin light orange trim. His swarthy skin had an orange tinge, and black, snaky veins popped out in an almost tattoo-like pattern wherever his skin was exposed. Long, flaming red hair surrounded his head like a cloud. His elegant hands were striped and tipped with black claws, looking more human and skeletal than feline. His malevolent yellow eyes locked on Sohyeon.

When a woman stepped into view beside the man, Sohyeon was astonished to see a voluptuous if plump, middle aged woman standing behind Baram wearing a glittering gold sequined evening gown. Marietta Esposito!

Tamnyn fell against Sohyeon, and he quickly caught her around the waist, pulling her close so she could lean against him, not completely understanding her reaction as they confronted Birum, Baram or whatever his name was. Until a strand of her hair blew across his face. Red hair. Baram's hair was the same color, though Sohyeon didn't know why that would catch his attention.

Baram smiled coldly, his eyes glittering with cruel amusement as he let Marietta step between them.

Watching them in fascination, Sohyeon noted Pete's movements out of the corner of his eye. They weren't quite surrounded, but Pete could attack them if they got too distracted by the unholy couple now standing before them.

"What do you want with us?" Sohyeon asked.

Baram squinted and studied Sohyeon and Tamnyn a moment. His eyes paused when they reached the couples' hands. Was he looking at their weapons? A look of surprise crossed Baram's face, and his eyes shifted back to meet Sohyeon's, only lingering a moment on Tamnyn's face, his expression exultant.

"So I see I'm not the only one to have crossed the boundaries from Eokhmisseun! From that crest on her sword, I see she is favored to be a member of one of Eokhmisseun's ruling houses, the house of Elyeon. This is a crest I know, as I know her face."

Sohyeon felt as if he had been punched in the gut, and he wrapped both arms around Tamnyn to protect her and keep her from collapsing. Now he held his bat across her body like she had held her sword across his moments before.

"What are you talking about?" Sohyeon asked roughly. "How could you know her?"

Baram smiled slightly, unintimidated by Sohyeon.

"I would recognize her face anywhere, and her red hair, rarely known in Eokhmisseun, is typical only in one prominent family bloodline there, the bloodline of my own mother, Crysalin of the house of Hyeonbal. This woman is my blood relative, is she not?"

Sohyeon felt a shudder go through Tamnyn as Baram said the woman's name and remembered her story not long ago about Birum kidnapping her mother. Was Crysalin Cargal's missing wife? Sohyeon didn't know for sure, but it seemed possible given Tamnyn's reaction. Even if it was true, this would hardly be a happy reunion. Sohyeon wasn't inclined to draw more attention to

Tamnyn by asking questions about it. They needed to get out of this predicament as quickly as possible.

"Why did you really have Pete call me out here?" Sohyeon asked, trying to buy them some time as he mentally ran through a number of possible escape plans. "And what are *you* doing here, Marietta?"

Unlike Pete, Marietta showed no signs of the turning, though Sohyeon could detect something thoroughly unwholesome about her now. She had changed drastically since Sohyeon talked to her Friday night at dinner, and he wondered what had gone on at the late night meeting when she had first introduced Baram to him.

"If this is what it means to be on the Welcome Wagon committee, I don't want any part of it," Sohyeon said sarcastically, not waiting for her reply.

"Come now, Sohyeon," Marietta said, her voice oddly seductive. "Ognjen Baram is quite a special resident, and all of the leadership in Addison agrees that he has so much to offer our little town."

As she spoke, Sohyeon detected movement behind Baram near the property line beyond a clump of trees. In the scattered moonlight, he could see two figures emerge, their gaits reminding him of Pontol. Coming closer, the two figures appeared to be men, but Sohyeon could only recognize them now by their hair and clothing. Sohyeon could hardly believe it when they came forward. Baram had turned Detective Mazurek and Adam Johnson, and they were now ghost-slaves under Baram's power! They had no way to fight Baram now with such allies. These men were powerful people in the local community, and now Sohyeon and Tamnyn were outnumbered and surrounded by them. It was time for Sohyeon to make his move. They would only have seconds to make their getaway.

But before he had time to take a small step with Tamnyn to the left where there was a break in their ranks, something reflective whizzed through the air and hit

Baram from behind in the left arm. Grabbing the arrow where it pierced his flesh, turning with a roar to look toward the dark knot of trees on the right past Adam and the Detective, Baram fell to his knees. Marietta rushed to help him, while Pete, Adam and the Detective ran toward whoever was hidden in the underbrush at the back of the yard. Sohyeon saw his opportunity. Grabbing Tamnyn, who had now collected herself and was alert enough to fight, Sohyeon fled around the corner of the house without making any noise and jumped on the bike, knowing whoever had taken the shot at Baram had just saved their lives. They didn't have much time to escape while their adversaries were distracted. Sohyeon could only hope they were too busy to follow them back to his house.

18

They reached the house quickly, but Sohyeon couldn't text his father on the way, so they had to wait nervously for him to open the side door into the garage for them. Since he had been waiting in the dark garage for Sohyeon's text, Jangsun quickly unlocked it and pulled them and the bicycle inside. Locking the door and leaning the bike against it, they went back into the house to the upper floor where everyone was gathered. Most of the house was dark, and even in their parents' large bedroom which served as the gathering spot for the household, the lights were dim and subtle. Jangsun clearly didn't want to attract too much attention from passers-by in the street. Philip and Sukjin sat on a sleeping bag on the floor while Alanna and Joriya sat with Mapin on the bed. An assortment of swords, axes and walking sticks were on the floor in the corner, easily within reach.

"What happened with Pete?" Jangsun asked.

"It's as we feared," Sohyeon said. "Not only did Pete probably kill Daria, he has become a ghost-slave, and he lured me there to meet with that Ognjen Baram. Only

Ognjen Baram actually goes by the name Baram, whom Marietta called 'The Red Tiger of Eokhmisseun,' but we didn't know what that meant at first. I couldn't believe Marietta was there with him, and Baram has also turned the Detective and Adam. We only got away because someone shot an arrow at him and distracted him. Otherwise, we'd be dead or worse right now."

"Do you think you were followed here?" Alanna asked.

Sohyeon noticed from the glance between his parents that his father had told her some of the story.

"It didn't look like it, but since Pete and the Detective are with them, it won't matter anyway," Sohyeon said, pulling Tamnyn closer to him, knowing they would have to talk about Baram's bloodline claims at some point. "They could just lead Baram straight to us here, if that's what Baram wanted."

Sohyeon paused, noticing that Joriya had visibly paled at his report.

"Do you know what this red tiger is, Joriya? I thought you said your royal family turned into white tigers, but Baram was clearly a red tiger-like man with bright red hair. He also claimed to be related to one of the ruling houses of Eokhmisseun. Does that sound like your brother, or are there more of them?"

"The ancestors are white tigers with no variation in coloring," Joriya said slowly, thinking.

"How could there be a red one now?" Jangsun asked, folding his arms across his chest. "Magic?"

"Perhaps, but what Birum is doing now is beyond anything I've ever heard of in Khabu," she said. "How curious that he would mention being from Eokhmisseun instead of Khabu."

"It wouldn't be curious, because it's true," Tamnyn said, her eyes fixed on the shuttered windows, her voice hollow. "Baram isn't Birum. This is a different man, though he seems to be just as dangerous. I'm not sure that any of the people in my land know of his existence or have ever seen him."

"How do you know it's true?" Joriya asked.

"You don't have to do this, Tamnyn," Sohyeon said softly. "We don't really know yet that it's true."

"Yes, I know it's true. He told us the name of his mother. Crysalin of the house of Hyeonbal is my mother, whom Birum kidnapped shortly after my birth. This creature is likely my half-brother." Tamnyn sighed deeply and looked away from them.

"Birum had a child with a human?" Joriya asked quietly, as if the idea didn't quite make sense.

"He recognized Tamnyn, too," Sohyeon said quickly, changing the subject as a look of distaste flickered over Joriya's face. Tamnyn, facing the door away from Joriya, didn't see it. "Baram noticed the crest on her sword, though I don't think he knows exactly that she is Crysalin's daughter."

"If my mother raised him, then he probably guesses," Tamnyn said, turning slightly back toward Sohyeon. "I should go back and put a stop to this."

"Are you crazy? What can you do against him?" Sohyeon asked, grabbing her wrist and pulling her away from the door. "You can't go back outside. This is just like it was in your homeland. We have to find another, more indirect way to fight him, and even then if he has anything like Birum's power, we have no idea what might work against him. Oh, that reminds me, when I texted dad, I saw I got a few missed calls from when we were riding over to Pete's that I haven't checked yet. I should do that now."

Sohyeon pulled out his phone and checked his messages. Three calls had come in, all from the same number which Sohyeon had stored in his phone under Vince's name. Vince! Listening to the first few seconds of the first voicemail Vince left, Sohyeon knew they all needed to hear it.

Jangsun had a phone dock in the bedroom on his dresser, though he didn't use his phone as much as the Choi kids did, and Sohyeon put his phone there, adjusting the volume on low so the sound wouldn't carry beyond the room.

"Let me start this first message again. It's Vince," Sohyeon said.

"Sohyeon? I hope you get this message in time." Vince's voice was barely audible since he was whispering, as if he were afraid of being overheard. "I just got home, but no one knows I'm here yet since I walked from the store after my car broke down. I thought I should warn you some strange men were here talking to my wife, and your name came up. Something about how you and your sister had been seen in Okmisty or someplace. I think Pete was with them, and he wasn't looking too good. But wasn't Pete MacIntyre missing?

"He also told them you had a dream where one of them bit you that was actually real. It was a really strange conversation I just overheard, but I didn't like the tone of it. I think they may come calling to have a talk with you, though they weren't the type of people I'd want to spend five minutes in the room with, if you get my meaning.

"Anyway, this message is getting long, and they may notice me here soon. They all went outside with my wife a minute ago. I'll see if I can find out more and maybe tail them. I guess this is a good a time as any to bring you over that crossbow you wanted for our lessons. It would make a good pretext for me to happen along your house if they end up there."

The call ended abruptly, and the voicemail recording started giving them options.

"Don't delete that call," Jangsun said quietly.

Sohyeon hit the appropriate button to move on to the second voicemail.

"Hey, Sohyeon, I don't know where you are, but I hope you get this message in time. I've been following those men with my wife, and none of them look too normal. One is quite a monster, and I just saw them enter the MacIntyre house. Wasn't there supposed to be a bunch of people here for the search parties today? Maybe that's why I can't get in touch with you, eh?

"Well, the MacIntyre house had its front door hanging wide open and looked from the street like it was ransacked. I went around to the side to see what they were doing through the windows – they left all of the lights blazing – and there was blood and slash marks all over the walls in every room I could see into. What the blazes is going on around here? You should stay away from this place and don't let Pete come in if he shows up at your house. This looks like serious stuff going down, with my wife all dolled up right in the middle of it though I can't fathom what has gotten into Marietta. Wait, someone's coming."

The second voicemail cut off abruptly. Sohyeon moved on to the third and last message, the time stamp for which showing it was recorded when they were at Pete's.

"Sohyeon, I see you're already here," Vince said, this time his voice tense and rasping, almost too low to hear. "Marietta must have been stepping out on me all this time, but what are these creatures? I can see you're unable to take my call, but maybe I can help you get you out of here before they jump you. Let me try since I can't do much else right now. I brought you my regular bow and arrows instead of the crossbow."

When the third voicemail had ended, Sohyeon picked up his phone and took it out of voicemail mode. Everyone was quiet a moment.

"Then Vince was the one who shot Baram so we could get away," Tamnyn said.

"I wonder if I should try to call him back," Sohyeon said, plugging his phone into his father's charger.

"He might be dead, or he could have lost his phone since that call," Philip said. "You don't know who might answer if you do."

"We can't do anything for him right now," Jangsun said. "Wait a little bit until things have calmed down before you try calling him."

"Would the arrow have done any real damage?" Tamnyn asked Joriya, who looked up from Mapin as if she had been distracted. "Is Baram a true immortal?"

"The arrow didn't hit him in any vital area," Sohyeon said. "When I saw Vince Friday night, I didn't mention that Mr. MacIntyre suggested we could substitute something else like titanium arrows in place of silver, so he wouldn't have known to bring anything special that could really take him out."

"Only silver will work, even on a half-immortal," Joriya said. "If it wasn't a mortal wound and only hit him in an extremity, he could be healed in an hour or two, maybe a few days if it was really bad."

"Then what other choice do we have but to despair against such power?" Tamnyn asked, her voice rising in frustration. "Now I know why my father chose to sit back and let the city crumble when it seemed like we could do so much against Birum with the council in secret. He saw this happen in my homeland. I was too young, and I don't remember any other world than our pampered hiding place and uneasy truce with Birum. As long as we didn't go out into the streets, Birum wouldn't pursue us in our hiding places, and the council was ineffective against him as he consolidated his power."

"But that situation did change, and he lured you out to kill you," Sohyeon said grimly. "Addison isn't Eokhmisseun. We don't have elaborate gardens in our houses for unending supplies of food and magic to entertain us. Our house is small and cramped, and we are dependent on the community for regularly needed items. We'll have to go out into the streets soon, just to stay alive. Maybe Baram knows that."

"Does this mean Mirae is dead?" Sukjin asked suddenly.

Everyone looked at her in surprise.

"Why would you ask that?" Jangsun said.

"If he's here, and there's no sign of her, maybe he killed her and the ancient king. Why would they come here anyway? Is there any other reason?"

"Space pirates," Sohyeon said, glancing at Tamnyn. "Didn't you say people thought Khabu had dealings with other worlds beyond the inner seas for a long time?"

"Birum was very restless and constantly in search of more power to rip the throne from me," Joriya said. "He didn't need a reason, but if he guessed at Mirae's true purpose and discovered her origins, then all bets are off."

"All we can do now is hope for the best and sleep here tonight," Jangsun said. "We will need to sleep in shifts with some of us standing guard, just in case. Maybe nothing will happen, but we can't take that chance."

"I would like to send Mapin back out tonight to send a message to Minha, my high priestess in my homeland beyond the inner sea," Joriya said, stroking the white bird in her lap gently. "She can aid us from afar, send Pontol or whatever to us."

"Can it wait until daylight?" Jangsun asked. "It feels too dangerous at the moment since Baram's attention has been drawn to Sohyeon. They could be watching us here even now."

"We need to have a solid plan anyway," Sohyeon said. "This was the problem in Eokhmisseun, too. We have no idea what to do or how to kill them, so we are just left helplessly waiting for the next attack. What is our best option here? Have Minha send reinforcements here to us in Addison? Should Tamnyn and I go to Eokhmisseun to rescue Mirae and the king and attempt to kill Birum? Do we all flee to Khabu to get away from these creatures?"

"I think that we should do a two pronged attack," Tamnyn said, thinking. "My father used to talk about tactical strategies we could use all of the time, he just never seemed confident enough to use any of them, or maybe the other members of the council wouldn't let him go through with his plans. Joriya, send for Minha. I think her presence here will help tremendously in opposing Baram."

"Yes, I agree. She also has the ritual tiger mask, which will allow her to communicate with the other priestesses and the ancestors back in Khabu without the need for Mapin or the other birds. She is very resourceful and understands more about magic than I do, having spent years in the presence of the ancestors. Jangsun can lead our warriors here with the help of his daughter."

"Good. Then Sohyeon and I can return to Eokhmisseun and find Mirae, Litt and my father, if he's still alive. I don't think we should try to assassinate Birum yet, just sneak around and free his captives if we can. At that point, we can decide what to do. Agreed?"

"How will you get back to Eokhmisseun?" Jangsun asked, standing to stretch his legs.

"Mapin will summon both Minha and Pontol," Tamnyn said. "Minha will stay with you, and Pontol will take us back to Eokhmisseun. Joriya, should you return to Khabu now? Who is heading the country while you are away?"

"Minha and her assistants are, so yes, if she comes here, I should return there," Joriya said. "Minha has far more power and is much cleverer than I, so my presence here will not be missed. I will return to Khabu and await either Minha's or Mirae's instructions, if you find Mirae alive in Eokhmisseun."

Sohyeon glanced at Philip, who seemed slightly dazed by the conversation. He went over to him.

"You said you knew how to fight some, didn't you?" Sohyeon asked. "As you have heard, we have something rather supernatural going on in Addison right now, and it will take a different kind of mentality. Dad, will you be able to take Sukjin and Philip down to the basement for sword training tomorrow? You'll definitely need to connect with Vince somehow, since he can provide some military training for you, too. Hopefully, he survived tonight's encounter with Baram."

"Leave your phone with me when you go with Tamnyn," Jangsun said. "For now, we should just stay put for the night, then implement the entire plan once the sun rises. Alanna and I will take the first shift while the rest of you sleep, followed by you and Tamnyn, then Philip and Sukjin for the last shift. Agreed?"

"If the sun rises we will be lucky," Tamnyn said glancing toward the windows. "Once Birum took over Eokhmisseun, the daytime sky was always steely with a cold light, a storm ever on the horizon, just barely out of view. Birum can control the weather and the stars in the sky."

"No wonder you brought up despair earlier," Alanna said. "What force is there to stop such beings?"

"The ancestors have more power, even so," Joriya said, as if in a trance. "If we can save Litt, he may have some ways long forgotten in the 8,000 years since he walked in Khabu's royal palace. That was why Birum stole him out of the crypt in the first place."

19

As the second shift took over at 11PM, Sohyeon and Tamnyn did a quick, stealthy walk around the lower levels of the house before settling back in the hall outside the master bedroom where everyone was sleeping. They checked the windows, peeling back the tape Jangsun had fastened the blinds to the walls with here and there just enough to see out for a moment. Grabbing a few cans of pop beside the kitchen door before they returned upstairs, they took up their positions facing the stairs, using a small flashlight so Tamnyn could write the message they would send in the morning with Mapin.

"Do you really think Pete will try to come here tonight after Vince shot Baram?" Sohyeon asked, wondering if was overly cautious to whisper. "I myself wouldn't expect them for a few days."

"It's hard to say. It depends on how seriously Baram was injured and whether his half-immortal heritage will help him regenerate quickly. We need to implement our plan right away and be ready for him when he comes. Your family is in grave danger, and Baram is not Birum. He will not be so predictable based on my experience and knowledge of our history in Eokhmisseun, and Joriya will not be able to second-guess him either. He is a complete unknown, though his intentions here in Addison surely are not that different than Birum's were, I would guess."

"Should we take the helmet and dagger when we leave?"

"I don't know. We can let Minha decide since she knows how they function. We have agreed that we are not on an assassination mission in returning to Eokhmisseun, not this time, so perhaps it's best to leave them here with Minha or let Joriya take them back to Khabu until we can figure out who can successfully deal with Birum. We don't want to lose them since they are our only hope at killing him given the scarcity of silver weapons, though Birum may have others in his possession by now."

"What are you going to say to Minha? I'm surprised Joriya didn't insist on writing the note for Mapin to take herself."

"She seems rather uninvolved in her kingdom for a queen, that is clear," Tamnyn said. "Minha will know what to do. You told me you met her. What were your impressions of her?"

Sohyeon could feel himself blushing a little in the dim light, feeling slightly foolish once again by his fleeting infatuation with the mercurial priestess.

"She's everything that Joriya is not: decisive, commanding, unsentimental. If Baram has never been to his ancestral homeland, she may be a real force to be reckoned with. I wonder if he was raised entirely in Eokhmisseun. If he has never met Minha, he will be in for a great surprise. She may be the real power behind the throne in Khabu."

He watched Tamnyn sign her small note with a flourish. She handed the pen back to Sohyeon and began folding it, which Sohyeon didn't object to since he could see the lettering was not in any earthly language he could possibly read. It suddenly reminded him of something he had been meaning to ask her.

"When I was at Pete's earlier, I saw strange writing scrawled across one wall in a language that looked like that. Do you have any idea what they might have written there? The house was ransacked, as Vince noted in his voicemail, and the letters seemed like they were written in blood. We haven't discovered what happened to Pete's father yet, so maybe…I don't like to think about it."

"Yes, from the stories I heard, Birum was known at the beginning to use a special inscription in our language when he defeated an enemy, perhaps a magical spell scrawled in their blood. Some of the informal histories written by the council when they were first sent into hiding talked about it. I don't think any of them dared to write it down for fear a curse would spread to them if they did."

Tamnyn fell silent a moment as Sohyeon clicked off the flashlight and she pocketed the note.

"When should we send Mapin?" Sohyeon asked. "I'll feel antsy until we can send her out. No matter where we go, we're in for trouble, but I want to see Pontol again and can't wait for Minha to get here to protect my family. Then I can leave for Eokhmisseun feeling the responsibility has been lifted from me to stay and watch over them."

"Your father organized us into three watches of three hours each. We went to bed really early since it's very dark and we can't do much. We switch shifts again at 2AM. The inner sea will be most visible in less than an hour, at midnight. It would be the best time to send Mapin but also the most likely time Baram and his henchmen would expect us to use that as an escape route."

"Then we should wait until we change shifts with the third watch at 2AM," Sohyeon said.

"I'll talk to Mapin and prepare her."

"We can bring her out here now where we won't disturb anyone, if you like."

"Yes, we should."

Sohyeon stood up, leaving his bat on the floor, and felt for the doorknob. Entering the dim bedroom where everyone else was fast asleep on the bed and floor, he tiptoed over to the dresser where Mapin was sitting with her head tucked in, fast asleep. Sohyeon gingerly reached out his hand to lightly touch the bird's downy feathers, and she opened her eyes and turned her head to look at him warily.

"It's okay, Mapin. Tamnyn wants to talk to you. We have a mission for you that is very important, as I'm sure you are aware."

He held out his hand so the bird could jump up and come with him out into the hall. Tamnyn watched them from the door that he had left ajar. When Mapin was settled on Sohyeon's arm, he walked quietly back to the hall and shut the door behind him.

Tamnyn turned on the flashlight again as he leaned down with Mapin, who hopped onto Tamnyn's lap. Placing the note into Mapin's collar, Tamnyn stroked her feathers and whispered to her in their strange language. The rising and falling intonation, sounding so ethereal and musical, nearly put Sohyeon in a trance, and he marveled again at the bird's power. The immortals were so intoxicating, so beyond anything he had ever encountered, but in comparison Sohyeon could see how Baram was not full-blooded. He had a powerful presence, but it was not as intense as that of the immortals themselves.

When Tamnyn had finished, Mapin sat quietly with her. The air in the hallway seemed to crackle with some sort of energy that washed over Sohyeon like a calming wave. It clouded his vision and filled his lungs like incense. He slid down to the floor, feeling for his bat and waited.

"How long will it take when she returns to them for them to come here?" he asked, taking a deep breath. "What if Baram sees her?"

"Not long," Tamnyn said reassuringly. "Only a few hours as long as she isn't intercepted, but Mapin is an immortal. There's only so much that they can do to her other than capture her, and even then, the messenger birds are special. I worked with them since I was a child, and they are very resourceful."

20

When the third watch finally arrived, Sukjin and Philip came out to relieve them, yawning and whispering amongst themselves and carrying a sword and axe. Tamnyn rose with Mapin and led Sohyeon into his bedroom. The digital clock on his dresser noted the time, 2:14 AM.

"We can send her out now," Tamnyn said, waiting for Sohyeon to pull back the curtains and window blind and open the sash.

His was one of the few windows in the house that didn't have a screen, so it was a better choice than his parents' bedroom. Still, he was too nervous to open the window very far. He only opened it a foot and knelt beside it, studying the misty, deathly quiet neighborhood. Not one light was on anywhere he looked except for the streetlights, and no one dared walk the street. However, the night breeze that blew into the room felt refreshing even if there was a hint of something acrid in it.

"Fire," Sohyeon whispered. "Is that what I smell?"

Searching the skies, he couldn't see anything that suggested a fire. After a few moments, though, he saw a flash of lightning hit the air. No thunder followed yet, but Sohyeon had smelled the ozone in the air.

"The storm is rolling in again. It never rained Saturday when it seemed like it would all day."

"Baram's magic, most likely," Tamnyn said, holding Mapin down toward the windowsill where she could fly up to the inner sea. "Go swiftly and bring the others," Tamnyn said in English this time.

The graceful little bird took off like a dart, swooping in an arc toward the hazy full moon and disappearing into it.

Tamnyn closed her eyes slowly.

"It won't be long now. Are you ready to go back and fight Birum, Sohyeon? Do we have the strength for this?"

"If you want to find your father and I want to find my sister, then we have no choice."

"Then let's sleep here and wait."

By 5AM, they could hear the others stirring, and the storm still danced around the edges of Addison but hadn't come any closer yet.

"There you two are," Alanna said, coming into Sohyeon's room with a look of relief. Seeing the open window, she turned grim. "Is that okay to leave open? I thought we had taped up the house so no one could tell we were here or easily break in."

"We're waiting right now for a response," Sohyeon said sitting up on the sleeping bag on his bedroom floor, stretching and yawning. Tamnyn was still lying on his bed, though her eyes were open. "We sent Mapin out earlier to get reinforcements. Tamnyn and I will be returning to Eokhmisseun soon. You'll have to deal with Baram here while we're gone, but we need to look for Mirae."

"Will she ever really come back here after what Joriya said?" Alanna asked sadly. "She will become queen of this fairy land you all have been talking about, won't she?"

"She'll probably have to stay there," Sohyeon said. "But that's not where she is now. Maybe you can visit her in Khabu from time to time when all of this is over."

"I need to get breakfast ready. Luckily, we just went on a big shopping trip Saturday and have plenty of extra food to last a few months, as long as the electricity holds out."

Jangsun walked into the room and put his arms around her from behind.

"We'll figure out a way to survive this, no matter what, so don't worry about us," he said to Sohyeon.

"You'll have to reckon with Minha soon," Sohyeon said. "It's not exactly going to be a question of surviving once she's around. Just wait until you see her."

"There," Tamnyn said, sitting up on the bed and pointing toward the window. "Sohyeon, open the window more. It looks like Pontol is coming."

As the ferryman and his little boat reached Sohyeon's window, Sukjin, Philip and Joriya had joined everyone in Sohyeon's room to greet the visitors. Most of the spectators were awestruck at the sight of the flying boat and Pontol's degenerate appearance. Much more surprising, however, was Minha's entourage.

The priestess looked every bit the part of a royal immortal servant, her light blue chiton billowing in the breeze, her sleek midnight black hair floating like snakes around her head. The frozen scowl of the tiger mask was fastened across her body on a sash like a primitive flaying trophy, and two young female acolytes dressed in dark blue chitons flanked her, holding spears tipped with curved blades, like *hyeopdo*. Mapin and nine other white war birds fluttered around them. Seeing Joriya step up on the windowsill to meet her priestess on the boat, Sohyeon thought once again that he no longer was certain which woman was the true ruler of Khabu. Next to Minha, Joriya seemed meek and uncertain.

"My Queen," Minha began, bowing deeply before Joriya before stepping down from the boat into Sohyeon's bedroom. "I have heard the terrible news that Birum has a son who has taken over in this world and threatens the family who has lovingly raised our princess all of these years. Of course, you must return to Khabu and take care of kingdom business while I see what I can do here to hold back the threat."

Joriya only nodded, looking back at Alanna and smiling.

"We will meet again, Mrs. Choi, do not worry. I can only thank you for your unwitting help all of these years. We will always share that bond, no matter what lands we live in."

Turning, Joriya stepped into Pontol's boat and sat in the bow, waiting for the rest of the passengers to join her.

Tamnyn quickly hugged both Alanna and Jangsun before following Joriya onto the boat. Only Sohyeon lingered, unable to tear his eyes from the sight of Minha, who also eyed him with a slight smile playing across her lips.

"There's nothing more you can do here, Sohyeon," Minha said. "I will take over now. You will have your hands full with the Duke back in Eokhmisseun, but you must save Mirae and free Litt from Birum's magic. Litt is far more powerful than I, and he has deep knowledge of the world. Do not worry about the fate of your family."

"You're very confident you can handle Baram," Sohyeon said, his irritation mingling with relief. "I hope you aren't underestimating him."

"He has never been to Khabu and may not know much about us, if I know Birum's mind," Minha said. "He wouldn't have dared send a secret son of his to us given his ruse in Eokhmisseun. We weren't even aware of his activities there until you informed us of them.

"In the meantime, use the temple in Khabu as your base should you need somewhere safe to escape temporarily. I will not guarantee you will be safe coming back here unless you send one of the messenger birds to us. Use them to communicate with Pontol if you run into trouble or need to warn us of something you have discovered."

"What should we do with the executioner's helmet and dagger?" Sohyeon asked, walking past her toward the window where Pontol waited. "Tamnyn brought them here when we fled Eokhmisseun, though we didn't know the significance of the weapons."

"Ah, we should put them in a safe place," Minha said, looking toward the box where Sohyeon had pointed. "My queen, these should return with you to the ancestral temple. I will capture our little cat Baram here and bring him back for questioning if I can, and we must do the same with Birum. Once that is done, we can use the artefacts for a formal execution. For now, Sohyeon, hit them to wound them when you can to slow them down, but don't expect to kill them. There may be no other way to kill them but the dagger. Hana, take the box to the Queen."

Minha's acolyte handed the *hyeopdo* to Minha to hold while she retrieved the box and handed it to Joriya on the boat. When she returned to her position, she took back her weapon.

"Is that all for now?" Minha asked, watching Sohyeon board the boat and the ferryman begin to turn it around to return to the inner sea. "Good. I will take care of things here and get to know our esteemed helpers the Chois as we plan to deal with Baram. We will speak again soon."

With a wave, Sohyeon settled in the boat next to Tamnyn and watched his family get smaller and more distant with every twist of Pontol's wheel. The ferry caught the misty currents of the moonlight, which had become as thick as water and pulled them along to their destination. He could only trust his family would be safe with Minha. He had no other choice.

4 THE ANCIENT LOVERS

1

"I should move the capital here," Litt said, looking back over his shoulder at his aide, Nominus. The towering waterfall rumbled before them, its gleaming blue water splashing down in a white spray across the span of the broad cliff. "It is so much more moving than the location my father has chosen near the inner sea where it's only barren rocks and has such a dull view."

"I'm surprised you have time to worry about such things, my lord," Nominus said, pulling the hood of his dark blue cloak back over his head. "Your father will be marrying you off soon, and there is much work to be done establishing the new kingdom."

"Yes, I know, but that's father's plan, not mine. Ever since he brought us to this land and we left our home world behind, he has had such grandiose ideas about creating this 'land of titans' where we could be safe from discovery. The old land was bad enough, but now he's turning this into some sort of sideshow. Can't we just live in peace here without all of this pomp? I didn't think he fought to get away from the evils of our home world just to become five times worse as our king. And now an arranged marriage?"

Litt turned and walked past Nominus, his golden shoulder-length hair blowing in the breeze. His dark blue leather tunic and breeches were not fashionable by the new standards of the recently founded kingdom of Khabu, but soon Litt would be forced to play a part in his father's fantasy that they were royalty. Returning to their mounts, a striking mix of ox and horse native to their new land, Litt sighed in resignation as they prepared for their return journey. He couldn't be away from the palace for long, but he would savor the few days away from it that he now had with their impromptu trip to the waterfall.

As he and Nominus began their long ride back to the palace across the plains of Khabu, Litt thought back to all of his father's arguments in favor of leaving their home world and founding a kingdom of their own. They were outcasts there, freaks even, a class of ever-suspected people who had uncanny abilities like talking to animals and even turning into them at times. Huddled into ghettos in their home world because their leaders were very aware they were an experiment gone wrong, inadvertent test subjects who now had strange powers of regeneration and who seemed impervious to aging and death. His people had become a terrifying specter back home, and his father, a leader among them, had hatched a plan. Now a year after their escape, Litt was set to become heir apparent to the kingdom of freaks his father had masterminded. Litt and Nominus, companions since childhood though of different castes among those who had fled to Khabu, returned to the palace with great trepidation.

2

Mirae opened her eyes, wondering where she was, her right hand full of downy fur. All she could remember was holding onto Litt before the dark beast took them away from Khabu. Turning to see what she touched, she saw she lay on a wide bed covered with a red brocade quilt, still clinging to the man who had bewitched her. Even now, she clutched at him frantically, unwilling to let him go, though now he looked half-animal, his striped fur soft and warm against her skin. His back was to her, and she held onto his bare arm. Sitting up and leaning over him, she saw his face now had strong feline features under dirty blond hair and was covered with a light, barely noticeable layer of black and white striped fur. His breathing was ragged, and he looked uncomfortable. *What a strange-looking man*, Mirae thought, *yet how delicately beautiful nonetheless.*

The door opened at the foot of the bed. Startled, Mirae looked up, and Litt twisted restlessly next to her, his eyes still closed. A girl of about 14 entered the room, and Mirae stared at her in astonishment. Like Litt, the girl had an odd but beautiful mix of feline and human features, her face with a ruddier tinge striped with black veins and almost no fur, and her long, red curls tied up in a black ribbon. Her dress was also an antiquated, vaguely Victorian style in black satin.

"Who are you?" Mirae asked, scrambling to the edge of the bed. "Where are we?"

"You are guests of the great king of Eokhmisseun," the girl said dramatically. "I am his daughter, Kerinda. He sent me up to you to see if you had awakened yet. I'm glad to see you have, but *he* doesn't look so good." The girl looked curiously at Litt. "I have met him before since he works for my father, but I haven't seen you. Why are you with him?"

"He seemed distressed, so I came with him. We were friends," Mirae said, thinking it was better to keep things simple.

"You've been delirious for a few days now," Kerinda said matter-of-factly, placing fresh garments for them on the edge of the bed. "There is a heated stone bath at the end of this hallway you can use, but don't leave this floor, or my father's guards will take you immediately to the dungeon. You are our guests, but we ask that you respect our wishes and not wander around the palace."

"I see," Mirae said, looking down at her dress. She was still wearing her blue temple chiton, now stained black with dried mud and magical ink from the beast that had seized them. Glancing over at Litt, his green tunic was grimy and stained as well. She would have to wake him and take him down to the baths before this "king" summoned them, but first she would see to herself and try to wash the chiton. "When can we leave here? We're grateful that you rescued us, but I must get back to the temple. I'm needed at the palace.

The girl's golden eyes took on a puzzled expression.

"You *are* at the palace, and you can't leave us. He is needed here. My father brought him here for more consultations. If you are his woman, you must stay as well."

"A consultation?" Mirae said softly. "Who is your father again?"

"Birum, though here in Eokhmisseun, he's sometimes also known as Litt."

Mirae sucked in her breath, realizing for the first time what happened.

"But this man is Litt," Mirae said in confusion, "though he was known as Birum where we were."

"In Khabu? Yes, so I've heard. My father is very good at practical jokes, and he has sometimes switched identities with this man. You are from Khabu then? That will interest our other guests, who have not met anyone from Khabu except for…".

The door opened suddenly, and a woman waved sharply toward Kerinda, hissing at her. Like the little girl, the woman had long, luxurious red hair but looked fully human. She seemed to be much older than Mirae, though she was still quite beautiful.

"I have to go now," the girl said sadly, turning to leave with the woman.

Waiting until their footsteps receded, Mirae wasted no time searching for the bath. She and Litt would soon meet their archenemy, and she needed to be prepared.

3

In the early days of Khabu, Litt found his father Zurui more and more incomprehensible. Always too excitable for his own good, Zurui had been a competent leader of their people and led the revolt against their fully human overlords when it became apparent they had no future outside of the ghettos of their home world. In that far-off land a generation or two before, curious humans had discovered ways of tampering with human and animal life, creating hybrids and engineering their genes for immortality and other abilities. The results were more than the human scientists had bargained for.

Instead of being lauded, the scientists involved in the experiments had been quietly executed for treason, while their creations, a hybrid race no longer human in anything other than appearance, had terrified the leaders of that world, who denied their existence and walled them off from the rest of human society. As time had passed in that controlled environment, their odd tendencies had intensified. Chatter among those in the test subject ghetto arose, and they suggested finding a way to escape. Zurui successfully led them out of the ghetto, travelling with them until they reached the inner sea. Using methods unknown to humans, they were all able to escape to worlds beyond their homeland through dimensional doors where none of their enemies could reach them.

Only now, it was becoming clear to Litt, who had been born in the ghetto and fled with them to Khabu as a teenager, that they had inadvertently brought their enemies with them. Since taking control of the new land and now planning its society, Zurui had become unhinged. In the ghetto, the community freely mixed without regard to their strange and disparate affinities, but now Zurui had deemed that was not to remain the case. He was codifying into law a caste system that would require all of the test subjects who fled to determine their dominant abilities and animal affinities in order to be herded into clans. Litt had been watching this process with distaste as his father extended the law to include a clause that the clans could no longer intermarry. Instead of escaping to freedom, they had escaped to a different kind of slavery. Litt wondered how he could wrest power from his father and correct some of the extreme positions his father had taken, but it seemed impossible. He could only watch from the sidelines, wandering the countryside to dream of how he wanted the world to be.

"Your father is looking for you," Nominus said, peering into the room from the corridor around the half open door. "What is it now?" Litt asked, looking out the window of his luxurious apartment in the palace. "More madness?" he whispered under his breath.

"He has gotten the results of the animal census, from what I understand," Nominus said, stepping into the room and closing the door behind him. Nominus was the same age as Litt, and his wavy ash brown hair and swarthy complexion contrasted strongly with Litt's fair appearance. "I think he's about to formally announce the new clan based system and wants you to be present when he does."

"He's enjoying himself too much in his new role as king," Litt said, standing and smoothing out his embroidered purple tunic. "Is it really necessary to go so far, when we have fought so hard for our independence? It doesn't seem proper now to push our people to accept this."

"He'll be sending the guards to get you if you don't go voluntarily," Nominus said mildly. "You really should be there, if for no other reason than to understand the new law he has devised and maybe think of a way to talk him out of it."

"I know you are right. As his heir, I need to at least keep up appearances so no one suspects that I oppose all of this. I don't think my sisters and many of the ministers would be willing to let me remain in line for the throne if they knew, though I don't understand how they can't see where all of this will lead. Have you gotten the results of your DNA test?"

"So in spite of your opposition, you will ask for my animal affinity? I was excited to hear that I tested for the deer clan. I understand four clans will be established in the kingdom and a special ceremony honoring them will be held soon. Did you hear about the new family crypt your father plans to build under the palace? He plans for it to reach into another dimension."

"For what end?" Litt asked impatiently. "He is cut from the same cloth as the scientists who made us as we are, Nominus. I don't suppose you've heard what the animal totem for the royal family is? We're part of the tiger clan, but I wonder if perhaps the days when no one really knew what animal they were spliced to genetically will turn out to be better. Deer are the prey of tigers, after all. Will this create some danger in our midst since we come from such different stock?"

"I could see your father's plan as a wise one, perhaps," Nominus said thoughtfully. "After all, if we don't know our ancestry, and we feel some of those primitive desires, how will we control them? Perhaps it isn't a bad idea to separate us altogether so we won't harm one another."

"You and I have been best friends since childhood," Litt said. "When have we ever felt like predator and prey, just because of the animal DNA we carried? Wouldn't it be true that our humanity has negated some of those tendencies?"

"But there have been reports among the older generation since we have arrived that they've reverted back, so to speak."

"Reverted back how?"

"They've returned to their animal forms, completely rejecting their human ones. Your father has been encouraging this, too. We've always been able to go through the change and even appear half animal, though I didn't recognize my animal was a deer and this transformation back and forth was never encouraged because of the trouble it could bring to us in human society. We've never even really discussed the issue, but it has always been there in the background. Your father has analyzed the stories from the ghetto involving murders among us, and he suspects that the predator-prey aspect of our DNA was a factor in those grisly crimes."

"Even in the human world, people are brutally murdered, and they have neither animal genes nor powers of regeneration. The murders among us can be stopped easily enough by outlawing silver and keeping it out of the country. We don't need to form clans and castes to do that."

"Well, the proclamation will be made shortly, and you are expected to be there for the final reading of the documents in the audience hall of the palace. He will be declaring all four clans today."

"What are the other two besides the tiger and deer clans?"

"The wolf and the bird clans. Two predators and two prey."

Litt looked at Nominus in dismay, running his hand through his hair.

"I guess I should get this over with and go down to talk with him."

"Take a minute to collect yourself. You are too easy to read, Litt, and your father is about to name you crown prince. Soon he will ask you to stop going to daydream at waterfalls and work on kingdom business, and he will announce your arranged marriage soon. "

"My sisters are lucky that they were already married with children before we fled the ghetto," Litt said, sighing. "How long will you remain my attendant with these new laws? Does even friendship get to survive his reorganizing of the kingdom?"

"Your father hasn't set up a timetable yet, but from what I hear, all but the tiger clan will be asked to move to different parts of Khabu's countryside. Your favorite waterfall may end up in my territory for all we know." Nominus laughed grimly.

"It will be hard to see you go. Find me a suitable replacement among the court staff who will not be thrown out of the palace for belonging to the wrong clan. I need someone as reliable and trustworthy as you have been."

"It will be a sad day, my brother, but we are in no position yet to argue. Your father has been talking about the necessity of a law requiring abdication after a number of years for every ruler who will take the throne, so this situation won't last forever. When you eventually take the throne, perhaps you can summon me back. Look forward to the day when you can ease the restrictions under your own reign."

A trumpet blast split the air, announcing the reading of the new decree.

"Time to go," Litt said, grabbing his golden cloak and hat. "Accompany me to the ceremony for now at least. "

"I wouldn't have it any other way," Nominus said as he opened the door to let Litt walk past him. "Perhaps it won't be as bad as you imagine."

4

After the formal declaration of the new policy in Khabu, Litt fled his father's chambers and wandered the halls of the palace until he reached the garden walk near the newly built temple. Most of the ministers were still listening to his father drone on when he snuck out early, and Litt felt confident none of them had noticed him leave. He saw no need to stay and listen to them react to the decree since he knew well enough after their flight from their home world they would agree to anything his father said. Zurui had paid for their loyalty by saving their lives and their families. Now, they wouldn't question his choices, even when they should.

The corridors of the palace were deserted since it was after dinnertime and everyone was settling in for the night. Even so, Litt approached the figure wrapped in a dark gray gown waiting for him by the garden entrance in the waning light. Her hair was even more striking than usual as the sun set, her long, straight strands striped alternately white and black. Surely she had white tiger blood in her, and Litt felt relieved just being near her. He went out to meet her as she bent down to examine the flowers.

"Eoksu! I have been waiting all day to talk to you."

She looked up at him and smiled. Standing, her almost black eyes softened with love for him, and he quickly embraced her, aware that they might be seen.

"What have you planned?" she asked. "Nominus told me that your father intends to arrange a marriage for you. How can we be together now?"

"I have a plan to persuade him. It may not be easy, but after losing mother during our time in the ghetto, he should be more understanding."

"Didn't you just come from the audience room?" Eoksu asked, a look of worry spreading over her wide, round face. "Didn't you hear the new decree? How can you think we have a chance to be together?"

"What? Do you mean the new 'clans'? My father is a dreamer, and maybe he isn't taking all of this as seriously as you think. Besides, we are both of the same clan, so it won't matter in the end."

"What clan were you given in your DNA results? Mine came back the clan of the wolf."

Litt looked at her in astonishment. Her family couldn't possibly have wolf DNA. Wasn't it clear enough from her oddly patterned hair? She had to be part of the tiger clan. He wouldn't marry anyone else his father presented, only Eoksu.

"The royal family is from the tiger clan, of course, but so are you, Eoksu. Your test results must be wrong."

"Maybe the report is wrong, but what would be the reason for the error? No one worried in the early days about the details of the DNA experiments, so our people didn't know which DNA had been used on them when they married. It's possible I could have some dominant wolf ancestry somehow for the results to come back like this."

"That has to be a mistake. The testing wasn't supposed to be made definitive for anyone discovered to have mixed animal DNA. If you had more than one animal, you would be taken aside for more scrutiny. Are you sure this is correct? Can you take the test again to verify this?"

"I can try, but you will need to come up with another plan, Litt. We can't go in to your father now and argue that we should be allowed to marry when the tests clearly show that we violate the new law."

"I'll leave Khabu with you if I have to. We left one world to find a better life. We can leave this one too, move on, and live however we like."

"Is it really that simple?"

"Yes. It has to be. We can flee to my waterfall abode next week. I will have come up with a plan by then, and we can leave Khabu."

Eoksu looked at him helplessly.

"Tomorrow I have been asked to help the high priestess prepare the banquet formally celebrating the founding of Khabu. I won't be able to slip away at all under her watchful eye any time in the next month with all of the ceremonies and celebrations your father has planned. Will you be there at least? We can't talk at the banquet, but at least we can see each other."

Litt nodded, swallowing his anger.

"I'll be there. I can meet you before my father's appearance at the temple if I don't get summoned to meet with the ministers earlier. Eoksu, I need you to trust me. I'll think of some way for us to get out of this so we can be together, I swear to you!"

Kissing Eoksu quickly on the cheek, Litt went back into the palace and retired to his quarters for the night.

The next day, Litt woke to find Nominus standing over him, looking more morose than usual.

"Has something happened?" Litt asked numbly.

"Yes and no," Nominus said quietly. "Your father issued a late night decree, more than one actually."

"And? What does it matter at this point? I can't do anything about it, you know."

"He has summoned you to the audience hall for a discussion with the ministers about the new caste system he is putting into place."

"I was talking with Eoksu last night, and they told her her DNA sample showed she is part of the wolf clan! How can that be? Isn't it clear to anyone with eyes that she belongs to the tiger clan?"

A look of anger and hatred flashed across Nominus' face.

"How will you marry her now, especially in the face of your father's selection of your new bride, if Eoksu is from a different clan? Could the DNA results have been faked to keep you apart, so you wouldn't reject your father's choice?"

Litt looked up at Nominus in surprise. They had been friends a long time, but Litt had never seen him so despairing.

"I will do what I must to be with Eoksu. I will reason with father if that's what it takes. None of my sisters had to put up with this, and I have no brothers to shift the burden of my role as heir to the throne onto, only one nephew. I see no purpose behind creating such an antiquated system!"

"Your father's plans have already been solidified to separate the clans permanently once the transformation to our animal forms takes place later in our lives," Nominus said, his words coming faster and growing more emphatic as he spoke. Litt slipped out of bed and pulled on his ceremonial garb, the gold embroidered night blue tunic his father had favored.

"The transformation is a dubious expectation to begin with, but pray tell how he will keep us all separated?" Litt asked.

"He has now issued a decree to build a forest of huge proportions at the far edge of Khabu, which will be walled, for the deer and bird clans to go once they change permanently into their animal form. Like the ancestor crypt beneath the temple, he will use his knowledge of dimensional doors to create this forest."

"So will the wolf and tiger clans be house together in their eternal pens, too, somehow?"

"The crypt your father has been building even before the palace was finished is where he intends for the royal family to go, but I have heard nothing about plans for the wolf clan."

"What do you mean you have heard no plans for them? Then where will they go? What is this crypt anyway that he is so obsessed with?"

"He has found more doorways into other worlds around the kingdom, places with a different progression of time that he wants to take advantage of. I have heard nothing about plans for the wolf clan, as I said. I think that's an ominous sign, Litt. If Eoksu is truly the woman you want, you must flee Khabu with her before something goes awry. Let me ask an even more difficult question: could your father have rigged the DNA test to label certain people in our community whom he doesn't like as part of the wolf clan so he can deal with them as he pleases, creating a criminal class among our people?"

Litt only stared at him, startled at the suggestion. Could his father do such a sinister thing? Would he have led them out of the ghetto only to kill off some of their numbers? Litt shuddered at the thought.

"And what do my sisters Liara and Lessynda think about what father is doing?" he asked, changing the subject, not knowing how to answer Nominus' accusation. "Have they expressed any doubts about his sanity?"

"Your sisters have been sent into the countryside where their husbands will help build the enchanted forest. I don't know if they have even been told about the change in the laws. Rumors have been going around the palace that before they departed your father left their husbands untested, and your nephew has been kept behind here at the palace for now under your father's care."

"So I am singled out as the target for his machinations. What clan do you suspect my sisters' husbands are from? Could they even remotely be part of the tiger clan?"

"Maybe Lessynda's husband, but surely not Liara's," Nominus said, sighing loudly. "I would guess he is a deer, like I am. That reminds me, Litt. I also heard a rumor that the clans will be forcibly separated by the end of the month. We don't have many days left for me to serve you or for you to meet with Eoksu and decide how to make your escape with her. You must make a decision soon. I don't think your future lies in Khabu."

5

After Nominus had slipped into the shadowy corridors of Khabu's palace, Litt also left his chambers to wander the palace before he was expected at the audience hall. He knew it was risky with his father's spies to be seen talking to anyone but his close attendants, but Litt felt too unsettled by the recent turn of events to take precautions. He just wanted to see Eoksu and reassure her, as well as maybe himself, that there was a way to stop his father's disastrous law from ruining their dream of a life together.

As he walked down the corridor toward the doorway where the palace connected to the temple, Litt felt a chill when he thought of Nominus' declaration: *I don't think your future lies in Khabu.* He wanted to believe his friend was right, that there was a way out, but he felt trapped by the circumstances. When he could get away from the palace, he would go to his favorite spot near the Blue Waterfall to meditate and make sense of his jumbled feelings about Khabu and his role in it.

Turning the corner, he saw Eoksu near the door to the temple's main hall where the font with the odd meteorite was. Today she was wearing the gray chiton the temple priestess wore, taking on her new, formal role for now.

"You came anyway," she whispered, putting her arms around his neck and he embraced her and quickly kissed her lips. "I thought maybe your father would drag you away, and we'd have no chance to talk again for a while. I was worried after our discussion last night. How can you fight your father on this? We may have to settle for the fact that there is no way we can be together now, with the new law in place."

"Nominus also suggested we run away together," Litt whispered in her ear, still holding her close. Breathing in the scent of temple incense lingering in her thick, straight hair, he ran his fingers through it gently. "No, he went further than that. He warned me we must flee in order to save ourselves. I must admit, he seemed melodramatic, but I appreciate his concern and agree with him to a point."

"Where would we run to?" Eoksu whispered back to him, pushing him away a little, knowing the corridor would soon be filled with people preparing for the banquet. "We will run again? Just the two of us? You are the king's son, Litt, you can't just do as you please anymore."

"Our people have great longevity and regenerative ability, thanks to the unethical genetics experiments done on us back in our home world. My father doesn't need an heir, not really. He is building this medieval world to suit himself, not out of necessity. He will merely abdicate one day and let me rule for a time, then I in turn will be forced to abdicate because of his arbitrary law and live a sterile eternity of his choosing. I would rather be with you. My father isn't thinking clearly. I would rather flee Khabu and spend my days with you than live in the palace with all this fakery."

Eoksu smiled sweetly at him and sighed.

"You always were very idealistic, even back home in the ghetto. I would love to stay with you always. If only that were possible for us."

"Don't lose hope. Please, "Litt said fiercely, holding tightly to her hand. "There has to be a way."

"But the clans," she began weakly.

"Yes, the clans. Nominus said something about a rumor that the clans will be separated at the end of the month. He thinks that no plans have been made for the wolf clan, and he even went so far as to suggest that the wolf clan is being set up as a scapegoat of some kind. You may not be part of the wolf clan anyway, so embrace your fate and escape with me."

Eoksu looked thoughtful for a moment.

"Nominus may be on to something there," she said suddenly in a low voice, her brow wrinkling with worry. "The only way we can tell for sure if wolf clan designations follow a pattern is if we find out who else got those DNA results. We need to determine if they are all people your father has a grudge against."

"Does he really have a grudge against you?"

"Yes, he might. I never told you about this, but after your mother was taken by the medical people back to the laboratory ten years ago and never seen again, your father was despondent. I met your father, and he seemed interested in having an affair with me, but I met you shortly after then and we fell in love. Your father never made an issue of it, never mentioned wanting to be with me again after that, but is it possible he resents you where I'm concerned?"

"Really?" Litt said, shocked. "I had no idea my father knew you before we met. Then perhaps there is something more going on with the DNA test results."

"It was a hard time for him, but I never seriously thought about him as a romantic partner."

"You are right that he was devastated at the loss of my mother and hated the people who did this, but he never mentioned another woman, at least not to me. I'll have to ask my sisters if they ever heard him talk about you. But his new plans for the kingdom might indicate some more general problem he has with me. He let my sisters marry whomever they wanted and is now trying to force a marriage on me. He has to realize you will now be separated from me by clan designation."

"Once he saw you and me together, it was a dead issue. He never even acted like he remembered me. We must find out who else is in the wolf clan to test Nominus' theory."

"And if it proves to be true, will you leave with me without delay? We will find a place to live, in some world or other. I have nothing really holding me here."

"What did Nominus mean when he said the clans will be separated at the end of the month? Separated how?"

"I don't know, but he said my father would be encouraging everyone to transform into animal form permanently by some set time of life and then we would all live in our designated homes by caste forever."

"I'll see if the high priestess knows anything. For now, go to your father's celebration." She started to walk toward the entrance to the temple hall. "I'll see you at the banquet later."

6

During the morning audience with his father and Khabu's ministers, Litt studied each of the ministers' faces carefully, wondering which clan they now belonged to. He thought about asking directly, but he would have to catch many of them after the announcements had ended when his father disappeared into his chambers with his closest aides for the afternoon session. He didn't want to be overheard by his father or his most loyal ministers. Barely keeping his attention on the matter at hand, Litt tried to remember all of the stories he heard in the ghetto back in their home world about who his father had been quarreling with to know where to begin to ask about the DNA test results.

As his father droned on about kingdom business and the dreary forest-building project he had sent Litt's sisters to help out with, Litt zeroed in on the most likely man in the room to have been targeted by his father for liquidation. Now serving as a minor minister in his father's court, Jentzu was standing off to the side of the group of ministers, near the edge of the room. The frail, older man looked more than a little distracted, and Litt thought he should cut off the man's escape on the way out and lead him to his favorite garden seat for interrogation.

Litt remembered his father always talked about how much he despised Jentzu, even mentioning leaving the man behind when they were preparing to flee the ghetto. Litt's mother, however, found Jentzu, a classmate of hers when she was young in the early days of the medical experiments, to be indispensable. His mother's fond memories, communicated for years to his father, were likely to be the reason Jentzu had come with them to Khabu and had even been appointed to his father's cabinet in their new kingdom. Jentzu was a competent leader with a great deal of wisdom from what Litt could see. Perhaps Litt could get more answers than merely the results of a DNA test from the man. Perhaps he would even be a reliable ally as his father tightened his grip on the kingdom.

Finally the audience ended. Litt slipped out the side door of the hall without a word to anyone and quickly went down the corridor to meet Jentzu on the way out the main doors. As expected, Jentzu was last to leave the audience hall. Litt walked up to him, noting that his father was still in the audience hall, distracted over some new law and talking with his prime minister as they turned to retire together to the court's inner chambers. Good. Zurui wouldn't be able to interfere.

"Master Jentzu," Litt began, matching his stride to the older man's. Startled, Jentzu looked over at him in confusion. "I know it's a bit of an irregularity these days for us to talk freely, but I was wondering if you would sit in the garden with me and examine some of the medicinal flowers there. I have some questions about them that I think you might be able to answer. Mother always said you were quite a good botanist."

Jentzu seemed to relax at the suggestion, and Litt was pleased with himself for thinking of it. He put his hand lightly on Jentzu's shoulder and gestured for him to turn down the hallway in a different direction from the rest of the ministers. Jentzu obliged with a flattered, satisfied smile. At the end of the hallway was a tall, sweeping staircase that led down to the garden where Litt had met Eoksu the day before. Since everyone in the palace seemed to be too busy to spend any time there, he felt confident they could talk openly without any of his father's spies casually appearing. As the two men reached the landing at the bottom of the stairs, a cluster of the new temple acolytes walked past them toward the main temple hall, but the women didn't even look in their direction. Satisfied no one was around, Litt led Jentzu into the garden then turned to slide the doors shut behind them.

"What is it you wanted to ask me, my son?" Jentzu asked. "Which plant did you have a question about?"

Litt looked at him apologetically, wondering how to start such a line of interrogation. The wind currents, now trapped in the walled garden, tugged at their silk tunics. As Litt hesitated, Jentzu's smile faded and his eyes filled with sadness.

"Was this really about something else altogether?" he asked, stroking his slight beard nervously.

"I really need to talk to you, Jentzu," Litt said, stammering a little. "Surely you are aware of my father's decree about the new clans based on the DNA testing. Do you understand what he intends by this? Why wasn't our way of life in the ghetto good enough for him?"

Jentzu's expression turned to one of great caution, even sternness.

"This is what the king has decreed. Who are we to question its wisdom?" he asked.

"Enough of that nonsense, Master Jentzu. I want to hear the truth. So far it has come out that my childhood friend will probably no longer be in my employ because he has been determined by these tests to be from a different clan, and the woman I love…".

Litt could barely stand to continue the thought. Jentzu silently waited for him to finish, his face unreadable.

"Do you really believe we are all captive to our DNA? Does it matter if Nominus' DNA comes from a deer and mine from a tiger? Are we predator and prey instead of friends and brothers based only on such a thing as that? Why has my father latched onto such silliness to found the kingdom upon? I don't understand him at all these days."

"I understand your confusion, your highness, but now that it's the law, we really can't do anything about it. Will you be torn from your loved ones because of the law?

All of us will. It will take some adjustment, but in the end, it will be the better course."

Litt was dismayed by Jentzu's answer and thought frantically about what he needed to say to get through to the minister how truly evil his father's plan was.

"Then will you be leaving us, Master Jentzu? Are you of the tiger clan? What future has your DNA test dictated for you under this new law that you are so serene about its implications?"

Jentzu winced quickly before composing himself. Litt realized then that Jentzu was putting on an act just in the same way Litt was. He wouldn't admit what he feared in case it got back to Zurui.

"Well? I'm waiting for you to enlighten me with your wise guidance, Master Jentzu."

"I was informed that I will be leaving the palace at the end of the month, that my service here will no longer be needed," Jentzu said soberly, careful not to meet Litt's gaze.

"Which clan did you turn out to be a member of? Where will you be sent at the end of the month?" Litt asked angrily, careful not to let his voice get too loud where they could be overheard from the upper levels of the palace.

"The wolf clan," Jentzu said, looking down at his feet. He stared at them silently for a long time. Waiting for the man to come to terms with his emotions, Litt was furious that his mother's old friend wouldn't admit what both men knew to be true.

"And where will you go when your service here is done?" Litt asked again, his voice both firm and grim.

"I don't know."

The words echoed in the deserted garden. Litt snorted.

"Why don't you know? Doesn't every other clan know where they are going at the end of the month? You don't have to answer me, because I have my suspicions."

"Your father is a good man, he has just lost his way a little. In time, he will correct himself. Try to be patient, my boy."

"And what will you do if 'I don't know' ends up meaning something a little more than you bargained for? What if my father's patience with *you* has run out? You dare to lecture me, but your own head is at stake here."

"You must love her very much to be so worried," Jentzu said softly. He reached out his slender hand toward an amethyst-colored flower near the edge of the garden path and plucked it.

"Tell me what to do, Jentzu," Litt said helplessly, near tears.

"Trust that your father won't go so far, and all will be well."

"Who else do you know has been given the wolf clan for their DNA results? My friend Nominus has a theory."

"No one has confided in me they got such a result," Jentzu said, turning back to look Litt squarely in the eye all of the sudden. "All of the ministers I have spoken to are either tiger or bird clans. I am the sole wolf among them. Rumor has it that the temple acolytes are mostly tiger DNA with a few exceptions. You won't lose many when the end of the month comes. So few no one may even notice."

"Do you imagine that you will end up as my mother has? Disappeared?"

"What are you saying, Litt? The days of illicit experiments are long done now that we have come here. Your father has seen to that. Perhaps I will just go study in the newly built forest for the rest of eternity."

"And if you are wrong? What then?"

"You are making too much of it, my boy."

"Then tell me, who else outside of the palace had been given the wolf clan as their heritage? Prove me wrong by providing me with some names I can check out."

"Prove you wrong? How would providing you with names of people in the wolf clan prove you wrong?"

"You do know of other wolf clan members, don't you?" Litt asked, his anger rising again. "Didn't you hear my father's decree yesterday on the matter? The lists will be announced publicly at one point."

"Then I suggest you wait to see what he publishes as proof. I don't know anything that can help you. Good day, your highness."

7

Without saying another word, Jentzu stalked over to the doors, slid them open and cried out in surprise. Litt turned around. Eoksu stood before the entrance in a night blue chiton, her black and white hair flowing loosely around her shoulders. Collecting himself, Jentzu bowed slightly to her then walked determinedly past her down the corridor. Eoksu watched him go, then turned back to Litt.

"I didn't expect we'd talk again so soon," Litt said, his voice low and full of emotion as she came over to him and pulled him down the path along the edge of the garden.

"I heard some details from Gwanghui, the high priestess. It couldn't wait until after the banquet, although if I'm seen with you, there will be trouble," she whispered.

"And what did the high priestess have to say about the matter?" Litt asked. "I tried getting some information out of my father's minister Jentzu, but he wouldn't cooperate. He did admit he is also of the wolf clan, however."

"Is that who that man was? I remember him from the ghetto. Do you want me to question him? It may be easier for me since I am now of the same clan and am affiliated with the temple. There are a number of the acolytes like me who have been designated as the wolf clan."

"Really? Which acolytes? Is there any pattern to who has been given this clan designation?"

"Most of them are not high in the king's favor, though Gwanghui is quite happy with all of the recruits. There are maybe five or six of us out of thirty girls who must leave at the end of the month, three of which are of the wolf clan. Gwanghui will be devastated when we leave. A few are also deer, but most of the acolytes are tiger."

"Should we try to take them with us if we have to flee?"

"If Jentzu didn't sound that receptive to your concerns, the other girls may be just as reluctant to believe anything is amiss," Eoksu said, sighing. "There may be another way to find out what's happening than questioning them."

"What other way?"

"It would be risky, but we could break into the laboratory that conducted the DNA tests. It's so odd that your father set it up the way he did, retaining that old technology when everything else in our new kingdom is much more primitive and magic has taken its place. It's almost as if he wanted to remember the laboratory that turned us into the monsters our home world found so threatening, like he internalized that fear himself and is now taking it out on all of us."

"I can go tonight when the palace has wound down for the night. I'll ask Nominus what guards have been set there and how I can get in without raising any attention."

"Let me go with you. I know we could get in trouble, but it would be easy for me to slip out of the temple late at night. Gwanghui is far more reasonable than your father and would do anything for our people."

"You think she is trustworthy even with this? I wonder how my father found her in the ghetto in the first place and why he decided to make her our spiritual leader. But regardless of whatever plans we make now, we'll have to make it through the banquet first."

"Your father selected her because she had strong psychic ability and a deep understanding of the pure animals we were spliced with. I think that's why she was a little non-plussed when she heard about the clan separation and testing. Of all people, she can sense the animal nature of anyone she meets. "

"Has she said anything about your designation as part of the wolf clan?"

"The high priestess keeps her thoughts to herself, Litt. She would probably not dare to share any doubts she has, given the situation. She was flattered to be named high priestess by Zurui when we came to Khabu, but I don't think she likes your father. Only once has she made an odd prophecy about Khabu, that everything beautiful about it would mask an evil core. None of us dared to ask her what she meant, and she denied ever saying it later."

"So my father has everyone too snowed or afraid to talk."

The sound of a bell interrupted their discussion.

"It's time for me to go back. The banquet is about to start, and we will be serving at the feast as representatives of the temple. I will meet you by the palace's back entrance tonight, so we can go to the laboratory together. Otherwise, we shouldn't be seen together at this event."

Before Litt could answer, Eoksu turned on her heel and floated back down the corridor toward the temple precinct.

Everyone had gathered in the enormous gallery beneath the palace not far from where the new crypt was under construction with its interdimensional door. Portraits of the royal family and long, colorful banners depicting the animals of the new clans and the insignia of the royal temple hung along the gallery walls. Festively decorated tables had been placed between the gallery's tall marble columns, and the temple's male and female acolytes brought around trays overflowing with fruit and meat. A trio of musicians, also from the temple, played in the corner on old fashioned instruments. Litt marveled at how different their new land was now, a wave of frustration washing over him. Litt never thought he'd miss their home world and the ghetto. That gritty technological society they had left behind destroyed their bodies and minds for the sake of knowledge and ambition. Yet their new home was now an alien world where nothing made sense. He tugged at the embroidered blue tunic that marked him as part of the royal family, wishing he could wear something more comfortable and less conspicuous.

He wandered around the room, searching for faces he knew. Nominus sat across the room with a few other court attendants who were preparing to lead the festivities and formally present the new symbols of the royal family to the court. He caught a glimpse of Eoksu's striking hair across the room as she helped the other acolytes set the tables. Surprisingly, Litt noted his sister Liara had shown up at the festivities, but then he realized his father had never exactly said their work at the new forest would keep them from the founding ceremony. He quickly strode across the room to have a talk with her.

Her blue eyes zeroed in on him as soon as he started to walk in her direction. She was ten years older than Litt but shared his curly blonde hair and fair skin. Her thirteen-year-old son Azantes was by her side, and he smiled eagerly as he watched his uncle approach. Liara wore a blue gown trimmed with gold with her hair coiled on her head in an elaborate braid. Azantes was dressed more informally in a plain blue tunic with gold trousers, and his blonde hair reached nearly to his collar.

"How surprising that you should appear here today," Litt said good-naturedly. "I would have expected you to stay out in the countryside with your husband working on that new project."

"Everyone else did, and father had suggested we not come to today's banquet, but I insisted it would look bad if all of the royal family stayed away and won the argument. How have you been?"

Litt looked at her sharply, realizing word may already have gotten to her about what was happening in the capital. He had always been closest to Liara out of all of his family members, and he liked being around Azantes.

"Would you like me to show you around the crypt level? It's a little crowded here, and we're expecting even more guests to arrive momentarily."

"Lead the way."

Litt walked with them past the acolytes and the court ministers that were pouring into the room toward the unfinished western precinct of the lower palace level. No one lingered in this area, and the marble walls and columns were in the middle of construction. The face of a tiger had been lightly drawn on one wall in preparation for carving, and the far wall presented a fully finished, carved map of Khabu as it looked now. An odd-looking wooden barrier by the unfinished gray marble slabs blocked the entrance to the deepest part of the western precinct. Azantes noticed it and walked over to it to take a closer look.

"Is this where the famed crypt will be?" Liara asked softly so her son couldn't hear. "Have you heard about father's ghoulish plans for it?"

"So you have heard about the decrees. I wasn't sure if you had been sent away before any of the talk began or if you had heard any news out in the new forest. What father is devising is quite cruel, I think. And the clans. Some of us are worried what it might mean for our people, and even for ourselves. Father has been pushing for an arranged marriage for me, though he hasn't made any demands on you or Lessynda. What have we fled to, Liara? Was it freedom we hoped to find beyond the ghettos when we came here?"

Liara bit her lip before answering.

"We have heard rumors even about the forest itself, which is a beautiful, serene place much like the waterfall region that you found so mesmerizing in the central mountains of Khabu. Azantes of course has been forced to stay behind here, and he is my eyes and ears, though he doesn't always understand court politics. It's hard to imagine that things could go so wrong, but I think father shouldn't be in charge now. He was a magnificent leader when we fled our home world, but he was never stable enough for leadership in peace time. Now there's no way for us to deal with him, and these decrees…".

"Something is set to happen at the end of the month. Plans have reportedly been made for all of the clans but one. I'm concerned, since my girlfriend has been named as part of that fourth clan."

"Your girlfriend? Eoksu? No wonder you are worried."

"Based on the new law, we won't be allowed to marry since we aren't of the same animal clan."

"That isn't fair, especially since father didn't test my husband or Lessynda's."

"Yes, I knew you were spared the testing for some reason. I've been trying hard not to resent your happiness. But what am I to do? He's setting up this crazy system, and all I can do is stand by and watch."

"One of the advantages to the genetic experimentation we were subjected to is that we can nearly live forever. You have time on your side. If father will truly abdicate in your favor as he has promised, you can change all of these terrible laws and undo whatever damage they cause."

"And if he won't abdicate? Then what? My choice would be to flee or to kill him. What if his ministers consolidate power and demand the laws remain in place? Living with this system isn't possible. His abdication is still going to be far in the future, even under the best of circumstances."

"Think about where you are now before you say such rash things! There would be serious consequences if you were to kill him. We must come up with some other way to deal with this without resorting to bloodshed. Even now, father has written decrees to eliminate all silver from Khabu, making murder an obsolete memory from the old world." The blast of a trumpet from the eastern precinct interrupted them. "We should be getting back now before they wonder where we are."

8

When they returned to the eastern precinct of the palace crypt level, the celebration was already underway. Zurui arrived wearing a silver tunic trimmed with white and black fur reminiscent of the white tiger his clan had descended from, his black hair shorn to just below his ears. Because of the strange side effects of the DNA experiments, age barely touched his face. Still handsome and fit, he smiled courteously at his guests as he led the procession of ministers into the center of the room where a special chair sat next to a small table covered with a glittering silver cloth. Zurui came over to the table as his prime minister appeared at his side and unrolled one of the newest decrees to declare to the citizens of Khabu.

"We're gathered here today to celebrate the founding of our new country, Khabu," he said in a deep voice that carried easily through the room.

Zurui looked around the crowd before continuing, measuring the impact of his words on the room. Litt had to admit that they had quite a turnout. Almost a thousand of Khabu's most powerful citizens had come to listen to their new king and celebrate their freedom from the nightmares of the old world.

"We have a lot to be thankful for as we embrace our future here together, finally free to accept our transformed humanity and live in new ways."

After a while, Litt tuned out his father and studied the crowd. He noticed Nominus had slipped out the side door, and he saw Jentzu standing once again at the edges of the crowd of ministers, as if he didn't really belong among them. Azantes also caught his eye again as the boy whispered with one of the female acolytes and tested out some of the more exotic fruit on hand. Soon Litt lost track of how long he hadn't been paying attention to the ceremony, though he saw he was hardly the only one growing bored with the official nature of the gathering.

"Before we close today's celebration of feasting and dancing, there is still one more serious detail on the list of official announcements I want to make," Zurui said, smiling. "The matter of kingdom justice needs to be addressed, though now that we are here in Khabu, most of the things we feared are distant memories. However, as a responsible leader, it is important to have a plan should any among us turn to criminal action. How does one control an immortal in that case?"

Litt snapped to attention, a feeling of dread washing over him. Zurui finally pulled the silvery cloth off the table beside his chair, revealing a gleaming helmet carved like a tiger's head with rubies in place of eyes and a shining silver dagger. Hadn't Liara said their father outlawed the use or keeping of silver in Khabu?

"The royal jails have been constructed further down this corridor in the eastern precinct as the first level of punishment for any would-be miscreants in our new land."

Everyone in attendance clapped. Litt scanned their faces, and most of them seemed approving. Their reaction made him wonder why he felt so uneasy. His eyes met Nominus' across the room, and Nominus looked away, shaking his head with a dark expression.

Zurui picked up the tiger helm and placed it on his head with one hand while gripping the dagger in the other. Litt saw something like a mist surrounding his father as an almost visible beam of electricity sizzled between the helmet and the dagger. Zurui smiled, noticing the effect of the demonstration on the crowd.

"This helmet and dagger were specially designed as the second level of punishment for any who would dare go against Khabu's laws. Nowhere in the country will we allow silver except for the executioner's official blade. One stroke through the heart of the criminal, and his life force will dissipate with no chance of regeneration.

"The death penalty of course will be reserved for only people deserving of its cruelty. Know that it still exists as a deterrent and that all silver is not completely banished from the land."

The party ended a few hours later. Litt had spent most of it lost in thought after his father's display of the executioner's dagger, struggling with the idea that he might have been right to threaten the crowd with such a measure. Leaders needed to worry about such things, but Litt didn't know if he felt comforted by it or concerned by it given his father's mental state. As the crowd thinned and the acolytes took away the festive decorations and food, Litt walked back to his quarters, counting the hours until his meeting with Eoksu later that night.

Nearing his door, Litt saw Nominus waiting there for him in the flickering candlelight of the wall sconces hung at intervals along the corridor. Knowing Nominus had to be there for a good reason, Litt slowed as he approached the door. Nominus opened it for him and gestured for him to enter the darkened room.

"To what do I owe the pleasure of this visit?" Litt asked as the men went in.

Nominus struck a match and lit a candle in the corner of the room after shutting the door behind him.

"I don't have much time to talk, but we'll be leaving the palace tomorrow."

"We? Tomorrow? Why so suddenly? I thought you said we had until the end of the month, which is still a few weeks away. Weren't you the one who encouraged me into thinking that this wasn't going to be as bad as I thought?"

"The deer clan members in the palace have met secretly and made a decision to leave before the deadline. News of your father's presentation tonight made a lot of people nervous, though we all understand the need for order in the new kingdom."

"Did his methods seem primitive to you, too? We have the jail, however, so there will be no real need for the dagger."

"Everything about the new kingdom he's founding seems rather over the top. The world we came from was far from perfect, but at least our rulers weren't some sort of mystical hereditary king like he wants to play now that he has led us here. It can't be a good thing."

"Where will you go?"

"For now, we'll gather near the Forest of Bliss, which I have heard from your sister Liara has been very quickly constructed, as has the palace crypt. They are both nearly finished, not that many will take him up on the offer to transform and stay there for eternity just yet. Once we arrive there and we see how things develop later in the month, we will make a final decision about what to do."

"Who is the leader among you?" Litt asked.

"I have been asked to be the leader of the deer clan. They have chosen a more democratic governance than your father has set up, with a council rather than one man full of megalomania. I saw you talking with Liara. What conclusions have you come to now that you have discussed this with her?"

"She doesn't like the way I'm thinking, but she confirmed that father hasn't challenged them on their husband's DNA sampling! I tried asking Jentzu if he was part of the wolf clan and what he thought it meant, but he only got angry with me. He did admit he was named as part of the wolf clan on his report, and I remember he was someone my father disliked, so your theory may be correct. Does my father know the deer clan is leaving?"

"They don't want to admit what is plainly obvious," Nominus said. "I hadn't wanted to either until the last string of decrees, each more draconian than the next. No, your father doesn't know about our plans, though I can't say he will be unhappy with our departure. This was what he had in mind anyway, isn't it? The segregation of the clans? What will you do now, Litt? I won't be able to console you if things get worse in the palace."

"Eoksu and I are going to sneak into the laboratory and get a closer look at those DNA tests in a few hours. Have you heard anything further in the grapevine about the fate of the wolf clan members?"

"No, there has been a strange silence surrounding that topic ever since it first came up, though many people had talked openly about your father's plans for the bird and deer clans. Of course, his own clan of the tiger will rule, as he made clear tonight."

"Have you seen the crypt? Liara and I went down there to find a private place to talk, and tigers are being carved all over the precinct."

"I have heard that your father has even devised a special magical tiger mask with the new high priestess to communicate across the crypt portal when they begin to enter it. If it's anything like the dagger and helm he demonstrated tonight, it should be quite powerful. I wonder where he learned to harness such arcane powers, given our home world's scientific bent."

"From what I have heard around the palace, it's a mixture of our home world's more advanced, forbidden science with some old magical texts my father was studying in the ghettos. It's how he tore open the magical barriers to this dimension in the first place. He must have figured out how to manipulate the world in more powerful ways than we guessed back home."

"Which only makes him more unpredictable and dangerous. Regardless of what you find in the laboratory tonight, flee with Eoksu immediately. I have a bad feeling about this. If he catches you there in the laboratory, you won't survive his wrath, especially if you discover his secrets. The back door is guarded by a friend of mine from the deer clan who is also planning on leaving with us, so approach him, and he will let you in."

"I will miss you terribly, Nominus," Litt said, smiling slightly.

"We are no longer children, Litt, and the time to act is now. You will see me again. Just be sly about what you are doing, or you may lose everything."

With that last warning, Nominus slipped back out into the hallway.

9

After another hour passed, Litt put on a nondescript gray cloak and pulled the hood up as he walked the opposite way down the corridor to the palace's back entrance. The lanterns were dimmer here, and he saw Eoksu was already waiting for him, wearing a cloak very similar to his. Darkness engulfed the street that led to the laboratory, but Litt was relieved to get away from the bright candlelight of the palace where he would be recognized. The building they sought was only a few blocks away, so their task wouldn't take long.

The laboratory was the only authentic remnant they had recreated in memory of their home world. The organization running the fateful experiments that created them two generations before had been called the National Alliance for Animal Research, or NAAR, a group considered a shadowy, unpredictable but necessary part of the ruling class of their land. The experiments they had conducted on their human test subjects, Litt's grandmother's generation, stemmed from a desire to learn the secrets of life and create a superhuman. Its goals were to find a gene to eliminate death and to splice animal DNA into the test subjects so they could take on some of their unusual abilities otherwise inaccessible to human beings. Some of the test subjects could transform halfway into their animal forms, but others could only transform to be fully human or animal, not some combination, depending on the animal DNA used.

When some of the first generation of test subjects failed, those failures were kept under lock and key at the NAAR facility. The subjects who successfully had accepted the genetic editing and developed the target abilities were kept and interbred. The NAAR scientists eagerly discovered that the second generation not only retained the traits they had cultivated in the original test subjects, the children had even stronger manifestation of the superhuman abilities the scientists were looking for. By the third generation of children, the abilities were so smoothly integrated into their human forms and had surpassed even the second generation's power that it sparked dissent among the scientists. Some were enthusiastically in favor of continuing the experiment, but others were frightened by the power of the monsters they created. The latter group had held sway in the end, but the test subjects' powers of regeneration and near immortality scared them so much, they considered drastic measures to control the experiment. The possibility of a massacre using silver weapons could have brought a public backlash if it ever got out, so they forced the test subjects into ghettoes and denied the existence of the program that had created them.

Zurui had always been among the test subject leaders in the ghetto. A dour but strong man, he had challenged the NAAR authorities who administered the ghetto more than once, and his wife, Litt's mother, had been reportedly taken permanently back to the laboratory as a punishment to break Zurui's will. Instead, it made Zurui even more unpredictable.

Cultivating the dark arts that he was able to glean from old books in the abandoned section of town that housed the ghetto, Zurui learned how to augment the power of their genes. He talked with the leaders about his findings until he had gained their complete trust in his plan, even demonstrating for them his forbidden knowledge by blasting a hole in the air that led to another dimension. When the ghetto leaders agreed they had finally found a viable route of escape, they threw their authority behind Zurui.

The large ghetto held 30,000 test subjects and their offspring, but Zurui had devised a plan that allowed all of them to escape through the dimensional hole before NAAR could detect them. Indeed, they crossed the border with only a handful of losses to NAAR's armed guards before they closed the hole behind them. Now in their new land of Khabu, for the first time in their lives, they could breathe easier and enjoy a measure of freedom. Yet for some reason, Zurui decided to recreate the NAAR bureau to continue to monitor the experiments. Few of the inhabitants of Khabu knew about its existence at first, though once the DNA testing was required to determine everyone's clan, it became widely known. For the most part, no one complained even as its existence struck fear in the hearts of Khabu's citizens. Zurui was held in too high esteem for helping with their escape for them to suspect him or rebel just yet.

"This is the place," Eoksu whispered to Litt, taking his hand and leading him toward the blocky building across the street from them. It was constructed in an ugly, functional style from their home world, not like the whimsical and monumental architectural style that Khabu's buildings were constructed with. "How do we get in?"

"Nominus told me one of his clan buddies was guarding the back door, so it will be safer to go that way."

Turning the corner to the back of the building, they entered an even darker alley and made their way to the steel door leading into the rear. A man sat near the door, but he looked like a vagrant rather than a guard.

"Who's there?" the man asked, sounding drunk.

"I just need to go into the laboratory for a few minutes to take a look at some files," Litt said, trying to keep his tone casual. "Nominus said you would be able to let us in for a quick tour of the place."

"Nominus? Oh, sure, but you can't let on to anyone I did."

"I hear you're all leaving anyway, so there shouldn't be any trouble for you."

The man paused as if considering how Litt might know such information, but he jangled a ring of keys and unlocked the door for them.

"I'll bang on the door when it's time to leave," the guard said. "I can only give you 15 minutes, maybe 20, before you have to be on your way."

"Fair enough," Litt said, pulling Eoksu along with him over the threshold.

When the guard had turned on the old-world electrical emergency lights and shut the door behind them, Litt looked along the walls for the facility map. There it was! They just needed to get to the records room and take a look at a few of the test results to get a better idea of what was going on.

"This way," he said, motioning to the left hallway.

Eoksu walked behind him silently, allowing him to lead her through the dim corridors to the records room. The door to the office was unlocked, and the emergency lights were bright enough to read by but not bright enough to attract unwanted attention from the street.

"Where do we begin?" Eoksu asked.

Litt walked up and down the cabinets, reading their labels.

"Here. This is the cabinet with the recent DNA test results."

Tearing open the top drawer that was labeled for the temple acolytes and palace ministers, he pulled out a few of the files and handed them to her, including Eoksu's own test results. Litt took that himself and quickly flipped through the file, while Eoksu looked over the general demographic analysis of the DNA tests that split them into clans.

Litt scanned the pages in Eoksu's file to get to the pertinent information, past all of her family and work history in their home world. Finally, he reached the DNA analysis sheet. Eoksu's own DNA was shown in one block, and the four animal DNA patterns were in blocks next to it. The match was clear. She was a tiger! Sucking in his breath, Litt flipped back to the beginning of the file where a letter explained that she was actually a member of the wolf clan. How? The justification in the letter never noted that her DNA was a match for the tiger clan but glossed over the test results entirely. Deeper in the file, Litt found what he was looking for, a letter from his father's closest minister demanding that Eoksu's results be switched to wolf no matter what the actual DNA test showed.

"They are deceiving us by saying you're a member of the wolf clan. You're really a member of the tiger clan, like me. Do you see who authorized this deception?" He showed her the page then slammed the file shut and dropped it back into cabinet where it belonged.

"It wasn't your father, Litt. That was the prime minister's signature on that request. Maybe Zurui doesn't know."

"I told you it was a lie! Nominus said I should get you out of here immediately, even tonight. He's right, and I have wasted a lot of time doubting his advice. We'll have to correct that immediately. What have you found there?"

"The pattern of DNA test results was kind of skewed to begin with. Most citizens were found to have bird DNA. Deer were the second most common. Tiger was third, and wolf…was the smallest population, only 5,000."

"Who were given the wolf clan results? Is there a way to tell who might be part of it? My suspicion is that my father has designated people whom he hates to that clan in addition to those who genuinely have wolf DNA."

Eoksu flipped through the pages in the file.

"Here are some lists naming who fell into which clan. The deer clan is actually rather striking for the sorts of people who showed that DNA."

"But the wolf clan?"

"Here it is. Look it over. Do you see any patterns?"

Litt's eyes scanned the page. About 100 of the names were people Litt would consider his father's personal enemies. Not one of them was omitted from the list. Handing the file back to Eoksu, he looked in the cabinet and pulled out Jentzu's results.

"Maybe not all of them are my father's enemies, but too many of them are," Litt said, turning to the DNA analysis page in Jentzu's file. Clearly, he should have been a deer, but he was marked as the wolf clan. The same letter from his father's minister was present in the file.

"NAAR's early scientists did use wolf DNA as one of the four sacred animals they wanted to splice with humans," Eoksu said, thinking. "I had heard rumors back in the ghetto that they had used those four, not that it mattered much to us then. It was just a curiosity that people mentioned sometimes. I always thought their choices were strange and pointless perhaps."

"Had you ever transformed into a tiger, even partially, back then in the ghetto? I did when I was younger, and it was exhilarating."

Eoksu shook her head.

"It was too dangerous to do things like that. NAAR might have come to take you back to the facility and keep you there forever if they ever got word of it. Is that what happened with your mother?"

"I don't know. I wasn't home when they came for her, and I was just a boy. It always seemed to me that they took her to get back at my father." Litt put Jentzu's file back into the cabinet. Looking at the list of wolf clan members that Eoksu held, he pulled another name out of the cabinet that he didn't recognize. This one had a DNA match for the wolf clan and no letter from the prime minister. He replaced both files in the drawer and shut it.

"I think we're done here. It's not exactly what I anticipated, but I have confirmed that some of my father's enemies have indeed been shuffled to this list. That can't be a good thing."

"Am I your father's enemy? Is that what we determined earlier?"

"Apparently." Litt grabbed her by the shoulders suddenly. "Come with me now. Let's leave here with the deer clan and never come back. I don't trust the prime minister and can't imagine he acted without my father's knowledge. You're in some kind of danger. This is a trap. I can feel it."

Eoksu smiled slightly and looked at him with such love and compassion that he nearly burst into tears.

"First, let me return to the palace to say goodbye to Gwanghui, then I promise you I'll go with you wherever you want."

"The high priestess? What could you possibly say to her at this hour of the night? No, we shouldn't go back. Let's leave now, straight from here, while it's still dark. We can wait at the Blue Waterfall until we can decide where to flee to from Khabu."

"Litt, Litt, you are letting your imagination run away with you. We can flee, it will only be a few hours more even if I go see her. We'll go around the outside of the palace so we won't be so easily seen, then once I have had a talk with the high priestess, we'll leave."

"This is foolishness, Eoksu."

"I think you are unable to see your father clearly right now. It isn't as great a risk as you think. Come on, Gwanghui will want to talk with you, too, before you leave. You're the heir to the throne of the new kingdom, so it's only right you at least speak to someone before you flee, even if it isn't your father."

She led him out of the file room back to the door on the first floor where they had entered. In the dark alleyway, the guard waited for them.

"Did you find what you were looking for?" he asked in a friendly tone.

"Yes. Thank you for your help. Send my regards to Nominus when you see him tomorrow. We may be joining him."

The man nodded curtly as Eoksu pulled Litt back to the street and stopped abruptly. She turned to face him.

"What is it?"

"Nothing. I just thought it might be nice to have a kiss, tiger to tiger, before we begin our long journey away from here."

She pulled him close and quickly kissed his lips. Giggling, she grabbed his hand, and they walked along the street back to the palace.

Taking the long way around the palace to the temple precincts, Eoksu paused at the exterior doors to the temple hall.

"Let me go in first. You wait here. I'll send for you when Gwanghui calls for you."

Stepping through the doorway, Eoksu pulled back the hood of her cloak, letting the torchlight illuminating the sanctuary of the temple hall dance across her striped hair. Slipping the cloak from her neck, she handed it to Litt. He stepped just inside the temple doors and stood in a shadowy corner while she walked solemnly across the broad room to the high priestesses' inner sanctuary. Litt wondered why Gwanghui would be down here in the main part of the temple instead of her sleeping quarters at such an hour.

As Eoksu reached out to touch the doorknob to the sanctuary, the room flared to light, as bright as if the sun had come out. A beam of pure white light emanated from the pearl in the font on the dais. Turning in surprise, Eoksu took a few steps toward the font, pausing midway across the room to look at the light, confused. Suddenly, guards spilled into the room from the temple hall's two side doors, their lances pointed directly at her. Her confusion transformed into terror as two of the guards came up to her, grabbed her arms, then dragged her down the corridor to the palace without even a glance around the room.

Frozen to the spot and unable to make a sound as the guards took Eoksu away, Litt suddenly found the strength to walk over to the sanctuary and knock on the door. Gwanghui stepped out into the temple hall, looking at him in dismay.

"Your Highness, is there something wrong? Why have you come to see me so late at night?" she asked, following his gaze down the corridor.

"The guards just took Eoksu," he said softly.

Her eyes grew wide, and she looked back down the corridor, but the figures were gone.

"Come with me now," she whispered just loud enough for him to hear. "Something is afoot in the palace tonight."

Clutching Eoksu's cloak, Litt strode into the sanctuary chamber after Gwanghui. When she shut the door, he slapped her across the face, nearly knocking her over. As she touched her face and felt blood coming out of her lip, she looked up at him in alarm.

"Do you think I wanted this?" she asked angrily. "You only stood there and watched them take her, didn't you? Now you will blame me for what's happened?"

"I wanted to flee with her. I couldn't move when I saw them. It was too terrible to see her arrested like that, and I don't have any weapon to fight them. Do you know where they're taking her?"

"You were going to flee with her?" Gwanghui asked in surprise.

"What's all of this about? Did you betray her by asking her to come here? I couldn't convince her to leave without talking to you first," Litt asked, his eyes glittering with hatred.

Suddenly, he noticed his hand that held Eoksu's cloak had begun to change. His skin now was covered by a short layer of white and black striped fur tipped with long, lethal claws.

"I didn't lure her here if that's what you're asking," Gwanghui said firmly. "Now we can't do anything if the palace guards have taken her. What were you doing out so late at night together?"

"We just came back from the laboratory. Some of the DNA test results were doctored. I had been suspicious that my father might use the test results as a cover to deal with his enemies."

"Then that's the big demonstration he had planned for tonight."

"What do you mean?" Litt asked, taking a step closer to the disheveled woman. For the first time since they had come to Khabu, he took a really good look at her.

Younger than Eoksu, Gwanghui was very beautiful with almost feline features, raven black hair and monolid eyes a deep shade of ochre. Instead of her usual night blue chiton, she wore a long tiered gown of white fur that left her arms bare. On the table beside her bed lay a wooden mask carved into the shape of a tiger's face.

"What is it you're doing in here so late at night anyway? I was surprised Eoksu led me here."

"I had felt uneasy and was unable to sleep. I'm doing some experimentation with the tiger mask your father created to speak across the crypt's barrier once we begin to enter there."

"An odd choice of activity tonight. Why did the guards take Eoksu? How do you know he had something planned? I need to rescue her and get her out of here somehow."

"Litt, you can't save her. Tonight was the fateful night when everything must change. You could never fight it.

Your father had been spreading rumors that the changes would be made to the kingdom in a few weeks' time, but that wasn't his plan at all. I heard the ministers talking with him about it privately earlier today. He wanted to catch everyone off guard."

"What are you saying? Nominus told me the deer clan only just decided on fleeing last minute tonight. Now Eoksu has been arrested."

"No, not Eoksu, all of the wolf clan will be gathered tonight. If you show any great attachment to her, it will only make it worse for her. You must stay away now. There is more in your future than this."

"No, I won't stay away! Whatever my father has planned, I will put a stop to it."

"You'll regret this," Gwanghui said, pulling on Eoksu's cloak that Litt still held. "But if you must go, leave this with me, so they won't tear everything away from you completely."

Litt let her have the cloak and ripped his own from his throat, tossing it to the floor. His whole left arm had now turned bestial, and he felt a sudden taste for blood. Never had he let the animal DNA take over so completely, not even to experiment alone back in the ghetto. Now, the sensation felt overpowering. What would it mean to make the change now, to appear before his father as half-tiger instead of his human son? Would that jar him into abandoning his plan?

10

Racing through the temple hall and down the palace corridors, Litt's animal senses led him to the gathering spot Gwanghui had indicated. The great timepiece set over the crypt on the lower level struck midnight just as he reached the stairs leading down to the eastern precinct. The celebration had only been held there hours before, but now he could hear screaming and rumbles of discord.

Quickening his steps, he wished he brought some sort of weapon with him.

As he turned the corner and walked through the first colonnaded room leading to the gathering spot, he ran into a group of guards holding another prisoner, a bruised and bloody man. Litt stopped abruptly and stared at the man, who raised his head and whispered incoherently. Jentzu! The old man had been stripped of his ministry robes and hat and could barely stand on his own. Looking further down the gallery, Litt could see a crowd pressed against the far wall, waiting for whatever fate held for them. The guards dragged Jentzu toward them into the eastern hall, where Litt knew Zurui was waiting to strike the wolf clan.

Turning to follow them, Litt winced, feeling his face began to burn as if he had stuck it in a fire. Touching it with his still-human hand, he stroked the light layer of fur now covering his cheeks, and he ran his tongue over shockingly long canine teeth. He was changing again as his emotions got the better of him, and he realized he might not retain any vestiges of humanity by the time he reached the other room where his father waited. Still, he felt obligated to find Eoksu and see what his father had in store for the wolf clan. As he ran past the loitering guards to catch up with Jentzu, many of them looked at him in alarm, seeing not the crown prince of Khabu but a raging half-tiger man, an odd appearance even in their kingdom where few made the change publicly.

Walking into the main area of the precinct close to the corridor leading to the jail, Litt could see his father had set up the room for a spectacle. The ornate chair and table from the late afternoon celebration had been moved to a wide, low stage where a beam with four sets of shackles had been raised on a tall and ominous scaffold. Litt paused behind one of the thick marble columns before anyone could spot him. So far the guards dragging Jentzu forward had not bothered to look for him or let Zurui know a strange monster was roaming about.

Hearing his father's voice as he commanded the guards, Litt realized that the deer clan had already fled.

"The seers of the temple warned us the deer clan would disappear tonight, but we didn't have enough manpower to put a stop to it. I gave priority to rounding up the wolf clan. Now you must sort through the people we have captured. Those less likely to cause us trouble should be put in jail for now, while the troublemakers should be brought to me here immediately. We must finish with this plan before daybreak. Be sure no one has escaped."

Looking around the crowd being herded into the eastern precinct in greater and greater numbers, Litt couldn't find Eoksu. Where would she be? Dashing across the room, he moved from marble column to marble column, careful not to be spotted by his father's men, until he made it to the doorway leading to the jail wing of the crypt level. The guards who saw him recoiled, but since he was a tiger, clearly a member of the royal clan, they let him pass. He wandered unhindered through the jail corridors looking for his love, but Eoksu was not in any of the cells among the young children and elderly women he found there.

Re-emerging from the jail corridor, he darted back to a shadowy corner behind the columns to watch the group who had been brought to stand near the stage where his father and his closest ministers waited. His father sat regally in the chair, wearing the same ceremonial garb he wore earlier at the founding celebration. The prime minister, the man who sent those letters of condemnation to the laboratory to frame certain members of the community as descendants of the wolf, stood near the scaffold wearing the tiger helm and holding the ceremonial dagger. On some level, Litt knew what he was seeing, but he wouldn't admit to himself the terrible truth the spectacle indicated.

Zurui smiled at the prime minister and motioned for the guards to bring the first member of the wolf clan forward. Unsurprisingly, they brought Jentzu, who could barely stand before Zurui in his weakened state. The guards let him kneel before Zurui, and he seemed at that distance to be begging for his life. Litt was uncertain as to why his father hated Jentzu so much, what personal or political grudge had brought the old man here, but he felt only outrage, remembering Jentzu's trust in the fairness of the court and in his father's good will even when confronted with the ugly implications of a political coup in the works. What a foolish old man! Even so, Litt did not think this was the end the old man deserved.

After a moment, Zurui looked satisfied and nodded to the guards. Taking Jentzu over to the scaffold, they began to place the shackles on his wrists, though it seemed ludicrous since Jentzu was clearly too weak to fight them. Leaning him against a wooden board attached to the scaffold that served as its back wall, the prime minister came forward, the eyes of his tiger helmet blazing to life. His body seemed to be wrapped in lightning, the electrical current knocking the guards beside him back a few steps and causing their hair to stand on end. The silver dagger in the prime minister's hand gleamed as he pulled it back and paused mid-air. The room grew still.

When the prime minister's hand fell, the dagger plunged smoothly into Jentzu's chest as if it cut through silk rather than flesh and bone. Blood welled out of the wound, streaming down his body and the wooden board he leaned against, then down onto the platform. Jentzu threw his head back in a spasm of pain. A sharp, metallic scent filled the room. Somewhere a woman screamed. Zurui, watching the spectacle with pleasure, stood and clapped as Jentzu's body went limp. No one clapped with him at first, but soon the guards had pressed the crowd to join in, and they also began clapping. Litt only watched from the shadows, numb with shock. Why had he thought it would end any differently than this? He should have heeded Nominus' warning when he had the chance.

As one group of guards removed Jentzu's body from the contraption and the prime minister wiped the dagger clean in a bowl of water with luxurious towels, more guards brought another victim up to the platform, Eoksu. The solemn, defiant woman still wore the temple chiton Litt had seen her wearing when she was arrested, her black and white striped hair glimmering with more life than any of the spectators in the room. Her wide monolid eyes, filled with both contempt and terror, locked onto Zurui.

"You," Zurui said, his voice full of annoyance and some other emotion Litt couldn't place.

"You know I don't belong to this clan," Eoksu said, her trembling voice ringing out through the gallery. "Not that it matters, since there's no lawful reason for you to slaughter the wolf clan other than your own twisted logic. That's what you intend, isn't it? For the whole wolf clan to be cleansed from the face of Khabu? Jentzu was just the beginning, wasn't he?"

Zurui snarled at Eoksu, and he made a chopping gesture with his hand. The guards dragged her through Jentzu's blood to the scaffold, where they locked her in place with the shackles. Litt felt his body grow hot again, all over this time, the beast consuming every last trace of his humanity as he watched the woman he loved face her death.

Stepping out into the center of the room, Litt caught the attention of everyone on the platform, including Eoksu. His tiger face could no longer form human words properly, though he knew it would come with time if he stayed in this new form long enough. All he could feel was rage and helplessness. Wondering if he should spring onto the stage and tear them all apart, knowing the worst he could do was maul them and wound them temporarily before regeneration restored them to health, his eyes met Eoksu's. She knew instantly who he was, even if none of the others recognized him in this form. Raising her shackled hand up a few inches, her palm out to face him, she warned him not to attack. He froze, unable to disobey her, devastated at his failure in the face of his father's evil even with all of the inhuman power he commanded.

With a swift motion, the prime minister plunged the silver dagger into her heart. Eoksu struggled not to scream and twisted in agony against the shackles, gasping for breath as blood soaked her chiton. Zurui sprang to his feet, looking eagerly at her as the life-force seeped out of her along with her blood.

Seeing his father's enthusiasm for murder, Litt could take no more. Unable to think clearly, he sprang back through the eastern precinct toward the crypt, the terrified crowd on that side of the gallery parting as he passed. None dared follow him. Turning suddenly, Litt bound up the steps back toward the temple. Back to Gwanghui.

11

He found the high priestess waiting where he had left her by her chamber door in the temple hall, tears running down her cheeks. Watching him slow and stalk over to her, she gestured for him to follow her into her sanctuary chamber.

"It's only safe for you here," she said softly, locking the door behind her and barricading it with a heavy chair. "He has gone mad, hasn't he? They'll all be dead by morning. Your friend Nominus interpreted the signs correctly, and I saw it in my dreams over the past few nights, so I decided to keep watch."

"What am I to do?" Litt asked, his body transforming back into his half-human, half-tiger form. "I could have saved her if I had had more courage. I could still save the rest of them now, but I fled."

"You can't kill Zurui and his allies unless it's with silver. They would have regenerated quickly and executed you too before anything more could come of it. This way, you stand a chance. The kingdom, when it falls to you, can enact more humane laws. You could even sentence Zurui to death for treason once you are king, even if that meant dragging him out of retirement in the crypt. If they killed you now, your father would stand unopposed in his folly."

Gwanghui reached out and stroked the soft white and black fur on Litt's face, taking a deep breath. She leaned her forehead against his.

"I hate that we had to sacrifice Eoksu, too, but this won't be the end for her. I had a vision a few nights ago about her. You will see her again, just as you will witness the end of the kingdom of Khabu. As it began, so it will end, and you will see it. She will come for you again. Wait for her. You must bide your time until all that you have lost will be given back to you. Then you can get revenge on your father."

"I can't just stand by and watch this happen," Litt said, weeping. "What's left if I remain as heir to the throne and watch him destroy everyone? We came to this kingdom because we wanted peace. If we all wanted to die, we could have stayed in the ghetto back home and let NAAR kill us. I will not spend eternity in the crypt with him, even if it means I lose Eoksu. He has become a monster."

"Stay here and rest," Gwanghui said wearily. "Your father will be looking for you come morning, but you don't want to let on to him that you were the tiger he saw in the eastern precinct during the executions. There will be a lot of bodies to bury before the night is through, and the slaughter will continue until not one of the wolf clan is left. I have seen this in my visions. For now, this is what we must do."

She returned to her couch across the room to lie down.

"If I kill him, will it change the future you have seen?"

"What are you talking nonsense for?" Gwanghui asked, closing her eyes. "You would need to steal the executioner's dagger to kill him. Do you really think they'll leave it unattended for any reason after this?"

"I don't want to rule Khabu. I don't care about any of that anymore. I just want him dead. If I succeed in killing him, I could abdicate in favor of my nephew Azantes. He has been groomed to rule and won't be tainted by my crime."

"You would be forced by your father's new law to transform permanently to your tiger form and retire to the crypt if you did, that is, if you could escape execution yourself for his murder," Gwanghui said. "He still would have allies in power who could demand your death for parricide."

"Would they really execute me if I rid them of him after tonight? Do they really agree with this slaughter, or are they just afraid to oppose him? If I was punished with retirement and ended up in the crypt as you say, across the dimensional barrier, would I see Eoksu there?"

"No, Eoksu is gone. You would only see me. Only the high priestess and her two attendants can use the tiger masks to enter the crypt before it's time to retire with the ancestors."

"All of these rules! Why was my father so obsessed with rules? Fine, I will accept you in place of Eoksu for now. Help me come up with a plan to get the dagger. As high priestess, you have ways of dealing with the ministers. I'm sure you could think of a way to steal it without any of them wondering why you wanted it. I will 'disappear' from the royal court along with the deer clan and remain hidden here in your sanctuary until it's time to kill him."

"You aren't thinking straight now. Put out the candle and sleep. We can discuss this in the morning when perhaps you will be more reasonable."

Litt got up and walked over to her couch. Leaning over her, he put his hands on the pillow on either side of her head.

"Promise me you will help me with this plan, high priestess," he whispered, his voice lethal.

Gwanghui opened her eyes, the yellowish irises looking more amber in the dim light. Litt let his lips brush against hers and paused a moment before standing back up beside her couch. He was pleased to see she was angry. She lay very still on the couch, tolerating his impertinence, though she looked like she would attack him.

"Is this how you honor Eoksu's memory, by threatening me, your highness?" she asked, her voice low and full of fury. "All right, I promise to help you!"

Litt laughed a little and went back to the other corner of the room to sleep.

"Now we are bound together in this wicked plot, high priestess. Once the deed is done and I have accepted my punishment in the crypt, you will come to me often there, whenever I call."

He leaned over and blew out the candle, plunging the room into darkness.

12

When morning came, half of the wolf clan had been slaughtered, and the bird clan had been summoned to help bury them out near the Forest of Bliss. After Zurui ordered her to perform a ritual prayer over the dead, Gwanghui returned to her chamber in the temple hall and wept. Now, by their agreement, Litt remained in tiger form with no trace of humanity left so no one would suspect his true identity if he was accidentally seen there. Word spread throughout the palace that Litt had fled with the deer clan, though spies reported he had spent part of that fateful night rifling through the files at the laboratory with the now dead traitor from the wolf clan, Eoksu.

"Spies? My father has spies in the palace? How unbalanced he has become," Litt said when Gwanghui told him what she heard.

"No one suspects you're here with me now, so stay out of sight until I tell you to come out."

"Have you heard where the dagger is hidden?"

"Your father probably keeps it close. The executions will continue for a few more nights until the jail has been emptied," Gwanghui said sadly. "The wolf clan members in the jail probably believe they have been spared, but there were just too many of them to kill all at one time. And your father intended this from the start of the DNA testing, I suspect."

"So we sit back and let him kill them all? How degenerate we have both become, high priestess."

"Do you think I enjoy this terrible situation? I would stop him if I thought I could, but I have very little power that will help in such a situation. I'm a seer, not a warrior."

"He has given you power over the temple, has he not?"

"Yes, but how can I use that to stop him?"

"Give him a vision of the wolf clan's revenge so he will stop the executions midway."

"He will never believe that. He only half believes in my power anyway. I'm just a figurehead for those he thinks are too gullible."

"Your visions are accurate, though."

"Yes, sometimes, but that's no match for Zurui. Whatever forbidden books he studied back in the ghetto have endowed him with terrifying powers. I can't even begin to fathom him."

"Killing him will end it, won't it?" Litt asked.

"Maybe," Gwanghui said absent-mindedly. "Perhaps there's a way we can get the dagger, but it won't be in time to save the wolf clan. The ministers involved are keeping away from the main palace and the temple while the executions are carried out, but once it is over, they will return to their usual quarters."

"So?"

"I will send my acolytes along to the prime minister to 'celebrate' the new kingdom with him. They can get him drunk and find out how to get the dagger or steal it from him if he has it. Then you can do what you want. I wash my hands of the situation once you take possession of the dagger."

"Have you heard what the bird clan has said about this situation? The deer clan has fled, and now they are witnessing this winnowing of the wolf clan from afar. Surely it must frighten the bird clan, especially since they are tasked with burying the dead."

"None have confided in me that they have lost confidence in your father, but I doubt they would even if they felt it. I have heard some discussion regarding the deer clan, that they were able to use the same magic your father used to travel the dimensions to flee to safety."

"What do you mean? They have fled Khabu the same way we fled the ghettos and are building a new world elsewhere?"

"I don't think that's it exactly," Gwanghui said, bringing her breakfast tray over to him and letting him have a few morsels of meat and fruit from it. "There's a strange, magical sea that reaches into the caves in the cliffs beyond the temple. From what I understand, the sea there leads to other worlds through multiple dimensions that don't require magic to access. The deer clan reportedly took boats to flee along it."

"With so many of them, how could they find enough boats? The laboratory had them down as close to 9,000 clan members."

"I don't think they all fled that way, only the leaders. The rest may have swum downstream or are hiding out in the network of caves connected to the temple until they too can make the journey. Others could have used your father's method of creating a hole in reality to flee through."

13

A fortnight later, Gwanghui returned to her chambers in the temple hall with the dagger.

"I thought you'd never return," Litt said caustically, transforming from animal form to half-man half-tiger. Taking the dagger from her, he ran his finger across the blade, shuddering a little at the thought that this could take the life of any of them, though they were otherwise immortal. "You have been avoiding me, high priestess."

"I've been avoiding you because you are too impolite, your highness."

"We'll be spending a lot of time together once I enter the crypt, so it's best you don't forget our agreement."

She looked away from him and pulled out the tiger mask, the candlelight dancing across its fierce, painted surface.

"We will be bound by the murder of the king, and I accept this fate, but remember my words, that Eoksu will somehow return to you. But we must consider the details of our plan now. Will the dagger work without the helm? My acolytes were unable to recover it from the prime minister's room, but with some persuasion, he let me take this dagger for consecration rites. I had to make a particularly foul offer to him, I might add, pretending that the blood of the wolf clan will seal the crypt with a special magic and that the dagger alone holds the spiritual power from the sacrifice that we need for the ceremony."

"Little does he know our true intention. A dagger is a dagger, is it not? The helmet seems to add some power to it, but it's the silver that will stop my father's heart."

"When will you make the attempt? You will only have one opportunity to kill him. If you fail, the dagger will take your life the same way it took Eoksu's."

"And if I succeed?"

"The bird clan will support you. My acolytes were able to meet with some of their respected leaders to confirm their opinion of the situation. They were terrified by the slaughter of the wolf clan and the disappearance of the deer clan. A few of the bird clan leaders have been calling quietly for Zurui's deposition, not that they have any power to oppose him. They'll protect you should the tiger clan and the ministers of the court request your execution for his murder. If you succeed with the bird clan's help, you must agree to reign over Khabu for five years until Azantes comes of age and can take his place as king. Then you will be expected to retire to the crypt, as you have promised, as punishment for your crime. Only a few of the tiger clan elders have retired there, so it will be quite empty when you go in. Then you will only have those few elders and me to talk to until more retire in the next few hundred years."

"When will Eoksu return?"

"I don't know. Khabu's end will be the same as its beginning, and you will live to see both. This is what my visions have shown me. Eoksu will come then, too, somehow. I don't always understand my visions, but this is the prophecy I have to give. Believe it or not, as you see fit."

"The crypt is a type of sleep? It isn't the same as living as a human in this dimension?"

"No, it is beyond a portal, and many centuries of living as an animal may make you forget who you are now. Are you sure you want to go through with this?"

"What other choice do I have? I am the bird clan's best hope to get rid of Zurui. The responsibility falls to me to deal with the king. If I don't, they will either suffer under his reign or send another, less successful assassin. I wonder, though, should I reveal who I really am to him when I kill him? If I go as I am now, he won't recognize me. In the ghettos of our home world, we never took on animal or half-animal forms."

"Sometimes the children did in secret, though they weren't supposed to. I know you did this, too. Do you want me to also transform and hold him for you while you kill him?"

"You're not serious, are you, high priestess? Would you implicate yourself so intimately in my crimes?"

"He wouldn't recognize me either in that form. How else will you contend with his ministers and bodyguards?"

"Let me handle this. I grew up with him. I know his sleep patterns better than anyone. You've already done enough."

"Then I'll leave you to take care of the details," Gwanghui said, clutching the tiger mask close to her as she turned toward the door. "Return here once the deed is done, and I will protect you however I can."

"Even if it means bringing down the temple with it? Of course, I shouldn't come back here again. Go now. I'll come up with a plan. Just stay out of my way."

After Gwanghui left him alone in her chambers, Litt began to plot holding the dagger up before him in the candlelight, as if it had some way of advising him. Eoksu's blood was spilled by the dagger, and he forced himself to think about that.

"Help me get vengeance," he said softly to it, looking blankly into the candlelight for a moment. "If anything has the power to kill him, this dagger now holds it. The stolen life force of an entire clan is now connected to it. Even without the helm, this has to be possible. But what do I do now?"

Litt tried to clear his mind and think through different scenarios of how he could kill Zurui. Nighttime seemed to be the best option. It would be hard to get close enough during the day when Zurui talked with his ministers, though his father wasn't stupid enough to sleep in his quarters without armed guards hanging around, especially after the executions. He had to know many in the kingdom would want him dead.

Regardless of what plan Litt came up with, his father and the prime minister wouldn't let Gwanghui keep the dagger indefinitely. After a day or two, they would demand it back, assuming the ceremony she had promised would be completed. They wouldn't dare let such a dangerous weapon out of their sight, not with silver otherwise outlawed in the whole kingdom. Litt had to act tonight before he brought trouble down on Gwanghui.

Taking one of the priestesses black cloaks out of her wardrobe, Litt hid the dagger underneath in his gray tunic and pulled the hood over his head so his odd half-animal appearance wouldn't be noticed. In Khabu, as in the ghetto back home, any hint of their true animal natures would have raised suspicions, and Litt couldn't allow anyone to stop him.

As the timepiece in the crypt struck the first watch of the evening, Litt left the high priestess' chamber. No one was in the temple at this hour, though it was still brightly lit. Noticing the odd pearl in the font on the dais, a strange rock his father had found as they excavated the foundation for the palace and declared as having some sort of magical power, Litt went over to it. Wondering if it really could help him, he ran a clawed finger over the surface, watching the colors swirl as it churned in sympathy with his inner turmoil.

Nothing seemed to be happening as he stared at it, but suddenly the surface darkened, turning red as if the blood of the executed wolf clan had spilled from its core and was spreading through it. Intrigued, Litt leaned closer, and it seemed to speak to him.

"*Concidi.*"

The dagger beneath his cloak felt warm, and Litt took his hand off of the pearl. Immediately, it turned back to its opalescent white. A cloud of mist rose from its surface, and he jumped back to avoid touching it. Fleeing in terror, no longer thinking of how to successfully assassinate his father, Litt ran out of the temple into the corridor linking it with the palace. The candles in the wall sconces all burned brightly, leaving no shadows to conceal him.

14

Almost instinctively, he headed for his father's quarters. At this late hour, Zurui would be finishing dinner alone in his room and then would prepare to retire for the night. Two guards stood on either side of his father's door, holding swords and carrying rope to tie up any aggressor. In a land of immortals, the best any guard could do against any would be assassin was to maim him or knock him out and tie him up for further punishment in the jail as he regenerated. Suddenly, Litt knew what he had to do. Silver would only kill if it struck the heart, but a scratch from it could poison the blood and bring great pain until regeneration took place. He could incapacitate them if he acted quickly, but he needed to come up with a diversion so he could fight them one at a time.

Suddenly, he heard an odd whispering behind him. Glancing at the guards, Litt saw they hadn't noticed it. Doubling back the way he came, he approached the stairwell where the whispering seemed stronger. This spot was more shadowy than the hallways, and the sconces were spaced further apart. Looking around frantically in the dark, he thought he saw glittering eyes in the corner near the ceiling. Something stirred the air, making the candles in the sconces flicker. Holding out his hand, he beckoned it, wondering if his suspicions were accurate, thinking back to what Gwanghui had said about the bird clan's reservations about his father's rule after the slaughter of the wolf clan. Was it a bird clan member? Could they recognize him like this?

The whispering continued as the small body of a white bird descended and landed on his wrist, its flashing eyes fixed on his. Glancing quickly over his shoulder, assured that no one near his father's quarters had heard them, Litt brought the bird closer to his face, sliding back his hood a little so the bird could see it.

"Who are you, little one? Are you here for the same purpose I am?" Litt asked softly.

The little white bird whispered something more as Litt put his free hand under his cloak to pull out the silver dagger for the bird to see. The little bird jumped back a step on his hand, and Litt replaced the dagger, showing his open hand to the bird. The words it whispered started to sound more and more like a language he knew as the stream of sighing sounds came from it, scarcely louder than a breath.

"Must stop him. No more bloodshed."

"Then you and I are here for the same reason, little one," Litt whispered stroking the bird's head lovingly, wondering which of Khabu's citizens had transformed and come to his aid at such a crucial moment. "I couldn't save Eoksu, but we can end it tonight. I just need to get past the guards, but how do I distract them to get to my father alone?"

The little bird hopped excitedly on his arm, then paced lightly up and down his wrist.

"I can help you," it whispered. "Let me help you."

"Go, and I will follow behind you to do the dirty work."

The bird flew down the corridor toward the guards, while Litt silently returned to the corridor landing and peeked around the corner to see what the bird would do.

"Hey, how did that bird get in here?" one of the guards asked, unsheathing his sword as he watched the little bird hover in the air above them, still muttering unintelligible whispers.

The second guard saw the bird, then grabbed the first guard's hand, shaking his head.

"Wait a second, is that a real animal from the countryside or one of our citizens?" the second guard said. "Remember what the king said about the bird clan. Now we can't be too hasty in handling these things."

"If it's a bird clan member, he won't die anyway. We can just wound him and force him back into his human form for interrogation. By the way, I don't recall you saying what clan your DNA test put you in. I'm in the tiger clan and am proud of it, so you must be in the bird clan. Is that why you're so nervous about what I might do to one of your clan mates?"

The second guard was shocked by the insult and turned an ugly red. Grabbing the sword out of the first guard's hand, he turned the tip toward his neck.

"We'll see who has the upper hand here," the second guard muttered. "What difference does it make which clan I belong to? It never mattered in the ghetto, where all men were considered equal. Here, it's another matter. Try fighting the both of us if you're so powerful. I'll bet you don't even know how to change into your animal form. This guy's pretty advanced if he can."

"That thing? What can a bird do to anyone?" the first guard asked, growing angrier. He tried grabbing his sword back out of the second guard's hand.

Just at that moment, the little bird dove down and plucked a small ring of keys out of the first guard's pocket, tearing his shirt where it had been fastened. As fast as it had appeared, it raced down the hallway in the other direction with the keys.

"What the...?" the first guard sputtered, watching the bird.

"Where's that thing going with the keys to the King's storehouse?"

"I don't know, but maybe you'd better follow him before he gets you in trouble," the second guard said, still waving the first guard's sword at him menacingly. "Then again, maybe I can help him steal whatever is in it by putting you out of commission."

The second guard stabbed the first guard in the gut, then sliced the sword across his chest before running down the hall after the bird. Watching the first guard slide to the floor and lay coughing in a pool of his own blood, Litt knew it was time to act. The little bird had made a way for him to enter his father's chamber. He couldn't hesitate now.

Walking slowly toward the man lying in the corridor, Litt saw he was losing consciousness but not so fast that he didn't see Litt. As Litt reached the door, the first guard looked up at him, alarm and terror crossing his face at the sight of the tall hooded man. Glancing over the man's torso to see if he had any other items or weapons of interest on him and seeing none, Litt stepped over the man and grabbed the doorknob with a clawed hand. Pushing the door open, he stepped inside without a sound.

Litt looked around the entryway to his father's chambers. He could smell his father's favorite meal of broiled fish and roots wafting from the other room. No one seemed to be hanging around his quarters to wait on him. Pulling out the dagger just enough to quickly strike but not enough to expose the weapon, Litt stepped over the threshold into the room where his father dined.

Zurui looked up, alarmed at the intrusion, his eyes widening at the sight of the shadowy figure rushing toward him.

"Who are you?" his father asked, standing. "Guards! Stop him!"

"They can't help you. No one can help you," Litt said tonelessly, closing the distance between them by leaping over the table and grabbing his father by the throat with his left hand as he stabbed the dagger into his heart with his right. Blood gushed over Litt's hand as the life-force drained out with it. Looking into his father's ice blue eyes, he could see how quickly his father was losing consciousness and realized he would soon slip away forever. Feeling oddly conflicted at that moment as he was confronted with the man who raised him, he removed his hand from his father's throat and let him fall to the floor, the dagger naturally sliding out of his father's chest. Litt quickly pulled off his hood to let his father see his face.

"I have returned, father," Litt said, watching his father's expression turn from one of pain to shock. "Did you think I wouldn't get revenge on you for what you did to Eoksu and the wolf clan? Your terrible deeds had to be met with justice, no matter how it once was between us."

Suddenly the little bird reappeared in the open doorway, catching Litt's attention again with its odd whispering. Turning his attention to the bird, Litt walked like a sleepwalker back to the corridor where the first guard now was unconscious and continued past him down the stairs back to the temple, the little bird not far behind.

15

Litt made it back to the high priestess' chamber without attracting much attention, though his cloak was soaked with blood and he still carried the blood-stained dagger openly in his right hand. The few people who saw him took one look at his clawed hand holding the dagger and fled. Since it was unusual to show any type of manifestation of their animal DNA in public, Litt floated through the palace corridors like some demonic apparition after days of terror and bloodshed in the kingdom.

As he entered the chamber, the little bird slipped in behind him before he shut the door. Not even bothering to light the candle, Litt slid off his cloak and dropped the dagger on the floor, immediately falling onto his woven reed bed across from the cushioned couch Gwanghui preferred.

A strange fluttering sound caught his attention, and the air rippled around him. Holding up his hand to ward off whatever was coming toward him, Litt strained to see in the darkness. Reaching for the candle, he quickly lit it and looked around the room.

Standing at the edge of his bed stood a woman wearing a white chiton, her short hair the color of straw, her eyes red-orange. Almost glowing in the candlelight, she had the air of someone much older than Litt, and he surmised she must have been one of the first generation NAAR had subjected to its DNA tests.

"Who are you?" Litt asked, sitting up. "Are you the bird who aided me in murdering my father? Well, if so, we succeeded, in case you were unaware."

"I am Mapin," the woman said, her voice almost as whispery now as it had been in her bird form. It held the trace of a foreign accent Litt couldn't place other than to a small group of people who lived apart from them back in the ghetto. "I followed Gwanghui back to you when she sent spies to our clan, and I discovered your plot. I thought I could be of some use. I hope you don't mind."

"Do you see the dagger on the floor?" Litt said, laying back down, shielding his eyes from the glowing nimbus around her. "That's the last weapon of its kind that can send us into true death. I have done this to our king, my father. Now there will be peace in Khabu, perhaps."

"What are your plans now, your highness?"

"You know who I am, even seeing me like this? My plans are to retire as regent to the Blue Waterfall at the bottom of the mountain range that cuts our land in half, and then to retire to the crypt once my nephew is of age to take the throne."

"Ah, the bird clan will be very grateful for your help in putting a stop to his madness, though I don't think now we can ever go back to the way things were. The deer clan is lost, and we should probably search for them, the wolf clan is now dead...".

"The deer clan had good reason to flee, and though I will miss my friend who is among them, I see no reason to stop them now. Let them find their peace elsewhere if Khabu has not been hospitable. Lucky for them they missed the big show the night they fled."

"The bird clan did not miss the piles of the dead that your father left for us," Mapin said.

"What will the bird clan do now with their newfound freedom?" Litt asked.

"We will do what we must to make Khabu hospitable. Beyond that, there is only the forest in the end, like there is only the crypt for you. Don't worry about the repercussions of today's deed. The bird clan will handle any demands for your blood in payment for the murder of the king, as the high priestess has told you. Just do as you have promised, and we will protect you."

Without another word, Mapin went back into the temple's main audience hall to find Gwanghui. Alone in the chamber, Litt fell into an uneasy sleep.

16

The next five years flew by like a dream. Litt had a small fortress built near the huge, tiered Blue Waterfall that he had come to admire since their arrival in Khabu, and he conducted kingdom business there while his nephew Azantes met with him periodically to train for his new role as king. His sister Lessynda never spoke to him again and never returned to the palace after it was publicly revealed that Litt had assassinated their father, but Liara quietly supported him and lived with Azantes and her husband at the main palace in the capital. During that time, the bird clan had settled into their primary role as citizens of Khabu and provided many services for the nation. The deer clan was never heard from again.

When the day finally arrived for Azantes to be crowned king of Khabu, Litt made a rare appearance at the palace for his coronation, closing up the fortress of the Blue Waterfall in anticipation for his own sleep ceremony with the high priestess who would lead him once and for all into the dream chamber in the crypt of the ancestors. Satisfied that Azantes would rule justly and fairly, as the palace celebration waned and the new king returned to his own wing of the palace for a private banquet with his parents, Litt went once again to the high priestess' chamber.

"The time has already come," Gwanghui said, wearing her finest ceremonial robes of bright blue, her sleek black hair coiled in an intricate circular shape around her head.

Litt stood in the center of the temple while she attended to the pearl in the font. As the rite ended, Litt transformed into the pure tiger form he had only taken on once before during Eoksu's execution and his period of waiting to retrieve the dagger. A procession of acolytes, led by the high priestess who now wore the tiger mask, brought him down to the western precinct of the lower palace level where the crypt waited. The portal opened at her touch, and she entered with the restless white tiger, who grew larger with each step into the crypt until he was over ten feet tall. An archway appeared before them, and beyond it a bright blue sky full of wispy white clouds hung over a lush, grassy meadow of fragrant flowers.

Litt turned back to Gwanghui, unwilling to walk through the arch just yet, knowing he had a long wait ahead of him once he did.

Only two of her acolytes stood just within the portal doors well behind her. None of the others in the entourage were permitted to enter.

"Gwanghui, I will look forward to your visits. You'll be the only comfort I have here."

"Silence," she said firmly from behind the tiger mask with a trace of irritation, though her eyes glittered with tears. She paused to stroke the hair on his face tenderly a moment as he leaned down toward her. With a deep sigh, she retreated back through the portal with her acolytes, and the portal closed with finality behind her. Litt waited a moment more, then he walked slowly beneath the arch into the meadow, full of relief and dread as he sensed the air change and time seem to bend. Sleepy and confused, he lay down among the flowers, breathing in their fragrant scent as his eyes began to close and the dream overtook him.

As the ages passed, many more of the elders of the clan joined him, taking on their tiger form and forgetting most of their human existence. Litt held onto his past, which he eagerly recounted every hundred years when Gwanghui visited until she too entered the crypt. With every high priestess, it was the same. He would not forget Eoksu, or what Zurui had done. The prophecy would have to come true some time, wouldn't it? While the crypt was not unpleasant, he grew restless. Gwanghui had warned him he had been too young to enter the crypt.

Then, after an eternity of every day passing the same as the last, the boundary between the crypt and the palace flickered uncharacteristically. None of the other ancestors had noticed it, but Litt wandered close to the portal, sensing it was not just the usual temple ritual. Unsure of how much time had passed since he had entered the crypt, Litt wandered closer and closer to the archway leading back to the outside world, determined to get a glimpse of whatever was happening outside. Perhaps it was time for Gwanghui's prophecy to come true. Eoksu would return to him now.

When the portal between the worlds burst open, Litt was ready. Only one of the other ancestors had been aware of trouble brewing, but Litt pushed closer to the portal as a strange man entered to talk with them.

The young Duke Birum was ambitious, it was clear as he spoke with the ancestors near the archway, but Litt noticed that he seemed to be looking for someone in particular. When the young man had finally asked their names, his eyes filled with recognition as Litt stated his. So this Birum had come looking for him? As Birum tried to use low-level magic on him to sneak him out of the crypt, Litt readily complied. The time for Gwanghui's prophecy had come. Birum, completely snowed into thinking he had come to kidnap one of the old ancestral kings, had not been aware that Litt was manipulating Birum into freeing him from the crypt. And so they had both used one another in their ambition to rule Khabu.

17

"Does Birum know about your father?" Mirae asked when Litt finished telling her his story. After she returned from her bath, she found him lucid and awake, and Kerinda had left them a few small plates of food for breakfast. "Was that why he came looking for you in the crypt?"

"I'm not sure how Birum would have known about my father," Litt said, leaning back on the bed with his hands under his head. "Gwanghui and I decided to strike most of this from the historical record of Khabu, only retaining my father as founder of the kingdom. Perhaps Birum thought he would know how to travel the dimensions, as Birum has also found a way to do. Sometimes when I think of it, Birum reminds me so much of Zurui! They would have been birds of a feather."

"Yet you conspired with him," Mirae said, taking a bite of fruit. "How can that be a good thing, Litt? Shouldn't we fight Birum now? His sister Queen Joriya brought me to Khabu to do just that. Does he know about the other missing clans? Does Joriya or Minha? Or was that also stricken from the historical annals?"

"We did mention them briefly in the annals as coming from the old world, but we didn't explain what happened to them. They just disappeared from the records after the first few kings, which certainly has raised Birum's suspicions. He came looking for me because somehow he had determined that Zurui wasn't in the crypt, and I was closest to that generation to give him the answers he sought. One thing that seems to be a motivating force for

Birum now is his search for the deer clan, which has taken him across the worlds. I think he suspects the wolf clan has been annihilated, but there's no normal way he could know that. Joriya may know, since the truth has been handed down to the high priestess over the millennia since then. The high priestess alone has complete access to the crypt of ancestors, don't forget. Minha would know all of it.

"But as for your other questions, when Birum first took me from the crypt, he returned to the ruins of my old fortress at the Blue Waterfall and used his magic to bind me and use me as a decoy while he came here, assuming my identity so no one would know he had subdued Eokhmisseun. We didn't have much time for conversation before he left. I didn't know until you came to me exactly how bad things were here. I was just happy to be out of the crypt and home again in the setting that I loved, waiting for my true love to return."

Mirae leaned over Litt on the bed, her eyes full of confusion.

"Does this mean I'm Eoksu? You were expecting her, weren't you, when I came? That's why you used your magic to trap me so suddenly."

Litt merely smiled.

"Only you would know if you are Eoksu. She died all of those years ago, one of the few of our kind to experience true death. It was an unjust end, and I would like to believe her essence remained alive somehow, and maybe passed on into you. It's only right we should be together again."

Sitting up, he kissed her passionately before Mirae pulled away.

"But I don't feel like I'm Eoksu. Is it okay if I'm not? I wouldn't fulfill Gwanghui's prophecy if I'm not."

"Birum is like Zurui yet is probably not Zurui either. Does it matter in the end if he is my father reincarnated, if the end result is the same?"

"Do you think Birum is planning a massacre like Zurui did?"

"Look at what he has done in Eokhmisseun. We'll hear more of that tonight when we are summoned to dinner with his other 'guests.' Already you can see some of it from inside Eokhmisseun's palace. Many of the citizens who roam the streets are twisted shells of their former selves, they look very degraded, and even his daughter looks like a hybrid monster of a sort not even NAAR had dreamed of."

"Yet you yourself have taken on the same cast as Kerinda," Mirae said, pointing to the shapeshifting Litt had done while she was away in the bath. Now instead of soft white and black fur over his skin, he had normal hairless human skin with pronounced feline features, the skin very white with a tattoo-like pattern of black stripes, his mane of shoulder-length blonde hair almost white. His thin hands were still tipped with long claws, but the skin was also now hairless and had the same tattoo pattern as his face.

"I may as well try to fit in around here. Perhaps I can leverage this half-form to stop Birum."

"Don't tell him what happened with NAAR or your father, Litt. Don't give him any more power than he already has. Joriya and Minha are sure he's dangerous. I need to get you out of here."

Litt smiled slightly at her and reached over to take a few bites of food off of their plate.

"All in good time, Mirae. First we have to figure out what his plan is, which will require some playacting."

"Since I'm now part of the royal family, it also means I can shapeshift into a tiger, too, doesn't it?" Mirae asked, looking sidelong at Litt. "I wonder if I should try it now that I've seen so many of you half-tiger people, but I have no idea how to begin."

"I find it amazingly daring of Joriya to try to outwit Birum by sending her daughter to a far-away planet beyond the inner sea of Khabu. It's hard to believe, but since you are from a technological society like my home world, perhaps my story makes more sense to you than to the high priestesses over the centuries who never set foot outside of Khabu."

"Shouldn't we test the truth of Joriya's statements? If I'm really her daughter, I can also change into a tiger."

"Do you have a reason to doubt her? Do you really think she and Minha have been lying to you about your heritage as heir to the throne? As you wish, try it for yourself to prove the truth. Just promise me that you'll keep all of this to yourself while we are near Birum and never transform around him, even in a small way. Joriya was right to fear him, and if he knew why you were here now, he would surely kill you. We'll just tell him that you're a citizen of Khabu who happened to catch my eye, and I made you my wife. There shouldn't be any reason for him to doubt me."

"You've hidden your own double dealing plans from him that well? I wonder if you really have him fooled, Litt."

"Until your arrival, I was the perfect patsy for his games, a puppet bound by his magic. He shouldn't be aware yet that you've completely broken his spell."

"What do I do to transform?"

"Close your eyes and imagine the tiger in your mind. Focus on the part of your body you want to change and imagine how far you want the transformation to go."

Mirae did as he directed, but it took a long time before anything happened. Finally, her bare right foot seemed too hot. When she opened her eyes, she saw the bottom half of her right leg was now covered with downy white and black fur and her toes were tipped with claws.

"It's true then. I'm Joriya's daughter," she said in amazement.

"Now quickly do the same thing to get your human form completely back. They should be coming to get us soon to take us to stay with the other prisoners."

A few moments later, her body was back to normal, and Litt seemed less anxious as they finished their breakfast.

18

A few hours later, the red haired woman appeared at the door, alone.

"Both of you must come with me," she said. She wore a green dress in the same old-fashioned style that Kerinda had worn earlier, with lots of satiny layers and frills.

"Kerinda isn't with you this time?" Mirae asked, standing and helping Litt to his feet since he had been slightly injured in their journey to Eokhmisseun. "She seems like such a lovely girl. Is she your child?"

The woman smiled slightly, though mostly her demeanor remained cold.

"Yes, she is my daughter. I'm Crysalin."

"I see," Mirae said, remembering that Kerinda said she was Birum's daughter. That meant Crysalin was at the very least his concubine. "Where are we going? Will we be having an audience with Birum?"

"Not yet. For now, he wants you to mingle with the other guests staying in the palace before you all retire for the night. You can consider it a show of hospitality. Birum felt that keeping you in your room all of the time would make you seem more like prisoners than like colleagues. Otherwise, you must remain on this floor unless one of us summons you to another part of the palace. We ask that you respect our rules as our guests. Now, please follow me."

She led them down the long hall in the opposite direction from the bath. Since the hallway was fairly dim with few sconces and was decorated in heavy red and black fixtures and carpeting, Mirae didn't see that they were coming upon a sweeping staircase down to the next floor until they were nearly at the first step. At the bottom of the staircase, Crysalin led them through double doors leading to a richly decorated ballroom full of couches and a few dining tables. At the far end of the brightly lit room away from the windows sat five people, one woman and four men. The woman was particularly striking with her swarthy skin, nut brown hair and green eyes. The four men all had black hair with dark brown eyes and fair skin, and one of them looked toward Mirae with a sudden flash of recognition crossing his face, though he didn't say anything and quickly turned away from her. The others only stared suspiciously at Litt, whose appearance now resembled Kerinda's enough for them to wonder if he was one of their enemies.

"This is Litt and Mirae from Khabu," Crysalin said coolly, gesturing for a servant to bring more drinks and snacks. "They'll also be staying with us for a time and will spend some time with you for your mutual enjoyment."

Crysalin smiled, though there was no warmth in her eyes, and she walked out of the room without another word, leaving the group to mingle with a few servants. The double doors shut behind her, and two servants rushed in and left a tray of pastry appetizers and a few extra glasses of wine before retiring to the far end of the room. Litt came forward and took one of the wine glasses before deciding where to sit down. Finally, he took a spot between two of the men across from the woman studying him curiously. The man who had been looking away suddenly jumped up and came over to Mirae.

"You," he whispered, his voice ragged and his eyes feverish. "I know you, don't I? Would you be Sohyeon's sister? I know he said you were in Khabu on some task. You wear the ring of the royal family, don't you? Yes, he mentioned you had it."

Mirae was startled by how much detail the man knew, but she remembered the letters she exchanged with

Sohyeon in Eokhmisseun through the pigeon earlier.

"I'm Sohyeon's sister. Is he here now too? Who are you?"

"Sohyeon disappeared with my daughter the night of the purge. I can only hope they made it to safety. I'm Cargal, one of the former leaders of Eokhmisseun. That woman who brought you here was once my wife."

Mirae gasped and glanced back at the door.

"What's she doing here with Birum? What is this purge you are referring to?"

"Birum? Do you mean Litt? He kidnapped her not long after our daughter was born, and I haven't seen her again until the night they brought me here, the night of the purge. The purge happened last month, when Birum decided none of the human inhabitants of Eokhmisseun would be permitted to live any longer. Most of the remaining human inhabitants he turned into bloodthirsty half-beasts. A few of us he kept here, alive, without turning us like the rest to taunt us and break our spirit. Who is this man you are with?"

"The man I am with is Litt, the real Litt. He's an ancient king of Khabu that Birum, the Duke of Khabu and brother of the current queen there, had kidnapped many years ago. It's Birum who has taken over your land and stolen your wife, all in Litt's name. Litt has been bound by his magic back in Khabu, masquerading as Birum so no one knew he had come here to cause trouble. Few remembered the name of the ancient king, and most of the people in Khabu never leave their country. They wouldn't have heard about the Duke's activities here. But now Litt and I are also his prisoners."

"Sohyeon wondered why Khabu had wanted you to come talk with them so badly. What did you discover?"

"I discovered there was a war between the Duke and the Queen, and I was brought to help them put a stop to his activities. Now I will marry Litt."

"Yes, we had suspected a marriage was in the works, though it seemed odd for any of the immortal royal family of Khabu to marry a human. But is the reason Litt resembles Birum due to the connection between royal family members then? Birum also has that same feline cast and strange skin markings, just like his daughter does. Only Birum looks very sickly and evil, quite the counterpart to his degenerate ghost slaves."

"Yes, I think it does have something to do with having royal blood that they look, er, feline. I haven't met Birum yet, but Litt thinks it's a good idea to not say too much about my work for the Queen around him. He and his sister Joriya are not on good terms. We will just tell him I am to marry Litt and leave it at that. What is it that they have you doing here at the palace, and who are those people with you?"

"Two of them are my bodyguards they captured with me the night of the purge," Cargal said. "The other man is the bodyguard of the woman, Yarava, who served on the council with me. We heard she had been abducted by Litt, or Birum I should say, and we secretly met for a council meeting the night of the purge to figure out whether we should rescue her. We didn't know if Birum would have already killed her. Little did I know I would soon be here as a prisoner with her. We don't do anything now but play these little parlor games with Birum's staff and wait for death. What will you do now that you are here as Birum's 'guests'?"

"I don't know. I don't think Litt does either. Until we're sent for a talk with Birum directly, we will be no different from you."

"He is an ancient king, you say. How ancient? I had heard rumors of the way immortality was handled in Khabu, but I never paid much attention to the details of their history."

"He is something like 8,000 years old, and he has spent millennia in the crypt of the ancestors, away from the human world and normal day to day living. I fear he will be too slow to match wits with Birum, who seems very politically savvy from everything I hear. He'll need me to protect him."

Cargal's expression turned to one of mild amusement as he glanced back at Litt.

"Don't underestimate him. If he's 8,000 years old, he may have a few tricks Birum never thought of up his sleeve, and then some. Perhaps now we have hope that something will change."

"Is there any safe place my brother could be now in Eokhmisseun?" Mirae asked suddenly, changing the subject.

"Probably not, but he had my daughter with him, and if anyone would know of a good hideout, Tamnyn would. Could he have returned to your home with the ferryman?"

"Pontol? Maybe, but wouldn't they risk Birum following them back to earth?"

"Pontol is a strange duck," Cargal said, thinking. "Although he is a ghost slave, he's a servant of the high priestess of Khabu, so perhaps he was able to stop Birum in his tracks and take Sohyeon and Tamnyn to safety. I don't really know. All I do know is that while the capital sleeps, Birum walks the streets of Eokhmisseun, searching for anyone stupid enough to be out at that time. Daytime is no better, however, and it's important to remain cloaked and quiet when you travel anywhere. If he catches anyone who is still human, he uses his magic to turn them into beasts. Don't ever let him touch your bare skin with his hands."

"If you don't mind me asking, how did your former wife survive him then? She gave birth to their daughter, after all."

"From what I hear, they also have a son or two. I don't know if it is a specific spell he uses when he touches the citizens of the capital, but although my wife looks human, she certainly doesn't have much humanity left to her beyond her appearance."

"Has she recognized you at all or asked about your daughter?"

"She doesn't seem to recognize me, and we haven't spoken beyond her giving me orders to come to a gathering like this. It's like meeting a stranger after so many years, though I did hear rumors right away when she had been kidnapped. I was always afraid that they were true and tried to shield Tamnyn from them."

"Perhaps she is bound like Litt has been bound, by Birum's magic," Mirae said, her eyes meeting Litt's. He, too, had been talking animatedly with the bodyguards. "Perhaps you can free her, but would you want to take her back?"

Cargal suddenly looked sad and weary.

"You never know. Crysalin was always somewhat indifferent to our marriage, which was arranged. It has been a long time. I'm not sure it matters anymore, though it has been unpleasant to see her again."

"I wonder if Birum spared you from the turning and brought you here because he knew you were Crysalin's husband."

Cargal raised his eyebrows. Clearly, the thought had not occurred to him. Litt called to Mirae, and she and Cargal returned to the arrangement of couches and chairs where the others talked.

Yarava turned to Cargal, her eyes full of excitement.

"We may have our answer to what our demon leader intends to do with the ships leading to the other worlds, Cargal."

"What ships?" Mirae asked in alarm, looking back at Litt, who nodded.

"Birum is searching for the deer clan on other worlds through the dimensions, like I told you earlier," Litt said. "The other prisoners who have met Birum have heard some of the details about this endeavor."

"We just didn't know why he was going to such lengths, especially since he was from Khabu and had already conquered Eokhmisseun," Yarava said, turning now to Mirae and studying the girl curiously. "You beastmen have excellent taste in women, if you'll forgive me for saying so, Cargal."

Cargal sighed and sat back down in his seat near her while Mirae sat on the other side of Yarava.

"The deer clan? What does that mean exactly?" one of the bodyguards to Litt's right asked.

"Khabu is split into clans by animal ancestry," Litt said, his eyes meeting Mirae's again. She knew not to interrupt since he wanted certain details kept from Birum at this point. "I am from the tiger clan, as is Birum, whom you have known until now by my own name Litt. We also have a bird clan, which is where your war pigeons originated. Legend has it there was also a deer clan in the ancient land, during the reign of my father, and indeed one of my close friends told me he was leaving with them."

"Why did they leave? We have always heard what a beautiful and peaceful land Khabu was," Yarava said.

"Clearly it was not peaceful, maybe not at any point, though perhaps this was undetectable to outsiders," Litt said. "You now are acquainted with our conflicts quite intimately since Birum has taken over your land. But Birum was not the first to wander. My father did the same when he established the kingdom, and then my friend left with the deer clan when things were not to their liking. I have not heard anything of their activities in all of the years I had been in the crypt. I only heard that Birum was actively seeking them when he brought me out."

"So you don't know where they might be or what they have been up to since then?" Yarava asked. "Birum seems to have made some progress, however."

Litt looked at her in surprise.

"How do you know?" he asked.

"Sometimes Birum calls for me in the middle of the night to talk with me about his plans," Yarava said, smiling slyly. "He seems to like to surround himself with beautiful human women, although I have not been elevated to Crysalin's position."

"Not yet," Cargal said, snorting.

"I listen to his comments without showing too much enthusiasm," she said, smiling more warmly at Cargal. "He has sent one of his sons to a place called Earth, where they have made some progress in finding at least a stronghold of the deer clan. There are other places he has sent his other son and trusted followers to also search. I think the last count was 8 potential strongholds where they were living. He has yet to make contact with any of them to begin negotiations. He's just in the observing phase."

"I had no idea things had gone so far," Litt said.

"You've been stuck in Khabu while Birum was here," Mirae said gently. "He didn't keep you close enough to hear of his progress."

"So he didn't trust you that much after all?" Cargal asked, looking at Litt for a moment before his eyes were drawn to the windows across the room. It was getting darker out, and they would be taken back to their rooms soon.

"Wait a minute, Yarava," Mirae said, turning to face the older woman sitting next to her. "You said he sent his son to Earth? Do you mean my world? Cargal, do you know if this is where she means, since you have a better idea of where I am from?"

"This is the first I've heard about it," Cargal said apologetically. "It may very well be."

"Was it along the inner sea? Pontol runs his ferry through there," Mirae asked Yarava.

"I think Birum said it was a regular ferry from there to Khabu that first drew him to the location."

"Then even if Sohyeon returned home, he could be in danger," Mirae said, her fear growing. "When did you first hear of this?"

"Just a few weeks ago," Yarava said, puzzled. "I am unfamiliar with this Sohyeon whom you mention, but I do know Birum decided to send someone he trusted to that location after his network of spies at the palace of Khabu had warned him that Joriya, the current Queen of Khabu, had taken that ferry there, leaving the high priestess to rule the country."

"The Queen of Khabu went to Earth?" Mirae asked, stunned. Litt also looked alarmed at the news. "Why would she do such a thing?"

"I don't know, but he felt like it was a good time to act on his overall plan since she had left the kingdom vulnerable."

"And what is Birum's overall plan?" Litt asked, his voice hard and full of anger.

19

Before Yarava could answer, the double doors to the ballroom opened, and Crysalin has returned with Kerinda.

"It will be nighfall soon, and you must all get back to your quarters," she said tonelessly. "Litt and Mirae will go with Kerinda, the rest of you, follow me."

"Wait a moment," Litt said, standing. "When will we get together like this again?"

"We usually plan for a party like this a few times a week," Crysalin said vaguely, her attention drawn toward the windows rather than any of her guests. "You will get together in a few days for another party."

Everyone in the room fell silent as Kerinda stepped forward and gestured with a shy smile to Litt and Mirae to follow her. Nodding to the others, Litt fell in behind her first, then Mirae waved slightly to Cargal and Yarava before following him.

Crysalin looked at them briefly as they passed her, but Mirae couldn't read her expression. Her face just looked blank, as if she was uninterested in anything going on. Only Kerinda seemed genuinely happy to have guests to talk with and hopped down the hallway back to the swirling staircase that led to their room.

Once they reached the landing, Kerinda started to talk about how she would make them a special breakfast the next morning, like they were playmates her age. Mirae glanced questioningly at Litt behind her back, but he seemed lost in thought. When Kerinda dropped them off at their room, she didn't linger. Litt shut and bolted the door behind her.

"Will that really help? They're magicians, after all."

"I need time alone with you to make plans. We can't be interrupted. It's too dangerous if they overhear," he said in a low voice as he sat down on the bed beside her. "What do you make of all of this?"

"What do I think? We need to get out of here and find Sohyeon. My brother could be dead or in trouble back on Earth, and why would Joriya return to my home?"

"She led him there inadvertently, didn't she? You've been with me and haven't returned to the palace. Could they have decided to send her back in your place? It's more important than ever that we convince Birum you're from Khabu's countryside and are merely my companion. If he discovers the truth…".

"He likely already knows something if he has a network of spies in the palace at Khabu, even how Joriya switched me at birth with the Chois' real daughter to protect me. Neither of you can protect me now, Litt."

"We still shouldn't admit to the truth while we are here unless we absolutely have to, no matter what he knows. We could convince him that the spies were lying to him, which could be a useful tactic. Just follow my lead, okay? I won't allow him to harm you or tear us apart."

"What would it mean for him to find the deer clan? Are they dangerous? Or is he a danger to them?"

"A lot could have happened to them in 8,000 years, though it's likely that my friend Nominus is still alive and with them. No matter what happens with Birum, I could call on Nominus as an ally if we could find him. All I know is that the DNA experiments in our home world gave them certain abilities different from the other clans. Unlike the other animal clans, they could only shapeshift to the full animal form, not a partial form like I am now in. They were bred for their ability to run swiftly and blend into any natural surroundings. Some of the scientists surmised the deer DNA they used would also gift their animal test subjects with unusual strategic ability, since there were legends of deer outwitting their predators. There was also talk of splicing the genes so the deer could grow a single horn instead of two horns in the test subjects' deer forms."

"A unicorn?"

"Something like that. But keep in mind that deer have another obvious function, a more troubling one that was brought up when we lived in the ghetto: to provide meat for food. They were meant to be hunted and scavenged for the benefit of predators. Some thought that the scientists chose to use deer DNA as opposed to other more predatory animals' DNA because its peaceful, docile nature could be easily exploited by pure humans."

"So Birum's motives may not be to free them or anything good. Then what should we do?"

"Let me think about it overnight. One thing I know for sure, I want to be called before Birum to hear what he has to say directly about his plans, though I will have to pretend to want to help him.

"I want to be there with you! I don't want you to be summoned before him alone. We should never be apart now, or else his magic might ensnare you again."

Mirae put her arms around Litt's neck.

"I'll make sure to request it even if he doesn't call for you at first," he said, stroking her long black hair. "For now, sleep. I'll come up with some plan to stop him."

20

"What should we do now, Sohyeon? Do we dare risk a rescue mission on such short notice?" Tamnyn whispered, nudging him a little.

It had been two days since their return to Eokhmisseun, and now Sohyeon and Tamnyn crouched in the shadowy grove behind the palace. Once again wrapped in tattered cloaks that Pontol had scavenged for them, Sohyeon carrying his staff with a blade on the bottom and Tamnyn with her sword strapped across her body, they made their way around the plaza, avoiding the guards walking the perimeter of the palace every hour.

"I think we should wait. At least we got close this time without attracting any attention, though it will get trickier the longer we hang around. It's dark now, and that's when the palace seems to be the most active. We'll need to find a place to hide until we can get inside."

"At least we got past the guards early enough to catch a glimpse of them," Tamnyn said, waving for him to follow her as she led the way to a small group of small sheds and gazebos in the palace garden.

Moving swiftly from one set of bushes to the garden gate so she wouldn't be seen, she waited for him to catch up. Glancing around the palace lawn, Sohyeon saw the guards were occupied at the far end of the plaza. He dashed across the open space to Tamnyn's hiding place, trying not to make a sound. Looking back toward the palace, he saw they hadn't noticed him.

"Whatever they're doing, it must be really important since they don't seem to be looking around the grounds that much," Sohyeon said.

"They seem much more relaxed now than on the night of the purge," Tamnyn said, tugging on Sohyeon so they could run together to the shelter of the nearest building.

She pulled on the door handle gently, and it opened without making a sound. Holding up a small flashlight he had brought along with him from Earth, Sohyeon looked around the shed. It was about as big as Pontol's shack only neater, holding some garden tools and empty sacks. An old bench sat in one corner.

"I guess this was once out in the garden," Tamnyn said, going over to it.

Sohyeon entered, clicked off the flashlight and shut the door quietly behind them. A small window above them allowed some of the starlight to stream in, though the darkness was very thick and the air dusty.

"Did you get a good look at them in the window earlier?" she continued excitedly. "I think I saw my father there, and there was a woman who looked strikingly like Joriya. Was that your sister?"

"It looked like Mirae. They're still alive then, all of them," Sohyeon said quietly, sighing in relief. "We need a plan to rescue them, however. The setting looked very casual, but there are still armed guards walking around. I doubt that Birum is going to let them just leave anytime they want. Do you know much about the palace? Birum has been living here a fairly long time, hasn't he?"

"He has been here since my grandfather's generation, so although the ruling council used to hold meetings here and sometimes stay here, I haven't been here personally. Perhaps my father remembers it from when he was a boy."

"Then we don't know the layout. We can't just wander around and hope to end up wherever they're being held."

"No, that's true, but perhaps there's another way to handle that."

"The war pigeons? They're back at your house, and we don't know who might be living there now. Besides, we don't want to leave the palace now that we've fought so hard to get in."

"I left instructions with Pontol to send for the birds at my family home, to have them come here to look for us, unobtrusively of course."

"If they can find us here where we're hiding, then there's no hope for us to hide from the palace guards. You know that, right?"

"Hmmm, maybe it won't be so bad. The birds are very crafty, and they know our target and general plans. They can get past the guards much more easily and even slip into the palace itself with much less scrutiny."

"So we just wait for them to come to us?"

"For now, yes, let's just wait for them and observe the palace. Maybe by morning, some of the birds will have appeared. If Pontol can get to them, that is."

"There were a couple of half-tiger people like Baram in the room with your father and Mirae. Should that concern us?"

Tamnyn didn't answer right away, and Sohyeon remembered why.

"That's right, the red-haired woman with them is Birum's concubine, your mother?"

"So it appears," Tamnyn said, turning her face deeper into the shadows where Sohyeon could no longer even see her profile. "The little girl tiger is my half-sister, most likely."

"In the same room with your father, no less. What a horrible situation."

"He looked uncomfortable."

Both of them fell silent.

"Should we sleep until daylight since the palace seems to be waking up now?" Sohyeon asked. "Will it be safe to do that?"

"One of us should stay awake to keep watch, but maybe we should try to get some sleep. Our best time to act should be early morning, just at sunrise. I can look for the birds then and see what they have come up with."

"Do you want to sleep first then? I can sleep when you're watching for them in the morning."

Pulling her sword around her body so she could hold it while she slept and pulling back her hood, Tamnyn laid down across Sohyeon, putting her head on his lap. He let his hand rest gently on her shoulder while he let his mind wander. Going over every scenario to break into the palace he could think of, nothing seemed appropriate. He could imagine them getting caught no matter what they might try.

"This seems hopeless," he whispered to himself. "We might be in for a very long wait here."

Ten minutes later, Sohyeon suddenly felt a jolt and heard footsteps walking past the group of little buildings into the garden. The air crackled with a dark energy that Sohyeon remembered from the night they fled Eokhmisseun, the night of the purge. That could only mean one person was standing outside. Birum.

"Why are you upset, my lord?" a man's voice asked hastily.

Sohyeon realized then that the window above them was open a crack and held his breath, straining to hear. Tamnyn squirmed a little on his lap, and he put one hand gently over her mouth and his other hand on her hand holding her sword so she wouldn't drop it. His spear was propped up against the wall beside the bench.

"I just needed to take a walk," the second man's voice came caustically. "My best spy from Khabu arrived back in Eokhmisseun today. I need to consider my next move."

"Really? Has there been more movement there at the palace? I thought everyone had left but the high priestess?"

"Now Joriya is back and Minha has gone to Earth. Send a messenger to Baram to watch out for her. She truly is the brains behind the throne of Khabu."

"Isn't it better that she leave Khabu to your sister? Or is Earth now your objective since Baram has found the deer clan there?"

The deer clan? Sohyeon thought. Baram was sent to Earth on a quest of some sort then?

"If I could get rid of Minha altogether, it would be very helpful to my plan. I'll see if Baram can arrange something.

In the meantime, Joriya has returned home, which means Khabu will be a weak target. My sister always was an incompetent ruler."

"And the role of the girl in this?"

"The girl? That one who Litt has latched onto? What was her name again?"

"She was from the house that Baram has been warned to watch back on Earth, my lord. Mirae was her name, and the spy networks said she seems to be of some importance to Khabu if Joriya and Minha have both gone to her home there."

"All anyone in the palace knows is that she is now Litt's woman."

"Crysalin told you this?"

"Kerinda did. She said they are as thick as thieves. I'll summon them to me for a talk soon enough, once I can get a handle on the situation on Earth and a few of our other waystations better. There has been more than one sighting of the deer clan, and before long I will need to act."

"The deer clan has some ancient connection to Khabu, my lord?"

"Chancellor, they are the lost clan of Khabu. Rumors are from my agents abroad that they have developed spectacular powers over the centuries they have roamed the inner seas and walked in strange lands. They now have the unusual ability to extend their regenerative powers to any living being they choose and have learned how to shapeshift partially."

"Have they taken over any of these worlds, as we have?"

"It isn't their way, Geravus. The deer clan was always a mystery in the annals of Khabu, and when I questioned Litt about it after I kidnapped him, he suggested that they were engineered specifically to be exploited by the organization that created them, unlike the other clans. Harvesting food and body parts from a regenerating human hybrid monster could be very useful in some situations, don't you think."

"Is that why they fled and are now scattered among the worlds?"

"That seems to be the reason, though when I questioned Litt about it, I got the impression there was more to the story than what he was telling me. He's hiding something. Perhaps the best way to get to whatever secret he's keeping is now the girl. I should summon her alone and see what he has confided in her."

"And our other 'guests'? You surprised me by allowing them to all sit and talk together."

"They don't do me any good in the dungeons, and maybe if they feel free to talk amongst themselves, I can get at the knowledge and expertise that they won't otherwise give me. I have gotten at least one of the councilwoman's bodyguards in my employ."

"A spy?" The man laughed.

"I just need to get that man's bodyguard to turn as well," Birum said darkly.

"The one whose family you destroyed years ago when you took your new bride? I had wondered why you kept him alive when you smashed the rest of the council."

"Oh, there may still be one or two of them lurking around, living in fear of when I might come upon them again, but yes, those two are the last of my opponents here in Eokhmisseun."

"His daughter was seen on Earth in the company of that young man who came here to help the council. Baram's last communique mentioned seeing his half-sister there. Were you aware of that development?"

"Cargal's daughter? How odd that she should appear there too. Why does everyone seem to be drawn to such an insignificant place?"

"Baram also mentioned that the man who was seen with her is connected to the house that this Mirae is from. Joriya was seen near there, too. Who are they, my lord?"

"That *is* interesting. We'll have to investigate them further. Baram needs a mate, so perhaps he should take one of their women. That will leave them torn, just as it did the councilman whose life I turned upside down."

"Crysalin came willingly to you though, didn't she? Will it be sufficient for Baram to just kidnap one of them? If she isn't willing, it will neutralize whatever power taking her will have over her clan."

"There's always magical persuasion that can fill the gap, Chancellor. I had to use some myself with Crysalin at first, though she quickly became eager."

"To save her husband and child?"

There was a long silence before Birum spoke again.

"I don't think Crysalin remembers them. Even now, when she is in a situation where she sees her former husband, she shows no recognition or interest in him. She has turned completely to me. If you have your doubts, we can test it out. Bring the councilman to us tomorrow, and we will see who has power over her."

"I still wouldn't trust her. She could be pretending just to protect them. So your next move is to return to Khabu? What of Eokhmisseun then?"

"Yes, Khabu has always been my goal. Eokhmisseun was just a safe base to prepare and search for the deer clan, to attain power in a sphere far away from my sister's influence and Minha's reach, though somehow she was able to get that ferryman in her employ. I'll need to look into that one more, too. It may be time to stop his voyages across the worlds now that we're ready to take control of more than one of them. Baram will be my agent on Earth, as my other son and loyalists are placed strategically in other lands. We will move on them all together."

"Is your ultimate goal still to rule them all as a confederation from Khabu? What advantage is there in that, my lord?"

"I haven't made up my mind how we will arrange this in the end, but I do intend to topple Joriya and end her reign. If we can find the executioner's dagger and helm, those ancient artefacts I stole years ago when I took Litt from the crypt of ancestors but later lost once I came to Eokhmisseun, then she will be the first to die by them in Khabu in a long time. What? You look shocked, Chancellor? Don't you have the will to do what it takes to see the coup through to its logical end?"

"On what grounds would you execute your sister? She's a weak leader, but surely she hasn't been treasonous. Would the deer clan feel comfortable allying with you if you did such a thing? Would your own people accept her death by execution? Perhaps it's unwise. Just throw her in prison."

"For eternity? But perhaps you are right. I could put her in the palace dungeons where her daughter has wasted away for years on a trumped up charge, then execute them both quietly when everyone has forgotten them. As for the deer clan, at this time I have no plans to repatriate them to Khabu. It was so long ago that they fled our land I think they no longer consider it home. "

"So then are negotiations the goal with them?"

"The deer clan should become our strongest allies, and perhaps we can rule these new worlds through them. They already have bases on them, though they are very different from the inhabitants of those lands. I'm sure they'll be glad to find there are others like them in the inner sea, others whose origins are full of pain, and they'll be grateful for our help to take over the places they now occupy in secret."

"Baram and your agents have already approached them about this?"

"We have started the process, though they have not been apprised of all of the details yet. We need to negotiate carefully and present our plan to them only when we feel we're on firm ground."

The men's footsteps receded in the direction of the palace as their voices slowly died away. Sohyeon sat in the dark, astonished by what he had just heard, silently praying that Pontol had been able to get to the magical war pigeons at the house of Elyeon. Now more than ever, they needed to get to Mirae before Birum.

21

"They're here, Sohyeon. Wake up," Tamnyn whispered, shaking him gently as he lay across her lap.

Opening his eyes, he saw a white bird flapping near the window.

"Should we let it in?" he asked. "Will that look suspicious?"

"Get up, and I'll get the door," she said, looking up toward the cold, watery sunlight coming through the small window where the bird hovered.

Once Sohyeon sat up, Tamnyn raced across the small shed to the door and unlocked it quietly. Opening it a crack, she poked her head out to look around. Rubbing his eyes, Sohyeon heard her make a strange hissing sound, and after a moment, the bird flew into the room. Tamnyn shut it and locked it again as the bird settled onto a pedestal stored in the far corner of the shed. Sohyeon studied it, but he didn't think it looked particularly different from Mapin.

Tamnyn came over to it and stroked its back as she whispered calming words to it. The bird talked back in the same strange language Sohyeon was now getting used to even though he didn't understand a word of it. Tamnyn looked back at him, smiling.

"What did it say?"

"He said Pontol was able to climb the tree up to their roost outside my house and convince them to come help us. Most of my old servants have been forced to serve Birum's henchmen, who have taken over the house, but oddly, Birum hasn't turned them, not yet. The birds were upstairs, mostly forgotten except for my old nurse who went up to give them some food and exercise."

"Magical birds need to eat?" Sohyeon said to himself, stretching and standing up. "What are *we* going to do about breakfast? Did my mother give you anything we can eat before we get started here?"

"I have some oat bars she made for us and a container of dried soybeans in my pack on the bench beside you," Tamnyn said in a low voice. "In the meantime, I'll send the bird back with instructions for the rest of the flock. They'll need time to search the palace and look for ways they can get in."

She turned back to the bird, and letting it sit on her hand, whispered together with it as she opened the door again to let it out.

"Which prisoner should we rescue first?" she asked when she returned to sit on the bench with Sohyeon. He handed her one of the spicy oat bars his mother was famous for making.

"While I'll understand if you want to get your father out first, we have to think of who the most dangerous prisoners are in the palace at the moment and get them out. Then we can free your father and whoever else is in there."

"So would that be this ancient king Litt that we need to get out, along with your sister Mirae?"

"I have to admit I'm curious to meet him. They say he's something like 8,000 years old. Have you ever met someone like that? I can't even wrap my head around someone that old still existing. But he's probably really important to Birum if he's here, and that could make him really a dangerous prisoner to leave under Birum's control. Joriya and Minha seemed worried about it. Then of course, there's the fact that my sister is now the heir to Khabu."

"If Birum knew that, she'd probably be dead now, not just sitting around with my father in the parlor having tea," Tamnyn said softly. "I understand what our priorities should be. First, we need to find a way to neutralize Birum before we free my father. Our best bet to deal with Birum is to help Khabu. We have no other options, really, and I'm just grateful my father isn't dead. He'll understand if we don't rescue him first. He has been involved in Eokhmisseun's politics all of his life."

"Then it's decided? We look for Mirae and Litt and get them out first."

"When the birds return, we'll know where they are and how to safely get in and out of the palace. Hopefully, it will be easier than it looks."

Sohyeon bit his lip, wondering if they really stood a chance if Birum's men caught them, but he didn't want to dampen Tamnyn's hopes. Everything was riding on their flimsy plan.

The hours passed, and finally the bird returned with a couple of companions. Tamnyn opened the door for them. As they settled along the garden decorations stored in the shed, they all started to whisper to Tamnyn in their strange language at once. She stared at them all, eyes wide and full of confusion, until they calmed down and spoken in turn.

"Can we get into the palace like we planned?" Sohyeon asked from the bench.

"It seems like a real possibility. They'll sneak in and open one of the doors that seems to have been missed by the patrols, one they found in the back of the kitchen that allows the servants to go in and out that the daughter carelessly uses to reach the palace rose garden. One of the birds they sent in breached the palace through an open window on the top floor. They can re-enter that way and return to human form to open the door for us even if the back door is suddenly locked, plus they were able to sneak around the palace and see where they're holding everyone."

"They were able to find them with just our descriptions?"

"Litt and Mirae are being held together on the second floor, but my father and a number of other humans are being held on the fourth floor. It would actually be easier to get Mirae and Litt out from the lower floor, but we must make it seem like they vanished so Birum won't take things out on my father, if possible."

"I'm not sure we can control anything. We can't guarantee Birum won't kill your father if we spring Litt and Mirae from the palace and he finds out before we can get to the others. Are you going to be okay if that's the case?"

"I don't like it, but we have no choice. We need to get to them first, as we agreed. The birds think that the morning and early afternoon are times when the palace is least active, with things picking up in the early evening and at night. We need to act fast before evening."

"And if we get caught, then what?"

"Then I guess we become Birum's guests along with them, and the birds will send one of the flock to inform Pontol of our failure so Khabu can decide what to do next."

"Harsh," Sohyeon whispered, wincing. "When do we begin?"

"I see no reason to wait any longer. I for one am sick of sitting around here, and a few of the birds are already waiting for us inside the palace in their hiding places."

"Then let's get it over with," Sohyeon said, standing and picking up his staff, as Tamnyn picked up her pack and strapped her sword on.

22

Following the birds around to the back of the palace, they snuck past the windows and dodged whatever palace guards were out during the daylight hours. The lead bird took them straight to the door in the rear where another bird, now in human form, waited to let them in. Sohyeon looked around curiously. The door was almost hidden behind a clump of tall, overgrown bushes close to the far side of the grove of trees, so it was not very conspicuous.

The creature waiting for them at the door left Sohyeon in awe, however. Standing nearly six feet tall, a well-built man of indeterminate age wearing a white chiton with long white feathered wings stood in the middle of the room, his curly hair a silvery white, his eyes a strange shade of reddish brown. A small group of white birds fluttered around him excitedly in the background as the couple entered. No one else seemed to be around.

"Where is everyone?" Sohyeon asked once they all had gathered in a pantry area off the kitchen and shut the door. "Is this what the birds really look like?"

"The staff takes a nap after every meal they prepare, and now it's just after lunch," the angelic man said, his voice tinged with an accent Sohyeon couldn't place. "While not everyone in the palace is asleep right now, something about the magic used to subdue the city has made those remaining human slaves sink deep into lethargy, and they sleep inordinately. We should be able to get some of the prisoners out before anyone is aware we're here, though we'll keep watch and attack if they do wake up."

The man smiled a little before continuing.

"I am Orach, one of the leaders of the birds and second in command after Mapin, whom I believe you met."

"Yet you are now a man," Sohyeon said in amazement.

"Didn't you know? If you have had any dealings with Khabu, surely you should know by now that we all have animal powers. Once we reach a certain age, we stop using our human forms most of the time."

"I had heard it, but I hadn't seen any of you until now."

"Enough," Tamnyn whispered. "We don't have time to talk now. Let's get Mirae and Litt to safety at least before we're found out."

"Lead the way," Sohyeon said, turning back to Orach. "We want to rescue the prisoners on the second floor first."

"Where should we take them once we have led them out of the palace? You understand that we are in a better position to get them further away than you, don't you?"

"Well?" Sohyeon looked over at Tamnyn, who had pulled out her sword to prepare for their task.

"We need to get them out of Eokhmisseun, so lead them to Pontol's shack where he can ferry them to Khabu and Joriya. Then we'll get my father and the rest of the prisoners and take them to Earth to help your parents and Minha, Sohyeon. But we'll all end up at the ferry waiting by the inner sea near the docks of Eokhmisseun."

Orach nodded, and after opening the door, he turned back into a bird. Three of the birds split off from the group as the remaining four led Sohyeon and Tamnyn down the hall. Ten more birds waited outside. They could see the birds in the distance perched on bushes and branches as they passed a few windows on the first floor. Sohyeon marveled at how different the palace was from Tamnyn's residence. Here the windows were bare of curtains and were even open with no screens. With everyone still human their prisoner or purged, rebellion among the ghost-slaves apparently was not a concern for them. The palace had minimum security in place.

The group walked through the lower floor of the palace as quietly as they could. Sohyeon looked around in awe at the palace's magnificent décor, but when they made their way to the bottom of a dramatically curled staircase, he saw it led to an uncharacteristically darkened corridor. At the top of the stairs, the birds led them through the dim hallway to one of the doors. Indicating it was the correct place and returning to his human form, Orach knocked gently then stepped aside to let Tamnyn approach the door.

Grabbing the doorknob, she turned it quietly to see if it was locked. The door slid open, and Tamnyn crept into the room.

"Kerinda?" a woman called.

The room was large and well-lit, but as they entered, they didn't see the prisoners sitting on a small loveseat on the other side of the bed at first. The curtains were pulled back to let the weak light of day stream through the large windows, and Sohyeon had trouble adjusting again to the bright light.

"Mirae?" he whispered as he walked deeper into the room and saw his sister sitting with a tall half-tiger man with a shock of white-blonde hair.

The woman and man looked up at the intruders, a shocked expression on their face.

"Sohyeon? How did you get in here?" Mirae asked, standing. The light purple satin dress she wore had layers of ruffles reaching from her hips to the floor.

"We need to get you and Litt out of the palace to safety," Tamnyn said, glancing around the room as if expecting guards to be hidden there. "Who knows how long we have until we are discovered, and I still need to try to get to my father."

"Cargal? Yes, that's right. I think he's in the other wing of the palace somewhere," Mirae said. "I'm astonished you could walk right into the palace, in the heart of Eokhmisseun, given the situation."

"We encountered no resistance, that's true," Tamnyn said. "But we need to take advantage of Birum's carelessness while we can. Once he discovers us, he will fortify the palace beyond any reckoning."

Litt nodded and stepped forward, dressed in a blue shirt with a ruffled collar and long sleeves under a velvety black coat reaching almost down to his knees fastened with sparkling silver clasps. His white trousers were tucked into black riding boots.

"We have been called to an audience with Birum sometime later tonight, so Kerinda brought us formal clothing to meet with him," Mirae said, looking down at their clothing in embarrassment. "He'll discover our absence quickly once the sun starts to set and blame his daughter Kerinda if we are missing, so we must find her and take her with us."

"We're going to kidnap Birum's daughter, Mirae? Do you think that's wise?" Sohyeon asked incredulously.

"She's just a young girl, Sohyeon."

"We met her brother back home, and he wasn't just a child," Sohyeon said, trying not to lose his patience. "He was in fact as scary as Birum. What makes you think you can control the girl if we take her?"

"Never mind all of that for now. Where is this Kerinda?" Orach asked, the birds flapping excitedly around him. "We'll look for her and lead her out. We must leave now and get you to the ferry."

"Her room is down the corridor here a few doors, marked with a wreath of holly berries hanging on the doorknob," Mirae said.

Two of the four birds hanging around Orach flew back out into the hallway.

"Birum has been very generous with us, though it may be hard for you to believe," Litt said. "He has left us free to roam within a few doors of our quarters but has asked us not to go beyond them."

"His security in the palace is generally lax, and we can infiltrate just about anywhere," Orach said. "Do you know why?"

Litt smiled slightly, looking at Orach's wings and the birds hovering nearby.

"You are from Khabu's bird clan, are you? You would be a formidable force even against Birum, who has come here in secret since intimidating humans is far easier than manipulating our own populace in Khabu. How long had you lived in the Forest of Bliss before coming to Eokhmisseun?"

"Like Mapin, I am one of the early generations. It was 6,000 years before our reigning king commissioned me and my brethren to come here as a gift to Eokhmisseun after our high priestess had a vision of distress in the land at some future time. She felt we could protect them somehow from the danger to come, only she didn't realize that danger would be a member of Khabu's royal family!"

"Mapin is here too?" Litt asked.

"No, she has been commissioned to stay with the Choi family on Earth," Orach said.

"She has been very helpful to us since Birum's son took over Earth and the death toll started rising," Sohyeon said.

"Birum's son has taken over Earth?" Mirae asked, alarmed.

"I told you Tamnyn and I need to get back," Sohyeon said. "But first you and Litt need to return to Khabu, and we need to get the rest of the prisoners out of here. Enough talking."

"But we don't know what Birum's plan is," Mirae said.

"We do know. We overheard him before we came in," Sohyeon said. "He plans on attacking Khabu and going to Earth and other worlds to find some deer clan."

A strange glance passed between Mirae and Litt.

"Do you know about this deer clan?" Tamnyn asked.

"Yes, but now isn't the time to get into details. We should leave in that case and plan our next move from somewhere safe."

"We have Kerinda, Orach."

The two birds who went down the hall to retrieve the girl appeared at the door in human form, two men as striking and strange as Orach, each of them holding one of the terrified tiger girl's arms.

"Let's go," Orach said sternly, leading them back through the hallway to the staircase.

"Mirae, what is going on?" Kerinda asked loudly.

"Be silent. We have somewhere we need to go right now, and you will stay with us so you won't get hurt," Mirae said, reaching out to stroke the girl's hair.

Seeing that Kerinda was willing to go with Mirae, the bird-men let her go. Kerinda put her arms around Mirae's waist and stayed close to her as they reached the bottom of the stairs.

Turning toward the food preparation area where they entered, they found their way blocked by a voluptuous figure.

23

As Tamnyn choked back a muffled cry, Sohyeon put his arm around her and pulled her close to him. The red-haired woman who stood before them was Birum's concubine, Crysalin, and her face was full of fury.

"Who are you and where do you think you are going with them?" Crysalin asked, her voice sensuous and lethal. "Did you think you could just walk into the palace and not get caught? We were on to you from the start."

They just looked at her silently, too stunned to speak, though Sohyeon had noticed the winged men with them had already turned back into their bird shape before they descended the stairs. Five of them had melted into the shadows of the upper floors at the first sign of trouble. Only Sohyeon, Tamnyn, Mirae, Litt and Kerinda stood before her, and Tamnyn still had her sword drawn.

Behind her in the darkened room near the garden door rose a looming shadow with two huge yellow eyes. Though Sohyeon couldn't make out the hulking creature's exact shape, he felt the same sense of dread creeping over him that he had felt the night they fled through the city streets from the black apparition of Birum. But how could Birum get to that size? None among them had ever seen Birum except Litt, so Sohyeon only surmised their archenemy was standing before them, blocking their escape and letting his concubine speak for him. For now.

Suddenly, Sohyeon was aware of other figures emerging from the shadowy edges around the stair landing. Ghost-slaves. The eight of them looked much fiercer than Pontol and carried short, curved swords with jeweled hilts. *What do we do now?* Sohyeon thought, trying to keep despair at bay. He barely knew how to use his spear.

"You'll never get out of here alive!" Crysalin said. "Whoever you are, you must yield to the master's desires. Drop your weapons unless you want to be executed by the ghost-slaves."

"Shut up, woman" came a familiar man's voice from behind them. "Just because you capitulated long ago to the beast doesn't mean any of *us* have to."

Everyone turned to look at the group of prisoners entering the foyer from the opposite wing. Sohyeon thought he saw a small white shape flutter away to the safety of the shadows out of the corner of his eye. That's right, the other three birds went down to the far wing of the palace to rescue Cargal and the other council member. Cargal led the group now with a striking woman at his side. Behind them came four trained warriors, apparently bodyguards also being held by Birum.

Crysalin looked at him in anger and disgust, then a cruel smile spread across her face.

"Do you finally remember me now?" Cargal asked as he came to stand in front of Sohyeon and the others, while the bodyguards spread around the back of the group where they could quickly deflect the swords of the ghost-slaves, who were now outnumbered.

"It has been a long time, hasn't it?" Crysalin said, her voice cold and flat.

"I've been in the palace for weeks," Cargal continued, his voice strong and unwavering. "I find it astonishing after all we shared years ago that you wouldn't recognize me when I came."

"Did you imagine I would run to your embrace and confess the error of my ways?" Crysalin asked, unshaken by Cargal's accusation. "If I had not gone willingly with Birum, I might have succumbed to such sentimentality. But what does it matter now that we shared anything at all?"

"Indeed? Is that why you don't even recognize your own daughter Tamnyn standing before you, now a grown woman?" Cargal asked scathingly.

Crysalin's eyes fell on Tamnyn, who still held her sword in a defensive position. Her expression didn't change, and no recognition or warmth appeared in her eyes.

"I have no children anymore," Crysalin said coldly. "I belong to Birum alone, and everything is arranged for his pleasure."

Sohyeon felt a slight tremor go through Tamnyn's body, and he held onto her more tightly so she wouldn't collapse like she did at the meeting with Baram. He pressed his lips against her hair as inconspicuously as he could to remind her that he was near.

Cargal wasn't taking his former wife's reaction that well, either, and his face twisted into a snarl.

"Move aside and let your precious Birum face us himself then," Cargal said.

"Don't, Cargal," the brown-haired woman standing next to him whispered, putting her hand gently on his sword arm. "You are letting this get too personal," she whispered, taking a step closer to him. "You must think of our goals here, not revenge for past slights."

"Slights? Yes, of course, they were just slights," Cargal said, his voice now as flat and emotionless as Crysalin's. "Move aside, wench, and remove your beast to let us pass. That's the least you could do after everything that has happened."

Crysalin laughed, though it was a harsh, unpleasant sound.

"Birum?" Crysalin glanced over her shoulder at the huge shadow behind her. She then sauntered across the foyer and down the hall, disappearing into a room there without another glance at the group.

Suddenly, Sohyeon could hear a low growl, growing louder, coming from the room they had hoped to escape through. The shadowy figure there stepped forward, emerging into the light of the foyer, revealing a nine foot tall white tiger with light blue eyes. But his large size couldn't mask his sickly appearance, and they all gaped at the strange, skeletal creature that stood before them.

"The ghost-slaves," Cargal murmured, not finishing his sentence, as his eyes were riveted on their enemy.

"The ghost-slaves? Yes, they are my children after a sort," Birum said conversationally, unconcerned that they were a threat to him.

He took a few slinky steps through the doorway into the foyer before sitting down in front of them, lifting a thin paw in their direction, his claws looking like mere extensions of his bony forefoot covered with mangy white and black fur.

"My magic was unable to create whole creatures out of the human citizens of Eokhmisseun," he continued, studying each of the party for a few minutes, his intelligent gaze resting too long on Mirae and Litt. "Apparently, the only way to pass on the weretiger genes is through normal reproduction, not magic. The twisted forms of the ghost-slaves are a sad imitation of life, though it still has given them some advantages even if it gives them an animal's taste for blood. They will never die now through natural means, though they don't enjoy the same invincibility as the inhabitants of Khabu."

"So they are now members of the tiger clan through magic?" Litt asked, stepping forward in front of Mirae and Kerinda protectively, understanding instinctively Birum's interest in Mirae.

"They are half-tigers, unable to become fully human or fully tiger. Interesting effect from the magic, don't you think?"

"So they are test subjects for your own experiments?" Litt asked, his voice smooth and soothing. "Have they thanked you for the terrible condition you left them in? You know the history, Birum, how our forefathers conducted such 'experiments.' Have you learned nothing from their failures?"

"Failures? Had they actually failed? They created glorious beings with their experiments. Surely you are too insensitive, ancient father, in thinking none of us are glad for what they achieved. The clans of Khabu have far more advantages than mere humans, are blessed with unimaginable powers and an eternity to explore them. By whose definition is that failure?"

"Yet you are like this, Birum," Litt said, walking toward him slowly.

Sohyeon could feel the men in their group shift almost imperceptibly, as if ready to spring and fight. He, too, tightened his grip on his staff. Tamnyn even raised her sword a few inches.

"I am like this because the magic drained me when I took over Eokhmisseun," Birum said in mild amusement at Litt's chiding. "You know that nothing but silver can kill full clan members, but the enormous life-force I expended to use my magic has taken decades to regenerate. I still haven't returned to my normal energy level."

"Is this why you're looking for the deer clan?" Sohyeon asked without thinking. "You have discovered they can give other people their powers of regeneration, haven't you?"

Everyone turned to look at him. Birum's ice blue eyes bore into Sohyeon while the creature studied him, as if he was trying to remember who Sohyeon was.

"What's this?" Litt asked, looking back at Sohyeon with interest. "The deer clan has been found?"

Sohyeon saw Birum's eyes narrow, and the big tiger sprang across the room, landing only a few paces from Sohyeon and Tamnyn, who had suddenly moved into a protective, defensive stance in front of Sohyeon, pointing her sword at Birum's face. Now free of propping up Tamnyn, Sohyeon brought the metal tip of his staff up to point at Birum menacingly, too.

"You're the boy whose sister Joriya brought to Khabu, aren't you?" Birum said, his voice low and lethal. "We meet at last. How odd that Joriya would find you interesting since you are human, though inexplicably your sister isn't!"

Sohyeon looked at Mirae in surprise. She looked away, and Litt took a step closer to her and Kerinda, shielding her from further scrutiny. Sohyeon's eyes met Litt's, and in a flash, he realized the truth. Up until then, Sohyeon hadn't made the connection that if Mirae was Joriya's heir, she also had to be immortal, and a tiger.

Without warning, a ghost-slave struck down one of Cargal's bodyguards, and everyone moved at once in response. Mirae fended off two of them with her bare hands now transformed into half-tiger paws tipped with long claws, shielding Kerinda close to her body as she swung at them. Cargal, the woman and the remaining three bodyguards engaged the ghost-slaves with their swords. Seeing Birum about to take a step toward his prey, Litt stepped in front of Tamnyn and Sohyeon. Birum stopped short, glaring at him.

"Ancient father, step aside so I can teach this boy a lesson," he said, but Litt wouldn't move.

"Run now!" Litt yelled, and everyone in the room broke down the hallway to the left, as Kerinda led them to a different door.

"Don't let them escape!" came an ominous, gravelly voice from the other corridor Crysalin had disappeared down.

Everyone glanced back in that direction, but what they saw made them only run faster. A five foot scorpion had emerged from the room and sidled up to the ghost-slaves, its tail poised to strike.

"Don't kill her!" Kerinda screamed, grabbing Mirae's clawed hands. "Keep running."

"Why not kill it?" Mirae called as they all burst through the front doors of the palace and ran out onto the lawn overlooking the plaza.

"It's my mother."

"Your mother is a scorpion? I thought it was that red-haired woman," Mirae said, panting as she waited for Cargal and Litt to catch up. Sohyeon and Tamnyn ran further, all the way to the edge of the street, looking around nervously.

"Father taught her how to use his magic for transformations, though she is human. She prefers to fight in the form of a scorpion."

"How charming," Mirae said under her breath, grabbing the girl's arm and running with Litt toward the street.

"Where do we go now?" Cargal asked Litt and Sohyeon as they all gathered under the shadow of the trees closest to the plaza, well aware that their enemies were spilling out of the palace in search of them.

"The dock, where Pontol has his ferry," Sohyeon said. "This way."

24

When they reached Pontol's shack near the inner sea, he was already waiting. One of the birds had returned from the palace to warn him they would be trying to escape through that route, and he waved to Sohyeon, who led the group of prisoners into the thick grove of trees toward the path to the dock.

Sheathing their swords as they followed the winding path through the back of the grove, hearing the echoing roars of Birum behind them, getting closer with every step, they reached the low-lying rocky shore near the dock.

"We're going to be trapped once we enter here," Cargal said, eyeing the rocks and the shoreline suspiciously.

"Never mind that, we need to get to the boat and get out of here," Sohyeon said, waiting at the canyon chokepoint to let everyone pass and make sure they left no one behind.

"They'll be here soon. Are you sure they can't follow us?" Cargal asked.

"I can't guarantee anything. For all I know, they have another boat hidden somewhere around here. We just have to trust Pontol."

Cargal looked down the path where the others had followed the ghoulish ferryman and shook his head.

"I have to thank you for looking after Tamnyn all of this time."

"Now isn't the time for chit chat," Sohyeon said urgently, nodding toward the grove. "Here they come. Let's run for it before they see us."

Cargal glanced back in the direction Sohyeon indicated, seeing the scorpion bursting out from the shadowy copse.

"Yeah, she's the last person I need to see right now," Cargal said.

They ran down the path toward the boat where everyone was already waiting and jumped on. The ferry swayed dangerously under the weight of so many people.

"Hey, Pontol," Sohyeon called lightly. "Are you sure this thing is seaworthy? Can it hold a load this heavy?"

Flashing Sohyeon a toothy smile, Pontol turned the wheel and pulled out from the dock. The boat moved swiftly, leaving a large gap of misty water between the hull and the dock. As they drifted further and further away, they saw the ghost slaves and Crysalin emerge on the dock, helplessly watching them escape. The group on Pontol's ferry could hear their angry discussion, but all eyes turned toward the lumbering shadow emerging from the trees behind them. Birum had arrived, and the cadence of the spell he weaved carried across the waves to them.

"What is he doing?" Litt asked, listening to the words with a look of terror.

"Is it magic?" Sohyeon asked, standing next to Litt, looking out toward Birum.

"I'd recognize his spellcasting anywhere after years of being ensnared by it," Litt said, grabbing the edge of the boat with a snarl as his eyes searched the dock.

The water next to the shoreline under the dock turned blacker and blacker, and the waves started to swell and foam, as Birum spoke the strange, rhythmic words. Pontol watched the churning waves rippling closer to the ferry, and he spun his wheel frantically, trying to turn the ship before whatever was approaching emerged from the water.

"I know what it is, Litt," Mirae said, holding Kerinda closer to her. "It's the creature that took us from the Blue Waterfall to Eokhmisseun."

"The dragon? Yes, that's probably what it is," he said, murmuring, as something large, scaly and black rose from the water between them and the dock of Eokhmisseun. The billowing waves lifted the ferry and nearly dropped it in its trough as the creature reached out a clawed, webbed hand toward them, towering above them and showering them with seawater.

"Pontol, can we outrun it?" Sohyeon yelled.

"I know an alternate route," Pontol yelled back.

The ferryman's eyes were nearly popping out of his head at the sight of the leathery dragon. He turned the wheel a hard left, and everyone on board lurched right as Cargal fell overboard into the water and the waiting dragon's claws.

"Father!" Tamnyn screamed, nearly jumping in after him.

Sohyeon caught her around the waist to stop her, and one of the bodyguards leaned down into the water instead, proffering a spear for Cargal to grab hold of so they could drag him back to the boat. Using his teeth and a small dagger he had pulled from his belt, Cargal broke free of the dragon's grasp and reached for the spear. Litt leaned down to help the bodyguard pull him in and extended a hand for Cargal to grab as he got closer, but the dragon was faster.

As Cargal took hold of the spear and his fingers just missed grabbing Litt's hand, the dragon dove into the water behind him. High waves rippled across the water toward the boat. Cargal screamed and flailed in the current, even as his hand held fast to the spear. Blood spread across the surface of the water, and the dragon's head re-emerged, this time very close to Cargal, its eyes red and its teeth full of flesh.

Seeing a coil of rope beside Pontol, Sohyeon suddenly had an idea. As Cargal gasped for air, his face full of pain, Sohyeon took the rope, quickly tied it into a lasso, and threw it toward the dragon, trying to hit some part of its body where he could restrain it long enough for Cargal to make it to safety. The lasso fell harmlessly in the water not far from the dragon's face, but it was enough to draw its attention momentarily away from Cargal. Now it was solely focused on Sohyeon and drifted like an alligator toward the part of the boat where Sohyeon and Tamnyn stood.

"Get my spear and hit it if it comes close enough," Sohyeon whispered to Tamnyn.

She immediately picked up Sohyeon's spear from the bottom of the boat where he dropped it and pointed it at the dragon's head, aiming for the eyes.

Cargal was free of the dragon long enough to take hold of the spear the bodyguard held out to him with both hands, and Litt and the bodyguard pulled the spear close enough that they could each grab one of his arms and lift him back into the boat. Laying him on the bottom of the boat, they could see that the dragon had done considerable damage gnawing on one of Cargal's legs, though he hadn't lost it completely. Moaning in pain, Cargal closed his eyes as Mirae and Yarava came closer to attend to his wounds the best they could.

Litt looked up at Mirae as she tried to find a clean cloth to wrap around Cargal's leg. Handing her a handkerchief from inside of his waistcoat, he glanced back at the dragon, which had inexplicably decided to ignore Sohyeon and Tamnyn and dive back into the water. Birum and his followers still stood on the shore, though they were growing smaller and smaller as the boat picked up speed. Perhaps they could outrun it after all with Pontol's skillful sailing. Sohyeon and Tamnyn kept watching the water for signs of the dragon's return even though it seemed to be gone now.

"It looks like you'll need to seek out the deer clan regardless of Birum's progress in finding them," Litt said to Sohyeon. "He'll need their new powers of regeneration, if the rumors are true and they have developed a way to transfer that to others."

"We need to decide who should stay with him and who should go on to Khabu, then," Yarava said. "Where is Pontol headed now? This place called Earth where the deer clan is said to have been found and where these new champions are from?"

"Mirae, Kerinda and I should return to Khabu, but first we should take Sohyeon, Tamnyn and Cargal to earth," Litt said. "Orach and the other birds will remain our only contact in Eokhmisseun now that Birum has set that thing to guard the docks there, but I assume he will be looking for us in Khabu eventually. We can take our time returning there, so if we must take a roundabout route to get to

Earth and drop off whoever will stay there, then it's a good plan. Is this what Pontol has in mind, Sohyeon?"

"Yes, we're going to my home first, and then you can continue on to Khabu," Sohyeon said. "When Minha came, more birds arrived on Earth too, to join Mapin there."

Litt seemed surprised when Sohyeon mentioned Mapin's name.

"So she's with your family? You mentioned that earlier. Then we have many of the clan elders watching over the key locations. Good!" Litt said. "She can help you find the deer clan, too. I don't imagine it will be easy to find them, but somewhere among them is my old friend Nominus. Even if he isn't among them on Earth, his name may get you some attention from them. Just tell them you had my blessing to find them and talk with him, although it has been a very long time."

"We'll use the birds to cross the sea instead of relying solely on Pontol's skills when we need to send a message," Yarava said thoughtfully. "That is perhaps a development Birum didn't count on. He doesn't seem to have much affinity for Khabu's other clans from what I've observed as a prisoner in the palace."

"They'll be more reliable," Litt said sitting down on a bench near Cargal. "It will be hard for Birum to cope with them since, like me, they have entered the ancestral dreamland and are hundreds, even thousands, of years older than him. Their small, vulnerable bodies are nothing to judge them by."

"And what of Pontol?" Sohyeon asked, looking back at Litt as he pulled the rope back into the boat and coiled it up. "Now that he can't go home, where should he and his ferry dock?"

"He'll come with us to Khabu," Mirae said, pulling Kerinda close to her again once Cargal had been bandaged up. "He has served us well and is in the employ of the high priestess there, so he has earned the right to stay under our protection."

The boat reached a point where it sailed into an open sea topped with a layer of mist that Sohyeon never remembered seeing when taking the ferry before.

"Now I understand why you said the inhabitants of Khabu were considered space pirates," Sohyeon said, putting his arm around Tamnyn. "It would be wonderful to sail like this all of the time. It's so beautiful."

Everyone fell silent and looked around. A gentle breeze blew across the misty water, and the night sky glittered with thousands of stars high above them that seemed to grow ever nearer as they sailed toward the horizon. But soon, their interlude of peace would end, Sohyeon thought, and they would have to face Baram. He dreaded finding out what had happened on earth in their absence.

5 THE HUNTING PARTY

1

"Pete? Are you there?" Sohyeon whispered, looking across the paintball park's darkened outdoor course.

It had been a long time since he had played a round of paintball, and now it was late at night. What a totally stupid time to suggest a game! How stupid of Sohyeon to accept! He could barely see out of his googles in the darkness, and he almost tripped over one of the field barriers but caught himself in time.

Keeping one eye on the field, he started to adjust his paintball gun, but Sohyeon was horrified to discover he wasn't carrying a paintball gun at all but a crossbow. It resembled a regular gun except for the curved split limbs across the barrel. This was all wrong. How did he end up in this situation again? He could only vaguely remember Pete's call and coming out here to meet him. Running his hand over the strap across his chest, Sohyeon felt for the crossbow bolts in the quiver on his back and pulled one out. The triangular, filigreed head gleamed like silver in the moonlight. Suddenly, Sohyeon understood. Turning the crossbow so he could step into the stirrup and use the cord to cock one of the arrows, Sohyeon knew it wasn't a game this time. They were fighting to the death with rules quite different from a regular paintball match. Flipping on the safety, he positioned the bolt and waited.

Hearing a twig crack not far from the tree line across the field, Sohyeon ducked for cover behind one of the wooden structures Vince had set up along the obstacle course, hoping Pete hadn't seen him. His thoughts raced as he waited for Pete to come into view. Straining to see through his goggles and feeling generally like he was suffocating, he thought fleetingly that he should have torn them off before getting the bow ready, but there wasn't time to change position and still be ready for Pete's attack.

"Vince? Thank god it's you."

A woman's voice broke the thick silence as a figure appeared above him and came around the side of the wooden fence, making him nearly jump out of his skin.

Vince? Sohyeon wondered if he heard her correctly, but he recognized the voice instantly as Marietta Esposito's. Did she mistake him for her husband? Of course, with all of the gear in the darkness, it might be possible she thought he was Vince, though Sohyeon was taller and lankier than the middle aged proprietor of the paintball park. Remembering the last time he saw her with Baram and her unwholesome appearance, he wondered if he should play the game and let her keep thinking he was Vince.

"Marietta? Oh, I didn't expect you to be here," Sohyeon said, trying to imitate his friend's gruff but friendly style of speaking. He didn't think he would easily fool her, though.

He let his finger on the crossbow trigger relax but kept the crossbow in a ready position with the scope not far away from his face. The arrow's gleaming tip drew his eye one more time as Marietta came closer. She was still wearing her wildly inappropriate gold sequined evening gown, and she smiled grotesquely at him, waving for him to stand.

"The game's over, now, Vince. You need not worry about anything. Come have some coffee with me in the paintball park's café, and we'll talk things over. Where did you get that bow and arrow? I've never seen anything like those arrows before. What are they? Platinum tipped? They look like they're real and not for target practice."

Sohyeon paused, wondering what he should do. Once they went into the paintball facility and he took off his mask, his ruse would be over, and Marietta would have him as her prisoner. Now was the time to make a run for it, though he didn't know if Pete or Ognjen Baram were somewhere nearby in the woods, waiting for him. He couldn't think fast enough to know what to do.

"Yeah, they're broadheads all right. Steel blades with a titanium tip," he said casually, trying to downplay the significance of his answer. "They only use platinum in video games, hon. I just found them in stock and thought they looked pretty cool, especially in the moonlight. Good for hunting werewolves, you know? I didn't reckon on anyone being out here."

He laughed, but his eyes darted around the area as he stood up, looking for more of his enemies and an opportunity.

"It isn't deer season, dear, and isn't it illegal to hunt at night?" Marietta asked as she led him to the facility's main doors.

Sohyeon saw a light was on in the facility, which he hadn't noticed before. What was wrong with him? he wondered for the umpteenth time. He felt like his head was jammed with cotton, and he couldn't think clearly. If he wasn't careful, he wouldn't escape their grasp and would get hurt himself. He needed to snap out of it. Glancing back over his shoulder toward the tree line, he saw someone start to emerge.

"Don't worry about him, dear," Marietta said, suddenly very close to his ear, making him jump again and nearly lose his grip on the crossbow. Her voice was both seductive and spooky, like the tone vampires used in the B movies he liked to watch as a kid. Was she hypnotizing him? "Come with me."

Sohyeon felt he couldn't disobey this time, but the hair stood up on the back of his neck as he followed her, certain the creature would be coming in with them. Stifling the urge to scream, he looked around again frantically to see where he could run to, but his body felt very heavy, and it took all of the effort he had to put one foot in front of the other and make it into the paintball facility.

Once they went inside, the blazing lights hurt his eyes. Marietta turned and, looking behind him, waved for whoever waited there to come in with them too. Sohyeon tried to turn, but the goggled helmet he wore was too constricting. Smiling broadly, as if reading his mind, Marietta came over and pulled it off. Sohyeon knew the ruse was up, but gulping in the fresh air, he caught a glimpse of himself in the decorative mirrors over the coffee shop counter. Vince's face stared back at him, looking a little drunk and quite terrified. But how could he be Vince?

Marietta handed him a cup of steaming coffee that smelled terrible, her eyes bright and triumphant. Putting down the crossbow on the counter against his better judgment, Sohyeon took the cup and sipped the hot liquid. Whatever it type it was, it cut through the foggy feeling almost immediately. Looking back at himself in the mirror, he saw the creature enter the facility's front doors over his shoulder and stand a few paces behind him. Wasn't that Pete MacIntyre? Pete looked like a cross between a werewolf and zombie rather than one of the neighborhood kids who liked to play at the park. So it *was* Pete who called him here, just like he first thought, but for what end?

Marietta started laughing as Pete cornered him in the café. All he could do was stare at Pete's fangs as the boy came closer and reached a clawed hand out for him. Sohyeon grabbed the crossbow off the counter and wondered if he dared take a shot at Pete, his former friend. This wasn't how it was supposed to end. This facility had been a refuge to him for many years, full of friends and fun. Had Marietta turned it into a base for these monsters?

Sohyeon fumbled to keep Pete at least arm's length from him, holding out the crossbow between them, but he saw more shadowy figures beyond the open doors moving toward them. How many had been turned?

As Pete grabbed Sohyeon's arm and the crossbow, Pete squeezed hard enough on Sohyeon's pressure points for him to drop the weapon. Opening his mouth to expose his cat-like fangs, Pete dove toward him. Sohyeon screamed and jolted awake back in his room at the Choi house. Sitting on his bed in the darkened room with Tamnyn sleeping on the floor beside his bed in a sleeping bag, Sohyeon's mind flooded with conflicting images. When the helmet came off, revealing Vince's face in the mirror, it wasn't just an illusion. He really was Vince. It had been a dream. And now Vince was in some kind of danger at the paintball park.

2

"How can you be sure, Sohyeon?" Jangsun asked, whispering, as he sat on the edge of Sohyeon's bed, casually holding his steel *hwando* in one hand. He had been on night watch in the upstairs hallway and came in to check on Sohyeon when he heard his son scream.

"I don't know. It just felt real. Why else would I have dreamt of Vince like that, or seen Pete? Has anyone gone to the paintball park to see what's going on? Or heard from Vince while Tamnyn and I were away in Eokhmisseun?"

"There have been a few missed calls on your phone, but no messages. I didn't bother to look to see who since we've been busy with the high priestess' arrival, looking for Baram and trying to trace his movements. Minha's people have largely taken over, and your mother and I have just tried to keep the household together and running. Many of the local stores and businesses have shut down outside of very limited hours for customers, and there's not much in the way of goods and supplies to be had."

"The darkness never lifts for very long then?" Sohyeon asked, noticing Mapin creeping around the corner of his room and settling her little feathery body on the sleeping bag near Tamnyn's head. "Is it safe to be on the streets at all even during the day?"

"Not very, though a few of us still try," Jangsun said grimly. "I'm just grateful no one has tried to enter the house. After the situation you found yourself in at Pete MacIntyre's, I think that's the best we could expect. It may not be long before they attack, though, and we should stay on guard."

"Maybe Tamnyn and I should check out the paintball park and try to find Vince. I could call his cell phone since he used that to reach me before we left for Eokhmisseun."

"It might be very dangerous to do something like that, though I understand your loyalty to Vince Esposito. He's a good man who deserves better than Marietta, from what I hear has happened there."

"Let me try to call him now," Sohyeon said, fumbling for the cell phone on his nightstand.

Jangsun leaned over and flipped on the nightstand light as Sohyeon turned on the phone display and looked up Vince's cell phone number. Hitting the call button, the phone dialed and the number rang for a long while before Vince's voicemail picked up.

"Vince? Vince!" Sohyeon said urgently into the phone after the beep. "I need to talk to you right away, so please call me back. I was thinking about stopping by the paintball park so we could talk, but as you know, things have been kind of weird with the new people moving into Addison." Understatement, Sohyeon thought. "We also need to talk about hunting deer and maybe hunting a few other animals. I hear there's something special going on with the exploding deer population in Addison that we need to investigate, but I'll explain when I see you in person. Also, be sure to bring titanium arrows for our little training bout that we discussed before all of this happened."

Mapin suddenly caught his eye, and he quickly finished the message and hung up, watching the little white bird transform into her human form.

"Mapin?" Sohyeon said in a strangled voice.

Tamnyn jolted awake as Jangsun turned to look at the woman who now appeared. A small but beautiful girl wrapped in a white chiton from another era stood up and presented herself to them, her long straw-colored hair spilling over her bare shoulders and white feathered wings rising from her back.

"Let me come," Mapin said, her speech heavily accented, almost sounding to Sohyeon like she had a French accent. "I heard you talking when you came back from Eokhmisseun with Mirae and Litt about how Birum is searching all of the worlds for the deer clan. Litt and I are old friends, and perhaps I can help more than the others right now if your goal is finding the lost clan and Nominus, one of their oldest members. I will be more than a match for Baram, should you run into him or any that he has turned."

"That might be a good alternative," Jangsun said, standing. "Gas is being rationed, so we have to be careful how frequently we use the car. Everything we do will have to be on foot or by bicycle unless there's a good reason to drive. Taking a bird with you on your bicycle to investigate would be easier, certainly, and look less suspicious."

"Tamnyn can take Sukjin's or mom's bike. Just because we're stuck with low-tech transportation doesn't mean we should be going around alone, and I need her with me since she knows how to fight. I'm still pretty green at using any of these old-fashioned weapons. I don't understand what we're supposed to do with the deer clan when we find it anyway, if we can find it. I know Cargal needs help, but beyond some sort of special healing properties, I'm at a loss. Should I tell them I just dropped by to say hello from their old friends from Khabu? That's kind of ridiculous."

"What progress has Minha made since she has come here?" Mapin asked, looking at Jangsun with her fiery red eyes. "Where is she now?"

Sohyeon had wondered that himself. When they had returned to the Choi house after fleeing Eokhmisseun, Sohyeon had quickly noticed how nothing seemed different. His parents, Sukjin and Philip were in the exact situation they had been before Minha had arrived, with only a few more of the birds hanging around the house with Mapin. Minha had immediately moved out and had barely returned or reported to them.

"From what I understand, she and her acolytes have found more comfortable arrangements at a local hotel that has been taken over by those city leaders that haven't fallen into Baram's camp," Jangsun said. "She wants to gain influence over them so Baram can't take over the city completely. The hotel in question is now their headquarters in the fight to regain control of the city from the interlopers."

"Good luck to them," Sohyeon said dryly, thinking of Cargal and Tamnyn's plight back in Eokhmisseun. "Birum has likely taught his son the black magic he used to take over Eokhmisseun. While Tamnyn and her father held out as long as they could, it wasn't a pleasant existence, and they ultimately failed."

"Minha isn't human, however," Tamnyn said. "Because she is one of *them*, she may have more power to stop them than we had. She can turn into a tiger, plus she has had access to their ancestral crypt over centuries. This is far more than the resources father and I had to use against Birum. Don't underestimate her."

"And then there's Mapin," Sohyeon said, looking at the woman standing before him.

How old had Litt and Orach said she was again? A few thousand years old at least, though she looked very young, perhaps even younger than Sohyeon. Still, there was an aura of power around her that, paired with her odd, half-animal appearance, hinted at some greater power she wielded. Her presence at least evened the odds a bit.

"Yes, we have three of the immortal birds here with us," Tamnyn said, nodding with approval. "Minha didn't leave us without any help, and the birds are formidable. I grew up working with them when they appeared to be just a flock of special messenger birds."

"Now you know what we truly are," Mapin said, looking at her in amusement. "If you fear your friend is in danger now, let's leave and find out if we can save him."

Sohyeon glanced at the clock on his nightstand. It was three in the morning.

"At this time of night? What do you think, dad? Should we risk it at this hour or wait until daybreak? Not that it will matter that much since it never really gets light around here anymore."

Jangsun looked at him thoughtfully.

"I would like to go with you this time. I think we shouldn't wait."

"If you go with us, who will help mom? She has her hands full with Cargal, who can't fight to protect anyone right now, and while Sukjin has some training, we don't really know much about Philip's fighting ability."

"My father's bodyguard Esram is a skilled fighter," Tamnyn said. "He can protect them while we're away. We can also leave one of the birds here, though I think we should take the third one with us along with Mapin. I see no reason why we can't go now on a rescue mission to find Vince, just the five of us. Your father is a skilled fighter, too."

"I will ask Laqrisa to come with us and leave Tmolos behind," Mapin said, returning to her bird shape and flying to where the other two war birds had perched to confer with them.

"Do we have enough bikes?" Sohyeon asked, jumping out of bed and putting his shoes on.

He hadn't bothered to get into pajamas to sleep since they were taking turns with the night watch.

"We only need two or three, right?" Tamnyn said, getting out of her sleeping bag and pulling out her shoes, too. "I can ride with you, while Mapin and Laqrisa can ride in the bicycle basket with your father."

"What happens if we find Vince and want to bring him back? What if he's injured?" Sohyeon asked. "How do we bring him back on a bicycle?"

"He can ride with me," Jangsun said. "I picked up a double seated tandem bicycle after you left, since apparently no one thought they might need one. The store was open long enough for me to get that. We'll manage. Let's get our weapons ready to travel, and grab a quick snack on our way out. Where are we starting our search?"

"The paintball park for sure," Sohyeon said. "But I think we need to be careful because it's probably true something has happened there. We should go into this expecting to run into trouble and that we will need to rescue Vince."

"Go downstairs and get ready while I brief the others on what we intend to do and get the next shift on watch out here," Jangsun said, walking back down the hall to the master bedroom where everyone else had been sleeping.

3

Less than an hour later, Sohyeon and the others were racing down the street toward the paintball park. Tamnyn rode behind him on the tandem bike, while his father rode his one-seater, the two birds sitting in the basket. The streets were mostly deserted, and Sohyeon felt uneasy as he noticed the few people who were out receded into the shadows when they passed. *Everyone is so nervous*, he thought. It was risky for them to be out at all, especially at that hour. Addison definitely felt like Eokhmisseun these days.

Turning the corner into the part of town with fewer houses where the wooded areas began, Sohyeon saw the paintball facility up ahead. The long, one and a half-story building had vertical beige siding with green trim, and it housed the indoor field, gear rental shop and mini café. Studying it now, Sohyeon realized how hard it would be for someone held inside to escape. An old warehouse Vince had turned into a paintball field, he had added a line of small windows just under the flat roof that allowed some natural light into the facility, but they were much too high for anyone to jump out of or look in through. The building had few standard-sized windows close to the street level that Sohyeon could remember, only two in the observation area and one in each of the staff rooms that faced the side and back of the building. Sohyeon also remembered the building had an emergency exit on the far side facing the thicket of trees and a few loading docks in the back.

Coming from this side of the building where the parking lot and outdoor field were situated, only the double front doors faced them. Normally, Sohyeon wouldn't have paid much attention to them, but now that the situation had turned dangerous, he felt helpless as he realized how flimsy they looked. The entrance was constructed with metal frames holding glass panes the full size of each door with only a crossbar splitting them into a top and bottom panel, hardly anything substantial to protect them against intruders. He wondered if the glass was reinforced somehow, since it seemed easy to just smash them and enter the building. As he got closer, he slowed down to look at the cars still in the parking lot, the shadow of the wooden fences and barricades in the outdoor field rising up behind them. The streetlights were dimmer than usual out there, or maybe some of them had burned out. He didn't remember it ever seeming so dark after nightfall.

"Is something wrong?" Tamnyn asked, looking up.

"I'm just surprised that anyone would still have their car here, but I guess we left ours here for a few days, too, after the incident with the search party. It's probably nothing. The one car looks like Marietta's, though. I think it was here the night she introduced us to Ognjen Baram."

Sohyeon stopped the bike at the far end of the parking lot near the tree line and one of the larger wooden fortresses in the outdoor field, then flipped down the kickstand. They stood in shadows just deep enough a casual observer would not be immediately alerted to their presence. Jangsun and the birds came up beside them with the second bike. Mapin flittered around the side of the building to do reconnaissance, while Laqrisa transformed into her equally formidable, chiton-clad human form. Her silky white, shoulder-length hair and pearlescent eyes glowed unnaturally in the waning moonlight. Like Mapin, she exuded a strong aura of power although she was unarmed.

The paintball park was deserted. No sign of human activity was apparent in the outdoor course, and the front glass doors looked in on the darkened indoor course and observation area. The windows along the top of the building also were all dark. Even with no sign of anything amiss, Sohyeon was sure something was wrong. He could feel it.

Jangsun, Tamnyn and Sohyeon dismounted their bikes and, clasping their weapons, walked cautiously around the field before approaching the front doors to the facility. Sohyeon remembered Vince had been hiding behind a wooden barrier near the building in the dream and walked over to the one that looked like it. On the ground behind the section of wooden fence, Sohyeon saw something glittering. He bent down and picked it up. It was a crossbow bolt with a lethal-looking, sharp-edged filigree broadhead on the tip. Titanium, didn't he say in the dream? Perfect. He could use it like a dagger in one hand as he waved his spear in the other should they encounter any trouble.

"Did you find something?" Jangsun asked, coming up to Sohyeon as Tamnyn and Laqrisa walked toward the tree line at the edge of the outdoor field.

"Vince's arrow. What I saw in my dream really happened. He had some of these. He's got to be here somewhere then."

"So he was here with a bow and arrow?"

"He had a crossbow, and he was waiting for Pete MacIntyre, but Marietta found him instead and led him inside, where they were waiting for him."

"Everything looks deserted now," Jangsun said. "If he's here, he's incapacitated or dead. Trying to rescue him will be a big fight. I can't imagine they put him in there and just left the place. If we wander around, we'll probably get caught."

"Are we really ready to fight them if they're here?"

"Maybe. I don't know. I've never fought a real sword fight where it was life or death, only tournaments. The rules and techniques will be very different. Now, you live by your will and your wits. Just be careful and know that everyone is counting on you to make it back home alive, no matter what happens."

"You be careful, too, okay," Sohyeon said, trying to keep his voice light. "I'm much too small to be carrying two wounded, grown men back home on my bicycle."

As they stood talking, Mapin appeared and landed on the wooden fence near Sohyeon and Jangsun. Seeing her arrival, Tamnyn and Laqrisa came back toward their side of the paintball field.

"Did you find anything?" Sohyeon asked Tamnyn as she returned.

"We saw footprints, but it's hard to say who made them. The ghost-slaves can still wear some types of shoes, which will make their footprints look like everybody else's. We didn't see any signs of a struggle. Mapin?"

They all turned to look at Mapin, who was still in her bird form. Laqrisa came forward and began to speak to her in their strange bird language then turned to them to explain.

"She says there are people in the room at the far end of the facility. They have the lights off, so they may be resting, but she senses maybe four or five of them."

"Maybe one of them is Vince," Sohyeon said hopefully.

"Did you bring your phone?" Jangsun asked. "Send her back around and try calling him. If he is around and doesn't have his phone on silent mode, she may be able to hear it coming from inside. The building is sturdy, but it shouldn't be completely soundproof, especially with the windows around the top."

"If Vince doesn't have it turned off, then he's in trouble," Sohyeon said, holding the arrow and his spear in one hand and pulling out his phone from his jacket pocket with the other. "Go ahead, Mapin."

Mapin flew off around the building again. Waiting a moment, Sohyeon turned on his phone and called Vince on speed dial. It rang a long time, but this time Vince's voicemail didn't pick up. As Sohyeon was about to hang up, however, someone answered.

"Hello?" It was Marietta.

Sohyeon knew he couldn't just hang up since his number was probably visible to her on the phone. He'd be found out no matter what he did.

"Hi, where's Vince?" he asked, scrambling for some plausible excuse to tell her why he called. Remembering their last meeting was quite unpleasant, Sohyeon decided not to let on that he recognized her voice.

"Not in right now. Don't call again. We're really busy, okay?" she said before hanging up on Sohyeon.

Just then, Mapin flew around the corner, her eyes flashing wildly. As she came to rest on Laqrisa's shoulder, she whispered another word in their language to her, and Laqrisa nodded, turning to the others.

"She could hear the phone ringing inside near the porch at the end of the back side of the building. He's here just around the corner."

"The porch?" Sohyeon said to himself, thinking. "The storage room window near the loading dock! We need to find a way to break in and get him out, but I guess Marietta is nearby since she heard and answered the phone."

"There will be more of them if your dream and Mapin's senses are anything to go by," Tamnyn said. "We need to use great caution."

"I wonder if the front doors are locked," Sohyeon said, eyeing them up again.

"Just walk right in the front doors?" Jangsun asked. "That would be very predictable for our enemies, and if the doors are locked, you'd have to smash them, wouldn't you? So much for sneaking in. Is there another way we can enter the building quietly?"

Sohyeon thought a moment.

"Everything is likely to be locked, and the loading dock doors are too big to open without attracting attention. We need to find an open window or something they may have carelessly left unlocked."

"Then we need to try all of the doors and windows," Tamnyn said.

"And if we don't find any way in, then what?" Sohyeon asked. "Do we just go home and wait for a better time? Then again, we shouldn't just stand around here too long either. They may be watching."

"Let's do this," Jangsun said. "You, Mapin and I will try to get in here through the front doors, and Tamnyn and Laqrisa will stay out of sight and cover us in case we get attacked or have to smash the doors open. This way, we all won't be captured at once, and someone can get help or potentially get us out of there if things go bad."

4

Sohyeon and Jangsun headed for the front doors, Mapin flittering around behind them.

"So what are the chances it has been left unlocked?" Sohyeon whispered to his father when they reached the doors. Sohyeon studied the lock under the metal handles, but he didn't see anything that gave him a hint as to whether the doors were locked just by looking at it.

"If it is, it's probably a trap," Jangsun said softly. "Don't the doors open onto the café and observation area? That won't provide us a lot of cover, and it will be easy for our adversaries to watch us from a safe vantage point where we won't notice them. There are a lot of tables and chairs, plus the long counters for the coffee shop and rental equipment area."

"Yeah, but it's the door Vince entered in the dream."

Sohyeon slid the arrow into his belt loop to free one hand and reached out for the handle on the left door. Pulling gently so he wouldn't make any noise, Sohyeon sighed in relief when it opened easily.

"Watch yourself," Jangsun whispered as Sohyeon swung the door open. "This doesn't mean we're safe, only that our entry was easy."

Sohyeon had his spear ready with the point out in front of him as he cautiously entered the foyer leading to the café and observation area. Mapin flew in the gap between the doors, and the sound of her flapping wings made Sohyeon wince since it seemed so loud in the thick silence. She flew in the direction of the inner paintball course. Nothing else moved in the facility.

Just a few steps inside the front doors, Sohyeon could make out the shape of about ten square tables with wooden chairs surrounding them as his eyes adjusted to the light. The café was in front of them, a mirror running along the short wall behind the counter just under the menu. To its left down a short hallway stood the gear rental counter, then the staff and storage areas were situated beyond that. The café and shops were separated from the inner course by a wall to the left that had large observation windows and another set of flimsy wooden half double doors like something out of a saloon in the Old West.

The weak light from the moon and streetlights streamed through the string of high windows looking down onto the indoor course, and as they surveyed the scene, Sohyeon realized with alarm that some of the chairs were turned over on their side and that blackish red streaks swept across the floor toward the rental counter. Clearly, the café had been the scene of a struggle.

As Sohyeon moved cautiously toward the coffee shop counter where he had seen Vince standing in the dream not long ago, Jangsun crept into the room behind him, letting the front door shut slowly so it wouldn't make any noise. With a slippery, swishing sound, Jangsun pulled his *hwando* out of its sheath and now held one of them in each hand, ready for battle.

Neither of them moved for a minute. Sohyeon suddenly had an idea. Taking his phone back out of his pocket, he turned on the display, letting the weak light from its surface provide a little more light so they could see. Sohyeon wondered if he should try calling Vince again to see where the phone was, but the dark streaks he saw on the floor and the memory of Marietta answering that last call made him hesitate.

Walking around the left side of the coffee shop counter toward the gear rental counter, questions rose up in Sohyeon's mind. Was that blood on the floor? What happened after Pete walked in? Sohyeon's dream had ended there, but the room had not looked like this then. The mirror behind the counter now had a few cracks, and one jagged piece had fallen out and shattered on the floor behind the counter. Fliers for the upcoming community picnic had been scattered across the floor, and a few of the paintball guns that usually hung on the wall behind the rental counter had fallen, their hooks ripped out as if someone had climbed up them and pulled them out of the wall. More dark, bloody skid marks pointed toward the doors leading to the storage and staff rooms, which were side by side at the far end of the rental counter. Rooms where Vince probably was.

"This way," Sohyeon whispered.

Pausing to glance at the staff room door, Sohyeon felt a strange uneasiness come over him as he considered which room to enter. Jangsun immediately followed him as he moved stealthily toward the storage room door instead to search it first. Sohyeon tried the doorknob, holding his phone under his chin up against his chest. As with the front door, the storage room door opened easily. It squeaked just enough to make Sohyeon jump, and he opened it slower to muffle the sound. Holding up his phone once the door was open so the weak light could penetrate the darkness and supplement the very dim moonlight streaming in on this side of the building, Sohyeon thought he could make out Vince's figure laying on his back, eyes closed with his hands tied together.

As Sohyeon entered and knelt down beside his friend, his phone started to vibrate, flashing a message about an incoming call. The number was Vince's! Sohyeon felt a chill go through him as he looked down at the supine man on the floor before him. Marietta had Vince's phone. She had to be somewhere nearby. Could she be watching?

"Choshimhaseyo."

Sohyeon said a sharp word in Korean to warn his father as he pressed the button to pick up the call and held the phone to his ear. Shrill cackling burst from his phone, startling Sohyeon so much he dropped it beside Vince with a clatter. Marietta for sure! He retrieved the phone, turned it off and stuffed it back into his jacket pocket, meeting his father's wide eyes in the darkness.

Jangsun understood and turned back to look out the door to the main lobby, putting his foot in the gap between the door and doorframe to keep it open as something crashed in the indoor paintball course. Without hesitating, Sohyeon bent down and sliced carefully through the rope holding Vince's hands with the edge of the blade on his spear, then he quickly felt Vince's neck for a pulse. Vince's feverish skin throbbed lightly under his fingers, and Sohyeon gave a sigh of relief, though he didn't have long to wake Vince up.

As Sohyeon shook Vince's arm and lightly slapped his cheek, the older man stirred and cautiously opened his eyes.

"It's me, Vince. It's Sohyeon," he whispered frantically, glancing back at his father, who still stood in his defensive position. Nothing moved in the area beyond the storage room. "We've come to rescue you."

Vince coughed quietly and sat up with Sohyeon's help before leaning on him to get back on his feet.

"Can you walk?" Sohyeon whispered. "We need to get out of here fast."

"Yeah, I can walk some, though they did their darnedest to me," Vince whispered. "That MacIntyre kid bit up my arms and sliced my legs. I don't think the wounds are serious, they just hurt something fierce, and I feel very weak. You're right we need to get out of here now. They're here somewhere, sleeping. Daybreak is coming soon, and they seem to prefer to sleep during the day even if they don't exactly need to."

"Then this is now their lair?"

"It was *my* lair until they came tonight. Marietta had them in our house before they came here, and I didn't want to stick around, especially after I saw how she played up to Ognjen Baram as if she was his girlfriend. That Baram creature has been using our house to travel between dimensions or some other such thing. I've never seen the likes of them. Creepy, like something out of a horror movie, though I can't say I ever like to watch the darn things. Is that your father there, Sohyeon?"

"Dad came in with me to find you since we didn't know what was going on. I had a premonition you were in danger here. More of us are out front waiting to make a quick getaway. We just need to make it back to the front door to join them. Who's sleeping here?"

"Pete and Marietta that I know about. More of them were hanging out near the door when we were fighting, but I don't know who they were or how many there were. Maybe more of them have come since they locked me in this room. They want to get revenge on me for shooting Baram when you were talking with them. They know I'm their enemy, though what are they? Do you know anything about them?"

"Don't say anything more now," Sohyeon said, trying to calm him as they joined Jangsun in the doorway. "We can talk about that later when we're safe."

Everything was quiet again in the indoor course, but they all strained to see what was out there. Jangsun waved for them to follow as they stepped cautiously back into the rental area to reach the front door. Alarmed though he didn't know why, Sohyeon realized he didn't see Mapin anywhere, though perhaps that was nothing. The birds could come and go as they chose. She probably just found a better vantage point.

Marietta, however, was another matter.

5

The men made their way slowly and cautiously toward the exit, but when they reached the swinging doors to the indoor course, Sohyeon saw a shadow cross in front of the glass doors, cutting off their only escape route. He and Vince looked up in alarm as Jangsun jumped to hide against the wall to the right of the glass doors before the figure could see him. A moment later, Baram appeared beyond the glass, his long, red mane and black cloak fluttering in the night breeze.

"No," Vince whispered, starting to lunge toward the doors though Sohyeon could now see the bloodstains and wounds all over his body where he had been ravaged with bite marks and deep scratches. Quickly pulling the gleaming arrow from Sohyeon's belt loop, he raced toward the door, wobbling unsteadily, then reached for the thumb latches and flipped them quickly to lock the creature out. Vince stood at the door a moment, staring at Baram, though the weretiger gave no indication whether he could see Vince from the outside.

"What do we do now?" Sohyeon whispered frantically, knowing that no matter which way they tried to run now, Baram would see them and could orchestrate an attack.

"Where are the girls?" Jangsun whispered from his hiding place. "Aren't Tamnyn and Laqrisa out there?"

"Hopefully they had the sense to hide," Sohyeon said. "I don't know what we can do against him, though I would have assumed Laqrisa should be more than a match for him. Hopefully they aren't dead. Would Baram have any silver weapons?"

Suddenly, as if on cue, a little white bird dove into the foyer, flying over the saloon style doors and hovering in front of the double glass doors facing Baram, her wings flapping rhythmically. With the quick word in her language, Mapin shrieked, causing all of the men to jump nervously as a golden-red glow began to emanate from the tips of her wing feathers with each motion. Mapin slowly turned into a ball of fire, the air crackling around her and whirling until each wave of flames licked further and further across the span of the doors, finally covering the entire glass surface in a wall of flames so thick Baram couldn't see through it.

Jangsun quickly backed through the saloon-style doors into the indoor paintball course, and Sohyeon and Vince quickly followed him, seeing the cover Mapin had provided for them to escape. Of course, Baram would assume they had entered the course, but at least he couldn't be certain that they weren't hiding behind the counters or had escaped out the back loading dock doors. As it was, Sohyeon assumed that was their next move, to sneak through the indoor course to get to the loading area where they had both a solid back door and two or three garage door mechanisms. All of them would be easy for Baram to stake out, but they had no other choice.

The inner paintball course normally was scary enough, but in the dark, knowing that bloodthirsty creatures lurked, it was a nightmare. The walls of the warehouse had been outfitted like a fake underground bunker with distressed concrete. Barriers assembled for paintball games included horizontal stacks of large corrugated plastic drain pipes secured in place with cords, simulated rusted 55-gallon metal drums built up on top of one another in a single layer wall and secured with solder, various large balloons made of canvas or vinyl camouflage, and a few abandoned cars painted over to look damaged and decayed. It was an impressive set up that Sohyeon had loved to play in with his buddies during middle school and high school. At least it offered plenty of places for them to hide, but that was exactly the problem with it. It was also easy for their enemy to hide from them, plus it was set up for modern weaponry, not old fashioned weapons like swords and spears. Even the arrow Vince held would be handled more like a dagger for hand to hand combat.

"This way," Jangsun said, rushing through the course as Vince whispered to them how to reach the facility's back door through the obstacles.

"We should stop here and let him rest a minute," Sohyeon said as they reached one of the towers of drain pipes taller than a man. "He's weak, and we need time to really think through what to do next. We won't be able to see if Baram or Pete are waiting for us when we run out the back door. We might run right into their arms!"

Standing beside Vince and holding him steady as they stopped a moment, Sohyeon saw from the shifting shadows and flickering light coming from the observation area that Mapin's fireball had died out. Glancing back toward the windows overlooking the indoor course, Sohyeon could see part of the glass front doors. Mapin was no longer there, but Sohyeon saw that Baram had not left the facility. A long, bony red-skinned hand with black tattoos and sharp black claws reached for the door handle beyond the glass and shook the handle gently.

"How sturdy are the doors really, Vince?" he whispered, unable to tear his eyes from the sight. Mercifully, he couldn't see much beyond the corner of the left front door. "Will the lock really hold against him?"

"All he probably needs to do is shoot a bullet through the glass or hit it with a crowbar," Vince said dryly in a low voice. "If someone wants to get in badly enough, they can. It's not like I had the place set up like Fort Knox, you know. The battles were only supposed to be fake."

"What's happening, Sohyeon?" Jangsun asked, turning to look at his son. He stood at the far end of the drain pipe tower, peering around the corner to see what might be lurking in the obstacle course.

Sohyeon didn't need to say anything. A loud snapping sound and the crash of breaking glass gave Jangsun the answer. Baram had broken the glass in the front door just enough to slip his hand in and twist the thumb latch to open the left side. A sharply scented current of cool air swirled through the facility, carrying the sound of crunching glass across the room as Baram stepped over the threshold.

The three men looked at one another in terror in the dim light, barely able to move as they all strained to hear. Finally as the facility fell silent again, Jangsun dared to peak in a voice so low Sohyeon and Vince could barely hear him.

"Which way is the back door from here? We need to get out now!"

Vince bit his lip and rubbed his upper arm.

"We need to get to the back hallway to reach the maintenance closet. The back door is next to that. The emergency lights should be on there, even at night. But we need to follow the far wall here on the right to reach it. We won't have cover everywhere along the way, though."

"Let's start that way now," Jangsun said, nodding in the direction Vince indicated.

All of them crept toward the far end of the tower of drain pipes, though Sohyeon realized the one observation room window ended not too far from the place where they were standing. Sohyeon glanced back over his shoulder at it, but he didn't see anything other than a long shadow edging toward it. He looked back at his father.

Only a few paces away was one of the burned out, distressed cars that popped up at intervals throughout the room. Behind that at a bit of a distance was a wall made out of a layer of metal drums stacked end on end, three drums high. In order for them to make it to safety, they risked being seen by Baram as they moved from obstacle to obstacle. Mapin needed to provide another pyrotechnic display to give them cover so they could make their escape, but she had disappeared after the fireball. Darn it, Sohyeon thought, where was she or Laqrisa, or even Tamnyn for that matter, when they needed them?

At least all three men had worn dark garments, Sohyeon in his navy t-shirt and dark denim jeans and jean jacket, Jangsun in black pants and a black windbreaker, Vince in his usual green camouflage park uniform. They wouldn't stand out too much as they crept around the course to make it to safety.

"What's straight ahead the way we were going before?" Sohyeon asked Vince quietly, gesturing to the right side of the room closer to the observation area.

"It's another way to reach the service hallway or to return to the main observation area, but if we go that way, we'll have no cover as we walk to the back side of the building. We'll be easily seen from the observation area through these windows if we make a run for that door, and it would be easy for Baram to just go through the door leading from the observation area and meet us in the service hallway there. If we go through the indoor course here, we at least have a shot at confusing our enemies and hiding for an extended period of time. Look, there goes your father."

Sohyeon saw Jangsun quickly race ten feet across the room from the tower of drain pipes to the car, falling carefully to the floor with his weapons ready as he reached the edge of the car and looking furtively around the room for Baram.

"Go, kid," Vince whispered. "Let me go last so I won't hold you back if I get caught. Don't stop to save me. Once you get there, have your father keep moving toward the next obstacle as I come out."

"We came here to rescue you, not to leave you behind," Sohyeon said, trying to reason with him, but he did as Vince directed.

Holding his spear defensively with the point toward the left, the direction Baram would be likely to approach them from, he raced out from behind the tower to where his father waited behind the car. As he squatted closer to the floor, reaching the edge of the front fender, his eyes surveyed the room, and he nearly fell backwards at the sight of Baram standing at the observation room window, looking into the indoor course at another part of the room.

Sohyeon crawled over to where his father crouched.

"Baram can see us if he turns now. I wonder why he didn't come into this room yet."

"Maybe he hasn't been in the park before and doesn't know the layout," Jangsun whispered.

"Vince told me that we should move to the next obstacle as he comes this way, in case he's too slow and gets caught."

Jangsun looked back toward Vince and sighed, nodding grimly.

"He's probably right, that's a good strategy, but we don't want to lose anyone. We need to make it back together. He isn't planning on doing anything foolish, is he?"

"I don't think so. Which barrier should we make a run for next?"

Jangsun looked around the room from the rear of the car. In front of them was the wall of drums, which would keep them close to the right side of the room, and to the left cattycorner was an inflatable camouflage pyramid that also could shield more than one grown man.

"Let's stay close to the wall and go for the drums," Jangsun said.

Moving from his deep crouch to a low stance, Jangsun looked back through the car windows toward the observation room windows and the swinging doors to make sure he wouldn't be observed before making a run for it. Pausing long enough to watch Baram move further toward the coffee shop beyond the observation windows, Jangsun skipped across the gap between the barriers and slid around the wall of drums on the right near the wall, flattening himself against the wall for a few moments before disappearing behind it.

6

Sohyeon could hear Vince's ragged breathing as he shuffled across the distance between the drain pipe tower to the car. Waiting long enough to catch Vince as he nearly collapsed behind the car still clutching the titanium arrow frantically in one hand, Sohyeon immediately took off toward the wall of drums where Jangsun waited. When he made it only three or four steps beyond the car, Sohyeon heard something that turned his spine to ice.

"You," said the familiar, raspy voice as the shadow of a man stepped out from behind the drain pipe tower to the far left of the car.

Freezing in place, Sohyeon turned, uncertain if he should give away his father's position by trying to make a run for it or just bide his time as he met his adversary.

"Pete?" Sohyeon whispered, his hair standing on end as he remembered his dream about Vince. But it already happened, hadn't it? What had he to fear now that the situation seemed to be repeating in real life?

"We meet again, Choi," Pete said, coming toward him slowly, his half-animal appearance and slightly hunched posture becoming more visible as Pete walked into the moonlight streaming through the high windows. This time, Pete was armed with a club. "We hadn't finished our conversation last time."

"You just wanted to talk, didn't you?" Sohyeon asked, trying not to raise his voice too much and keeping his tone light.

"We have unfinished business," Pete said matter of factly.

"If I remember correctly, you just wanted me to come over to your house for a meeting of some kind, and I had to leave," Sohyeon said, grasping his spear tighter and slowly bringing up the point into a defensive position.

"Yes, and now we have another opportunity for an introduction," Pete said, taking another step toward

Sohyeon. "My friend is back in the observation room, and one word from me will bring him here."

Sohyeon watched in fascination as Pete actually licked his lips when he made reference to his power to summon Baram. His eyes were glued to Pete's face, and he could barely breathe or move. His palms felt sweaty as he held the spear. Vaguely aware that Vince and Jangsun were still in the room as he flashed back to his dream, Sohyeon felt like he would crumble to the floor if he had to stand there any longer. Yet neither of the boys moved.

"Should I call him now?" Pete asked, smiling grotesquely. Still wearing the same tattered clothing he wore when Sohyeon had seen him at the MacIntyre house, Pete rubbed his chest a moment with his free hand and turned his head slightly toward the observation windows. "Baram!"

Pete's voice rang out in the stillness, strong and clear. In that moment, everything seemed to spin, and the sound of the weretiger's name freed Sohyeon's arms. In a panic, he stabbed at Pete with the tip of his spear, but Pete grabbed the spear above the blade and jumped out of the way. With a fluid movement, he took two running steps toward Sohyeon and swung the club at him. Sohyeon moved aside fast enough for the blow to only brush him, but he still felt a stinging pain run up his arm.

"Move!"

Sohyeon heard his father's voice, and his mind racing, he made a run for the camouflage pyramid with as much speed as he could muster. As he slid behind it, he turned just in time to see the wall of steel drums crash down on Pete and the car, smashing out one of its windows. Jangsun now stood exposed, breathing heavily and looking down at Pete, who had been pressed to the floor under the weight of the drums. Pete's club was a few feet away from his hand now, and Jangsun crept forward slowly, raising his *hwando* and the sheath of the sword in each hand, his face twisted into a ferocious scowl.

"Whoa, watch out!" Vince screamed hoarsely from his new position against the wall at the back end of the car. One of the loose steel drums rolled toward him through the shattered glass from the front car window.

Sohyeon could see Vince from his vantage point behind the pyramid, but he could only watch helplessly as Baram emerged not far from Vince, coming through door leading from the service hallway. Too far away to defend Vince, he couldn't think of what to do to stop Baram's attack. Baram's focus was entirely on Vince, his clawed hands reaching out for him, while Vince crept backward toward the wall, waving the arrow menacingly toward Baram.

Pete's eyes opened as Jangsun approached, and he twisted like a cat back onto his feet, retrieving his club in one lithe swoop. Facing Jangsun, he held up the club in a defensive position. For a moment, everyone seemed frozen in place again, and Sohyeon tried to think of the best strategy he could muster. Should he run around the room to Vince's side and help him get away from Baram? Should he come at Pete from the other side to protect his father? Should he run out of the back door to find Mapin, Laqrisa and Tamnyn and bring them back to help? Sohyeon wished he could do all of it at once, for making a choice would mean dire consequences for either his father or Vince.

Before he could make up his mind, he noticed something about the way Baram's hand was moving that reminded him strongly of the night he had fled Eokhmisseun with Tamnyn. It was the same motion Birum had used to turn one of the guards at the Elyeon estate. The turning! Could Baram do the same wicked magic that Birum had used on the citizens of Eokhmisseun? Is that what created the monster Pete had become, what made him like Pontol? If it was, Vince was in serious danger of losing his humanity.

But Vince seemed to instinctively know what was coming, and he lunged at Baram, scraping Baram's outstretched hand with the arrow tip enough to draw blood as he made a dash for the other side of the car where the metal drums had fallen to stand not far from Jangsun. Baram snarled, drawing his hand in to protect the wound. The titanium didn't seem to be having much effect, Sohyeon noticed with disappointment. It might not even slow Baram's regenerative powers.

Baram roared in fury as he watched Vince flee, and saying a magic word, his body began to grow and change. Vince watched, a look of terror convulsing across his face. He was trembling so much from weakness, pain and fear, he had to hold onto the trunk of the car to remain standing.

Pete looked from Jangsun to Vince and gave another twisted smile, trying to gauge which of the men was closest for the first blow. Jangsun didn't wait any longer. Leaping forward with a practiced ease, he swung the *hwando* at Pete and caught his shoulder with the sword, then jumped skillfully out of the range of Pete's club, taking a few steps closer toward Sohyeon's position behind the pyramid and watching Vince out of the corner of his eye.

Sohyeon realized he should come out of hiding and help, so he edged closer to the side of the pyramid, ready step out into the open just as Baram burst into full tiger form. At least ten feet tall, he looked as massive and terrifying as Birum had at the palace in Eokhmisseun. With one swoop of his paw, he tore apart the cables holding the huge plastic drain pipes together and sent them flying across the room toward the other barriers, knocking some of them down. Roaring, he took a few steps toward Vince, who fled down the right wall leading toward the corridor in spite of his injuries. Nearly tripping, Vince ran blindly to the facility's back door. Baram, however, was no longer interested in his prey but turned his fiery yellow eyes onto Sohyeon and Jangsun, who were held at bay by his minion.

Suddenly, a shot rang out, and the inflatable pyramid Sohyeon was standing behind popped and slowly collapsed. Glancing around the edge of it, Sohyeon saw Marietta standing just inside the swinging doors, a shotgun with a smoking barrel in her hands.

"Bullseye," she said, laughing.

7

Sohyeon couldn't take anymore. Seeing they were outnumbered and had no defense against gunfire, he lunged forward and, grabbing Jangsun's arm holding the *hwando,* dragged him in the direction Vince had fled.

"No! You can't do this!" Sohyeon screamed. "Mapin! Where are you, Mapin?"

The two men dashed down the edge of the indoor course against the right wall like Vince had instructed, dodging behind a few more barriers as Marietta shot wildly in their direction. Clearly, she wasn't trying to kill them or else she would have done more damage. Fleetingly, Sohyeon wondered if she knew the layout of the building well enough to guide Baram or Pete to the other exits.

Bumping into a darkened corner, Sohyeon felt for the door with his free hand. Somewhere behind them, he heard what sounded like a flock of birds, cawing and flapping their wings. Good! Mapin had returned to distract Baram at least. Finding the doorknob, Sohyeon pulled the door open and pushed his father in ahead of him, wincing at the bright light that momentarily revealed their position as they stepped into the service hallway.

Constructed of concrete block and painted a crystal blue, the hallway made a few sharp turns but otherwise was well-lit and clean. Suddenly, Sohyeon understood why Vince said it would have left them sitting ducks if they had entered the hallway at an earlier point. From where they stood, he could see the door which led to the indoor course down at the far end of the long hallway to their right. Shuddering, he pushed his father to the left, seeing a few telltale bloody handprints along the wall where the corridor turned.

"Vince?" he called softly.

"This way."

Sohyeon heard the whisper, but Vince's voice seemed even weaker than before if possible. After turning a few corners, they found him by the back exit, laying across the floor on his stomach and hyperventilating. The arrow lay on the floor near his head, and blood smeared the floor where he had fallen.

"Get the door open. Hurry!" he said hoarsely, trying to hold back a cough that would give away their position.

Jangsun jumped forward and, sliding his sword back into its sheath, flipped the bolts to unlock the door. Pushing the heavy steel door open into the night air, he stepped out a few paces and looked around before coming back to them. In the distance, deeper in the facility, they could hear an ominous banging punctuated by a few warning shots from Marietta's gun.

"Help me get up," Vince said, looking up at Sohyeon, who knelt down to roll Vince over on his back and offered his arm so Vince could steady himself.

Within a minute, Vince was able to stand, and Sohyeon pulled him out through the back door, quietly shutting it behind them. The three men stood outside, taking deep breaths in the cool, early morning air. It was 4:30 AM, and sunrise would come in another hour.

"We left the bikes at the far edge of the outdoor course, so we should be pretty close to them. Will you be able to ride, Vince?" Sohyeon asked, still whispering as they walked toward the tree line near the back edge of the farthest barrier in the course.

"We need to find the others," Jangsun said gruffly as they walked, still looking warily back at the building.

"I thought I heard the birds when I screamed for them. I don't think it was just Mapin," Sohyeon said.

"Did you bring trained birds?" Vince asked, confused but clearly feeling a little better now that they had reached relative safety.

"Not exactly," Sohyeon said, quickening his pace as he saw the bikes and Tamnyn waiting nearby, alone. "There she is. I bet she couldn't hear a thing all the way back here."

Jangsun chuckled a little, rushing to catch up with them as he fell behind.

"Where do we go now?" Sohyeon asked. "Home?"

"No, it wouldn't do in case we're followed," Jangsun said. "We need to go to Minha's headquarters at the Renaissance Plaza Hotel in downtown Addison. I told you she was staying there. She'll have a better idea of how to handle the situation. She can send one of her birds back to find Mapin and Laqrisa if need be."

8

"Let me get this straight, you're immortals, yet you try to avoid situations where you can get injured?" Sohyeon asked angrily, looking in amazement from Mapin to Minha in the Renaissance Plaza Hotel ballroom.

A few hours had passed since their fight with Baram in the paintball park, and after breakfast had been served in the main dining room for Addison's displaced citizens, everyone had settled in the ballroom to talk to the local council. Sohyeon had texted Sukjin to let her know where they were and that they were okay, though he wasn't sure yet when they would return home. Now, Jangsun and Sohyeon sat at a small table across from where Minha stood on the ballroom dance floor. Vince, who had been given one of the guest rooms to shower and change in, sat in an extra hotel uniform on one of the cushioned lobby chairs the staff had brought in for him at the next table. A few of Addison's council members sat scattered among the tables on the other side of Minha, looking more than a little shell-shocked from the recent shift in power and the appearance of monstrous entities from beyond the stellar seas.

Sohyeon had to admit this time Minha looked even more intimidating than usual. With the threat of Baram's attack now so close at hand, she did the unthinkable for a citizen of Khabu still among the living and let her arms and legs turn into half weretiger form while keeping her head and torso fully human. Her bare arms now bore the strange pattern of bone-white skin laced with black tattoo-like veins, ending in thin hands now tipped with black claws. Beneath her light blue chiton, her legs seemed to have gotten more bowed, and her bare feet that poked out beneath the dress' hem bore the same black curved claws. A thin, whip-like white and black tail curled around her body. Sohyeon thought, with her Asian facial features and long mane of silky black hair pulled back into a chignon with a layer of loose curls, half-animal was a good look for her.

Next to her stood Mapin in her half-bird form, her long gleaming wings protruding from her back and her wavy, straw-colored hair covering her nearly to her waist. Both women seemed chagrined by Sohyeon's question.

"Khabu has been a land of peace for many millennia," the high priestess said as her acolytes returned with their *hyeopdo* spears in hand after walking the perimeter of the hotel and nearby park, but she waved them off. "Much like you here in your land, we do not train routinely for war, and only some of us have skill with weaponry. You yourself are not warriors, so you should not be surprised when I say that we are not either.

"As immortals, we have special powers and skills of regeneration that make us nearly indestructible, but this does not mean we wander foolishly into situations where we can be harmed. I understand your frustration that Mapin and Laqrisa were not able to attack Baram and his minions more effectively, but you must remember that the women have lived for a very long time in the Forest of Bliss, like Litt did in the crypt of the ancestors. They are unused to the human world and lived in lands where there was no conflict, in a land of dreams. Mapin, our ancient mother, has developed other powers, as have all of the citizens of Khabu who make the change and retire from the world. Hence you saw her fireball transformation. It's bad enough that Baram now is aware that the birds of Khabu are here, but they are limited in the ways in which they fight, as are most true birds. Fear is their primary weapon against Baram and the ghost-slaves."

"We need to train for war if we are to defeat Birum," Mapin said in her thick accent, biting her lip. "The boy is not wrong, but our animal natures are not predatory, so we are no match for the tiger clan even as immortals." Mapin gave Minha a sidelong glance before coming over to stand in front of Sohyeon's table. "But we must discuss news of a different kind, that Birum is searching the known worlds along the inner sea in the hopes of finding the lost deer clan."

"It's true," Sohyeon said grimly. "I had heard that Litt's old friend Nominus should still be among them and that Birum's followers have made contact with them here. Like you, they also have acquired new abilities over time."

Mapin's red eyes glittered with interest as she studied Sohyeon's face for a moment. Turning back to Minha, Mapin walked slowly toward her as she spoke.

"Let me take a few of the birds to stake out Baram's many lairs in that case," she said, her voice ringing through the ballroom. "We will follow him and trace him to wherever this deer clan may be hiding. It must be in Addison for them to try to take over here, or were they more interested in this town because of Joriya's connection to the Choi family and Mirae?"

"To our knowledge, Birum doesn't know about the child," Minha said flatly, then she looked thoughtful. "Even if his interest was in the Chois, they must be close enough geographically to the deer clan to make contact with it from their base in Addison. What will you do when you find out where they are?"

"I will send Laqrisa to talk with them when the tiger clan is not present and see if Nominus is still with them. If he is, I will request to speak with him."

"We have no reason to believe Nominus would be on Earth with his clan than any of the hundreds of other worlds along the inner sea where they scattered millennia ago," Minha said. "Why would you expect to speak with him here?"

"It's true he could be anywhere, but if I name him and reveal myself as one of the originals from the old ghetto, they may be willing to summon him here. It's important that the deer clan not fall into Birum's clutches."

"Go then," Minha said, waving one clawed hand toward the hotel's front lobby. "I leave the assignments of the birds among us to you. Report back on the deer clan when you hear something."

Mapin smiled sweetly before walking through the ballroom doors to the front of the hotel.

"You will excuse me for a moment," Minha said, gesturing to her acolytes who were waiting in the corner of the room. "I must speak with them before the day wears on too long. After hearing your story of how Baram entered the paintball park, I worry that the hotel will also be vulnerable. It has a lot of large glass doors and walls, too."

She walked over to her acolytes, leaving the humans sitting at the cluster of tables alone for a few moments.

Vince glanced over at Jangsun and Sohyeon, his face full of wonder and amazement.

"So they're some sort of magical creatures?" he asked in a loud whisper, leaning across the aisle toward their table.

"It's complicated," Sohyeon said slowly, getting up to sit at Vince's table. Jangsun stayed in his chair and was texting back and forth with Sukjin on Sohyeon's phone. "They definitely aren't human and aren't from around here. You look a lot better now that you've washed up."

"I feel a lot better, though not enough to go through another fight like that," Vince said, laughing a little. "Will you be going back to your house? I should stay here and see how I can help since I know the enemy's lairs better than anyone. They've totally taken over my home and business."

One of the five councilman assisting Minha, a man in his mid-thirties named Anton Zhao, came over to talk with Sohyeon, Jangsun and Vince.

"On behalf of the remaining council of Addison, I really have to thank you for all of the help and information you have given us. When this whole thing struck, we had no idea what we were dealing with."

"Is Mrs. Miller okay now?" Sohyeon asked, remembering the story his father told him about the meeting between Minha and the local mayor, Megumi Iwase Miller.

"Megumi was dead set against Marietta encouraging Ognjen Baram to move in here from the beginning. The rest of us thought she was overreacting, maybe even being a bit discriminatory, but in the end," Anton left his thought unfinished and sat down at the table across from Jangsun. Glancing back over his shoulder at Megumi Miller, who even in the middle of a civilization-changing crisis still managed to wear her best tailored suit and a string of pearls, Anton could hardly repress a giggle. "She's a piece of work, I know, but she's the best mayor we've ever had in Addison. She was equally stubborn about working with Minha and was a bit prickly over the woman's wild appearance, but Minha has earned her respect. Well, that and the fact that we're dealing with an otherworldly monster convinced her that she needed to rethink her priorities. We're very grateful she didn't become an ally of Baram's but has stayed on with us to fight for humanity instead."

The men paused in their discussion as Tamnyn approached the tables, still looking as pallid as she had when they found her outside the paintball park in a fog of confusion. Sohyeon stood up and embraced her, then pulled her into the chair beside him. Jangsun looked at her questioningly. Meeting his gaze, she nodded.

"The medics found this in my back," Tamnyn said, holding up a needle a few inches long. "They think it had some sort of poison on it that drugged me without me noticing. Do you think Marietta would have done such a thing? Obviously someone didn't want me to come to your aid when Baram arrived at the paintball park."

"It looks like the kind of old-fashioned weapon they used to soak in poison and blow out of a bamboo tube," Jangsun said, looking at the needle she held. "I'm surprised they gave it to you. Are you sure you can't get poisoned again from handling it? Put it here in the ashtray for the staff to dispose of before you get hurt."

"I suppose you're right, but we should try to figure out who used it and why," Tamnyn said, placing the needle in the ashtray as Jangsun requested. "It's important to know the enemy's battle tactics, and if they use something like that, it will be nearly undetectable."

"We were just talking with Anton when you arrived," Sohyeon said. "He's in the group of council members opposing Baram. I was thinking we should see if your father is well enough to come here to talk with them about Eokhmisseun when Birum took over and how it proceeded."

"Is your father not well?" Anton asked gently.

"He was injured on the way here, and it's serious enough that we are hoping we can find a member of the legendary deer clan from Khabu here in Addison to heal him. Mrs. Choi is handling it the best she can, and he is at least comfortable even if he can't move around much or fight. Have you gotten any texts from Sukjin about his progress, Sohyeon?"

"He's able to eat and sit up now, but the wound still looks very bad, and he's in a lot of pain."

"Maybe I should go there with you to talk to him, or even bring Megumi along since she's the boss around here."

Anton smiled weakly, knowing the council members had to be careful traveling around town with Baram in power. Like the remnants of the council in Eokhmisseun, they worried about getting caught and turned into ghost-slaves or kidnapped and held prisoner. Sohyeon knew Anton's offer was an empty gesture. They had to get Cargal to the hotel somehow before long.

"So tell me," Anton said, changing the subject, "there's a *deer* clan now too? I thought I misunderstood when Mapin and Minha were discussing this before. I find it amazing we now have all these half-animal people running around Addison all of the sudden."

"We don't know where they are yet," Jangsun said, sitting up and looking restlessly at the door. "Right now they're just rumored to be here. Mapin will see if Baram has truly found a way to contact them, and then we can make our move."

"What do we do in the meantime?" Sohyeon asked, knowing his father would want to get back home soon.

"Wait," Jangsun said shortly, nodding to Anton. "We have nothing but time on our hands." He got up abruptly and walked over to the hallway leading back to the lobby.

"Your father's right," Anton said in a low voice. "Hunker down in your house and keep watch, do some drills to prepare to fight if you can, and keep in touch through phones, shortwave radios and the magical birds. We'll keep you posted as to when various supplies are safe and available and what parts of town to avoid. If it gets too dangerous, we'll start bringing more of you here to stay and man the hotel like a fortress against them."

"We'll be back then," Sohyeon said, standing. Tamnyn quickly got to her feet, too, holding onto Sohyeon's arm though she tried to appear calm. Pausing only long enough to fist bump Vince's hand and make a quick promise to stay in touch, Sohyeon led Tamnyn out of the hotel after his father.

The hotel lobby was surprisingly crowded with the various groups of local authorities who had split with Baram's faction and joined Minha's, as well as hotel staff who had retrieved their families and become boarders at the hotel. It was the largest, most famous hotel in Addison, so it could hold a lot of people.

Sohyeon felt a heaviness come over him at the thought of leaving the hotel and the comforting sense of normalcy it provided. Out in the street, the citizens of Addison lived as if they were under an order to shelter in place, but inside the hotel, the hustle and bustle was the same as any other day with guests checking in and out. Nowhere else in the city had life continued as normally as it did at the hotel.

It was almost noon, not a time likely for Baram and his people to be out waiting for them, but still dangerous nonetheless since the streets were now potentially his battlefield at any time, day or night. Catching up with his father as he reached the edge of the lobby near glass revolving doors now monitored by armed guards holding machine guns, Sohyeon helped his father prop up their bikes and wheel them through the door one of the guards had unlocked for them.

This time his father took the single rider bike while he rode the tandem with Tamnyn. It was only a 15 minute ride, but Sohyeon had to take a deep breath and tamp down his terror at the thought of running into the creature again.

9

A week passed before Sohyeon heard any news about Mapin's surveillance of Baram and his contact with the deer clan. During that time, Jangsun led daily weaponry drills among the small group in the Choi household. The drills took place before dinner in the basement and in the very early morning hours out in the backyard since they had determined from Vince that Baram's allies preferred to sleep during the day. Jangsun figured it also would put anyone watching on notice that there were fighting men in the household and make them less of a target for looters and other criminal elements in the neighborhood.

Sohyeon joined in the drills with his father, Phillip, Sukjin, Tamnyn, the three birds who all temporarily transformed back into human form, and Cargal's bodyguard so he could learn some basic moves, and Alanna came to at least the evening session. Everyone in the group needed basic skill with a sword or spear, and Sohyeon, Alanna, and the birds had the least training of anyone in the household. Cargal, too weak to participate, often gave tips and advised Jangsun on other weapons and tactics to use in a real battle.

During that week, Jangsun took Sohyeon back to his *dojang* to get a few extra *mokgum* and *hyeopdo* to practice with, though the group also discussed using normal items like baseball bats and crowbars to defend themselves. Jangsun only had two *hwando* steel swords to use, so he gave one to Sukjin since she had the best training to handle it and since the professional warriors in the group brought their own weapons from Eokhmisseun.

Between their drill sets, the birds returned to animal form. Mapin and Laqrisa conducted surveillance and went about their errands for Jangsun or Minha until nightfall, while Tmolos hung around Alanna in case she needed him to relay a message to Minha in an emergency.

Alanna kept the household running and ran errands when Megumi Miller announced on the shortwave radio that it was safe to go out and which store would be open for a short period of time. She made large batches of rice-based meals for everyone staying at the house and tended Cargal the best she could with limited medical supplies since the local hospitals had been burned down by Baram's allies shortly after he took control of Addison, aware of the human population's greatest weakness.

Disappearances had continued at a trickle, but they still made Jangsun in particular uneasy as Mayor Miller announced them over the shortwave radio every few days. There didn't seem to be any pattern to the disappearances, and a few occurred close enough to the Choi house to make everyone anxious as they listened to the reports in the master bedroom before retiring for the night. Targeted houses were discovered by small, armed patrols riding in military Humvees which the remnant council sent out at regular intervals to check on the neighborhoods. Baram's minions had left doors and windows smashed open, the houses' interiors torn apart with bloody claw marks and strange writing all over the walls, the people gone, never to be seen again. Thinking this sounded exactly like what he had witnessed at the MacIntyre house, Sohyeon sent a message through Mapin to Minha asking about getting access to photos of the writing, wondering if maybe Tamnyn would recognize it since Baram had been raised in Eokhmisseun, but she hadn't responded.

In every neighborhood, residents at two or three houses had drawn a black symbol in soot on their front doors, looking like a mouth full of sharp teeth, to announce their allegiance to Baram. Sohyeon wondered at first why they were so open about it, why Baram would allow his followers to make it easy for them to be apprehended, but Mayor Miller had spoken on the shortwave about discovering those houses abandoned without any of the signs of violence that the others had shown. She suggested Baram might be gathering them at a different location for some purpose, while the others had been targeted for attack for unknown reasons.

The situation had everyone on edge, and Sohyeon arranged for the household to play cards and other board games daily to keep everyone in good spirits, while Sukjin had gathered boxes of books and magazines they had around the house and left them in the living room for their guests to flip through. Sohyeon, Sukjin and Tamnyn also decided to handle the housework, which was continual with so many people living in close quarters, mostly on the upper floor which had three bedrooms and two bathrooms.

Although they went down to the main floor and basement during the hours of weak daylight to cook, practice with their weapons and try to live normally, they were alert to signs that the house was being watched or approached. Every day, Jangsun checked all of the doors and windows on the first floor at least three times to make sure the locks were in good order, the glass intact, and the tape and other barricades still in place. He had set up a schedule for one of the people in the household to always be watching around the clock through the upstairs windows, alert for any sign of approaching danger or other trouble in the neighborhood. Although the lifestyle was confining, no one dared to complain, and they all got along well enough in spite of the strain.

"It's just like having a sleepover," Alanna said frequently to Sukjin, and Sohyeon had to agree it did feel a little like that, though their vigilance made it far less relaxing than the children's party the image evoked.

Sohyeon knew the other neighbors were sheltering in place like they were, that not all of the houses were empty or had gone over to Baram's side, but the Chois hadn't talked with any of them since the night everything had gone wrong. Most of the remaining citizens were reluctant to be outside at all unless necessity drew them out to one of the shopping times. When Sohyeon went out with his mother to the store, one of the rare times they used the car to transport all of the heavy items they needed back to the house, Alanna tried talking to some of the other residents to find out what they knew about the crisis. Most avoided speaking with anyone and stuck to their own families. Everyone looked serious and tired, and only one or two dared to discuss the situation with her.

"I told Devon this would probably last awhile when Megumi first went to the hotel and starting making announcements on the shortwave," an old lady of about seventy who lived with her son and daughter-in-law a few streets over said conspiratorially when his mother smiled at her and asked her what she thought.

The old woman looked at Sohyeon with pleasant curiosity, and she seemed rather energized and alert compared to the others waiting in line. A few people tossed her dirty looks for her enthusiastic commentary, but she was undaunted.

"Do you have a cell phone or land line?" Alanna asked, flipping the page in her grocery list book and clicking her pen to get ready to write. "We should keep in touch, especially if you live nearby. We have a lot of people staying at my house who know how to fight. Sohyeon, give the lady your cell phone number."

Sohyeon complied and also put the old lady's number into his phone as his mother wrote it down along with her name and address.

"Gemma Brightman," the old woman said, running a hand absent-mindedly through her short white hair. She was otherwise dressed in a nice plum-colored pantsuit with a long chain holding a purple tassel draped over her chest and brown moccasins. "Nice to meet you, Mrs. Choi. My older son Terrence is on Addison's council and works with Megumi out at the old hotel now. I get to hear a lot of first hand details. I think they're doing a great job along with the help of that foreign woman, what's her name? Minha, yes, they've been doing very well at keeping the community together and getting everyone supplies."

"Did they tell you what's happening?" Sohyeon asked quietly when his mother stepped up to the counter to pay for their supplies, suspecting that she didn't if she only considered Minha "foreign."

Gemma's eyes glittered shrewdly as she looked at Sohyeon then glanced around them. Suddenly, Sohyeon realized she did know and was only putting up a good front.

"Enough to know to be cautious," she said in a whisper, her voice more serious this time. "I know Megumi is quite distraught over the things that have happened in the community. She and I have been great friends for years. I used to work at the library for years and worked with her on the community bookmobile.

"The disappearances are worrisome, and I myself have seen strange half-men walking around our property at night. You know, I don't sleep well anymore, so I happened to be looking out when they came. And they often come, just to stare at our house. I don't know why. Do you know what they are? They look like ghouls, like something that clawed its way out of a cemetery, and come to think of it, we do have one a few blocks over near the old Anglican church. I wonder if there's a connection."

Sohyeon looked at her a minute, thinking. Did she mean ghost-slaves were watching the Brightman house? Pete and Pontol looked like ghouls after a fashion. He felt uneasy just listening to her.

"Maybe, but I think it has something to do with black magic, if you ask me," Sohyeon said cautiously, knowing he was probably saying too much. "Do you believe in things like that?"

A sudden flash of fear appeared in the old woman's gray eyes. She seemed speechless but regained her composure quickly.

"I have a gun in my nightstand drawer. My son doesn't know about it. Maybe I should keep it loaded in case they try something like they did at the MacIntyre's down the street."

Sohyeon snapped to attention at her comment. She lived near the MacIntyres? Then she had to know what was happening.

"Pete was a friend of mine," he said. "Did you see the house after they hit it? I went in, before we heard any of the stories about the disappearances. It was really scary, not a normal crime scene. I think you're right that the creatures watching are ghouls. Maybe they're near your house because of Pete's disappearance."

"Sohyeon, what are you doing? Come help me with the supplies and tell Gemma we'll talk to her later," Alanna said, looking at him in alarm.

They said their goodbyes and returned home in the car, both lost in thought.

10

Halfway through the second week since Sohyeon returned from Eokhmisseun, Mapin came home with the news they had been waiting for. Now more comfortable with her human form and human language, she turned back into a woman as soon as she returned to Sukjin's bedroom window to speak with them about her activities that day.

"Baram has made contact with them, with the deer clan," she said in her silky, thickly accented voice. "I know where they are now, though perhaps they don't stay in one place long. I have asked Minha for instructions on how to proceed."

"What did you find out?" Jangsun asked, sitting with Sohyeon, Tamnyn and Sukjin in Sukjin's bedroom. It was 1AM, and they were in the middle of the evening watch shift change.

"I know why Baram took over the paintball park," Mapin said, standing in the middle of the room, the moonlight streaming through the open window transforming her into a glimmering vision with her pure white wings and white chiton. "Because that area beyond the outdoor course is partially forest and is a fairly large tract of land, it attracts deer. The frequent deer sightings there drew Baram's attention."

"If it's a matter of just looking for deer sightings," Jangsun said, a little surprised, "then there are all sorts of places in Addison where they appear regularly. A month ago before all of this happened, a doe and three fawns crossed the road a few blocks away from here when I was driving to work. Is it just any random deer that we are trying to find?"

Mapin smiled at him indulgently and shook her head.

"Of course, any sightings of deer in the land would be a place to begin our search, but no, the mere presence of deer is not going to indicate they are the lost deer clan. They are very special, though they will look like earthly deer when you just glance at them. I think Minha believes they usually hide from other creatures by pretending to be completely animal, unlike those of us who stayed in Khabu who only turn into animals once we retire to the forest or crypt. The ancient wolf clan, which was systematically slaughtered, is no longer a consideration, but I'm sure the deer clan remembers their punishment quite vividly even after so long and have taken measures to protect themselves against all enemies, human or otherwise."

"So what do we do now that we think they are in that location?" Sohyeon asked, crossing his arms over his chest. "And how to we get them to reveal what they truly are so we can prove they aren't regular deer?"

"We should go investigate the forest and meet with them secretly," Mapin said calmly.

"That's where we took the search party when Pete was missing," Jangsun said, rubbing his chin. "Creepy place. We should go in the morning, shouldn't we, after drills?"

"How will we find them?" Sohyeon asked. "Deer aren't that easy to approach, even in suburbia, and if they are allied with Baram, won't they see us as enemies?"

"Laqrisa and I have been monitoring the forest since we saw Baram and his concubine Marietta wandering out there regularly last week. There is deer movement, though their movements are erratic since there's so little human activity at any time in the community with the crisis. They feel less afraid to go out in daylight than at night now when Baram's minions are on the prowl. We can indeed go to the location after drills, just a few of us, to see what we can learn.

"They are expecting me to bring someone to them today. Laqrisa was able to get near enough to one of them in her bird form to speak with them in the language of the ancestors of Khabu, and she got a surprising answer. They have maintained a strict neutrality with Baram, and not all of them in the local clan are eager to help him at all. They want some alternative. Some fear him since he openly wears his tiger clan heritage, which they still remember in dreams and legends. The tiger clan slaughtered the wolf clan, and as predators, they carry the DNA of the deer clan's natural enemies. They have, in fact, asked us for a meeting, seeing that we are docile animals like them and also are half-human, as a counterweight to Baram. Plus Laqrisa has asked them about Nominus. They were intrigued that she should know about him, their revered leader, even now."

"Who should go with you as our human representatives?" Jangsun asked.

"I will take Sohyeon and Tamnyn with me when Laqrisa and I meet them in a few hours. They need to hear of Birum's activities in Eokhmisseun and Baram's here on earth to understand what they are dealing with. Tamnyn also knows our language some since we served her family as war messengers for a long time, which will be useful in persuading them. Do you agree, Jangsun?"

"Leave at sunrise, before we finish drills then," Jangsun said.

11

Five hours later, Sohyeon and Tamnyn rode the tandem bike across Addison toward the paintball park with Mapin and Laqrisa flying along behind them to not look conspicuous. Although Baram would have figured out by now that the old bird clan from Khabu was aiding them, the birds tried to keep a low profile around their human allies, even when they went to the Renaissance Park Hotel to meet with Minha and Mayor Miller. It was better Baram and his followers didn't know the extent of their aid.

As they approached the turnoff to the paintball park's lot, Mapin flew around Sohyeon, signaling for them to take a different road along the back of the outdoor paintball course. As they passed it and reached another residential area, Sohyeon did a double take. The drain pipe! This was the area where the search party had lost Analisa Gomez that day, which meant they would be near the strange house that looked like Pontol's shack. Of course, there really was something significant about the place after all. Maybe they would even find Analisa alive.

However, instead of turning off the road to reach the house and drain pipe directly, Mapin led them to a path between a few of the houses winding through the yards to the back of the small forest. The houses on either side looked deserted, their broad facades shuttered but with none of the strange, sooty markings showing allegiance to Baram scrawled on the front door. *The owners must be hiding out like we are*, Sohyeon thought, realizing the people inside might be nervous if they noticed Sohyeon's party's approach. They didn't stop until they made it into the trees at the far end of the houses' backyards. Stopping when they were just inside the forest, Sohyeon and Tamnyn propped up their bike against a tree, then followed the birds down a narrow path through the underbrush.

Sure enough, when they got close to the creek bed where the drain pipe was, Mapin signaled for them to turn right. Ahead of them sat the little house that had caught Sohyeon's attention the day the search party came through. This time, a strange magical aura emanated from it, and Sohyeon suddenly felt apprehensive about approaching it. Mapin and Laqrisa dropped on the doorstep and began their transformation into their now familiar half-beast half-human forms.

When Mapin knocked, the door opened immediately, revealing a small woman with nut-brown skin and almost black eyes. Small white spots dotted her cheeks like white freckles, and her head full of straight, glossy black hair was tied up in a ponytail. Her features reminded Sohyeon of Cambodians or Filipinos, since her skin tone was more suntanned, and she wore a plain brown dress that looked more native than modern which Sohyeon thought might be made of soft leather or suede. Her eyes filled with recognition when she saw Mapin, and she stepped aside to let them in.

"We have returned with help, Lidonia," Mapin said as the group entered the room.

The interior of the house was very plain with a rustic atmosphere and walls of wood paneling, quite unlike Pontol's frightening, grimy shack in Eokhmisseun. A low couch, a wooden frame covered with a thick brown cushion with wildly colored crocheted blankets and throw pillows, sat under the window. The woman motioned for them to sit down, though Laqrisa and Mapin remained standing near the front door like ancient caryatids. Sohyeon and Tamnyn quickly sat on the comfortable couch and waited politely while Lidonia brought them a viscous green drink that tasted a little bit medicinal but made Sohyeon's senses perk up.

A man, a teenage girl and a little boy sat down on a few chairs across from Sohyeon and Tamnyn, the three looking very similar in features and coloring to Lidonia. All of them dressed simply in brown just like her, too.

"These are my human allies," Mapin said, waving a graceful hand toward Sohyeon and Tamnyn. "Sohyeon's family has been aiding the royal family of Khabu, mostly unknowingly for many years, but they have helped us set up a base here to monitor Duke Birum's shady activities. Now that his son Baram is here on Earth, we must also deal with the Duke's ties to Eokhmisseun, another far away human land that Birum has attacked and subdued in far more destructive ways than Earth has experienced. I understand that the deer clan did not establish a presence over the millennia in Eokhmisseun the way it did on Earth, so perhaps you are unaware of the crisis there. This girl, Tamnyn, is a daughter of one of the leaders in Eokhmisseun and is half-sister to Baram, who has been pushing you for a treaty. They may be able to answer your questions that we could not."

Lidonia looked at Sohyeon with great interest.

"Since your household has been the entry point to Earth for the royalty of Khabu, the Duke is unhappy with you and your family, Sohyeon. Baram has mentioned this to us when we have had talks, and so I was eager to meet with you and see what kind of person you are."

"What was your impression of Baram?" Tamnyn asked.

Lidonia's dark eyes shifted to Tamnyn with a look of amusement.

"Baram is an apparition of terror, and everything he does here is calculated to increase fear in humans," she said gravely. "He wants the population to succumb to his overtures and join him, either as food for his blood sacrifices or turned as his ghost slaves, who are really a new clan created by the Duke." Lidonia laughed grimly.

"They are degenerate, however, retaining little of their humanity and only sickly aspects of their animal heritage.

"Baram intends on making Earth a colony of his branch of the family, modeling his approach after the Duke's attack on Eokhmisseun," Lidonia continued. "Baram thinks of Eokhmisseun rather than Khabu as his home, which I find interesting. Until he and Mapin came to us here, we also did not think of Khabu as anything more than ancient history, though we are in touch with other deer clan settlements beyond Earth."

"And Nominus?" Laqrisa asked, turning her pearlescent eyes from the window to Lidonia. "Have you been in touch with him since we last came to you? Mapin is an old friend, and she would like to meet with him in person."

"Litt has also returned from the crypt of the ancestors," Mapin said, "so Nominus should also consider returning to Khabu after so many years away to speak with his old master."

Lidonia nodded, smiling a little.

"We have quietly sent a messenger along the inner sea to his base. It's far from here, though he has visited Earth before and knows about our situation here. In all of the lands we inhabit, we remain out of sight to the native populations, only working our magic to help them secretly when needed. When we go out, we only appear in our animal form so we will not be recognized as intruders."

"What exactly are the deer clan's magical abilities?" Sohyeon asked. "We've heard they have learned to extend their powers of regeneration to others, and we have a seriously wounded man, Tamnyn's father, at our house. We've heard that it's this power that Birum is seeking since his magic makes him so weak that even as an immortal his powers of regeneration are too slow to heal him."

Lidonia seemed surprised at Sohyeon's comment. Exchanging glances with her family, she went into the next room and brought back a jug of the strange liquid she had given to Sohyeon and Tamnyn, placing it on the end table beside the couch.

"Take this home to your father, and have him drink it," she said. "We have learned over the centuries, at Nominus' direction, to extract our healing powers through our milk and enhance it with native herbs to help our host worlds cope with their troubles. Nominus has always felt we should be a benevolent influence on the worlds we inhabit, as both a sign of our true natures and also to protect us from their fear should they ever find out what we really are."

"When Baram came to us, he only mentioned the past," one of the men said suddenly.

"Hush, Cautis," Lidonia said softly.

"They need to hear this, Lidonia. I will not hold back these details," he said angrily. "Baram only found us because of the human woman who helps him. She placed a feeder out for deer in the area with the city council's permission and liked to encourage the true deer to hang around the paintball park across the forest from us."

"So you know Marietta Esposito," Sohyeon said. "Interesting."

"She brought *him* here, which was bad luck for us. One day my son saw his followers grab a girl and eat her right here at the creek."

"Analisa!" Tamnyn said, horrified.

"We lost a girl around here the day we conducted a daylight search," Sohyeon said by way of explanation. "It was after another girl's murder and the disappearance of a friend who ultimately turned out to be a follower of Baram's, a ghost-slave."

Cautis nodded, his face full of sadness.

"He knew we saw what they did but still had the audacity to come here and try to befriend us. So he wants our powers to help his father?"

"And probably Baram wants it for himself. He's using similar magic here to do some of the same things Birum did in Eokhmisseun," Sohyeon said.

"He told us the reason he wanted a treaty with us was because Birum had been researching Khabu's ancient history and had discovered the missing deer clan. He said he wanted to find us to welcome us back to Khabu under his leadership, though he is not its leader at the moment, am I right?"

"His sister, Joriya, is still Queen of Khabu," Mapin said, nodding. "Her heir, Mirae Choi, who was raised as Sohyeon's sister, is now there with Litt to take the throne upon Joriya's retirement. Birum is not in line for the throne, though he wants to be king and to destroy Joriya. He has always had an unreasonable hatred of his sister."

Cautis looked up at Mapin in disgust, then sighed and dropped his gaze.

"Perhaps we shouldn't cooperate with either side, Lidonia," he said softly. "This fight among the royalty of Khabu has nothing to do with us. We have lived in peace across the known worlds for millennia, but Khabu has always brought us trouble in our history. We should discuss this further with Nominus when he arrives." He turned to Sohyeon. "We will do nothing more than provide the healing drink for you until we do."

Cautis stood up and stormed out of the room. The girl and little boy followed him quickly, glancing at Tamnyn and Sohyeon before they disappeared into the back of the house.

Lidonia couldn't meet their gaze but took a few deep breaths as if holding back strong emotions. When she finally looked up at them again, her eyes glittered with tears.

"It is as he says. We will wait until Nominus' arrival the day after tomorrow to conduct further talks with you. He will know what to do. We are too vulnerable here to take sides without his guidance. You are asking us to give up the peace we worked so hard for, to bring us back into the terrifying political whirlwinds of Khabu.

"Yes, we still remember when we got the news of the wolf clan's slaughter by Zurui, the first king of Khabu. Nominus has not let us forget it and has taught us many songs and stories about the incident in our clan history, mostly to remind us why we left and why we should not go back. Baram and his father can do as they please without our intervention. We will not help them regenerate after murdering populations of other worlds for their own benefit. How like Zurui they are if they do such things!

"For now, you must go. When Nominus arrives, we will send for you. Leave your address with me."

Tamnyn jumped up and took the jug of healing liquid as Sohyeon went over to Lidonia, taking out his cell phone.

"Does the deer clan have cell phones? We can exchange numbers, and it will be quicker for you to let us know that Nominus is here."

Lidonia shook her head and wrote down Sohyeon's address on a notepad as he dictated it.

"We don't have such things as cell phones here. Go now. We will send our message our way when we are ready. Good day."

12

Sohyeon and Tamnyn made it back to the Choi house as quickly as possible with the jug Lidonia had given them in the tandem's basket, while the birds continued on to the Renaissance Plaza Hotel to give a report of their meeting with the deer clan to Minha and Megumi Miller. When they arrived, Jangsun opened the side door leading into the garage where he had been waiting since Sohyeon texted him, and they brought the tandem in before he shut and locked the door again. He had changed into black slacks and a gray sweatshirt after breakfast.

"Did you come up with anything?" Jangsun asked, looking at Tamnyn curiously as she opened the lid on the tandem's basket and pulled out the jug of green liquid.

"They want to wait until Nominus comes to talk to us. They already summoned him, and he'll be here soon, but they're afraid of getting drawn into the war in Khabu after they fled so long ago," Sohyeon said.

"What's in the jug then?"

"This is for my father," Tamnyn said, heading for the door leading to the living room where Phillip was waiting to let them in. Phillip locked the door to the garage and followed them. "He's supposed to drink it, and it will heal him. Where is he now? Is he awake?"

Jangsun led them down to the finished side of the basement where Cargal sat on an old couch looking at some of the *kumdo* magazines Jangsun had collected there. The wide, carpeted basement floor was where they usually conducted their evening drills, but now Cargal was the only one down there. He looked up as they approached.

"You seem to be doing better, father," Tamnyn said, sitting down beside him on the couch with the jug while Sohyeon got her a cup from the bar in the corner. She poured it in the cup and held it out to him. "Drink this. It should help with your wound."

As they watched Cargal drink an entire glass of the green liquid from the deer clan, the sound of one of the Humvees pulling up outside penetrated even down to the basement. Alanna came to the top of the steps where the door had been left open to yell down to them.

"Hon, someone's here to see you," she said. "It's Terrence Brightman making the rounds with the armed guards. Should I open the front door for him, or do you want to come up to handle that yourself?"

"Terrence Brightman? Is he with the Addison police? Why is he going around with the patrols?" Jangsun asked as he ran up the steps, Sohyeon on his heels.

"No, no, he's a councilman," Alanna said, walking behind him in her flip flops and gingham blouse over jeans, her long brown hair up in a braid around her head. "I told you we met his mother at the store the other day, didn't I? She lives near the MacIntyres. He called me earlier to say he would be dropping by, but you were busy with morning exercises, and I forgot to mention it."

Jangsun looked out the window next to the front stoop and saw a middle-aged white man wearing a plaid shirt and cargo pants standing with uniformed men flanking him on either side. The guards looked like military wearing in camouflage and holding automatic weapons, and their Humvee was parked at the edge of the sidewalk in front of the Choi house. Walking over to the front door, he flipped open the deadbolts and opened it.

"Yes? Can I help you, Mr. Brightman?"

"Mr. Choi, I'm sorry about my oversight, but I stopped by to make amends," the man said. "May I come in a minute? The guards will remain outside."

"Fine, fine," Jangsun said, stepping aside and waving Councilman Brightman in. He shut the door on the commandoes with a slight salute. "What can I do for you?"

"I believe it was your son Sohyeon who made the request, so I brought this," Terrence Brightman said, holding out a large manila envelope to Sohyeon.

Sohyeon took it, immediately remembering he sent a message to the council at the hotel about getting information on the strange markings left at houses where people had disappeared.

Opening the envelope, Sohyeon saw it was full of crime scene photos, and he pulled them out. Flipping through them, Sohyeon saw various shots of the strange words and symbols written in blood all over the walls, the ransacked rooms, and the walls torn by knives or claws. Sohyeon saw they all resembled the markings at the MacIntyre's the night of Doug MacIntyre's disappearance.

He looked up at Terrence Brightman, who along with his father and mother watched him thoughtfully.

"Well, what do you think?" Terrence asked.

"I need to go downstairs and show these to Cargal and Tamnyn," Sohyeon said. "They look like the same things I saw on the walls at Pete's house that night after the second search for Pete went so wrong. We should check with them to see if they recognize the writings as something in the language of Eokhmisseun. Since Minha doesn't seem to know what they mean, they must not be in Khabu's."

Sohyeon went back down the stairs with Terrence Brightman. As he approached the couch where Tamnyn sat with Cargal, he was shocked to see how quickly Cargal had changed. Gone were Cargal's sunken, pale features, the silvery tips of his hair, even the deep lines in his face when he smiled. Now, Cargal's skin radiated health and even had a pink tinge to it, like he had been drinking too much wine. His eyes sparkled with life, his black hair now was solidly black with a glossy sheen, and his skin looked like that of a young man with all of the roughness and weariness gone. Sohyeon was speechless as Cargill stood up and met him halfway across the room, the first time he had been able to walk around the house unaided and with vigor.

"What do you have for me?" he asked, holding out his hands to take the photos Sohyeon held. "Is this the evidence you hoped to get from the authorities that we have been waiting for?"

Sohyeon gave him the photos and the envelope and looked over at where Tamnyn sat holding the jug. It was still full. Cargal only drank one glass of it, and this was the effect.

"You should take that jug up to my mother to put away for later when anyone needs it," Sohyeon said. "It's astonishingly effective, and we should be careful with the rest. No wonder Birum's looking for the deer clan with power like that."

"Father looks very healthy now, doesn't he?" Tamnyn said, walking over to where her father was flipping through the pictures to look at them over his shoulder. She gasped. "Aren't those ancient sigils from some of the books we had back home in our library?"

Cargal nodded.

"Some of the writings are in our modern language, but there are a few that were known to be used by magicians in Eokhmisseun's distant past. Baram picks up his father's legacy in studying black magic. Birum does not have merely passing knowledge of Eokhmisseun's history, that's for sure. Perhaps my wife has guided him to the sources since we did have them in our library and she grew up with them, though such profane details would only be mentioned in a few of the books we had there. The signs here are quite distinct, which is why Tamnyn recognized them. A few centuries ago, we had a cabal of underground wizards who used them to terrorize our people, so it was quite in fashion, though the council eventually put a stop to their activity. But they have been used throughout the centuries by outlaw groups in our land."

Cargal handed the photos back to Terrence, who listened in fascination.

"So we really are dealing with some form of alien magic?" he asked, looking a little forlorn. "I'm not sure how we defend the city against something like that. What do you think is the purpose of the disappearances then? I understand the inhabitants of Khabu don't need food, yet we have found some of the missing persons who have turned up half eaten."

"That would be the meaning of the other half of the scribblings here," Cargal said. "It says in our language that these are warnings to you what will happen if you don't surrender. Eating one's enemies is an act of war for them, and it sates the ghost-slaves' taste for blood."

"But what good does it do to put such a threat in a language we don't know?" Terrence asked, shaking his head.

"You weren't meant to read the message but to feel it in your bones," Cargal said. "After years of living under Birum's reign of terror, effectively under house arrest for decades to watch as our citizens slowly were absorbed by his magic, turned into monsters we had to fear and had no way to control, this is only part of the method he uses to demoralize a world he wants to take for himself. He leaves nothing living left, nothing that was once good about a society, by the time he is finished. The world is an empty husk compared to what it once was. You need to find a way to rid yourself of this pestilence. Sadly, we were never able to."

Terence Brightman only stayed for a half an hour to talk a little more about the upcoming store openings with Alanna before he left in the Humvee. After the visit from the councilman, everyone in the Choi house was eagerly awaiting a message from the deer clan notifying them that Nominus had arrived to meet with them, but months passed without any word.

By July, everyone was tired of the routine they were in, stuck in the house, which was always locked up tight. Everyone had read all of the magazines and books at least twice, they were bored with the games after months of playing them on end, and to make matters worse, Baram began to attack the community's services, which the council had done so well to keep running. Between his attacks on the power plant and the 85 degree weather, Addison was forced to endure rolling blackouts, which set everyone more on edge than before. Some of their guests no longer stayed on the top floor of the house at night but chose to sleep in the living room or basement just to feel less smothered by the situation and the rising temperatures, though the watches continued around the clock.

Sohyeon's mother tried her best with the help of Sukjin and Tamnyn to keep the household running with as little disruption as they could. Tamnyn and Cargal started telling stories from their homeland to pass the time after dinner every evening before bedtime. Jangsun even wondered aloud if they should move to the hotel since many of the other citizens of Addison were abandoning their houses to do just that.

Then the house next door was hit by Baram's gang. All through the night, Sohyeon watched in terror as he saw the ghoulish figures lope across the yard to the house, heard the smashing of windows and even a few screams as he saw them drag their neighbors out into a waiting van. He tried to keep out of sight and not draw their attention as he watched them from his bedroom window. Seeing their methods first-hand, Sohyeon felt it was almost surreal. Their victims left the house alive and alert, but Sohyeon shuddered at the thought of what might come next for them.

At one point during the commotion, Jangsun walked into the room to look out Sohyeon's window for a better view, then he dashed down to the first floor to look over all of the locks on the doors and the barricades on the windows. Sohyeon could feel the tension in the house, though no one else moved or said anything. Sohyeon followed Jangsun downstairs and found Cargal and his bodyguard Esram sitting in the living room, looking spooked, listening to the commotion outside in grim silence. The night passed slowly, agonizingly, but finally the attack next door died down and morning came. Jangsun, Cargal and Sohyeon walked over to the house to see first-hand how it had been hit as Terrence Brightman and Anton Zhao brought their Humvee full of guards to search and document the attack. The councilmen didn't say anything to the Chois as they went about their business but only looked at them sympathetically as they passed to enter the house.

13

That afternoon, Sohyeon went back to his room to get one of his Calculus books and found Sukjin there on watch.

"What are you doing?" she asked casually, not looking up at him from her seat at his desk where she was staring out the window.

"Getting one of my textbooks," he said, opening one of the drawers beside her and pulling out the book.

"Finals were cancelled, and you'll never graduate now, so why bother?" she asked listlessly.

"So it's all getting to you, is it? Is that why you always seem to be up here on watch? I've hardly seen you at anything we do as a family now."

"Do we do it as a family? We have a lot of guests now, and Philip, well, it's not worth talking about."

"Did something happen with Philip?" Sohyeon asked, sitting down on the side of his bed.

"I don't know. Maybe. I might be in love with him, but I know, mom will say I'm too young. It's only a few years to wait right, as long as we don't get killed in the meantime? Does it upset you that you never got to go to graduation with all of this stuff going on?"

"A little, but I'm just glad to be done with school, either way."

"Are you going to marry Tamnyn now?"

"Tamnyn's special, and I'd like to think I'm worthy of her. Minha was way out of my league, but even Tamnyn is sort of. She's already helped rule a country, and what have I done?

"Minha is awesome. I want to be her when I grow up, and I'd fall for her too if I were a guy. The immortals are all amazing. But seriously, I really felt envious of you and Mirae for going off on this wild adventure and meeting people like them."

"And now you don't?"

"The world is a scary place, isn't it? There really are monsters out there." Sukjin looked out the window with a dreamy, puzzled expression on her face.

"So you've been sitting up here on watch alone for the past few months getting all existential on me?" he asked, teasing her gently.

She shot him an annoyed glance before returning to her pensive study of their neighborhood.

"What I've been doing is following mom around, learning how to cook with small meat and vegetable rations for an army. I've been sitting here bored, thinking about what I really want out of life. And I've read all of your comic books over and over until my eyes started to bleed. Can I come to the hotel with you next time? I just need to get out for once."

"I'll tell mom to let you drive the car for the next supply run. You need to get your permit soon anyway."

"If we ever get back to normal, you mean. What time are we expecting today's blackouts anyway? We need to get meals prepped before we can't use the stove."

"I didn't hear the announcements this morning on the shortwave," Sohyeon said. "Megumi is doing quite a job keeping everyone organized and everything running, even in the midst of all of the disappearances and limitations on travel. Was she in the military or something? She seems as tough as nails."

"The neighbors are dead, aren't they? I heard everything last night."

Sohyeon looked at Sukjin in amazement. The speed with which she changed subjects was giving him whiplash. Seeing her blank look when she asked the question, he felt uneasy about the answer.

"Probably," he said softly.

"Sohyeon! I need you in the kitchen," Jangsun said, his voice floating up the stairs.

Sohyeon immediately got up and walked toward the open bedroom door but paused, thinking he should say more to Sukjin before he left. Turning back toward her, he saw she had covered her face with her hands and her shoulders were trembling, though she was sobbing too softly for him to hear. Without another word, Sohyeon went downstairs.

"Did something happen?" Sohyeon asked when he got to the kitchen where his father was waiting, leaning against the counter with his arms crossed.

"I'm not sure. Minha and Anton Zhao have requested we send representatives of our household to the Renaissance Plaza Hotel for a meeting later this afternoon."

"We don't get summoned very often. It has been at least a months since we went out there. What does that mean?" Sohyeon sat down at the table and looked at his mother, who was taking inventory of the dry goods in the pantry.

"I think they do this with every neighborhood where there's been a house hit close by," Jangsun said.

"Who's going to represent us?" Sohyeon asked.

"I think you and Tamnyn should go, and this time I will send Cargal and Esram with you, too. I want to stay close to home after what happened last night, and Sukjin, Philip and I should be able to handle any trouble while you are away. Laqrisa and Tmolos will also stay with us, and they know how to fight a little now. I already told Cargal my plan. Did you charge your phone? The blackout will be coming in our district in a few hours before you go, and I want you to stay in close touch with me while you're out."

"I'll see to it right away." Sohyeon paused before going to find Tamnyn, looking helplessly at his mother and father.

"Was there something else?" Jangsun asked, noticing Sohyeon's hesitation.

"Well, Sukjin seems a little upset today."

Alanna turned around and looked at Jangsun.

"One of us should go talk to her," she said. "Is she in your room on watch now? I think she should be taken off night watch for a few days after last night's commotion. It really has her upset since their daughter was a close friend."

"Do you want me to do it?" Jangsun asked, smiling slightly. "You know I can't really handle women weeping."

"Eh, maybe not. I can check inventory later. I'll go up to see her now." She kissed him lightly on the cheek as she passed on her way out of the kitchen.

"How do the two of you manage to seem so normal in the middle of all of this?"

"We keep each other sane," Jangsun said with a short laugh.

"I'll get ready to go with Tamnyn and Cargal. Are you sure you want so many of us to leave the house this afternoon? We probably don't need Esram to tag along now that Cargal is back to normal. We've only had three of us out of the house at the most at a time."

"See what Cargal says. I'll leave it to him to decide to do as he thinks best. He has a lot more battle experience than I do."

14

"There's really no reason for Mapin to come with us if you're concerned about protecting the house," Esram said as they were taking the bicycles out of the garage. "We'll have plenty of protection once we get to the hotel."

"It's alright," Sohyeon said, watching his father close the door behind them and hearing the lock click. "We can take Mapin to alert someone in case we're attacked on the way and I can't reach my cell phone. Hopefully we won't be gone that long for the meeting and will get home before nightfall."

Sohyeon let Tamnyn take her father on the tandem bike while he let Esram ride behind him on the single passenger bike. They quickly made their way through the neighborhood to the park where the hotel was located. A few of their neighbors passed them, some on foot and some in cars. Everyone had been summoned from their street, confirming Jangsun's remark to Sohyeon that the meeting had been called because of their next door neighbors' disappearance the night before. Sohyeon waved to a few of them as they passed, though no one looked to be in the mood for lighthearted greetings. Seeing their guarded reactions, Sohyeon realized he had gotten used to such attacks after living in Eokhmisseun under Birum's rule for that short time. Everyone else in Addison was still shell-shocked.

When they reached the hotel, the armed guards at the door let them in as they wheeled their bikes into the lobby and parked them off to the side. Cargal and Esram looked around in awe at the hotel's beautiful interior. Sohyeon realized they had only seen the inside of his home since coming to Earth, and this building was similar to the ornate style of the palace of Eokhmisseun. Smiling, Tamnyn took her father's arm and led him toward the ballroom where Minha waited with the local council, Mapin landing on her other shoulder. Sohyeon knew she wanted to present her father to Minha as proof of the deer clan's new powers.

As Sohyeon turned to guide Esram towards the ballroom, too, he noticed Esram was flirting with one of the young women on the hotel staff as she finished giving the guards cold glasses of water. Then the pretty young woman passed them with the cart of refreshments, wheeling it toward the ballroom. Annoyed, Sohyeon clapped him on his upper arm and gestured in the direction they should go. Esram was pleased to see they would be following her.

This time, the tables had been moved to the edges of the ballroom and the chairs placed in rows in front of the stage and small dance floor. Minha sat with her two acolytes on chairs off to the side of the stage while Mayor Miller paced back and forth between them, making comments to a few of the other remaining allied council. As Sohyeon sat down next to Tamnyn, he was startled to find Mapin suddenly sitting in his lap. He noticed only briefly that Cargal sat down on the other side of Tamnyn and Esram had moved to sit on the other side of Cargal at the end of the aisle.

It had been awhile since he heard his mother and Vince talking about the council, but he thought he recognized Stephen Columbo and Nicolette Erickson talking with Megumi Miller, all of them dressed in casual clothes this time in the July heat. Anton Zhao talked with the staff in the back of the room, and Terrence Brightman was out by the front desk in the lobby. The birds that had come with Minha were inconspicuously scattered around the room, perched on chandeliers or the arms of the decorative floor lamps in the corners of the room.

As their neighbors straggled in and took their seats, the hotel attendant Esram had eyed started passing out drinks and warm cookies. Sohyeon felt too agitated to be hungry, and he waved the woman past him. Tamnyn followed his lead, refusing any refreshments, but the woman gave drinks and cookies to Cargal and Esram. After about ten minutes, when it appeared everyone had arrived, Megumi Miller stepped down onto the dance floor to say a few words.

"I'm so sorry to have to call you here, but there has been bad news in your neighborhood, and given the nature of the crisis and how it has been prolonged, I wanted to make sure to speak with everyone involved in person to reassure you that the Addison city council, those of us who remain and are allied with Minha of Khabu in the fight against Baram of Eokhmisseun, are doing our best to keep you and your families safe. We have managed to keep the utilities running to some degree, and food and other goods from our local community as well as a limited amount brought in from areas not affected by the invasion has been available. We will continue to work through these challenges and keep our distribution channels open. I know we've been living under these difficult conditions for a long time, and everyone is under a great deal of strain."

As she was speaking, Megumi Miller's eyes stopped moving around the room to look in the direction of the front lobby. For a moment, her voice faltered, and she paled visibly, looking around the room frantically for someone.

Sohyeon turned around to see what was going on, but at first he didn't notice anything. Then he saw what had drawn her attention. Although it wasn't supposed to get dark for another five hours, the hallway leading to the lobby had now been plunged into darkness. Sohyeon wondered how that could be since the lobby had a large set of windows over the revolving door leading into the hotel, and only ten minutes ago the lobby had been bright with daylight. Did the deepening shadows mean it had gotten dark outside?

Mapin was getting restless on his lap, and she suddenly flew up with the other birds. As he watched her cross the room to one of the chandeliers, Sohyeon noticed the woman sitting on the right of him had dropped her cup and was now slumped over in her chair. Alarmed, he reached out and shook her, but she didn't wake up. When he touched her neck, he felt a pulse. Looking down at the cup, he realized what had happened, then looked around the room. Everyone among the guests who had taken the cookies and fruit-infused water now were asleep. Everyone except for Esram, Sohyeon, Tamnyn!

The woman Esram had flirted with earlier was also alert and had a triumphant expression on her face as she looked defiantly at Megumi. Megumi's suspicious scowl showed she realized something was up, and she studied the hotel staff spread around the room, taking a step closer to Stephen, whom she whispered something to. Minha looked up in alarm and rose to her feet when she saw what was happening. Pulling out a strange, flat mask that looked like a roaring tiger, she placed it on her face quickly. Her acolytes immediately flanked Megumi holding their *hyeopdo* ready for battle.

Whispering a warning to Tamnyn, he stood and pulled out the *mokgum* he had grabbed before leaving the house. Tamnyn did the same with her steel sword, but they both noticed Cargal wasn't just asleep but had slumped over. Sohyeon stared at him for a moment, trying to figure out what was wrong, but when he saw blood dripping down the chair, he pushed past Tamnyn to get to him, noticing Esram's chair was now empty. Tamnyn, seeing the blood, also came over, her face full of fury and fear.

"What happened to him?" she whispered, looking around at the other people who also had slumped over and were sleeping. "Isn't he just sleeping like they are?"

Sohyeon pushed Cargal's body gently, and he fell to the floor, twisting partially onto his back. His eyes were open, his face frozen in an expression of pain. Tamnyn knelt down and pulled open the cowl around his neck, which was bloody and slashed. Beneath the jagged tear in the fabric, Cargal's neck had been sliced, and the wound was now turning black around the edges. Tamnyn gasped in shock.

"He's dead! How can he be dead?" Sohyeon whispered, putting his hand on her shoulder to calm her and as a warning of where they were. For now, the hotel staff was too riveted on the reaction of the council and Minha to be interested in the few stragglers from their housing plan who hadn't taken the drug-laced drinks.

Tamnyn looked up at him, tears glittering in her eyes.

"Esram!" she whispered, standing slowly. "He used a type of poison famous in Eokhmisseun for instantly killing a victim targeted for assassination when it hits their bloodstream. The black edges of the wound are an indication of its presence. It only takes one slice. But why would he kill my father? He served us loyally for so many years."

Fighting back her sobs, she looked around the room at the silent standoff between the hotel staff and Megumi. Something lumbered down the hallway from the front door, and the shadows there deepened as it moved into the ballroom. Without waiting, Sohyeon grabbed Tamnyn's wrist and led her slowly out of the rows of chairs to the back of the room near an out of the way spot where a group of birds were perched on a lamp.

"I wonder how long it will be until they try to deal with us since we didn't fall asleep," he said under his breath so only she could hear him. It felt safer near the birds, though they were limited in how much they could help should a fight break out. "What's going on around here?"

"Baram," she whispered, standing closer to him. "We need to go out the service door back there, away from the front lobby entrance."

"Why? I don't see how he could think an open attack on the leadership could work out in his favor," Sohyeon said, carefully studying the staff members hanging around the doors, including the service entrance she mentioned. They'd have to kill someone to get out of the ballroom now if they were all Baram's allies. Glancing back at Cargal, he regretted they would have to leave his body behind and that the healing provided by the deer clan's tonic had been so short-lived.

Suddenly, Minha's voice grew louder as she chanted in her native language, her face obscured by the wooden tiger mask. The cloud of darkness spread across the room from the lobby, obscuring the lamps to the point that the ballroom looked like it was bathed in dim candlelight.

"What's happening?" Sohyeon whispered to Tamnyn. "Do you know?"

One of the birds dropped down from the chandelier onto his shoulder between them and started to speak in low, musical tones. It was Mapin.

"She is trying to call on the ancestors in the crypt beneath the temple in Khabu, though they are very far away to hear her," Mapin said in Sohyeon's ear. "The mask bridges all time and distance so she can draw on their wisdom and power. Hush now. Baram approaches."

Indeed, the towering shadow of an orange tiger at least nine feet tall appeared at the center of the cloud, flanked by Pete MacIntyre and a few other ghost slaves. Seeing the challenge in the creature's eyes, Megumi Miller's jaw dropped, her face looked haggard, and she backed up a couple of steps on the stage. Minha came up behind her, pulling the mask off of her face and putting it back into a pouch at her waist.

"Let me deal with him," Minha said to her firmly, her eyes never leaving Baram's face. "You deal with his human allies. Hana, Ashira, take your positions."

As the four human council members stepped back to the wall behind the stage, looking warily at the hotel staff spread around the room, they all could see many of the staff now wore arm bands with Baram's sigil on it as a sign of their true allegiance. Minha walked out to meet Baram, her body shifting completely into that of a huge white tiger. Hana and Ashira, her acolytes, dropped their *hyeopdo* on the stage and shapeshifted into white tigers too.

"We finally get the opportunity to meet, Grandmother," Baram said, his voice oddly formal and deferential even if his stance was still very threatening. "While I understand you are here on principle and at Aunt Joriya's behest, you surely must know your place is not among humans. Why is it you have taken it upon yourself to protect them, as insignificant as they are to our kind? Remember all of the things they had done to us millennia ago? What loyalty should you show them now?"

"I am not one of the Originals," Minha said, her eyes glittering in fury at Baram's statement. "I have no memories of the ghetto from that distant world where human ingenuity created us and then feared us so much that they inflicted such torment. It is for them to decide the fate of humanity, not I. Besides, this community has aided Khabu unwittingly, so I do have a debt to repay and a reason to put a stop to your attack. You must leave Earth now, Baram, or be annihilated with your new degenerate clan of half-breeds!"

"Would you have me go through the execution ceremony back on Khabu once you get your hands on me?" Baram asked, sneering. "As you can see, I showed restraint in not turning all of my followers here on Earth. Many of them remain human yet still willingly serve me. You can at least give me that much credit. But they will fight to keep me here. Even on Earth, there are jails with bars strong enough to hold you for a very long time."

Mapin jumped off Sohyeon's shoulder and transformed into her human form, waving to the other birds perched on the lamps. Laqrisa soon followed her lead, though Sohyeon wondered when she had arrived since she was supposed to have stayed back at the Choi house. They stealthily snuck around the edges of the room toward the stage, picking up the fallen *hyeopdo* and pointing them at their enemies surrounding the ballroom, ready to fight anyone who attacked the human council members standing behind them. Jangsun's training would finally pay off since the birds only had a few flashy defenses otherwise.

If Baram noticed their movements, he didn't react. He was totally focused on his rhetorical battle with Minha, which was getting sharper by the moment as they switched between English and their otherworldly languages. Finally, Minha and the two acolytes charged him.

At a word from Baram, two orange tigers that looked exactly like him emerged from either side of his body and lunged at the startled acolytes. Minha didn't hesitate, however, and swiped one of her paws at Baram where he stood between the two phantom beasts that had joined him. Scratching his face, she snarled and leapt at him. The two of them rolled across the ballroom floor, their large bodies locked together with their fangs hooked into each other's flesh, claws scraping wildly at each other. The chairs with the sleeping guests tipped and overturned, too, as the tigers crushed a few of them, unaware of anything other than their fight.

The acolytes tried the same maneuver, one with each of the new tigers facing off against them, but they found the figures too ephemeral to fight effectively. Sometimes their paws hit flesh, sometimes they missed their mark and their paws met only air as the visions of the tigers flickered, throwing the acolytes off their balance. As the tigers moved in and out of the physical world, they landed a few strikes on the acolytes too, but the acolytes were swifter, grabbing the parts of the tigers that had become real long enough to drag their adversaries to the floor.

Meanwhile, the ghost-slaves, ten in all led by Pete MacIntyre, charged the bird-women on the stage, unmindful of their odd appearance in their half-form which made them look like angels. Some of the other birds joined in the fight, staying in their animal form and whispering magical incantations they had learned over the ages to turn themselves into balls of fire or to hypnotize the ghost slaves who looked their way. Some grew their claws and beaks to huge proportions so they could tear at the ghost-slaves' flesh, while at least Mapin hit her mark with the *hyeopdo*, running it through Pete's stomach and slashing two other ghost-slaves who approached with the blade's edge.

15

As the battle between the immortals and the ghost-slaves intensified, Baram's human allies made their move toward the stage with Esram suddenly reappearing among them wearing an armband with Baram's sigil. Sohyeon noticed how Tamnyn was staring at Esram with abject hatred, and he knew she would try to kill him in revenge for murdering her father. He grabbed her arm and leaned close to her ear.

"Let's get the council out of here before Baram's people kill them and Addison has no leadership left. We're the only other humans who have weapons here. Everyone else is asleep, and Megumi looks so distraught, she won't be any match for the whole group of them if they charge the stage."

Tamnyn looked in alarm at the four council members who were watching the monstrous melee with terrified, confused expressions.

"This way," Sohyeon hissed sharply, catching Anton's attention with a wave of his arm as the humans who had helped orchestrate the attack began to pull out daggers and even a few handguns.

Whistling softly to himself in alarm, Sohyeon pushed Tamnyn toward the service door, which had been left unguarded as the human staff joined the fight. As the council members zigzagged their way across the room to join Sohyeon, Baram's human allies edged toward them but were distracted by the battle between the ghost-slaves and the birds. At least one had been hit inadvertently by a tiger's paw and lay twitching on the floor, mortally wounded.

As Megumi caught up with him, Sohyeon pushed her behind him as he held his *mokgum* in a defensive position. Tamnyn led the other three council members to the service door, slicing one of the hotel staff running toward her across the chest and neck without hesitation. She fought so fiercely and killed the man so swiftly, some of the staff watching them warily took a few steps back. They had not been trained in hand to hand combat like Tamnyn, and Esram, her only match in skill, was blocked into a corner on the other side of the tigers across the room where he could not reach her. In the lull, the six of them dashed toward the service door, Sohyeon coming last. When everyone else had gone through the door, he slashed one last wide arc around his body toward the room to keep the human attackers at bay before diving through the door after them.

The room the group now found themselves in was full of five shelf steel banquet service carts as tall as Sohyeon holding various empty steel platters and other items, and another door on the other side of the room led to the kitchen.

"How do we get out of here?" Sohyeon asked Megumi, who was standing closest to him. "Can we get out through the kitchen?"

She looked around the room for a moment then led them to the other side of the room past a door leading to the lobby. In the back of the room beside a tall cupboard was an emergency exit with signs stating it would set off an alarm if opened. Without hesitating, Megumi pushed on the door and fled down the darkened alley leading to the plaza. The rest of them followed, quickly escaping the eerie, piercing siren that had begun to go off in the hotel.

"I have a van around the corner," Stephen said, walking briskly toward the street and looking back over his shoulder every few steps to see if anyone had followed them out of the hotel. "We should have enough gas to get just about anywhere since I haven't left the hotel for weeks. Any idea of where we go from here?"

Everyone looked at Megumi as they cautiously left the alley and stood on the sidewalk in front of the building beside the hotel, away from the hotel's front windows and lobby entrance a half a block away. Although it was still early, the sky was as dark as midnight, and at least half of the street lights had come on. The plaza appeared to be deserted except for a man standing across the street under the shadowy trees just at the edge of the park, only the tip of his cigarette illuminating the scene. Sohyeon recognized him at once.

"Vince," he whispered loudly. The man turned around, startled as they raced across the street to him.

"What are you doing out here?" Sohyeon asked, glancing back toward the hotel. The glass doors, now smeared with blood, glittered black under the streetlights. "Did you see them come into the hotel?"

"I came out with a few of the hotel staff earlier when it was still light and fell asleep in the park," Vince said. "On that bench over there. I know it was dumb of me with all of these creatures running around, but I felt cooped up in the hotel and came out to get a bit of fresh air." He looked at his cigarette, smiled a little, and put it out against the lamppost, placing the stub in his shirt pocket. "I must have been out here a long time. What time is it now? Ten o'clock? I haven't worn my watch in a while."

Sohyeon didn't know if he could trust Vince now that he had seen how many of Addison's citizens in the hotel had secretly sided with Baram. Alarmed by Vince's flimsy excuse, he looked back at Stephen.

"Where's the van? We need to get out of here now," he said, his voice harsher than he intended.

Stephen nodded, and he started to lead the group across a grassy area to the parking lot on the other side of the plaza.

"Are you coming, Vince?" Sohyeon asked, taking up the rear again and turning around to look at his friend.

"Why do we need to get out of here now? Did I miss something?" Vince jogged a few steps to catch up.

"Miss something? Baram and his friends stormed the hotel and are fighting with Minha and the other immortals. The hotel staff betrayed the council and put the entire neighborhood they invited here for a meeting to sleep. Wait a minute! Did you drink some of the water they were giving to everyone when you came out before?"

"Yeah, I ran into one of the maids in the lobby, and she had some beautiful pitchers full of cold water filled with strawberry slices. I couldn't resist. Can you believe that we could get that kind of fruit with all of the rationing? I hear one of the council members has a fenced off farm he was able to keep guarded since the crisis started, so that's where they've been getting a lot of the fruits and vegetables for us in limited supply. I'm tired of eating pasta and other bland dishes. Come to think of it, I did feel sleepy after I polished off that glass and went to lie down on the bench."

"This darkness appears to be magical. It's not even night time yet," Sohyeon said as they reached the parking lot. Suddenly, he bumped into Tamnyn, who had stopped in front of him.

"Is something wrong?" he asked, looking around at the wary council members who had stopped in the middle of the thin patch of trees to stare into the darkness. "Why are we stopping?"

"Something's coming," Tamnyn whispered, glancing back at Sohyeon and bringing her sword up into a defensive position. "Across the plaza. Do you see them? Who are they?"

Sohyeon looked up in the direction she indicated, toward the opposite side of the plaza. A wide line of people walked down the street toward them from beyond the plaza, a tall man in dark clothing leading them. The figures in the front line held 8 foot spears tipped with gleaming metal points. As they got nearer, Sohyeon could hear a clamor of angry voices and hoof beats. Hoof beats?

"The deer clan?" Sohyeon asked, running along the edge of the park toward the group while the others stayed behind.

As he neared, he almost tripped on a tree root, and his free hand accidentally caught hold of a furry body standing under the trees.

"Sohyeon!" Tamnyn called softly, her voice full of fear as she ran to him.

The council members and Vince took a few steps toward him, glancing cautiously at the approaching band of warriors. Sohyeon regained his balance and pulled his hand away from the creature he had caught hold of as if touching a hot stove. The fur was rough, and the back of the beast reached as high as Sohyeon's shoulders. Turning to look at its face, which was now pressing close to his, he saw two black eyes staring at him out of a long, thin face and the slight outline of antlers reaching up into the tree limbs.

"We have brought our clansmen to aid you in your fight against Baram," the deer said in an elegant, masculine voice. "Nominus approaches. Prepare to meet him as you requested."

"Now?" Sohyeon asked in astonishment, looking back at the crowd.

The deer clan warriors were close enough to see clearly under the dim streetlights. The first line carrying spears had human torsos with antlers on their heads and the four-legged bodies of deer, looking similar to a traditional centaur, but their backs were covered with white spots marking their breed. In the lines behind the warriors, male and female clan members walked on two legs, wore clothes resembling medieval hunting garb, and looked fully human except for the men's antlers.

"I will take you to meet him," the deer said. "Follow me."

"Wait, should I bring the others? We're fleeing Baram's attack on our city leadership and against the high priestess of Khabu right now in the building behind us."

"An attack against the high priestess of Khabu? Yes, bring your friends. We must tell Nominus immediately."

Waving for Megumi and the others to catch up, Sohyeon and Tamnyn followed the graceful animal into the street where the approaching deer clan could see them. From their vantage point under the streetlights, Sohyeon watched the crowd slow as the leaders met them in the middle of the street.

At the center of the line of warriors stood a tall man about 6 and a half feet tall wearing a light brown cloak over a dark green tunic and trousers. His body fully human, his face showed none of the markings of the deer clan that Sohyeon had observed so far. His shaggy, grayish brown hair the shade of elm tree bark floated on the night breeze around his stern face. Instead of a spear like clansmen held, this man held an even longer stick with a faceted diamond at the top of it, edged like an arrow tip. As his eyes scanned the group of humans waiting for them, he saw Sohyeon and smiled, quickening his pace.

"Who are you?" Sohyeon asked as the man approached, aware he was probably being impolite when he heard Megumi gasp behind him. "Are you the leader of the legendary deer clan we've heard so much about?"

"I am Nominus, if you have heard of me, though I doubt you know much about my clan, boy," the man said with a cool but good-natured tone. "You are the new Queen's brother? I have heard that you are one of the few inhabitants of Earth who has seen Eokhmisseun and Khabu. None from this world travel the inner sea as we in the deer clan do, so I must congratulate you for your willingness to wander the known worlds and involve yourself in the affairs of the immortals."

"What is it you have come for?" Tamnyn asked, her voice strong and even commanding. Nominus regarded her with noticeable admiration. If Nominus knew who Sohyeon was, he likely already knew who Tamnyn was, too. "Your clan representative here told us you have come to fight Baram with us. Is this true?"

"Cautis here has accurately given you my message," Nominus said, gesturing to the noble animal that now stood off to the side of the group of centaur-like warriors.

"Baram has attacked the high priestess of Khabu, my lord," Cautis said, quickly interrupting their discussion.

"There is no more time to waste. We must deal with the creature before he kills more humans."

Nominus shouted a command in another language to the warriors behind him, and they charged across the plaza toward the hotel, their hooves kicking up the grass, Anton Zhao running ahead of them to guide them into the correct building. After scores of deer clan members had passed them, Nominus turned back to Sohyeon and his friends.

"Aren't you going to confront Baram?" Megumi asked, standing on Sohyeon's right.

"Personally? Why should I?" Nominus said with a wry grin. "Few get an audience with me among the known worlds where our clan has hidden enclaves, let alone some far out world on this side of the inner sea. Why should I let a two-bit tiger prince, not even a full-blooded member of Khabu's royal family, expect such favor? His father Birum is another matter, however, and I have half a mind to return to Khabu to see the end of this nonsense fight with his sister for the throne before I return home."

"Why did you come if you consider Baram beneath you?" Tamnyn asked.

"Lidonia said Baram had gained the upper hand here. She felt I should bring a band of our fiercest warriors to stop him, but they were scattered across our settlements and needed time to prepare for this battle. But I also came to help because I heard that this boy and his family have personally helped the royal family of Khabu. As I said before, there are not many who travel among the worlds, especially not humans, and I sense you have a different destiny than your brethren, Sohyeon.

"Although I left my homeland millennia ago, I still know what has transpired there, and even now I am willing to help to a limited degree. It's better Baram doesn't know how deeply involved I am in his defeat."

"He sought out the deer clan to take advantage of your powers," Sohyeon said. "Has Lidonia explained that to you?"

"She has, but my clan is one that likes to move in the shadows and merely help our native allies in quiet ways. We have flourished in our hiding places across the worlds over the ages, and I for one will not change that situation. We have made peace with our unique existence and our painful origin."

"Will it be that easy to set things right, I wonder?" Megumi asked, almost to herself.

"Let my clansmen drive the beast and his allies from the borders of your world, and you can return things to their rightful place," Nominus said, looking curiously at the mayor. "Find a safe place to bunk for the night while we fight them. Human weaponry is no match for immortals and their magical ways, so it's best to let us handle our own. In the morning, you can return to clean things up. Baram will not defy us by remaining, and we will flush out all of his followers to send on their way with him with the local deer clan's help. They are our eyes and ears here and know the land and the inhabitants better than you would think."

"Will even the human allies leave with him?" Sohyeon asked, wondering about the hotel staff who placed armbands with Baram's sign on their uniforms. "Will it be so easy to get rid of them?"

"Try not to worry about it now and leave things to us," Nominus said, walking past the group toward the hotel with the remaining crowd of deer clan members. Sohyeon noted that the deer clan members varied in appearance. Some of them had long nut-brown or sooty black hair, some had Asian facial features or looked very swarthy, almost Arab or Mexican. Nearly all of them had the strange white freckles across their cheeks. "Go home. We will send word when it's settled."

"Wait! My father," Tamnyn said, turning back to look at the hotel as Sohyeon led her to Stephen's van in the lot.

"Your father is dead, dear," Megumi said gently, going over to her and patting her gently on the back. "We'll come back tomorrow to retrieve him and give him a proper burial along with the others. There have been so many who have disappeared and died over the past few months. We have a lot of work to do to get back to normal when this is all over, and I'll need your help, as I would have needed your father's with all of his leadership experience in Eokhmisseun. For now, let Nominus handle things."

Looking defeated, Tamnyn followed the group into the maze of cars in the parking lot.

"Let's go to my house" Sohyeon said to Stephen. "They'll know where to find us since they know my sister and Lidonia has my address."

6 WAR OF THE IMMORTALS

1

Mirae sat on the dais in the temple of the ancestors' audience hall, alone. The beautiful pearl sitting in the font nearby glittered warmly in the sunlight pouring through the ceiling dome, but the room was deathly quiet since the acolytes were away attending to other palace matters. Since Minha's return from Earth with her acolytes and the war pigeons, Mirae had been named temporary high priestess by Joriya while Minha recovered. In the small room reserved for the high priestess' use off the main hall, Minha lay in agony on her bed, her body covered with wounds that would have killed any mortal. Joriya had reassured Mirae that Minha would be fine in a month or two, though Joriya had kept her condition quiet since she knew Birum had spies in the palace.

"Why me? Why should *I* take over her role as high priestess since so many of the other acolytes have served her for over 100 years? I know my training in the temple was always supposed to be a cover for my training to take the role of queen when you retired, but isn't this going a bit further than we intended?" Mirae had asked, astounded when Joriya suggested it.

"I want you to get used to taking on more responsibility for Khabu's affairs and for the other ministers of the court to see you and gain some familiarity with your skill," Joriya said, pouring her a cup of cardamom tea as they talked in her luxurious quarters on the palace's fourth floor. "No one can know yet that you are my daughter and heir to the throne, though I'm sure some have guessed. Birum's spy network is very active in the palace. While rumors of your true identity may have reached him, I don't want to confirm it for him until he is neutralized. Besides, there still are details regarding Litt and your new adoptive daughter Kerinda that need to be worked out, and giving you unfettered access to the crypt is best for now until Litt's fate is determined."

"You know Litt's plans already, don't you?"

"That he wants to marry you and rule Khabu with you instead of going back into the crypt? Yes, I am aware, but the ministers and the ancestors will make the final judgment on him for his crime of helping Birum. However, if this is what you hope for, your role even briefly as high priestess of Khabu will do a great deal of good and will convince them of the rightness of such a move once they discover your true identity."

Although Joriya's plan was a good one, Mirae had to admit things had not gone well upon their return to Khabu. Joriya's ministers had demanded Litt be kept in the palace jail until they could determine his fate, and the interrogations he had been forced to endure in the Queen's chambers with the ministers had been very confrontational.

"Many of them can't comprehend the idea they're talking to one of the ancient kings," Litt said to Mirae later when she had gone down to visit him in the lower levels of the palace. The ministers had given him a cell that looked more like an austere bedroom with a few couches and a desk, and the door had a small cut out window instead of bars. Mirae had been allowed in to see Litt, but a guard stood at the door watching them through the window. "It's a good thing Mapin has stayed out of sight since her return. Who knows how they would react if confronted with one of the Originals at this point? I'm too close for comfort for them, since I'm second generation out of the ancient ghettos of our home world, but Mapin would just be too much for those narrow-minded old men. I also test the limits of their tolerance because I won't choose a completely human form here, but I am neither animal nor human anymore, not after emerging from my sleep in the crypt after such a long time. I will not pretend my time in the crypt never happened and go back to a pristine human form."

Litt indeed looked wild, wearing a loose black silk robe, his skin still bearing the tattoo-like pattern of black tiger-stripes over his pale white skin, his long wavy white blonde hair blending in and giving his feline features a more human cast, his pale blue eyes almost glowing with unnatural power. His long, bony fingers tipped with claws looked more ghoulish than human, yet Mirae found him as attractive as any human man she had known back on Earth. However, she could well imagine the ministers' consternation when facing such a monster.

"What should we do about Kerinda?" Mirae asked. "I feel a little guilty for bringing her along now that the ministers object to her staying in Khabu."

Litt nodded grimly.

"They're as closed-minded as my father was on the issue of blood and clans, and her half-human heritage which she wears openly in the odd color of her hair is an affront to them. We can't do anything about it. She came knowing she would never see her outlaw father again. I have suggested to Joriya that she be trained in the ways of temple acolytes to keep her out of the public eye and out of the ministers' path. Where is she now?"

"Kerinda is staying with me in my quarters since I've taken on Minha's duties while she recovers. A few of

Minha's closest assistants in the temple are teaching her about Khabu. Apparently Birum hadn't taught her much about it other than to say Joriya is a bad queen."

"Has she been upset by what the ministers have said about her or her father?"

"No, not as much as I would have expected. She must have known something was already wrong when she lived in the palace at Eokhmisseun, and she had been curious about Khabu. Will Birum come and try to get her back?"

"Birum? His sons have been sent to other far-off worlds to subdue them. I can't imagine Birum would be that sentimental to want his daughter back unless she could provide him some tactical advantage by doing so. Admittedly, Mirae, he actually has a great advantage by her being here in Khabu. We're his ultimate target. If he comes, it will be to declare war on Khabu, not to retrieve his daughter, I assure you."

"Litt, she's just a young girl! Are you saying she could help him takeover by infiltrating the palace?"

"As much as I want to believe she's as innocent as you say, Birum has trained his other children to do such things, and she has come here without so much as a whimper of upset at her losses. She must be watched until her true allegiance can be determined."

Mirae stood up and headed for the door in disgust.

"You are as bad as the ministers!" she said, sighing as she looked back at him.

"No," he said gently. "I'm just realistic. If Kerinda is genuine in her desire to stay with us and live in Khabu, that will ultimately be apparent, and you and I can accept her even if the rest of Khabu will not. But we shouldn't be too hasty given the seriousness of the situation we face."

"But Litt," she stammered.

"Trust me on this, Mirae."

"My lady, there is word from the temple that someone has come to speak with you," the guard at the window said.

"I was just leaving." She turned back to Litt, her expression softening. "I will try to trust you. *You* try not to get yourself killed in the meantime. I can't stand that you have to stay down here in the jail instead of with me."

"It won't be much longer, my love," Litt said lightly as the guard opened the door and she stepped into the corridor.

2

When Mirae returned to the main hall of the temple, she saw the acolytes had gathered just outside the entrance linking the palace to the temple, talking excitedly in hushed tones. They fell silent and looked away as she approached. Reaching out to push the door open, she paused and looked at them curiously.

"Do you know who our visitor is?" she asked in a low voice to the nearest acolyte. A few of the girls behind her giggled. "What's all of this commotion for?"

"You really don't know, high priestess?" the acolyte asked. "Truly, this is an amazing time to be alive in Khabu. First the ancient father, Litt, has returned, and now, well, do you know who Nominus is? I know you studied our history some when you first came, but perhaps you are unfamiliar with him and his role."

"Nominus?" Mirae said to herself, thinking. Of course, she hadn't read about him in the histories she was given when Joriya first brought her to Khabu, but Minha had mentioned him a few times since returning from Earth, and she recalled Litt had been friends with a man named Nominus who had fled Khabu millennia ago. "He's the one who chased Baram from Earth and saved Minha and the others from Khabu aiding my people, wasn't he?"

"Yes, that's the man."

"The same one who reportedly fled Khabu with the deer clan in ancient times?"

"Yes, he is legendary. No one was certain such a man existed, though a few of our histories mentioned him."

Mirae looked at the acolyte's awestruck expression and realized Nominus' appearance with the deer clan was quite fantastical to the native inhabitants of Khabu, much like Moses suddenly returning with the Israelites from a distant star would have been a sensation on Earth. Eight thousand years was a long time.

"Is there some protocol I should follow?" Mirae asked her in hushed tones so the other acolytes wouldn't overhear.

"Oh, probably nothing other than standard court etiquette since we have no expectation of such a figure appearing out of the blue. Normal hospitality should be enough, though may we come in with you and get a glimpse of him and the deer clan? The guards who brought them from the inner sea said they are quite unusual looking, with the body of a human melded with the four legs of a deer."

Realizing the regular citizens of Khabu never saw each other in animal or even half-animal form until they retired to either the crypt or forest, Mirae understood their curiosity and nodded. She entered the temple hall with the acolytes shuffling in behind her and kept her attention focused on reaching the chair on the dais before dealing with her visitors, though she heard the muffled gasps of the acolytes. When she was seated, the acolytes bowed quickly and went to stand behind the dais and flanked the door leading to Minha's sickroom. Mirae looked up and studied Nominus and his entourage.

As the acolyte said, they looked strange by Khabu's standards. The man standing in front of the group was tall with nut colored skin and long grayish brown hair. Looking fully human, he wore a simple brown cloak and green tunic and breeches. The male warriors behind him were centaur-like, only with deer markings on their backs and even on their faces, deer horns of varying lengths coming out of the tops of their heads. They wore brown or green cloaks, too, but their human skin gradually turned into a layer of rough brownish gray fur with white spots.

"You are Nominus," Mirae said matter-of-factly, aware that her position as high priestess gave her more right to speak with such a figure on equal ground. "I hear from Minha that I owe you a debt of gratitude for saving my home from Baram. My brother and family are safe?"

Nominus smiled warmly, as if expecting her comment.

"You are Mirae Choi, then, the girl from Earth who has been sent to Khabu?" he asked, nodding. "I hoped I would get to meet you."

"Of course you would meet me here," she said. "Your old friend Litt is also here in Khabu, though he is in jail since he was supposed to remain in the crypt of ancestors. He and I are very close."

Nominus looked at her in amazement.

"I heard rumors not long after I left that he killed his father and abdicated in favor of another family member before retiring early to the crypt. I thought it was a shame since he always had it in him to be a good leader."

"Had you also heard Birum kidnapped him from the crypt secretly 60 years ago and bound him by magic?"

"I regretfully have not kept up with the events of my old homeland in such great detail in the past 8,000 years, high priestess. I know only the most basic facts of its politics and its people anymore. My clan has found peace across the worlds, far away from the turmoil of Khabu, and although we were summoned to help your home world, it was only limited help that I have been willing to offer."

"So you will not be staying in Khabu to aid us in our fight against Birum? I heard Baram joined him in Eokhmisseun with his human followers and ghost slaves he turned while on Earth. They will need to be dealt with eventually, and I know that Queen Joriya intends on trying to apprehend her brother and his family before he does more harm in the known worlds. Eventually, they could find their way again to another world where your clan has a settlement."

Nominus looked at her grimly and nodded.

"I understand your position, and I had thought about coming to Khabu's aid more than once over the days since I got word of your plight, but after some consultation with my federation of clan leaders, we have concluded our clan has grown very far apart from our brethren here in Khabu. As you can see from our wild appearance and uncouth ways that we would only shock the inhabitants of this land and have no foreseeable way of returning to our former place here among the clans of the old world and the ghetto."

"Then why have you come here, Nominus?"

"I felt it necessary since I have helped your leaders back on your home world to at least visit Khabu before I return to my settlement. Although I will not stay to help you in your fight, I will leave a map and instructions on how to summon me in an emergency in the future, though I will not deal with Birum. He is your responsibility, as was Zurui so long ago. Remember, if you have heard anything about my history from my dear friend Litt, I fled Khabu as the king slaughtered the wolf clan. While I felt it was my duty to protect a human land from Baram since they are so much weaker than immortals like us and my own clan has long lived among them, as we do in so many worlds, I don't feel any obligation to help my own kind. You are not helpless, and the trouble that you stir up is your own doing. I'm sorry."

"On what grounds will you refuse to help Khabu? Because the inhabitants are immortals?"

Nominus looked at her with a shrewd glint in his gray eyes.

"Because *they* are immortals? Do you imagine you can fool me the way you can fool them, high priestess? I have lived among humans and know them well. I can identify them by their smell and the way they carry themselves. How is it you came to be on Earth, and what exactly are you doing here now?"

Mirae looked at Nominus in alarm, and he seemed to understand what her reaction meant.

"I am sorry if I offended you, high priestess, but know you don't have everyone fooled, even if the leaders of Khabu are too blind to see. That's why I left long ago. You know now, do you not, what power you hold in your hands?"

Mirae looked away from him toward the pearl, worrying that Birum's spies might be among the acolytes. It was dangerous for anyone to know her true identity just yet, and Joriya had been careful to only let a few of the most trusted leaders in the palace know. Yet this man, this ancient father, could see clearly? She wished Litt were there to speak with Nominus and change his mind.

"Won't you go down to the cell where they're holding Litt and speak with him before you go?" she asked, standing and stepping off of the dais toward him. Nominus was only a few feet from her now.

"As much as I want to see my old friend, I think given the circumstances that it's best I don't this time. Consider me too suspicious if you will, but I don't like the confined feeling of the palace's old jail and certainly don't want to see my friend in such a place. Why is he being held there instead of coming out here to meet me? Have the ministers, in their ever convoluted way of thinking, decided he's some kind of threat to public order for coming out of the zoo they keep beneath the temple?"

"Yes, something like that. They want to verify he's truly free of Birum's magic and influence and make a determination as to what to do with him since he had been in the crypt so long."

"How typical of them," Nominus said with a slight sneer. "So you see now why the palace and the court are not for me. Perhaps one of these days, you can come to my world and see how I have arranged the deer clan's settlements for comparison. But for now, I will depend on you to relay my letter and my words to Litt. Unless they execute him, we will see each other again."

"They wouldn't dare execute him, would they?" Mirae asked in a whisper. She was close enough to Nominus to not be overheard. "He is, after all, one of their most ancient kings."

"Probably not, but you never know with court politics," Nominus said. "They aren't the most rational at times, and the ministers certainly aren't imaginative enough to realize his value. They only look at the laws they've set up. He should be in the crypt, but now he's out here running around, undignified, sullying their memory and misconception of who he was. Sometimes that's the greater problem, not anything he actually could do. I trust you'll do your best to keep him out of their clutches. I must go now."

3

"Nominus has gone home?" Minha asked, sitting up in bed when Mirae entered the high priestess's room.

Minha was still pale with deep scratch marks and bites all over her exposed skin, and her white shift had bloodstains from some of the ruptured wounds, but she seemed more energetic than when she had arrived a few days earlier.

"I hoped he would stay longer," Mirae said. "He could help get Litt out of this predicament and avoid punishment for leaving the crypt with Birum. We still need to find Baram and Birum and end their madness. But Nominus wouldn't listen."

Minha smiled slightly.

"Of course, he wouldn't. The histories do mention he was quite adamant about leaving Khabu, and there has been no other recorded visit from the deer clan since. Most of Khabu's citizenry would be surprised to know we ever had a deer clan at all, let alone expect some obscure figure from our history to reappear like this. We should be sure to send one of the acolytes to accurately record your meeting this day and correct some of those perceptions. Are you really worried about Litt? Has Pontol returned from his latest reconnaissance voyage with word on Birum's activities?"

"I am worried about Litt, but mostly because he told me what happened when Khabu was first founded. I worry this could be a replay of those tragic events, given how obtuse the ministers were back at that time. Nothing seems to have changed over the millennia. I haven't heard anything from Pontol yet. But Minha, Nominus suspects my identity, and he made reference to that in the audience hall. Should that also go into the histories? Could that create difficulties for Khabu?"

"Nominus knows that you are the next in line for the throne?" Minha asked, looking serious.

"I'm not sure if he figured that out, but he seemed to indicate he knew I wasn't human. He said something about being able to smell humans." She bit her lip, looking off into the candle flame.

"Then he knows you are an immortal like us. I don't think that should be terribly sensitive, though it might tip off an observant person that you are much more than merely one of us, somehow living for all of these years in a different world. Joriya's main concern about keeping it secret is that Birum be given no advance notice about who will take her place when she retires to the crypt. I think you are safe for now. In the meantime, send one of the birds to check in with Pontol if they can find him on the inner sea. We need more information about what has happened after Nominus chased Baram from Earth."

"But Birum has spies in Khabu's palace, doesn't he? Could one of them have been among the temple acolytes?

Even the fact that I am part of the tiger clan may be enough for him to put two and two together, and Baram came to Earth and knows of my family's importance since they helped you."

"We can't do anything about it if there was a spy," Minha said matter-of-factly. "All we can do is hope for the best and move forward. The girl is still with you in your quarters?"

"Kerinda? Yes."

"Then go talk some with her and see what you can find out. We have a lot of work to do before the transition of power. Try to get some rest and go about your duties without worrying about it."

When Mirae returned to her room, she found Kerinda awake and waiting for her instead of sleeping in her bed in spite of the late hour. Almost a teenager now, Kerinda had not changed into the Greek-style dress of the temple acolytes but still wore the long frilly black satin dress she had worn during their escape from Eokhmisseun. Like Litt, she didn't shapeshift into a completely human appearance to humor the ministers of Khabu but defiantly kept her weretiger attributes, including her long red hair and her orange-toned skin with the black tattoo-like markings.

"You're late, Mirae. I've been waiting for you. Did you see Litt today? Will he be joining us soon? I can't wait until you two are married, and then we can all be a family."

Mirae sat down across from Kerinda on the long couch in her sitting room and thought a moment.

"Do you miss your parents and the palace in Eokhmisseun?" she asked.

"I didn't see father much, and mother was a little too somber to have any fun around," Kerinda said sadly, looking down at the floor. "We were locked in the palace all of the time as the people outside got scarier and scarier."

"Now you're locked in the palace here in Khabu, too. I'm sorry that's the situation, but surely when Litt is free and joins us, we will go to his old fortress and enjoy the countryside. Have you finished your studies today?"

"I learned a little about the crypt of the ancestors and Forest of Bliss from the temple acolytes. Is this the role the real high priestess has decided I should take on here in Khabu? The acolytes don't do that much, I think."

Mirae laughed.

"They actually do quite a lot. They keep the official histories of the land, for starters, and they maintain contact with the ancestors who have retired to the both the forest and the crypt. They run special ceremonies for the royal family and keep an eye on the country's borders, holding diplomatic meetings with anyone from outside of them. In some ways, they are more powerful than many of the queen's ministers, who only handle domestic affairs. The fact that they speak with the ancestors means they have much greater access to old secrets of the land and can draw on the ancestors' power. It's quite a complement that you would be asked to join their ranks as an outsider."

"You means as the half-breed daughter of their wayward Duke, don't you?" Kerinda asked sarcastically. "They want to isolate me from their people since I'm not one of them, not really, because my mother is human. Isn't that why they put you there, too? You're from Earth and not really one of them either. But are you also half like me since you can do the change?"

Mirae could only sit in silence in response. She had to protect Joriya's secret and couldn't correct Kerinda's impression.

"They're afraid of me, aren't they?" Kerinda asked when Mirae didn't answer. "Hadn't they ever seen our animal forms before?"

"I don't know that they ever change like you do or even like the ancestors who have retired do. They don't ever change until the day they leave society," Mirae said.

"It must have been a shock for them to see you and Litt in your wild forms, wearing your animal heritage so flagrantly before them. They want to put Litt back in the crypt and force him to renounce his human form there entirely again, but he's fighting them."

"I didn't think it would be like this when I left home to come here with you."

"What did you expect it to be like?" Mirae asked gently.

"I don't know. I was tired of the palace at Eokhmisseun, and I knew there was something wrong going on with everybody. I liked you and Litt right away and wished you were my parents instead."

"Did your father tell you much about Khabu? He clearly taught you to speak some of the language."

"I didn't know much at all, only that the Queen was evil and that we had tiger blood and amazing abilities which my father augmented through magic."

Mirae could only smile at her characterization of Joriya. How predictable of Birum.

"But let me tell you something that maybe will help me in Khabu," Kerinda said, coming over to sit beside Mirae on the couch.

"Tell me what?"

"I had a strange dream this morning that has me worried. It might be important. I used to have dreams that came true all of the time in Eokhmisseun."

"Tell me then," Mirae said, leaning forward and studying the girl's face. "What did you dream?"

"I was walking in a beautiful place, like a field that became a forest, and as I reached the edge of some body of water, I saw an astonishing waterfall in front of me. To my right behind me was the ruins of an old mansion of some kind, but I thought the blue water looked so inviting, I walked closer to it. I was never allowed out of the palace to play in Eokhmisseun, even when I was a little girl, and this place smelled so fragrant and crackled with life and color. I wanted to jump into the water and lose myself in the depths."

Kerinda paused, seeing Mirae's look of surprise.

"Is something wrong?"

"No, continue," Mirae said in a strangled voice. "Was there more?"

"Yes, I heard someone call my name, a man's voice that sounded familiar, before I could take another step near the beautiful water. It came from the ruins, and I turned to see who it was. He was still too far beyond the trees, so I backtracked along a short path through them past the cliff to the plain where the mansion remained. Then I saw him. The man who spoke to me, my brother Baram, whom I haven't seen in about five years since my father sent him and my other brother away, stood before me."

"Your other brother?"

"I also have a brother named Abbason who is a little older than Baram. But in the dream, Baram wasn't like I remembered him. He also had taken on the half-tiger form, and he had gained a fierceness, even an evil cast, in the years we had been apart. I wanted to run to hug him like I had when we were children, but he seemed dangerous now. I couldn't move for a moment, and he started walking toward me, pulling out a spiked club as if he would kill me. A number of ghost-slaves followed him, and I was so scared I dashed back to the water and dove in, but the water around me turned black. A reptilian head arose from the water, like the dragon father sent after us when we were in the boat. Why are you looking at me like that, Mirae? Do you know what the dream means?"

"I myself have had a dream like that many months before I was brought to Khabu to stay," Mirae said, standing and pacing around the sitting room. "I don't understand why you would have nearly the same dream."

"You dreamt of my brother Baram?"

"No, the waterfall, the Blue Waterfall to be exact. You haven't had your lessons on Khabu's geography yet to know the significance. The Blue Waterfall is a very important landmark, especially connected to Litt."

"To Litt? Then was it maybe Litt I saw in the dream, not Baram. I can't imagine since Baram had red hair in it. Why would Litt come after me with a weapon?"

"He wouldn't. It might be Baram," Mirae said softly, half talking to herself. "My dream actually happened when I had it, though I hadn't dreamt of a tiger-man. I had dreamt of the dragon. When I came to Khabu, I was drawn there by a man I thought was the Duke, your father, but it wasn't Birum, it was Litt. Birum's magic took us to the palace at Eokhmisseun using that water dragon."

"Oh, so that's how you came to be at the palace with him! So could it mean something is happening at this Blue Waterfall now? Could my brother actually be there, if your earlier dream turned out to be true? "

Mirae looked at her, horrified.

"That would be a problem, wouldn't it, if Baram is here in Khabu?" Kerinda asked, standing and grabbing Mirae's arm. "Should we go there to see?"

"Go to sleep for now, Kerinda," Mirae said, pulling the girl into the half of the suite that split into two bedrooms. "We can't do anything now until morning, and I will need to talk to Litt about this, and Joriya as well. If we go investigate your dream at the Blue Waterfall, Litt should be with us. It was his home when he was prince of Khabu, and the ruins you saw was his fortress before its more recent restoration. Maybe Joriya can convince the ministers to let him out and help us. If we're wrong, Litt would come back and face their final sentence on him, but if we're right, it could free him from them and the crypt."

"Wake me up before you go to the palace jail. I know I can't come, but I want to be ready to leave for the Blue Waterfall. You'll trust me once you see for yourself it's true, won't you? The ministers will change their minds that I am a traitor like my father?"

Mirae looked at Kerinda in dismay as the girl went into her room without waiting for her answer. *Could Kerinda be lying to make her troubles go away?* Mirae thought to herself. Perhaps it didn't matter. Now that Baram had left Earth, he could turn up anywhere.

4

At daybreak the next morning, before Mirae could request a meeting with either Joriya or Litt, word came to her from the acolyte who had served overnight in the temple that Pontol had returned with Mapin. He had news of Eokhmisseun. Throwing on her light blue chiton and brushing back her long black hair, Mirae ran through the corridors of the still-sleeping palace to the temple hall where he waited.

"Pontol, what news do you have?" she asked as she took her seat on the dais near the pearl. "What has happened in your homeland? Is it as bad as we expected?"

Pontol looked at her through distorted features Mirae now recognized as degenerate weretiger, his face looking unusually haggard. At her command, the acolytes busily prepared the room he had been given in the temple after his exile from Eokhmisseun.

"It's worse," he said grimly. "Birum got rid of the dragon in the port near my home when that Baram came by ship with his wench and ghost-slaves from Earth."

"When Nominus expelled them from Earth, Baram left with quite a large group of people, even humans, who were his allies. I heard he had a few large ships, though I don't understand where he got them since I am not native to the worlds of the inner sea. So he did return to his father, did he?"

"Aye, and I was able to sneak back to my old place after they entered and disembarked. I went ashore to see what else I could find out since Birum had left the place unguarded for a time, and my old friends told me that Birum was outraged by Nominus' interference, though he was quite interested otherwise in the deer clan and had hoped to get their tonic to help heal himself when he uses his magic.

"So Birum had both of the ancients, Litt and Nominus, slip through his fingers, and he went into a rage, burning down the east side of Eokhmisseun's capital city. He knew all of his adversaries had returned here to Khabu, so it won't be long, I think, until he makes his move on you. He reportedly talked with Baram about how it's time to claim Khabu. When I left Eokhmisseun, they were preparing more ships, bigger than I ever saw run on the inner sea, to come here with their people. I worry he may evacuate Eokhmisseun and bring them all here."

"Pontol, is it possible for them to sneak into Khabu at a different port than the one here at the temple?" Mirae asked, thinking of Kerinda's dream. "Does the inner sea reach any other parts of Khabu directly?"

"Well, there are waterways, real ones rather than the ephemeral inner sea, that run across Khabu's countryside. A few lead directly to the Forest of Bliss, which has a natural moat from what I hear, though I have not been to that shore."

"How about the waterfalls? Could they reach inland waterfalls?"

"Waterfalls?"

"Do you know Khabu's geography?"

Pontol scratched his head a moment, looking thoughtful.

"Aye, there are some waterfalls in the middle of the country, and they connect back to a major river leading from the inner sea. I think it would be possible for someone to land there and be sneaky about things. Unlike the boundary of the Forest of Bliss, the region surrounding the waterfall has no dimensional or geographical barrier, and Khabu doesn't have any guards at the ports along that river. One could probably just sail right up to the falls."

"Thank you," Mirae said, standing. She turned to the acolyte who had guarded the temple overnight. "Please take Pontol to his special quarters where he can rest and give him some of the food reserved for the high priestess' retinue to refresh himself. I have a few things I need to attend to before I return for my morning audience with the ministers."

The acolyte bowed and led Pontol through the corridor connecting the temple to the palace. Mirae followed but turned to the right where they turned left, walking toward the private wing of the royal family where she reached the stairs leading up to Joriya's quarters.

5

"Kerinda had a vision of Baram out at the Blue Waterfall?" Joriya asked, her eyes growing wide as she shut the door behind Mirae. Both of them remained standing since this wasn't a social call.

"Pontol just returned from Eokhmisseun and said Birum's plan is to capture Khabu. He described the way the inner sea connects to a river leading inland past the Blue Waterfall. If have no guards stationed along the river, what would stop him from landing there?"

"There are no guards, but Litt did traditionally have his fortress there," Joriya said thoughtfully, her brow furrowing. "You're right, we didn't think through the danger Birum posed and never tightened security."

"Even when he reportedly studied black magic and took one of the ancestors from the crypt? Why weren't you more concerned with the threat he posed, Joriya?"

Mirae wanted to say more, but she bit back her words. It would do no good to alienate Joriya now, but Mirae thought fleetingly of how the Queen seemed too lethargic and unengaged, always taking the path of least resistance and not proactively doing what was best for Khabu. Dismayed, Mirae realized this was probably why Birum hated his sister so much, why he considered her incompetent and had wanted to take her place. What was it that made her so complacent? She had done well in hiding her child, though it was obvious Mirae would have been in danger had she stayed in Khabu instead of switching places with the Chois' oldest daughter, but that action was uncharacteristic of Joriya. Perhaps Minha, her more decisive, even ruthless, mother was the reason Joriya had taken that precaution.

"We can't do anything about it now, Mirae," Joriya said, pulling her out of her reverie. "It's possible Kerinda has inherited the oracular powers we typically seek for those who serve in our temple, and if she's right, it would be disastrous for Khabu for him to gain a foothold in the heart of our kingdom. I should send a contingent of our ceremonial warriors, or maybe the war pigeons, to investigate the matter before things get worse."

"Send me and Litt to the Blue Waterfall to deal with Baram if he's there," Mirae said without hesitation.

"You and Litt? Litt is imprisoned right now at the request of the prime minister while he's under investigation, and what will you do, Mirae, if you find Baram there? Do you expect the two of you can subdue him alone or can talk him out of invading Khabu? We need professional warriors to do that. Unfortunately, Nominus has already left us to our own devices.

"And what happens if Baram discovers you are my heir? He and Birum would rage against you and pursue you to the farthest edges of Khabu before they would let you take the throne. We may have no choice but to admit defeat, however, if he has already gained a foothold here."

Mirae looked at her incredulously.

"You're going to admit defeat? Why don't you just throw open the palace doors and invite Birum back in if you're going to go that far? Why bother protecting me all of those years? There won't be a kingdom left to rule if you can't even muster enough concern to oust Baram should he be here!"

Joriya glared at her, but then her face softened as she glanced toward the window at the far end of her suite.

"Let me go with Litt to the Blue Waterfall and take a few of the birds with us," Mirae said. "We'll see if anyone is there and report back for reinforcements if we actually find anything. Litt will willingly come back and return to his cell to complete the investigation if that's what the prime minister requires. Just don't leave things the way they are, or you may find Baram on your doorstep ready to rip out your throat while you fight with the ministers of the court over nonsense."

"The girl will stay behind then?" Joriya asked, turning back to Mirae.

"If you think that's wise."

"If her brother is here in Khabu, it would be dangerous for you to reunite them. She should remain in the capital in case she's luring you into a trap, that way she can't aid him by turning on you once you get out there. I'll ask Minha to allow Kerinda to take one of the tiger masks to communicate with Litt since the mission you're going on is very serious and it will take a few days to reach the waterfall then return to the palace. Is that acceptable?"

"You'll ask the prime minister for permission to release Litt temporarily to come with me then?"

"I'll release him myself with a personal guarantee of his return. The prime minister can't oppose me if I choose to do so. Wait for Litt in the temple with the girl while I make arrangements."

Without another word, Mirae bowed deeply to Joriya before returning to the corridor, thinking that was the first truly risky thing she had seen Joriya do since she had come to Khabu.

6

"The mask has special powers, little one. Did your father explain to you what they were or that they even existed?"

Kerinda looked up at Minha where she lay in the high priestess' sanctuary recovering from her fight with Baram. This was the first time Kerinda had been called before her grandmother, and when she held the delicate wooden mask carved in the shape of a tiger's face, she could feel it pulsing, like it was alive. Afraid to hold onto it too long, she quickly placed it on the cushion beside her where she sat on the low sofa across from the high priestess' bed.

"I know nothing of Khabu, my lady," Kerinda said softly, looking down at the floor.

"Mirae tells me you shared a dream with her of the Blue Waterfall. We will confirm over the next few days that you have the sight. If you do, you will be a valuable addition to our temple. Not many any more experience it like they did in the old days."

"Yet Mirae did."

"Yes, Mirae did, but she's a special case."

"Why is she a special case?"

"We'll talk about that later, little one. First, let me explain how the mask works so you will know what to do with it while we wait for the birds to return with news of their arrival at the waterfall."

"It feels funny when I touch it."

"Funny how?"

"Uncomfortable."

"Hmm, then perhaps the ancient father isn't as confident of his abilities as I had hoped."

"The ancient father? Do you mean Litt?"

"Didn't Birum tell you about the crypt and who Litt is?"

"The crypt? I've only heard a little about it since coming here. It's where the tiger clan of the royal family retires after living life in the kingdom as a human."

"Yes, and Litt was one of the early kings. He is more than 8,000 years old, and your brother is no match for one with such a long memory."

"So the mask is connected to his thoughts somehow?"

"The mask connects the high priestess to the ancestors who have retired to the crypt to live in a dreamlike sleep as tigers. Now that one of them has returned to the human world, the mask has latched onto him. Instead of taking the acolyte who wears it ceremonially to the crypt to talk with the ancestors in the other dimension, it takes you to wherever Litt may be on the outside. Only the high priestess has enough power to control it to return to the crypt under such a circumstance. But you must use it sparingly, only when the bird returns and tells you what they have found at the Blue Waterfall. The mask will transport you to where they are when you wear it, and you will be at the ancient father's mercy, under his control due to the power of the mask."

"Will he be able to feel my emotions when I touch the mask, too?"

"I don't know. That's a very strange question, little one, and I have not considered how the mask might work in reverse. Until one of the birds returns with news, stay here in the sanctuary with me where it's safe. I know the ministers fear you and that they are not fair in their judgments."

Kerinda placed the mask on the table beside the sofa and lay down as Minha extinguished the lamp.

In the sanctuary room, it was hard to tell how late or early it may have been since the room had no windows. Suddenly, Kerinda woke with a start and sat up in the darkness. Across the room she could hear Minha's breathing, still ragged from her wounds. Whatever had woken Kerinda had not caused Minha to stir in the deep, uncomfortable sleep of her sickbed. Kerinda turned to look at the door where a thin band of light filtered through at the bottom. A slight shadow moved across it, causing the light to dim and shift a little, and voices on the other side of the door grew louder until she could make out the words.

"Where is my mother? Now that my sister has been removed, I want an audience with the high priestess!"

Kerinda recognized her father's voice, and it jolted her completely awake now. Creeping over to the door, she put her hand on the doorframe and pressed her ear gently against it as the voices were getting softer again.

"Please, my lord, don't touch the font," she could hear one of the acolytes say. *"It's a very old artefact of our land even if you don't respect its power."*

"Where is Minha? I hear this Earth woman Mirae was made high priestess to replace her while she recuperated. What a sham! Where is she, for that matter? I demand an accounting of the temple right now."

"I understand, my lord, but Minha has been sent away to recover, and Mirae has left the palace on an errand for the Queen," the acolyte said quickly, her voice quavering in fear.

Her father must be threatening the acolyte in some way, as Kerinda knew all too well he could, having witnessed his rages all of her life. She also heard familiar clattering footsteps echoing through the main hall. Her mother joined her father there in her favorite magical form, the grotesque half-woman half-scorpion she had learned to shapeshift into using her father's black magic. Kerinda shuddered and felt around the edge of the door to make sure the lock was in place. It wasn't, and she gently moved it over so her father couldn't barge in. She would at least try to protect Minha from him since the acolyte had gone to the trouble to lie.

"The Queen is now imprisoned beneath the palace with her dead whelp at last. She matters not at all now to the future of Khabu. I will have my way with her before this coup is done. Did you see my battalion of ghost-slaves outside? They have the same sharp claws and teeth as I do even if they still retain some of their humanity. If you aren't telling the truth, I will find out, you know that, don't you?"

"What will you do, my lord? What is it you plan for Khabu now that you have returned and taken the throne by force?"

"My first order of business is to appoint my own high priestess. Crysalin!"

As the clacking footsteps grew louder, the acolyte began shrieking in terror, her voice growing distant as she either fled the room or fainted in the temple hall. Kerinda wasn't sure what happened, but she could only imagine the effect of her mother's nightmare magic on the temple attendants. Even Kerinda, who had grown up in the palace with Birum's black powers, could never get used to the unnerving appearance of her mother in that shape.

Never close to either of her parents, Kerinda felt the most warmth toward her brother Baram than any of her family, and when they were little they played together and comforted each other instead of turning to their parents. Her father was always preoccupied with his magic and ruling Eokhmisseun, while her mother seemed cold and unmoored from just about everything but her husband. Now that Kerinda had betrayed her favorite brother, she felt a little despondent, but when it came to her parents, she shared the acolyte's terror and was relieved by the warmth and sweetness she saw in Mirae and Litt when they arrived at the palace.

As an eerie silence fell over the temple hall, Kerinda held her breath a little, straining to hear more, but Minha coughed softly. Glancing back in the darkness toward the high priestess' bed, she tiptoed over to it, afraid Minha would speak to her and her father would hear her in the next room. Paying no more attention to the drama beyond the door, Kerinda sat down gingerly on the edge of Minha's bed and put her hands on Minha's face as if feeling her temperature. Minha woke with a start.

"Quiet, now, they're here," Kerinda whispered as loud as she dared.

"Who?" Minha whispered back, her question barely audible.

"My father Birum is out there. He has done something to Joriya and appointed my mother high priestess. I locked the door so they can't come in. We can hide in here for now."

"What?" Minha tried to sit up, but Kerinda stopped her and pushed her gently back down on the bed.

"Don't move, or he'll hear you. Go back to sleep. I'll keep watch for a while."

"Don't use the mask to escape yet, Kerinda. I need you here for now, and Litt and Mirae can take care of themselves. Wake me if anything happens."

"What are we waiting for?"

"A moment when the temple hall is unobserved long enough for you to slip out. You must disguise yourself and wander about the palace to find Joriya then report back to me what you find. Can you turn yourself completely into a human girl?"

"I'll think about it. I've never done that, not since I was a baby. I guess it's possible."

"You have to try, or else he'll recognize you and capture you."

"I understand. Go to sleep, and I'll wake you if it seems we have a moment for me to do as you ask."

Minha fell silent, and Kerinda went back to the couch and sat down. Wondering how it felt to be completely human again, Kerinda thought about it a lot before focusing her attention on her hands. Strange noises and gibbering voices still were coming from the temple hall, but it sounded like the ghost-slaves had taken over and come for her mother's instructions. Kerinda blocked out the sounds. Finally sparking the sensation her hands were burning, she felt them change as she concentrated on them. Rubbing them together to ease the pain then touching them slowly, she noticed her skin was now smooth and her claws had receded. She began to work on each part of her body where she normally wore the colors of her tiger heritage like a banner. When the transformation was complete and the light beneath the door grew brighter and brighter, Kerinda felt exhaustion sweep over her, and lying down on the couch, she fell into an uneasy sleep.

7

A day and a half later, Minha felt safe enough to light the lamp again. The temple hall had been quiet long enough to assume they would not be noticed in the sanctuary room, so she began to implement her plan. Getting out of bed, she went over to the couch where Kerinda had been sitting and studied the girl.

"The transformation is complete, isn't it? You didn't keep any of the tiger attributes this time?" she asked her charge.

"They're all gone. I'm completely human now. What do you think?"

Kerinda's smooth skin was still swarthy with a slight orange cast though now it was all one hue, and her eyes were the color of amber. Minha looked in dismay at her long red hair.

"That isn't a natural shade in Khabu and will attract too much attention when I send you through the palace. In Khabu, the bird clan typically has light blonde, white, dark gray or more rarely *cinnamon brown hair, and the tiger clan typically has black or white-blonde hair, sometimes a combination reflecting the animal's stripes. Your father will know it's you right away with a shade of red that dark, so we'll have to come up with a disguise. But first, put on the acolyte's chiton. The dark blue should suit you."*

Kerinda quietly did as she asked while Minha returned to bed, groaning a little in pain though her wounds seemed lighter now.

"Use the light blue scarf in my closet to wind around your hair like a turban. That would still look unusual in Khabu, but it would be less noticeable than your hair. Come here if you can't get it to stay in place, and I'll help you," Minha said, sighing as she lay back on her pillow.

Kerinda had quickly changed from her black dress, which now lay in the middle of the floor, to the dark blue chiton, which made her look older than 14. Taking out the scarf as Minha had instructed, she brought it over to her and began to twist her hair back into a ponytail to keep it from coming undone and escaping from the turban. Sitting down next to Minha, she let the high priestess wind it and fasten it around her head. When she had finished dressing, she stood in the center of the room for Minha's approval.

"How exotic and grown up you look, little one. Be sure to put the tiger mask in its pouch and wear it across your chest so it will be close at hand. Then you will be set to go. Do you know what you need to do out there?"

Kerinda did as Minha instructed, crying a little at the thought of leaving Minha behind.

"Will you be okay, grandmother? Is it safe to leave you here alone while this is going on in the palace?"

"Don't worry about me," Minha said off-handedly. *"There's not much that can kill an immortal, so you needn't concern yourself. It will be time for me to retire to the crypt before long anyway. I just need to see to the transition of power when Joriya abdicates the throne. Go now."*

Leaving the sanctuary room after preparing a signal with Minha for her return, Kerinda crept through the deserted temple hall toward the palace. Her first order of business was to go to Pontol's room and warn him of the coup, if he wasn't already aware of it. Of course, her father's spies would already know he was hiding here in the palace, so perhaps it was already too late to help him. On her way to him, she ran into one of the acolytes Kerinda recognized.

"Ashira?" Kerinda said softly, glancing around the corridor. It was still very early in the morning, before anyone was awake, though the candle sconces lining the corridor burned brightly and flickered as the air stirred.

"Who are you?" Ashira asked suspiciously, squinting at the girl. Then her eyes opened wide as a look of recognition crossed her face. "Kerinda? I would never have recognized you if I hadn't heard your voice. What are you doing here? And dressed like that no less? Weren't you supposed to be with the high priestess?"

"Minha and I heard my father arrive. We know the palace is in the middle of a coup. They didn't search our room, so he doesn't know I'm here. Minha sent me to be her eyes and ears around the palace and had me dress like this so I wouldn't be recognized."

"It's a good disguise. We were afraid to come into the sanctuary room in case Birum saw us and found her. It's good that you escaped his notice. The Duke has been like a madman since he stormed the palace with his ghost-slaves. I'm sure he knows you're here somewhere by now, if not through his spies but through torture of the ministers who don't trust you anyway. Where else could you have gone, since you were with Mirae and Litt when they fled Eokhmisseun?"

"He'll be angry if he finds me since I left with his enemies and sold out my brother. Any word from Laqrisa? She went with Mirae and Litt to the Blue Waterfall."

"Not that I've seen. What tasks has Minha given you? Are you here looking for Pontol?"

"That was first on my list, but she also wants me to look in on the Queen."

Ashira's face turned grim.

"We snuck Pontol out of the palace this morning and took him to his boat at the shore of the inner sea. Perhaps the Duke has someone watching the ports, I can't say for sure, but we thought Pontol had a chance of talking to the deer clan and maybe even persuading Nominus to help us, though I know the high priestess said he won't."

"Then what should I do now? Go to the crypt level to find where they are holding the Queen?"

"Oh, no, you shouldn't go there," Ashira said in alarm, grabbing Kerinda's arm. "There's a rumor around the palace that today Birum is holding a big farce of a meeting with the palace ministers there, and they have rallied around him against the Queen for allowing the release of the ancient father, Litt, from the palace prison."

"She never consulted with them?" Kerinda asked, horrified.

"No, she made the decision herself, as is her right as queen, expecting them to go along with her, but the palace ministers are afraid of the ancient father and want him to be banished or executed though they have no grounds exactly to do so. They've been trying to reassert their authority on the issue since the ancient father returned with the Earth woman, but the Queen has blocked their will at every turn. Now with this blunder and Birum's arrival, they have their wish, though Litt and Mirae are thankfully not in the palace for them to deal with. Word is the Duke will be sending troops to meet them out at the Blue Waterfall soon if they haven't already done so."

"And what will happen to Joriya?"

"Maybe he will leave her in prison, but he used the special silver executioner's dagger on the princess, whom he imprisoned years ago."

"The executioner's dagger? He has the dagger? Could he execute Joriya now, or even Minha?"

"Yes, anything could happen, but there's no way to stop him. He has both the twisted, degenerate humans he has turned into heirs of the tiger clan as well as human followers from Earth who have joined him as loyal warriors after going back to Eokhmisseun with Baram. They can intimidate any of the palace ministers still wavering in their decision. Baram is your brother, isn't he? I haven't seen him around the palace."

"Didn't you know that Litt and Mirae went to the Blue Waterfall because I sensed his presence there? That's the news the birds will bring."

"Then the ministers don't need to send troops at all to get them and bring them back here. Baram will deal with them once they *arrive at the old fortress there."*

"It can't end like this, Ashira. It just can't." Kerinda couldn't hold back her tears any longer. *"What should I do?"*

Ashira noticed the pouch hanging from Kerinda's waist and recognized it.

"She sent you with that, didn't she? Then there's only one thing to do. Walk around the palace and gather as much information as you can without being caught, then use the mask to reach the ancient father and warn him of what has transpired here. Perhaps the birds will beat you to it, but it's the best you can do given the situation."

"But Minha...".

"I will see to the high priestess myself in your absence."

"Warn her about Joriya, and that my father now has the dagger."

"She won't be able to stop him, Kerinda. If that will be the Queen's fate, then so be it. She will be the first besides her daughter to feel the executioner's dagger in at least 800 years, and Khabu will fall completely into your father's hands, as he has planned for so long."

Ashira bowed slightly to Kerinda without waiting for a reply to her dire pronouncement, but quickly walked past her down the stairs leading to the temple.

8

By nightfall, Kerinda had wandered the palace halls for hours and walked out into the garden on the first floor near the temple to rest a moment. Among the tall flowers and exotic trees, Kerinda noticed it was already much darker than it should have been, a sign her father had taken over the land and brought his cloud of gloom that never let the sun shine too brightly anywhere his influence touched.

The situation in the palace was equally unnerving. Only the palace ministers and the temple acolytes walked freely through the halls, though most barely noticed her as they hurried to their destination. Kerinda saw the ghost-slaves wandering in some of the palace wings, particularly near Joriya and Mirae's quarters, and it sounded like they were tearing their rooms apart. When she crept nearer, she saw pillows torn and scattered in the hallway, broken furniture left beside the tufts of batting and tattered cloth, broken mirrors and even piles of clothing. More items were flung out the doors into the corridor from multiple rooms, though the ghost-slaves stayed out of sight. Kerinda left quickly before she was seen.

Before retreating to the garden, she had gone down to the crypt level where she heard angry voices, including her father's, shouting down the right eastern corridor, echoing off the majestic colonnaded marble galleries. Shivering at the sound, she felt drawn to the left western corridor toward the relief showing the tiger mask. The air there crackled and intoxicated Kerinda as she cautiously walked closer to the deserted wing, the sounds of the voices dying out behind her, muffled by something more kinetic in the air as she reached the strange carved portal. The crypt of the ancestors, the letters above it read. Now she could read the written language of Khabu and saw that the portal was covered with a map in relief, saw the words carved into it for the Blue Waterfall. Closing her eyes, she could feel it was almost time to go there.

When she ran her fingers lightly over the map, their tips tingled with the same power she felt in the air. Something was moving on the other side, though there was no way at the moment to cross the portal into the crypt. Suddenly, Kerinda understood the power of the high priestess and what it meant to be one of the immortals who lived in their most magical, unnatural forms on the other side. Litt had lived this way for 8,000 years, and she must join him soon. But first, there was other work to do, so she returned to the garden to wait.

Behind her in the garden, she heard a shuffling, then the fluttering of wings. Turning, one of the birds suddenly landed on her shoulder and in its soft musical voice spoke in her ear.

"He has come to the Blue Waterfall," it said.

"We should go now and join them, shouldn't we? I need to inform them of Birum's arrival. Do they know yet? Father will be sending guards after them to arrest them, Laqrisa."

"They only know what Baram tells them. They were on the verge of a fight when I left," Laqrisa said. "But what of Joriya and the high priestess?"

"My father and the ministers of the court are arguing about Joriya's fate now in the eastern precinct downstairs and have been all day from what I hear. Minha is safe, and Ashira is going to attend to her in my absence."

"Then we must go down to the crypt level and watch the proceedings before we leave."

"But why? I don't want to get caught. My father might see me, or worse yet, my mother."

"We need to know what they intend to do so we can report it to the ancient father. You must be strong and do this, Kerinda."

Nodding sadly, Kerinda walked grimly through the corridor toward the palace with the bird on her shoulder. Once again, the palace seemed quiet and deserted, as if waiting for something. Kerinda felt afraid to even breathe and break the silence. Descending the wide marble stairs once again, this time she turned to the eastern corridor where the shouting had turned to chanting.

"The verdict is being read," Laqrisa whispered.

"Is that what it means? It would be beautiful if it weren't such a sad situation."

"Stay in the shadows, but enter the room."

Kerinda snuck through the doorway and stepped into the room full of people. Here, the air was stuffy, and many of the people in attendance appeared to be exhausted. Ghost-slaves lined the room, menacingly holding curved swords nearly as long as their bodies. As Kerinda found a spot beside one of the columns in the back, she saw a stage had been set up in front of the gallery with Joriya tied to a board hung on a scaffold. Without warning, Joriya's eyes fell upon Kerinda as she scanned the faces around the room. Joriya smiled, and her brow cleared. At first Kerinda wondered if it was coincidence. Perhaps something had been said in the proceedings she had not noticed that had pleased Joriya, but Kerinda's hopes were dashed as one of the ministers angrily stepped forward and pulled a black cloth bag over Joriya's head.

As Kerinda watched the man, everything seemed to move slowly, as if time had stopped, and the mask resting lightly against her body in its pouch began to feel heavier and colder, as if it had turned to ice. The coldness penetrated everything it touched and had deepened to the point it was painful for Kerinda to keep it near her. She looked frantically around at the people nearby, afraid they would also feel the cold and notice her. Still, she couldn't look away from the scene as it played out on the stage. After placing the bag on Joriya's head, one of the guards sliced his blade across her exposed skin in many places, knowing the wounds would sting but not kill her. The man then waited as blood oozed out over her arms and her breathing became labored.

Kerinda gripped the pouch without looking at it, irritated and afraid as she watched the terrifying spectacle that her father had demanded as punishment for the Queen. His bloodthirsty methods had never been clearer to Kerinda, but in her shock, all she could think about was how cold the mask was. Pulling it out of the pouch after fumbling with the strings, she let the pouch flutter limply to the floor. Holding the mask by the edges of both hands, she saw that the surface actually was covered with a layer of frost, the ice crystals glistening in the lamplight. Laqrisa's claws dug into her shoulder, but she could barely even feel the pain, her senses were so overloaded from everything going on around her.

As a scuffle began on the stage, Kerinda looked up at Joriya again. The prime minister who had so strongly opposed Kerinda's own presence in Khabu walked forward in strange ceremonial garb holding the legendary dagger of Memnoth, its silver surface gleaming like ice as if in sympathy with the frosty mask Kerinda held. He stepped in front of Joriya, and Kerinda felt tears spill down her face unheeded as she watched him pull back the knife, preparing to plunge it into her.

"Now," Laqrisa whispered in her ear urgently.

Before the prime minister's hand changed position and sent the Queen to her death, Kerinda felt her hands move reflexively and place the tiger mask on her face. Stifling a scream as its coldness burned her skin, she felt herself falling into darkness as the scene of the execution before her faded.

9

When Mirae and Litt left the palace with two of the birds, Mapin and Laqrisa, the palace guards had given them a carriage pulled by beasts that were a cross between horses and oxen and sent two of their trained warriors along with them to serve as bodyguards. They sped across the plains of Khabu, stopping only at night to sleep and let the animals rest. When they finally reached the Blue Waterfall two days later, it was the middle of the day, though the usually brilliant sunlight had turned wan and even held the hint of a storm. In the subdued light, the water looked steely blue with white foam where it poured over the falls down into the plunge pool at the bottom.

"He isn't here," Mirae said looking around at the cliff side and trees as Litt came up behind her from where the carriage waited. Mapin had taken off to fly around the area, and Laqrisa still perched on the back of one of the beasts. "Was Kerinda wrong?"

"He isn't here at the waterfall, but that doesn't mean he isn't around," Litt said, standing at the edge of the water, his half-feline face in profile as the breeze gently tousled his blonde hair. "We need to search the whole area and my fortress to know for sure."

"Mapin already went that direction. Should we wait for her to return or follow her?"

"It's nice to be here, isn't it? I'm free for now, and we're together."

"So we wait for Mapin then?" Mirae smiled, looking back at the carriage a moment. Suddenly, she noticed a woman standing off in the distance beyond it, but just her face was visible in the trees. She looked familiar for some reason, though Mirae couldn't think of where she had seen her before. "Litt," she said in a strained voice. "Someone's here. Who is that?"

Litt turned to look in the direction Mirae had indicated.

"She looks familiar doesn't she?" Mirae asked.

"Isn't it that woman who was being held in Eokhmisseun along with Cargal?"

"The councilwoman? Yarava, I think her name was. Yes, she came back with us when we fled Eokhmisseun, but come to think of it, Joriya never mentioned what became of her or her bodyguards."

"Apparently we're about to find out." Litt walked back toward the carriage as Mirae quickly followed him. "Hey!" he yelled as they got only a few feet away from the clearing where the carriage sat.

The woman turned to look at them and stepped into the clearing, though her face showed no recognition. Mirae hung back a moment, puzzled by the woman's strange reaction, and an eerie feeling started to come over her. As Litt stopped only a few feet away from the woman, Mirae noticed in alarm that Yarava's dress was stained from the waist down with dirt and dried blood. Then movement caught Mirae's eye as Laqrisa flew to the back of the carriage out of sight.

"What has brought you out here today, Yarava?" Litt asked as Mirae crept closer toward the carriage on the other side, out of the woman's line of sight.

For some reason she couldn't name, she felt very afraid and looked around them on all sides, wondering what direction the attack she sensed would come from. She couldn't hear Yarava's muffled answer, but as she reached the other side of the carriage, she saw the path that led to the fortress. Her sense of panic rising, Mirae wondered if she should make a run for the fortress to get away from the woman. Even the thought of abandoning Litt didn't stop her from planning an escape, so terrifying was the feeling washing over her, but Mirae was too confused to wonder what she was afraid of. She only needed to cross a little patch of trees to reach the fortress.

As her eyes scanned the suddenly darkening forest, she noticed Mapin perched nearby on one of the tree branches and thought in passing how odd it was since Mapin was supposed to be doing reconnaissance. Turning where the path branched off, Mirae was too distracted by the bird to watch where she was going. Mapin suddenly cried out a warning with an unnaturally high pitched screech Mirae had never heard any of the birds use, but before she could react to Mapin's warning, she felt herself falling, and her hands flailing out in front of her suddenly touched soft fur!

Mirae sprang back, recoiling from whatever stood in front of her in the shadows. When the creature before her shifted position and took a step forward, she found herself face to face with a huge, ten foot tall orange tiger. Baram.

"Litt, he's here!" Mirae screamed, trying to run back the way she came but tripping over a branch. Falling to the leaf-strewn bed of the forest on her hands and knees, she looked back at the creature as it bore down on her.

"Tranform," Mapin shrieked from her perch, flapping her wings in agitation.

Transform? Oh, yes, I'm a tiger, too, aren't I? Mirae thought in her hazy brain. She realized Baram had used some spell to confuse and lure her here. Concentrating on her body, she watched it change before her eyes into the shape of a white tiger. Within minutes, she stood before Baram, eye to eye, beast to beast.

The sensation of her new animal form was almost too much for Mirae, and it distracted her from her fight with Baram. Before she could react to the new situation, Baram swatted at her with his paw, and she ducked out of the way just enough for his claws to catch her ear and tear at it. Blood dripped down her face as she felt a searing pain, but she leapt toward his throat, bearing her fangs. Startled, he wrapped his other paw around her back and dug his claws into her as she clamped her jaws down on his throat. Locked into this painful, bloody embrace, neither of them could move. Baram growled deep in his throat, sending blood bubbling out of his wound into Mirae's mouth, forcing her to let him go just long enough for him to pull away from her and retreat a few steps back into the thick undergrowth.

Mirae went after him, thinking she had him on the run, but as she stepped into the prickly brush, it caught on her fur and sliced across her skin, leaving her with more stinging wounds. Caught in the thicket, she realized Baram was more adept than she in this form. She cursed herself for not asking Litt to train her how to fight as a tiger, and now she just felt tired and heavy in the lumbering, unfamiliar form. Crying out with a high-pitched yowl, she hoped Litt or Mapin could hear her. It took too much effort to make her mouth move in the correct shapes to say anything a human would understand, and she saw Baram watching her carefully, as if preparing to pounce, since he clearly had no similar limitations and was comfortable in his skin as tiger or weretiger.

"Mirae, hold on, I'll be right there!" Litt yelled in the distance.

A glint of anger appeared in Baram's eyes as he heard the voice.

"Tell him to stay away unless you want me to rip him to shreds," Baram said in perfect English. "This is between you and me, princess. That's what you are, aren't you? My father is such a fool not to see it. And to think his spies never caught on either. Joriya wasn't much of a queen, but she kept that secret well. At least I thought to make inquiries back on Earth as to your true identity. That has to be it. Nothing else makes sense unless you are the heir. But this will be the end for you!"

Hearing his taunts, Mirae felt a surge of strength flow through her body, and she pulled herself out of the thicket, letting the thorns and brambles tear at her, knowing she was an immortal and couldn't be killed so easily. Litt had spent most of 8,000 years locked in the tranquility of the crypt of the ancestors, and she wasn't sure if he had much ability to defend himself any better than she had. Baram just watched her in bemusement.

"Going to try another round, are we? You look pretty clumsy like that."

"I ripped you across the throat last time," Mirae said, though her new mouth would hardly let her form the words intelligibly.

Starting to veer off to the path leading out of the forest toward the fortress, Mirae confused him enough that he took a step to the right, and she quickly shifted position and leapt at his left flank with the full force of her weight. The two of them caught onto one another with their claws and rolled around, biting and scratching at each other. Each time one lost their grip, the other slunk a few steps closer to the cliff side by the lower level of the Blue Waterfall. Trees shook, leaves fluttered to the ground, and tufts of grass flew in every direction as they struggled together.

Finally when Mirae felt she couldn't fight anymore, Baram shapeshifted into a tall weretiger, keeping his head completely in animal form. Now a ten foot tall man built like a weightlifter, he repeatedly grabbed Mirae and tossed her closer to the edge of the cliff by the waterfall, and at first she landed a few trees away but soon was only a few steps away. Mirae felt too exhausted to fight anymore and couldn't latch onto him with her claws because he was so agile. As he bore down on her and knocked her to the ground, wrapping his clawed hands around her neck as if to strangle her, she cried out again in despair and pain as they finally reached the cliff's edge. The sound of the water rushing over the edge fifty feet away nearly drowned out her cry, which was slowly dying into a whimper.

"Litt, grab her," a woman said as a figure with a long bladed spear appeared behind them and the branches swayed and cracked on the other side of Baram.

Mirae could barely see, her vision blurred by the blood dripping from her head wounds, but suddenly a tall woman wearing a white chiton with golden-tinged white wings and flowing blonde hair ran up behind Baram. Holding the spear in a defensive position, both the woman and spear ignited into a ball of flame, and she moved closer to Baram, her face twisted into a fierce grimace as she plunged its metal blade into his back.

Screaming in pain and surprise, Baram jumped off Mirae, and she nearly slid over the edge of the cliff to the plunge pool. Hanging onto the thorny vines draped across the side of the cliff with her claws, looking down at the frothy blue water below her, she tried to think what to do to save herself, but someone grabbed her by her paws and dragged her to safety just as small pebbles beneath her rolled down off the edge. She looked up at whoever had saved her. Litt, now grown to titan-sized stature to match Birum's, pulled her into his embrace and then to safety while Mapin kept Baram at bay.

"Take her back the carriage, and we'll get out of here," Mapin growled, her eyes locked on Baram, still full of fury. "We can deal with him and his followers when she is safe."

"We need to come up with a better plan to deal with him, Mapin," Litt said, his voice as angry as Mapin's. "He killed the last of the leaders of Eokhmisseun and turned her into a puppet to lure us into his trap. Who knows what he is capable of? Let's be done with him and his family. There's only one way, and we shouldn't hesitate this time. Release the ancestors to deal with him. Let him fight all of us who have congregated in the Forest of Bliss and the crypt for millennia and see if he can stand against our numbers."

"Yes, we can do that," Mapin said, her voice low and lethal as she took one more swipe with her bladed spear at Baram before slicing him across the stomach. Watching him fall to his knees and double over, she turned back to Litt, unmindful of the blood splatter on her chiton.

10

Before Litt could answer, the forest lit up like a lightning bolt had struck it. In an empty spot on the ground beneath the trees, a small figure appeared, a girl in a blue chiton wearing the tiger mask with a white pigeon on her shoulder. Nearly falling over sobbing, the girl peeled off the mask and looked around, her eyes filled with tears.

"Kerinda!" Litt said, looking at her in surprise. Mirae turned her head slightly toward Kerinda, though she was sure Kerinda wouldn't recognize her as a tiger. "What are you doing here? Has something happened at the palace? How strange to see you look like a human girl."

Kerinda looked from the two weretigers to Mapin and Mirae. Pulling the cloth from her hair, letting her long red locks fall around her face, she started to wrap the tiger mask in it.

"Wait, what are you doing?" Mapin asked excitedly, leaning over her. "We can use the mask to summon the ancestors from the crypt, and now that Laqrisa has returned, she can go to the forest and get the rest."

"Yes, we can do that," Litt said, putting Mirae gently down on a bed of leaves away from the cliff and shapeshifting back to his half-human, half-tiger form at his normal height. He walked over to Kerinda and bent over to take the mask as Mirae shapeshifted back to her normal form.

"Stop," Kerinda said angrily as Laqrisa flew over to land on Mapin's hand for a quick conversation in their odd, musical bird language before flying off through the trees. "You haven't even asked me why I'm here. I didn't come here to help you, not exactly, though I see my vision of Baram was correct. There's big trouble back at the palace, though it's too late now to save her."

Kerinda started sobbing again as Mapin and Litt looked at her, waiting for her to calm down.

"Birum came and jailed Joriya. He took over the whole palace, and the ministers were angry that she let you leave, Litt. They did everything Birum wanted. Can you guess what that means? Can you? Joriya is dead. I can't believe it myself, but I was there as the execution began."

Mirae sat up and turned to look at Kerinda.

"What are you saying?" Mirae asked. "Joriya is dead? They executed her with the silver dagger? Is Minha at least safe?"

"I'm saying it is too late to stop the execution. Run them out of Khabu, or else it's all over for the rest of us."

"Ha, princess, what good news for you," Baram said sarcastically, spitting out a mouthful of blood. "All hail to the new queen of Khabu!"

Litt watched him a moment, his face full of passionate hatred as Litt's fangs grew longer and his mouth more prominent.

"Litt, use the mask," Mapin yelled, her expression ferocious and her eyes full of bloodlust, pointing her spear at Baram's throat again. "I have already sent Laqrisa to the forest. End it now by bringing out the royal clan! Neither he nor his accursed father will ever set foot in Khabu again. Do it now!"

Litt brought the mask up to his face with a swift movement of his arm, and it stuck almost of its own accord. Mirae wondered fleetingly what would happen if the ancestors wore it instead of the high priestess, but she wouldn't have long to wait to find out. Raising his palm up to the same height as Baram's face, he said ancient words that Mirae only vaguely recognized as the litany the high priestess used as a greeting to open the crypt.

As the litany ended, the sky flashed with a light even brighter than the noonday sun before Birum's arrival. The beating, rushing waters of the Blue Waterfall pulsed with an unnatural life as the air and even reality itself buckled around them. Golden light poured out of Mapin's body like flames as the sky suddenly filled with small white bodies, all of the birds from the Forest of Bliss, as far as the eye could see. A wave of voices that sounded like drumbeats came from the direction of the palace as time and space shifted and the ancestors of the tiger clan surged toward the Blue Waterfall. Mirae even thought she could hear screaming from the palace all the way back in the capital as the ancestors there dealt with Birum.

Baram raised his hands to his ears as if being bombarded by a deafening, painful sound, a howl of despair coming from his lips.

"Get out now while you still have your life, Baram," Kerinda screamed at him, and Mirae remembered for a moment that Kerinda had once told her Baram was her confidante as a child. Feeling sorry for her, she almost wanted to stay Litt's hand but didn't dare. "Even if you don't want to believe it, even if you are immortal like the true bloods, the ancestors can destroy you. Leave now!"

Baram opened his eyes and seemed to see his sister for the first time. Kerinda stood up and walked over to him slowly, letting her usual tiger appearance take over her human features once again so he would see her as he always knew her.

"You too, Kerinda? You will betray us in this way and stay with Joriya's whelp?"

"Get out!" Kerinda screamed again.

With that last exchange between brother and sister, Baram shifted back into his full tiger form and ran from the forest to where his followers waited by the river's shore downstream. If he couldn't get them out quickly enough through the river leading back to the inner sea, the ancestors would eat all of his human followers alive and tear the degenerate ghost slaves limb from limb until none of them survived. Moments later, the Blue Waterfall descended into a cacophony of angry voices as the ancestors swarmed over it in search of Birum, Baram and any of their enemies.

EPILOGUE

1

Six months after the ancestors of Khabu drove out Birum and Baram, Kerinda sat in the temple hall near the corridor leading to the shore of the inner sea, waiting for Minha to arrive. After the commotion of the fight, the temple acolytes spent months restoring the ancestors to the crypt and the forest, resealing the boundaries between the worlds, then sadly burying Joriya and the long-suffering Pareya in the palace garden in a small tomb together. Before long, Khabu was back to normal, though this time the ministers were more subdued as Mirae took the throne, the ancient king Litt at her side as her chief advisor and companion. One of her first acts as queen was to establish a bureau of inner sea exploration, headed by Pontol, after centuries of Khabu gazing inwardly upon its own land and its citizens never leaving its shores. Birum's rebellion and Joriya's desperate act to save her child were the first time anyone from Khabu had ventured beyond its borders in a very long time.

Minha had finally healed and resumed her role as high priestess of the temple, but she made it clear to her acolytes that she had chosen Kerinda to be her successor.

While she had considered retiring to the crypt during the restoration of the ancestors, she knew Kerinda would require years of training to take over the role, especially since the temple would have to oppose the ministers who had never wanted Birum's half-human daughter to play a dominant role in Khabu's politics. Instead, Minha brought Kerinda from Mirae's wing of the palace into her own private quarters to raise and train, safe from the court ministers' political intrigues.

"Will you keep your human appearance or remain in the form you always preferred, the half-tiger?" Minha asked one night in her suite as Kerinda sat with her studying Khabu's history and language. "You will be more acceptable to the ministers and will cause less trouble for Mirae if you remain fully human before them."

"Do I have to? Litt hasn't changed back into his fully human form but has kept his tiger features, and no one is opposing him now that Mirae has been crowned queen."

"The ancient father has scandalized the ministers beyond their limits in every way imaginable," Minha said, smiling mischievously. "But you are not 8,000 years old, and you don't have the advantage of time spent among the old ones in the crypt as he has. Such cunning the man has developed in that time. He can challenge the very foundations of our society, and indeed, his coming has restored to us our lost history.

"You, however, are a child, and Birum's daughter to boot. They'll always fear you as the seed of a traitor. Birum has not been apprehended, and he isn't likely to be killed on any world whose shores he may reach. Please understand their position."

Kerinda sighed, looking down at her book sullenly.

"Then why did you choose me to be the next high priestess? Wouldn't Ashira have done better and been more acceptable to the ministers?

"I think Mirae and the ancient father intend to make changes to our land. We have attained a place of safety and live a nearly indestructible life, yet still we are missing many things that perhaps we need."

"Litt remembers his father's mistakes and is still haunted by them, as am I of my own father's," Kerinda said. "I have talked with him some about it when I visit Mirae's quarters. He just wants to correct aspects of Zurui's legacy that have never been uprooted enough to disappear."

"Yes, I think that's why it's time for you to also take the position of high priestess." Minha paused to pour Kerinda a cup of cold root tea before continuing. "Besides, it is clear you have the sight. Not many of our line have been so gifted. It will be helpful in guiding the country in the next few hundred years. Joriya is dead and I will be entering the crypt soon, so Mirae will need more than the ancient father to rely upon."

"And what of Pontol?" Kerinda asked, taking a sip of the thick, aromatic brown liquid.

"Pontol? Why do you ask?"

"His mission is an extension of the temple's diplomatic reach, is it not? I will also be liaison to those other worlds he finds beyond the inner sea, including Mirae's homeland." Kerinda paused, looking out the palace window at the stars in the clear night sky. "Will she ever return there do you think?"

"Her brother will come here, perhaps other family, but I think she will not return."

"Has Earth recovered from my brother's attack? I was sad when I heard how my father had destroyed Eokhmisseun when he fled. Baram didn't do that to Earth, did he?"

"You heard Nominus' report," Minha said, looking at Kerinda curiously and nodding. "Earth will survive and serve as a link of some importance along the inner sea, though it will never get back to normal. Khabu's old reputation as 'space pirates' will spread, especially now that we're linked to the elusive deer clan that has settled among the human worlds to live quietly and watch over them.

"Are you curious about the other lands beyond Khabu now? I know your father kept you locked up in the palace at Eokhmisseun since you were born. I can ask Pontol to bring me books to teach you about them, if you wish."

"Yes, let's ask him to do that, and I will also have him keep tabs on Earth for Mirae and send her regular reports."

"Enough plotting. It's time for you to study. Please write out your vocabulary list for me."

Putting down her tea on the table between them, she picked up a feather pen, dipped it into a shallow cup of ink and began to write.

2

Two years after Nominus drove Baram from earth, Addison was thriving again, and the strange episode with the otherworldly weretiger Baram was mostly forgotten, as were the ever-present deer clan. The transition that year from Baram's invasion back to normal American living had not been easy, though. The next morning after the arrival of Nominus and the deer clan warriors, Baram and his ghost slaves were gone without a trace, and the smoky, magical clouds dimming the sunlight in Addison had also been banished along with them. The neighborhoods woke to an eerie silence and the feeling that the crisis was over. They had passed whatever cosmic test it served to provide.

The remnant of Addison's city council roamed the neighborhoods with their guards and Humvees to check on all of the citizens, readjusting the number of registered members of the community and accounting for the missing and the dead. After the first month, a list of those presumed dead was released side by side with a list of names and photos of those thought to still be missing. Slowly, businesses opened up for regular hours, and supply trucks once again rode along the suburban routes. Houses in the neighborhood opened their blinds and repaired the damage inflicted by Baram's gangs. New people from other districts bought the houses of those missing as time passed. The high school reopened in the fall and held an impromptu graduation ceremony for the students whose ceremony had been postponed in the spring as preparations were made for the new school year.

News from outside of Addison trickled in, giving the local residents a glimpse of how strange it all appeared to nearby districts. Rumors persisted that there had been derechos of unusual proportions lasting for weeks on end one after another, causing the main roads into Addison to be blocked to through traffic. Neighboring weathermen had commented on odd storm cloud formations that lingered over the city, even blocking out any radar or photography from the air. The president had considered sending in the national guard at one point in June, but Pentagon officials, terrified of what they saw on photographs they could capture of the strange weather phenomenon and magnetic readings of the Addison area, advised a wait and see approach, sending supply trucks through at long intervals, though the deliverymen who returned were unable to account for the missing time once they entered the storm cloud.

Conspiracy sites chattered about the strange events in Addison, floating theories of bigfoot, chemtrails and even an Area 51-like crash. Megumi Iwase Miller, now winning her fifth term as mayor of Addison by a landslide, had convinced most of the survivors to keep what happened to themselves, though she publicly supported a lighthearted version of the bigfoot theory and marketed the idea as a highlight for tourists to the city. Vince Esposito, upon reopening his paintball park, contributed to the bigfoot fervor by adding a few huge ice-age style furry animals with lethal claws and teeth to both his indoor and outdoor courses.

SOHYEON AFTER MIDNIGHT

Sohyeon, now 20 and preparing to be married to Tamnyn, was one of the few who still thought about the incident and looked to the sky regularly for the inner sea and the silhouette of Pontol's ship. After formally graduating from high school and helping Tamnyn bury her father properly in a local military cemetery where she could visit the grave regularly, he took a job at the paintball park helping Vince with parties and working the gear rental counter. Sometimes Tamnyn joined the staff, helping with the coffee shop. Vince was well aware of the real reason for Addison's crisis since his wife was on the list of the missing and he still bore the scars from Pete MacIntyre's attack, so he had no problem letting Sohyeon work at the park and still have time off regularly with Tamnyn to attend to otherworldly duties.

Both Sohyeon and Tamnyn had joined Jangsun's *dojang* to continue to their sword and spear training. Life otherwise went on as usual at the Choi household, with Sukjin preparing to attend George Washington University in the fall with her boyfriend Phillip, now a senior, and Mirae reportedly working for the consulate on top secret projects in Bishkek, Kyrgyzstan, with no time off to return home to visit. Alanna started working more with Megumi on the city council since there were vacancies, and Jangsun helped Sohyeon map the inner worlds by painting detailed maps and compiling his travel notes from their night journeys.

As Nominus noted, they were now part of a small, unique group of men and women to regularly travel the inner seas beyond Earth. When Pontol came with the ship, Sohyeon and Tamnyn joined him in searching among the known worlds for signs of Birum or Baram and their allies. This was the commission they were given, coming down from the Queen of Khabu after Birum's expulsion, and Sohyeon couldn't forget his experiences in both Eokhmisseun and Addison under their cruel reigns to let them begin the tragic sequence of events on yet another unsuspecting world somewhere beyond the stars. He knew Tamnyn also couldn't forget her doomed homeland, no matter how well she seemed to have adjusted to life on Earth with the Chois, with whom they lived.

One night a few weeks after their wedding, Sohyeon sat at his desk in their room reading a book on the ancient mariners of Earth. Rubbing his eyes and wondering if he should go to bed, he glanced at the clock on his nightstand. It read 12:30 AM. Turning off the light on his desk and standing, ready to go downstairs and see if Tamnyn had fallen asleep in the living room while watching a movie, he paused as the curtains blew into the room on a gust of warm summer air. Returning to the open window, he looked up at the sky. A smoky, silver cloud enveloped the full moon, blurring its features, yet even though the night was not clear enough to see much starlight, Sohyeon could make out the shape of Pontol's boat coming for them.

Smiling and nodding to himself, he dashed out of the room and down the stairs, yelling Tamnyn's name. She quickly appeared at the bottom of the steps, looking up at him in alarm.

"What happened?" she asked.

"He's here. Get your sword and get ready to leave for a while. We'll be back as soon as we can, mom."

Alanna stood by the kitchen, watching them race back upstairs.

"I guess we get the house to ourselves for a few days with the kids all gone," she said to Jangsun as she walked back into the living room.

They quickly changed out of their pajamas into something more suitable for exploring. Sohyeon pulled on a pair of camouflage green cargo pants, a loose flowing burgundy shirt and a retro-looking green velvet overcoat that reached a few inches above his knees, while Tamnyn wore her old white leather armor with a satiny black vest reaching past her hips over it, her long red hair half braided and half loose. Strapping their swords to their backs, they waited for the ship to get close enough to the window to board. Tamnyn also picked up another bag which held pens and notebooks so they could record data.

"Where do you think we should look this time out?" she asked.

"I don't think we'll find them tonight," Sohyeon said, watching Pontol floating closer to the house. "We haven't had much luck in the past two years out at sea, and I'm sure they know better than to hide anywhere obvious after their defeat. Right now we need to get a sense of the shoreline along the inner sea, mapping out where the various lands are along the way, and listen for rumors of their arrival. Perhaps we can contact one of the deer clan representatives at port, if we find somewhere hospitable. Ready?"

Sohyeon stepped onto the windowsill and leapt across the gap to the hull of the ship, and he turned to catch Tamnyn as she did the same. Pontol watched them a moment before flipping through his ship log. Once they were seated, he nodded a curt greeting before spinning the ship's wheel to turn the boat back into the inner sea's currents. They would be exploring downstream tonight.

AFTERWORD

This project grew out of a plan I had to write a bilingual Korean-English novel since I became intrigued with stories I read of foreign literary writers who routinely wrote and published in two or three languages. This English language edition is only phase one, and I still hope to work on a dumbed-down Korean version for language students.

In preparation for writing about Jangsun Choi's expertise in *kumdo*, I consulted the *Muye Dobo Tongji: The Comprehensive Illustrated Manual of Martial Arts of Ancient Korea*, which was translated by Sang H. Kim. This book is the actual 1790 manual written by Yi Duk-moo, Park Je-ga and Pak Dong-soo by the order of King Jeongjo, Korea's renaissance king. I've compiled a short chart of the related technical terms I use throughout the book to refer to the weapons my characters use from this discipline.

검도   *kumdo* – a Korean martial art derived from Japanese *kendo*

목검   *mokgum* – a wooden practice sword, similar to a Japanese *bokken*

환도   *hwando* – a historical steel single-edged bladed sword, similar to a Japanese *katana*

| 협도 | *hyeopdo* – a crescent-bladed spear 4 feet tall, similar but not the same as a Japanese *naginata* |
| 죽도 | *jukdo* – a bamboo practice sword, equivalent of a Japanese *shinai* |

Inspiration for the crypt of ancestors in Khabu came from ancient Near Eastern sources, especially the Sumerian King List's antediluvian rulers and first dynasty of Kish. This stone tablet listed kings who ruled for hundreds and thousands of years.

ABOUT THE AUTHOR

Wendelin Gray is a linguist, writer, dancer and long-time volunteer with the Silk Screen Asian Arts Organization in Pittsburgh, PA, and is a regular contributor to Pittsburgh Japanese Culture Society events. She has also written the novellas *The Weary City* and *Kumori and the Lucky Cat* and novels *The Vulpecula Cycle* and the award-winning *The Haunting at Ice Pine Peak*. She blogs about East Asian language and literature at http://icepinepalace.wordpress.com and https://sunrisesintheeast.wordpress.com. In 2017, she founded an Asian education project, the Enlightened Rabbit Scholastic Society and published *Lady Xiansa's Guide to Beginning Korean*.